FRESH KILLS

FRESH KILLS

BILL LOEHFELM

G. P. PUTNAM'S SONS
NEW YORK

PUTNAM

G. P. PUTNAM'S SONS
Publishers Since 1838
Published by the Penguin Group
Penguin Group (USA) Inc., 375 Hudson Street, New York, New York 10014, USA • Penguin
Group (Canada), 90 Eglinton Avenue East, Suite 700, Toronto, Ontario M4P 2Y3, Canada
(a division of Pearson Penguin Canada Inc.) • Penguin Books Ltd, 80 Strand, London
WC2R 0RL, England • Penguin Ireland, 25 St Stephen's Green, Dublin 2, Ireland (a division
of Penguin Books Ltd) • Penguin Group (Australia), 250 Camberwell Road, Camberwell,
Victoria 3124, Australia (a division of Pearson Australia Group Pty Ltd) • Penguin Books
India Pvt Ltd, 11 Community Centre, Panchsheel Park, New Delhi–110 017, India •
Penguin Group (NZ), 67 Apollo Drive, Rosedale, North Shore 0632, New Zealand
(a division of Pearson New Zealand Ltd) • Penguin Books (South Africa) (Pty) Ltd,
24 Sturdee Avenue, Rosebank, Johannesburg 2196, South Africa

Penguin Books Ltd, Registered Offices: 80 Strand, London WC2R 0RL, England

Library of Congress Cataloging-in-Publication Data

Loehfelm, Bill.
Fresh kills / Bill Loehfelm.
p.   cm.
ISBN 978-0-399-15531-4
1. Fathers—Death—Fiction.   2. Murder—Fiction.   3. Loss (Psychology)—Fiction.
4. Staten Island (New York, N.Y.)—Fiction.   I.Title.
PS3612.O36F74   2008   2008023462
813'.6—dc22

Printed in the United States of America
10   9   8   7   6   5   4   3   2   1

Book design by Lovedog Studio

This is a work of fiction. Names, characters, places, and incidents either are the product of the
author's imagination or are used fictitiously, and any resemblance to actual persons, living or
dead, businesses, companies, events, or locales is entirely coincidental.

While the author has made every effort to provide accurate telephone numbers and Internet
addresses at the time of publication, neither the publisher nor the author assumes any
responsibility for errors, or for changes that occur after publication. Further, the publisher does
not have any control over and does not assume any responsibility for author or third-party
websites or their content.

To my parents, Steve and Diane McDonald,
thanks for the greatest gift a son can get, your always being there.

And to my wife, AC Lambeth,
thank you for being here now.

Dead men are heavier than broken hearts.

—Raymond Chandler, *The Big Sleep*

"Junior, open the door. It's important."

"Says who?"

"C'mon, Junior. I've been calling you all morning. So has your sister. It's Purvis."

My sister? Purvis? Why was he talking to my sister? Why was she calling me? I looked down at the gun in my hand and realized I was naked. And that the guy at my door was actually *Detective* Purvis.

"What happened to my sister?" I asked.

"Julia's fine," Purvis said. "This concerns something else."

"This official business? Can it wait?"

"Yes to the first," Purvis said, "No to the second. Open the door right now."

"I need to get dressed. Another minute won't kill you." Through the door, I could hear him swearing. Fuck it, why not try the truth, I had nothing to hide. "Thing is, I got a gun and a naked girl in here."

There was a long silence. I figured he'd moved down the hall to call for backup.

"They're both legal," I said, lying about the gun. "And neither has anything to do with the other."

"Thirty seconds," Purvis said. "Put some clothes on and do not open the door with the gun in your hand."

I set the gun on the end table and ducked into the bedroom for jeans and a T-shirt. Molly stirred. The bedcovers had drifted down to her hips. I took a moment to admire her, then pulled the sheet and blanket to her shoulders. Mumbling, she asked who was at the door, snuggling deeper into the bed. I didn't answer, wondering as I dressed how much trouble I'd have keeping her out of whatever I was about to get into. I walked, barefoot, back into the living room, closing the bedroom door behind me.

ONE

I DON'T OFTEN ANSWER MY DOOR WITH A GUN IN MY HAND. LESS often at noon on a Sunday. But that day someone beat on my door like they were gonna kick it in, jarring me right out of a perfectly good sleep next to a perfectly naked woman and right into a brutal hangover. I told the woman to go back to sleep, reached for the nightstand, yanked open the top drawer, and grabbed my gun.

It was a nine-millimeter, loaded, that I used mostly as a prop. Every five or six months a new junkie moved into the neighborhood, marked my comings and goings, and figured I was easily rattled out of a few bucks by a skin-and-bones wraith that held his fighting weight eating the cheese out of rat traps. He'd bang on my door, ask if he could wash my car, or watch my mail, or some other money-hustling shit like that, and I'd answer with the nine. I'd explain how the gun not only took care of my car and my mail, but my stereo and my liquor cabinet, too. Negotiations always ended there.

In the apartment above, the neighbor's dog barked like crazy.

"Jesus, all right already," I hollered, crossing the living room. "I'm coming." I leaned close to the door. "Whadda you want?"

"All right," I said, unlocking the dead-bolts and twisting the doorknob. "I'm dressed and the gun is sitting on the table immediately to your right as you walk in." I opened the door.

Purvis grimaced, waving a hand in front of his nose as I let him into the apartment. "Long night? You smell like it." He glanced at the gun. "I hope you didn't drive home."

"What're you doing here? And what's it got to do with my sister?"

He crossed his arms. "John, your father's dead. He was shot this morning, not far from the house." He waited for me to say something. I didn't. The pounding in my head doubled and I felt sick. "Outside the Optimo deli." Another pause. Maybe waiting for a question. "I'm sorry."

I chewed the inside of my cheek, trying to catch my breath and will my stomach to be still. I wondered what was stranger, that my father had been shot, or that it was Purvis standing there telling me. We'd known each other since we were kids, grew up across the street from each other. He knew my family. Then, in high school, Purvis and I had a falling-out he's never been able to leave behind him. "No, you're not sorry," I said. "And neither am I. And you know it."

"Gimme a little credit, John. I don't like seeing anyone die. I don't like telling anyone about the loss of a loved one." He paused. "Even you." He almost grinned. "Either way, I'm gonna need that gun."

"Take it. I got nothing to hide."

"I hope that's the truth," Purvis said, pulling on a pair of rubber gloves.

"Whatever, Purvis." Despite his news, he bored me already.

He just snapped the rubber at his wrists. He picked up the gun and dropped it into a clear plastic bag. He put the bag in his jacket pocket. "You may want me on your side on this," he said, peeling off the gloves.

"Enjoying yourself?" I asked. I hadn't shot the old man, and Purvis, despite his tough-cop act, knew it. If he really thought I'd done it, he'd have been at the door with his gun and cuffs out, and about fourteen other cops. If I wanted, I could tell him right now what the police lab would tell him in a couple of days, if the gun ever made it there. That gun had never been fired.

"We're going to your parents' house," Purvis said. "My partner's waiting for us. He wants to talk to you about this, obviously."

"You talked to my sister?" I asked.

"Called her myself this morning." He checked his watch. "She's arriving soon. Said she was leaving right away." He looked down at my feet. "Put some shoes on and let's get going. I'm sure you want to get this over with."

"How about you don't give me orders," I said. "I can get there on my own."

"Waters told me to bring you," he said.

"I'm not riding over there in the back of a cop car like a goddamn criminal." I walked to the window, pulled aside the shade, and looked down at Purvis's terribly obvious, unmarked white sedan. "Shit, it's bad enough the whole block'll be thinking I'm a narc."

"We've waited long enough," Purvis said. "Waters is getting pissed."

"I'll drive over myself," I said, walking back over to him. I nodded toward the bedroom. "I've got company to attend to." Then the name he'd dropped finally fell into place. "Nat Waters? He's in on this?"

"He's my partner. *We've* got the case."

This was getting richer by the moment. "I'll be there," I said, shooing him toward the door. "Scurry back to your boss and tell him I'm on my way."

Purvis stopped in the doorway. "You are still a fucking asshole."

"Whatever," I said, and slammed the door in his face.

MOLLY SAT IN THE MIDDLE of the bed, the bedclothes kicked down to her ankles, her knees drawn up to her chest, her black cherry hair loose over her shoulders. She glowed in the afternoon sun shining through the window behind her. She blinked at me, apprehension on her face.

"Did I just hear Purvis call you an asshole?" she asked.

I crossed my arms and leaned in the doorway. "That you did. Neither the first nor the last time that'll happen."

She rolled her eyes, kicked her feet free, and slid to the edge of the bed, reaching down for her clothes. She knew my history with Purvis, found the enduring antagonism rather pathetic. She knew it had started with her. "What was he doing here? I thought you two fell out years ago."

"We did," I said. "It was business." I hesitated, unsure of how to tell her the news, unsure if I wanted to. "Police business." She stopped dressing and stared at me, waiting. I couldn't leave it there; she'd make all the wrong assumptions if I did. Hell, I figured, it's not like she won't find out anyway. "My father's been killed. Somebody shot him this morning."

Molly stood up straight, her eyes wide, mouth hanging open, her jeans pulled only halfway up her thighs. "Jesus." She crossed her arms over her bare chest, fingers splayed open over her col-

larbone, as if hearing the news half-naked shamed her. "Good
Lord, John, that's awful." She pulled her jeans up to her hips and
sat back down on the bed.

"I guess so," I said. I pulled a Camel from the pack on the
dresser. I cupped my hand around the end and lit it, tossing the
lighter on the bed. Molly grabbed it and lit one from her pack on
the nightstand.

"Jesus," she said, perching her face on her palm, elbow resting
on her knee. She didn't ask any questions, didn't get up to hug
me, didn't wave me over to the bed. She just sat, staring at the
wall, smoking, saying nothing.

After she'd finished half her smoke, she set it in the ashtray
and stood to finish getting dressed. I watched, sorry she was
wrapping up that long, fluid body she'd shared with me through
the sunrise hours. Still, I was anxious for her to go. I needed to
get to my sister. And I knew Molly wanted out of my apartment.
She checked the clock three times as she dressed. I figured I'd
make it easier on her.

"I hate to rush you out the door," I said, "but I've got to get
to the house and see my sister. The cops are waiting there for
me, too."

She strapped on her watch, staring at it for a long time. Cal-
culating, I knew, her schedule, her excuses, and the right thing to
say about the news I'd shared.

"I should've been out of here hours ago," she said. "I'm supposed to be grading papers. David's picking me up for an early
dinner."

"Tell him I said hey."

She raised an admonishing finger at me. "Leave him out of this."
She frowned at the bed. "This has got nothing to do with him."

She slipped past me through the doorway, careful to avoid contact. I fought the urge to grab her wrist and drag her back into bed. Fuck Purvis and Waters, fuck David, fuck my father. I didn't want any of them anywhere near my afternoon. But all I did was hold out my hand, letting Molly's hair run through my fingers as she went by.

She stopped in the living room, halfway to the front door, searching through her purse for her keys. "Don't do that, either. That's the rule. When it's time for me to go, you let me get from the bed to the door without touching me."

I smiled. Molly with all her rules. Don't pick on David, don't ask about work, don't ask about her brother or her folks. Don't call her, she'll find me. I guess it kept our thing under control for her, let her keep me out on the edge of her life, where she could reach me, but I couldn't touch anything but her. It worked for me. I had no interest in the things she didn't want me touching. I lived with them, these rules about the people in her life. In exchange, she gave me free reign over her body, put no limits on what I could touch there. Seemed like a fair trade to me.

She stopped again at the door, turning to me. "Are you gonna be okay? I guess I could call David and cancel." She looked up at the ceiling. "If I could think of some excuse."

"A friend's dead father doesn't cut it?"

"Stop," she said. "You know he doesn't know we're even in touch again, never mind . . . doing what we're doing."

"I'm fine," I said. "Go see your boyfriend. Do I look like I'm about to break down? I don't need anything from you." I shrugged. "We're old friends, we fuck every now and then, nothing more, nothing less. I'm not asking you for anything."

She stared at me a long time. "You've never been one to mince words, John. Sometimes it stings."

"C'mon, Molly," I said. "I can see the relief in your face. You're off the hook. You know you want it that way. Don't bullshit either of us." I crossed the room to her. Stood close enough to smell us on her skin. "That's what makes this work between us, bare, stone-cold naked honesty." I backed off, turned away, and walked into the kitchen. She followed.

"You know the old man died to me years ago," I said, pouring ground coffee into a filter. "This morning is a technicality. I'd have nothing to do with it if it wasn't for my sister, cops or no cops." I filled the coffeepot with water and turned it on. I leaned back against the counter. "If you hadn't been with me all night, you'd be wondering the same thing as Purvis, whether or not I capped him myself."

"I'd never think that," she said. "And I'm sure Purvis doesn't, either."

"Why not? You think I wouldn't do it?"

"Never, in a million years," she said. "I don't care how many fistfights the two of you have had. Be serious. You? Kill your own father? Even Purvis knows that's ridiculous. Bare-knuckled honesty. Isn't that what you were just talking about?"

"More or less," I said.

I yanked the carafe out of the coffeemaker and sat my mug under the spout, staring into the black stream pouring down. I debated the wisdom of trying to convince her I was capable of killing my father.

"You want honesty?" I said. "Fine. I'm not indifferent, I'm glad. It's about time. He had it coming. You know what he was like. Shit, you spent two years of your life listening to me rant about him. How do I feel about it? I don't know if I'm grateful to the guy who did it, or if I'm jealous because he did it first."

"You should hear yourself," Molly said. "You sound just like you did when we were seventeen." She walked over to me. "Half a minute ago he meant nothing to you. Now you're spitting poison all over the counter." She put her hand on my chest, looked me in the eyes. "I think you're in for a bad time, John. Be careful. If you need me, I can be around."

I sipped my coffee, backing harder against the counter.

"Yeah, we fuck every now and then," she whispered to me, "but we're old friends, too."

I wouldn't look at her. "Tell David I said hey."

Molly turned on her heel and walked out, slamming the door behind her. I wasn't sure, but I thought I heard her call me an asshole on her way out.

T W O

AFTER I WATCHED MOLLY DRIVE AWAY, I STUFFED SOME CLOTHES
in a bag, hopped in my Galaxie and sped south across the mal-
formed, mutant offspring of Brooklyn known as Staten Island.
The forgotten fifth borough. The Cultural Void. Home of the
world-famous ferry, the world's largest garbage dump, and the
world's largest collection of identical people.

I was worried about how my sister was taking all this; she has
a tendency to overreact to things. Julia wasn't wild about the old
man, either, but she'd tried hanging on to him. She worked even
harder at it after Mom died. Julia and Mom were more like sis-
ters than mother and daughter. They even looked alike. Straight,
blond hair that they both wore long, deep green eyes, pale, burn-
ready skin. Thin but hippy, with long legs. When Julia hit her late
teens, in the last couple of years before Mom died, they swapped
clothes all the time. From a distance, it was difficult to tell them
apart. They were best friends.

To me, their closeness was all the more reason for Julia to
hate the old man, considering how he treated our mother. But
Julia isn't the hating kind. I asked her once why she even bothered with him.

"He's my father," she'd say. "And he's alone now. And Mom loved him." That's Julia. She's quite a pistol, my sister. Of course, it was easier for her to be more forgiving. She hadn't had quite the hands-on experience with the old man that I'd had.

Mom did love him; how I don't know. I never felt any obligation to him whatsoever. I'd told him so a few years ago, and as I bobbed and weaved through traffic on the Staten Island Expressway, the stink of the Fresh Kills Dump filling the car as I passed it, I felt glad we'd had that conversation before he died.

WHEN I PULLED THE CAR into my parents' driveway, Purvis was waiting on the front porch.

"Took you long enough," he said.

"Whatever. Where's Waters?"

"Around back," Purvis answered. "He didn't want to attract the neighbors' attention." He gestured toward the front door. "You wanna open it up for us?"

"I don't have a key," I said. "Haven't for years."

Purvis led me around the side of the house to the backyard.

Standing on the patio, studying his shoes, was Detective Nathaniel Waters, a hulking, balding man in his mid-fifties, all loose, pale skin and wet, yellow eyes.

"Fat Nat," my father had called him. They'd grown up together on Katan Avenue, alternating between being inseparable and brawling on sight. Sometimes, after a glass or two of wine, my mother told me stories about them. They played varsity football at Farrell together. My father started at left defensive end. Waters was his backup. Their weight room rivalry was the stuff of legend.

Their senior year, at my father's encouragement, Waters

switched to linebacker and broke his leg in the first quarter of his first start. Done. My father went to Wagner College on a scholarship and met my mother. He found a new rival in a guy named Stanski. Waters failed his army physical and went into the police academy. The first time my father got arrested for bar fighting, it was Waters who busted him.

Though raised in the same neighborhood, Dad and Mom only got to know each other at Wagner. She was his tutor, assigned the challenge of preventing my father from failing off the football team. My mother was smitten, she told me, by the fact that such a powerful, handsome man needed her help. It had never happened to her before, she said.

They'd met only once before, when she was Waters's date for the senior prom. As soon as she and my father started going steady, Waters decided he was in love with her, too. He had to. He and my father were those weird type of guys who hated each other so much they couldn't stay out of each other's lives. They drank in the same bars all their lives, preferring for decades to trade insults and glare at each other over their light beers rather than cede territory. Waters only gave up on my mother when she got pregnant with me. I guess even Fat Nat had standards.

Not long after my parents' wedding, he met a girl of his own, married her. Less than a year later, they had twin sons. Two years later, Waters came home from a twelve-hour shift on foot patrol in the Bronx to an empty house on Staten Island. His wife, who my father came to refer to as "the Disappearing Blonde," vanished with their sons into her huge Italian family. She had relatives scattered all over the Eastern seaboard. Some still lived in Italy. Waters tried, but he never found her. A hard case for an aspiring detective to leave unsolved.

Waters went on to a thirty-year career as a New York City cop, never working anything but homicide after he made detective. He made a record number of busts, but he was too honest to make the right friends, on the job or in the city government. So like a lot of other cops who did good work but who nobody liked very much, as soon as he lost a step, Waters got sentenced to a police precinct on Staten Island, running in circles for the last ten years after Mafia sycophants and chasing teenage vandals, teenage car thieves, and teenage drug dealers. I'm sure it burned his ass something serious, being put out to pasture when he felt he still had good races left in him. He never heard from his wife again. Never took off his wedding ring.

My mother's voice glowed with admiration for my younger father as she told the stories, but it always softened with embarrassment when she spoke of Waters. Who that twinge of shame was for, her or him, I never knew.

I'd last run into Waters three years ago, during the big St. Patrick's Day parade on Forest Avenue, not long after my mother's funeral. My father burst hollering and stumbling into the pub where I worked. I eighty-sixed him, waving for the bouncers as soon as he got to the bar. He launched the empty beer bottle he'd carried in at my head.

I went over the bar after him like I'd been sprung from a cage, teeth clenched, adrenaline surging, a half-full bottle of Bushmills in my hand, but my foot slipped on the beer-soaked bar and I crashed down into the suddenly empty bar stools. The whiskey bottle shattered and shredded my hand. Waters pinned me to the floor before I could right myself. My father kicked at the both of us. It took three bouncers to haul my father outside. Waters bolted for the door, cuffs swinging in his fingers, leaving me cradling my bloody hand in my lap, tears of rage streaming down my face. He came back with empty cuffs. My father had disappeared into the crowd. Laughing, I was sure, at Waters and me all the way to the next bar.

Now, as my father lay dead on a slab, Waters stood in his yard, waiting on me. As I approached him, Waters frowned at me like I was a dog that had shit on the rug. A dog that knew better, but did it anyway. I'm sure I looked like the long-lost son he was glad he never had. Black boots, dirty Levi's, black T-shirt, leather jacket. Silver hoops in each ear. My father's eyes.

"Speak of the devil," he said, "and the devil appears."

Goddamn if his white T-shirt didn't, as always, show through the buttons of his dress shirt, right above the belt buckle.

Purvis extended his hand. "Again, sorry for your loss, John."

Carlo Purvis. Jesus, what a mess. Slicked-back hair, stubby legs, big beak of a nose, huge head. He went through Farrell with me. The football team used to kick his ass twice a semester. Detective by thirty-one? He must've learned to give one hell of a blow job. He wasn't sorry and neither was I and neither was Waters and we all knew exactly how each other felt.

I stared at Purvis's hand until he pulled it back. "Let's not have any bullshit here, fellas," I said. "Not among men. The only regret among the three of us is that we didn't pull the trigger."

"You sure about that, Junior?" Purvis asked.

"Positive," I said.

"And you were where this morning?" Waters asked.

"I was at work until five. You can check my time card. After we closed down, an old friend and I went out for breakfast and then back to my place." I looked at Purvis hard. "She was next to, above, or below me until I left to come here." I turned back to Waters. "Where were you this morning, Detective?"

"We're going to continue on as if you never asked that ridiculous question," Waters said. "This intimate friend of yours, Junior, she have a name?"

Purvis flipped open his notepad.

"I'd rather she didn't," I said.

Waters raised his eyebrows.

"Her involvement with me might complicate other situations for her," I said.

"Like a marital situation?" Waters asked.

"Not exactly, but close."

"We'll be discreet," Waters said. "Your story checks out, we forget about her."

"It's not you I'm worried about," I said.

"Detective Purvis understands the importance of professional conduct," Waters said. He reached over and closed Purvis's notebook in his fist. "Right, Detective?"

Purvis nodded.

"Molly Francis," I said.

"You're sleeping with Molly?" Purvis blurted. "Still?"

Waters sighed. "You know Ms. Francis?"

"Well, we dated in high school," Purvis said. "For a while. Not long."

"Until she met me," I said. "And it's not still, it's more like again. We haven't been doing it all this time. Just the past three months."

"What about David? Shit, they were together almost six years. When'd they break up?"

"Who says they did?" I said.

Waters sniffed loudly. "Maybe you two can take this trip down memory lane another time?" He pulled a business card from his wallet. "You can ask Ms. Francis to contact me?"

I took the card and nodded. Molly would never see that card.

Purvis flipped his notebook back open. "We should have results from ballistics in a few days."

Waters cocked an eyebrow. "Ballistics?"

"Well, John here had a gun on him when I went to the apartment," Purvis said. "I confiscated it." Waters just stared and Purvis blushed. "He and his father have a violent history." Waters said nothing. "I mean, Mr. Sanders *was* shot." Purvis dropped his eyes to his shoes.

"What kind of gun was it that Junior had?" Waters asked.

"Nine-millimeter," Purvis answered, not looking up.

"Mr. Sanders was killed with a thirty-eight," Waters said. "You know that. *You* recovered the weapon at the scene." He stared at Purvis. It was outstanding. I was glad I'd bought the gun just for the way Waters stared at Purvis, like he'd just caught him jerking off. Nobody spoke for a good thirty seconds.

"You seen my sister?" I finally asked.

"Her flight from Boston should be landing as we speak," answered Purvis.

"How do you know all this?" I asked. "Where'd you get her number?"

"Detective work," Purvis said. "I've been in touch with her all day. No need to worry about a cab, I sent a car to pick her up at the airport."

"That's just fucking fantastic," I said. "She'll love that, being picked up by cops at the airport." I looked at Waters, who rubbed his temples with his forefinger and thumb. I figured he did that a lot, working with Purvis. "You approved this?"

"I asked Detective Purvis to arrange her arrival, yes," he said. "I should've given more specific instructions."

"Her father was just murdered," I said. "Maybe she'd want her brother to pick her up? Just a thought."

"Her brother was nowhere to be found," Purvis snapped. "Or more specifically, we couldn't get him out of bed."

"Hey, fuck you, Purvis."

"Boys, boys," Waters said. He stuffed his hands in his pockets, rocked back on his heels. "Detective Purvis, go wait for me in the car."

Purvis looked up, his mouth agape, and I thought for a moment he'd protest with an "aw, Daaaaaaaaad," but he stalked off silently.

Waters turned to me. "It's probably best if I hang on to that gun for a while, anyway."

"Look, Detective," I said, "I wanna pin a medal on the guy who did this, not shoot him."

Waters grimaced. "You won't feel that way for long. Trust me."

"Have it your way." If I wanted another gun, I could have it by sunrise.

"Is there a will, anything like that?" Waters asked.

"Not that I know of. I doubt it," I said. "The old man hated lawyers. Anyway, I haven't talked to him in over three years."

"Bank accounts?" he asked. "Insurance, maybe through work?"

"Beats me."

"Help Julia find these things out. And you'll have to arrange for a funeral home to receive the body," Waters said. "Discuss these things with her. Gently."

"Far as I'm concerned, we can stuff him in my trunk and take him to the Dump."

"Keep that to yourself, Junior," Waters said. "And show some respect. I got friends out at Fresh Kills."

I spat on the patio. "Keep Purvis away from my sister."

"I'll discuss it with him." Waters turned to walk away.

"Wait," I said. I didn't know why, but I didn't want him to go. "What about the body? Do I need to do the ID? I don't want Julia having to do it."

"Me neither," Waters said. "So I did it. Also, depending on how the investigation goes, we may need to go through your father's things. Don't throw anything away just yet. Don't touch anything at all."

"Yeah, sure," I said. "That's fine about the ID. Thanks."

We stood there, staring at each other, despite the fact that Waters looked desperate to get away. I felt like I should be asking more questions, but they were hard to come by. I dug my hands into my jacket pockets. No matter where I tried to settle my eyes—my mother's long-dead forsythias, a cigar butt in the spotty lawn, the empty bird feeder on the back fence—they wouldn't stay.

"Okay then," Waters said. "You two need anything, call me."

"When you saw him in the morgue," I said suddenly, "what did he look like?"

Waters wiped his mouth with his hands. His eyes, which had held steady on me all through our conversation, darted around, as busy as mine. He puffed out his cheeks then blew out his breath. "I guess you're gonna find out anyway," he said. But he still didn't tell me anything.

"In the face?" I finally asked.

"Back of the head. Twice. The exit wounds did do severe damage to his face."

I ran my fingers through the hair on the back of my head. They'd shot him execution style. Who? And what the fuck for? What the hell had the old man gotten into? This was gonna destroy my sister. It was gonna break her heart. I couldn't think of a way to soften any of it for her.

"You're sure it was him?" I asked.

"We have witness verification at the scene. He had his wallet on him," Waters said. "ID, credit cards, a picture of the four of you, from when you and Julia were still little kids."

"Motherfucker."

Waters put his hand on my shoulder. I walked away. "What're the chances you'll get somebody for this?" I asked. I kept my back to him, spoke over my shoulder. "Do you have any idea what this will do to my sister? You have to at least give her that. You have to get somebody."

"I won't make any promises," Waters said, "and there wasn't much useful at the scene. But I've been doing this a long time. I've made cases with less."

"Sounds like bullshit to me," I said. "Sounds like the company line."

"I'm sorry you feel that way, Junior. When I find him, you still want to give him a medal?"

THREE

WHEN I WAS EIGHT YEARS OLD, I TOLD MY FATHER I HATED BEING called Junior. He took it personally, and, who knows, maybe I meant it that way. He did his best to smack me around to it, and I've been stuck with it for twenty-three years. In the back of my mind, I know it's fitting that I'm named after my father.

I got his face. Irish as a famine in the fog. Bright blue eyes, thick, dark brown hair, a few stray freckles. When I don't trim it, my beard grows in red. Much to the old man's chagrin, though, I didn't get his body. Dad was the size of a backhoe. He was a superstar at Wagner. I'm lean and wiry, always have been. Molly once called me lithe. I liked that; it's a sexier word than skinny. Dad called me "sickly thin" and demanded my mother feed me and fill me out. He took it upon himself to toughen me up.

Mom tried, but at sixteen I was still a beanpole and the slowest butterflyer on the high school swim team. Dear old ass-kicking Dad couldn't stand having a skinny son in Speedos, but Mom called me "graceful" and said I had "great form." That was her way of telling me I wasn't much of an athlete and that was okay with her. She had a kind heart, my mother, especially when it came to her kids, and no matter how much my father tried, he never did break that part of her. He didn't need her anymore, but we did.

I missed out on the big body, but I inherited other things from my father. His big temper, for instance. From the beginning, that never needed any feeding or filling out. I could split ears screaming as a toddler. I routinely emptied my crib of all toys, bottles, blankets, pillows, and sheets, and when I was really inspired, the contents of my dirty diapers.

By grade school, I'd developed a propensity for destroying my toys. Not by accident, mind you, in fits of youthful enthusiasm, but purposefully and elaborately. For a while I did it in the privacy of my room, hiding the broken pieces in my closet or under my bed. Then, one warm fourth-grade evening, I took half a dozen complicated dinosaur models I'd spent the better part of a month building out into the driveway. One by one, I smashed them to pieces. To this day, I have no idea why I did it. My father arrived home from work to find me stomping the wreckage, and proceeded to smack me dizzy right there in the front yard.

He dragged me into the house by the arm and threw me at my mother's feet in the kitchen. He demanded she do something with me and stalked off upstairs. My mother sat me at the kitchen table and held a bag of ice to my face. I winced at the coldness and swallowed a mouthful of blood, but I didn't cry. My mother hurriedly explained to me that the beating had been an accident. She was sure my father and I were both sorry. I knew she was afraid of him when he came back to the kitchen. She put the ice in my hands and rushed me outside to clean up the mess I had made.

I walked out onto the porch and hurled the bag of ice into the street. It was then that I saw Purvis across the street. He stood there, watching me with his mouth hanging open, clutching a soccer ball against his stomach. He looked terrified. I knew he had seen everything my father had done. I wanted to explain it to him. I wanted to punch him. I lifted my hand to wave and call him over so I could do one or the other; I wouldn't know which until he was in front of me. But he just turned and ran back to his house, leaving the ball bouncing in the gutter. I felt a flicker of pride that I'd scared him, and then humiliated that he'd seen me getting punished.

Confused, and shaking with shame and anger, I walked over to the driveway to do my job. It was the first time I saw my own blood on the ground. Just a few little black spots scattered among the dinosaur parts. My mouth and jaw throbbing, I collected the plastic shards of the models and threw them down the curbside drain. All that remained was the blood. I didn't know how I'd get that off the concrete. I couldn't go back into the house. I thought about getting rags and bleach from the garage, but I was afraid to go anywhere near my father's stuff. So I knelt down and rubbed at the stains with the hem of my T-shirt. I was still at it when my mother called me in for dinner.

Later that night, from my room, I heard my father yelling at Julia. The rush of footsteps up the stairs told me Mom had scooped her up and spirited my sister up to her room next to mine. I went over to ask Julia what had happened. Dad had gotten angry with her for dragging a chair up to the fridge. She'd been trying to reach the freezer. To get me more ice. I told her not to worry about it and picked up a Dr. Seuss book off her floor. Julia sat cross-legged on the floor and I stood up on her bed. "I am the Lorax," I began, holding the book open but reciting from memory, "I speak for the trees."

———

I GOT TO STAY HOME from school the next day, until the swelling went down. At recess the day I went back, Purvis asked what I'd done to make my father so mad. I pushed him so hard he banged his head when he fell. A teacher came running over, and I told her, before she even asked what happened, that it was an accident.

Purvis never asked any more questions, but he always looked at me funny when I missed school, whether it was because of my father or not. He made me nervous. Purvis was well-known at school as an excellent rat. We resented him for it, but silently respected his skill. None of us could ever catch him telling a teacher on us. I feared he'd bring his excellent ratting ways back to the block and tell my folks when I got in trouble in class. I knew I'd never catch him at it. Every now and then, as a precaution, I warned him to keep his mouth shut. In response, he would drag his pinched finger and thumb across his closed lips and nod knowingly at me, like we shared the location of buried treasure. I didn't know what made me more angry, that he knew secrets about me, or how much he enjoyed ownership of the knowledge.

Purvis and I continued hanging around together as we got older. He was always the one making the effort, waiting for me after school, showing up on the front porch every Saturday morning. I don't know if I ever really liked him, but it got me out of the house and away from my father. Secretly, I feared betraying Purvis because of what he knew. I towed Julia around the neighborhood with us when I could detach her from my mother's side.

My father and I had more accidents, though he learned after the first call from school to stay away from my face. I wouldn't talk to a soul about what was happening. I don't remember if it ever even occurred to me. I doubt it did. I was no Purvis. I was no rat.

After a while, I at least learned to run. I ran to my room, to the bathroom, anywhere I could put a door between us, and never to my mother. My father had a long reach but wasn't much for chasing me. In my early teens, things changed. My father went for quality instead of quantity. For a big man, my father was surprisingly quick. Closed fists replaced open-handed smacks. I was growing up, and it was time, I guess he decided, to treat me like a man. I turned dark, became a brooder, steeling myself against him. I trained myself not to flinch when he raised his voice, not to make a sound when the punch landed. I appeared like a spirit for dinner every night, then vanished to my room for the evening.

Using a stolen switchblade, I carved through the covers of my textbooks, into the desk my mother bought me when I started high school. I sliced thin red lines in my shoulders, drawing stares at swim practice. I answered their stares and the coach's questions with crazy rants about Celtic warriors and tribal markings. I got suspended for telling the guidance counselor to mind his fucking business. I never talked to my parents about anything. I just haunted the house, my high school, my small slices of the island, pissed off at the world.

"This has to be your genes, Susan," my father said one evening as I cleared the dinner table, eager to escape upstairs to write bad poetry, to read, or just to stew in my own inarticulate venom. "We got us one of them faggoty artist types. He sure as hell didn't get it from me."

"Please don't use that word in reference to our son," my mother said. To his last day, I'm sure my father thought she was referring to the word "artist."

———

I WAS IN THE SHOWER when my sister arrived from the airport. Julia pounded on the door and yelled at me to hurry up. I yelled back that I was already hurrying. I'd slept through the first inning of the Mets game. Already, they were down by two to the hated Atlanta Braves. I hate the fuckin' Braves almost as much as I hate my father.

I glanced at the TV as I passed it, saw things hadn't improved, and found my sister sitting at the kitchen table, photographs spread out in front of her. I bent into the fridge for a beer, tossing the cap into the sink, an odd habit I'd developed I don't know when, and sat in the fake leather nook that wrapped around the kitchen table.

"'Sup, sis."

Julia swept her hair out of her face and sighed. "I didn't think you still had a key."

"I don't," I said. "Broke in through the dining room window."

"Glad to see you're staying sharp," she said. She covered her eyes with her hands and rested her elbows on the table. "Can you believe this shit? Someone murdered our father. It's unbelievable. Who would do this? What for?"

"Forget that for now." I leaned across the table and touched her elbow. "How're you doing?"

Julia didn't answer. Her face was blank, unreadable when she took her hands away. Her eyes fell back on the photos.

"Whatcha got there?" I asked.

Julia moved some of the snapshots around, apparently at random. She was looking at them but seeing something else entirely. What that was, I had no idea.

"Just some stuff, some pictures I had at my place," she said.

"Of us?"

"Of all of us," she said, still staring.

She shoved a few photos across the table to me. They were square, four-by-four or something, with fat white borders, curling at the edges. I picked one up, then another, then another. My sister and I standing in front of a vintage car in a museum somewhere. My sister and I running across a beach. My sister and my father on a carousel. My father seated behind her on a toy horse. He's wearing a loud shirt and wraparound sunglasses. He looks seasick. Julia's wearing a bright yellow dress and a brighter smile. I looked at my grown-up sister. Her eyes were wet.

"What museum is that?" she asked. "What beach?"

I tossed the photos on the table. "I don't know."

"Where is that carousel?" she asked. "Coney Island? Jones Beach? I don't remember any of these." She swept her hands over the pictures. "These people, they could be anyone. I don't remember this family."

"Jesus, Julia, how old are these pictures? We were little kids. Of course you don't remember." I picked up the one with the car. "When was this? 'Eighty-four? I was seven, you were, what? Three? Of course you don't remember."

"Do you remember?" She shoved the carousel picture at me. I was ten in that picture. Old enough to remember, if I tried.

I concentrated. We'd been to Coney Island. I thought so anyway, I thought someone told me about it once, but I couldn't recall anything specific. "I remember that ugly shirt the old man's wearing."

"Do you?" she asked. "From that day? Or from looking at these pictures with Mom? Or from her cleaning out the closet? Or do you just think you remember it?"

She pushed another photo at me. Mom and I are holding hands, running toward the camera through a field of short dead grass. We're both laughing. I'm going on four years old. Autumn, judging by my mother's sweater and the yellow grass. Just me and my mother. She is thin and young. Red-cheeked. Beautiful.

"Tell me about that one," Julia said. I couldn't. I didn't remember a thing about it. That moment, wherever it was, may as well have never happened.

I pushed up from the table. "Julia, I don't know. What's the difference? So we don't remember. Big deal. I don't remember my first day of school. I don't remember the first book I read. I don't even remember the first day of high school. I barely remember the day I met Molly." Julia looked up at me, confusion in her face. I threw the picture on the table. "These are just . . . this is just the highlight reel, the wish list. It wasn't like this and you know it. It wasn't toy horses and beaches and sunny fields." I took a big hit of beer. "There's plenty I do remember, like bruises and broken furniture. I don't need any pictures to remember what he was like."

"It wasn't all misery, either." She wiped her eyes. "You know why I'm crying?"

"Not for the old man, I hope." I flicked my cigarette ashes on the kitchen floor.

"Don't you let him cause you one more single moment of sadness."

"Are you going to answer my question?"

I blew out a plume of smoke. There were a million reasons for her to be crying. Because whatever misguided hope she'd held of making him a decent father died on that sidewalk. Because all that remained of her family now was me and some grainy, yellowing photos. Because she grew up watching her old man beat her mother and her big brother. Would it have been easier on her, I wondered, if he had hit her, too? I drained more beer from the bottle.

"Fucked if I know," I said.

"I'm crying for me," she said. "I don't miss him. I never realized it until now, but I haven't missed him for years. I don't know who he is, this man in this awful shirt. I feel like I never knew him. Isn't that sad? My father, the man our mother loved for most of her life, was shot dead in the street and all I feel is numb." She reached out and grabbed my hands, squeezing hard. "What kind of daughter does that make me?"

"You were a better daughter than he ever deserved," I said. "And you know it. You tried as hard as you could. You wrote, you called. You tried."

"I did those things because I was supposed to, because that's what daughters do," she said. "Because Mom would've wanted me to. It wasn't because I missed him."

"It's not your fault he never answered," I said. "It was more than I ever did."

"What kind of sister am I, John? Tell me the truth."

"You're a fine sister," I said. "The best a man could hope for. You're too hard on yourself, and too forgiving of the old man, like always. When will you learn not to care anymore?"

"You care," she said.

"The hell I do."

"Sure you do, Junior," she said. "If I still know you at all, you're feeling a whole world of things, maybe none of them good, but at least you feel something. I don't. I can't. I can't feel anything. It doesn't matter to me that Dad is dead, that neither of us will ever see him again."

"Then why are you even here?" I asked. "I'm only here because of you. Why didn't you stay in Boston and go on with your life? You should've saved us both the trouble."

"Because Mom would be heartbroken if we didn't do the right thing."

"Mom is dead. Besides, she was heartbroken for most of her life. It's too late for either of us to make it up to her now. What the hell's the difference?"

"Mom's not dead in here," Julia answered, tapping a small fist above her heart.

She started crying again. Quietly. One deep breath and a steady stream of tears. I lifted her from her chair into an embrace.

"It's just us now, Junior," she said. "Don't be a complete bastard. Not to me." Against my shoulder, I felt her eyelashes beat back tears. "Stay here, in our house, with me. Until this is done." She looked up at me. "Don't leave me here alone."

I sat with her and held her hand until she stopped crying, but we didn't look at any more pictures. I started to tell her what Waters knew about our father's death, but she stopped me. Purvis had already told her. I wanted to know more about her conversations with Purvis, but I bit my tongue. He was a touchy subject for her, too. I just got up from the table and went back into the den.

After she tidied her makeup in the bathroom, Julia joined me on the couch, sitting close beside me, and we watched the Mets fall further behind.

"Has Jimmy called back?" she asked.

"Jimmy who?"

"McGrath," she said. "I called him when I got in."

"Jeez, what'd you do that for?" I asked.

"Because I knew you wouldn't," she said. "Just like when Virginia dumped you. For Christ's sake, your father just died and Jimmy's your closest friend."

I sank back into the couch. "Jimmy and I don't talk so much anymore."

"Why am I not surprised?" Julia said, shaking her head. "What happened? What'd you do?"

"I didn't do anything," I said. "Nothing happened. Just life, you know?"

"Call him in the morning," she said. She stared at me, waiting for a promise to do what she said. She'd have a long wait.

"Can we talk about something else?" I asked.

"Actually, we do need to talk about the arrangements for Dad," she said. "The wake, the funeral Mass, all that."

"The hell we do," I said. Me and my big mouth. She so set me up for this.

Julia chuckled like she knew exactly what I was thinking. "I'm sorry you feel that way," she said, "but things have already started. I called Scalia's and arranged for them to receive and prepare the body. They even agreed to handle the insurance for us. I didn't want to make any of the formal, final arrangements without talking to you."

"About what?" I said. "I'm not interested in formal arrangements. How much of a bribe would it take for the coroners to take him right to the Dump?"

Julia crossed her arms and sank back in the couch. "That's disgusting," she said. "And it's rude. A lot of people from the Towers were laid to rest at Fresh Kills. It's where they found Eddie Francis. That, at least, should matter to you."

"You're right about the Dump," I said. "It's better company than the old man deserves."

Julia snatched up the remote and muted the game. "Enough. There's going to be a wake, and there's going to be a decent funeral. Like in a normal goddamn family."

I turned to face her. "That's what you wanna do? Fine. You wanna try and make some pretty pictures out of this mess? Fine. But don't expect me to participate in it."

"This isn't about pretty pictures. It's about doing the right thing."

"You spent years trying to do the right thing by him," I said. "What'd it get you?"

"This is about more than him," Julia said. "It's about Mom. It's about us. Give me one good reason you can't take a week out of your oh-so-exciting life and do the right thing by your family."

"I don't want to," I said. "That's reason enough. The best thing you could do for *us* is leave *me* out of it. What's the point? All right, you'll be there alone if I don't go, but other than that, why should I go? It's bullshit. Everyone knows how he and I felt about each other. It'd be a joke."

"There will be other people there," she said. "I want *you* there. That's not a good enough reason to go?"

"Don't do it, Julia. Don't make me choose between how much I love you and how much I hate him. It wrecks my head. I'm getting a headache already."

I got up to get another beer. I brought one for my sister, pouring it into a glass first. She drank it just like Mom did.

"You tell me to ignore how I feel about Mom," Julia said, turning to me as I sat beside her. She sipped her beer and set it on the coffee table in front of her. "Why don't you do the same with Dad? You got your wish. He's dead."

I cocked an eyebrow at her. "First of all, I didn't get my wish.

He didn't suffer extensively before he died. So, while I'm satisfied, I'm not happy. There's a difference. Second, can you forget how you feel about Mom? It hasn't stopped affecting your decisions. It's the whole reason you're here. I still hate the old man and I will make my decisions accordingly."

Julia's eyes got very deep and she patted my knee. "You can't know how unhappy it makes me to hear you say that." She turned her head to the TV. "Delgado just homered. They're only down by one now."

"They scored?" I stood and pointed to the TV. "See? See how the old man ruins my life? First time in weeks I get to see a goddamn Met game in peace and quiet and I miss the big hit because we're talking about him."

Julia grabbed a belt loop on my jeans and pulled me back onto the couch. She smacked me across the back of the head.

"Gimme a break," she mumbled. "Not everything bad in your life is his fault."

"He's haunting me already," I said. "Look, there he is. Sitting on the Braves' bench, in uniform. The betrayal never ends."

She rubbed my back and laughed, nodding toward the TV. "I don't pay attention to this silliness. I'm only in front of the TV because it's fun to watch you watch the game."

I screamed at the ump when he called an obvious ball four a third strike on David Wright to end the inning. "There is no justice in this world," I said. "The whole league is in conspiracy against me and my boys."

"Junior, you have the strangest set of loyalties I've ever encountered in another human being. All this emotion over millionaire strangers who probably wouldn't let you clean their spikes and yet you won't even call Jimmy about Dad."

I just rolled my eyes. This was an old conversation. At least as old as the Mets' enduring habit of getting torched by the Braves. I watched the Mets' second baseman fumble a ground ball, blowing a golden shot at a double play. Now, instead of the inning being over, it was first and third with the clean-up hitter at the plate. Get one back, give up two; that was how my boys did against Atlanta.

"I'm counting on your loyalty this week," Julia said.

"I thought we'd settled that," I said. I eyed the remote, wondering if I should grab it before she got the chance.

"I need you there," Julia said, "and I think you need to be there."

"Maybe you're right. I wanna see him put in the ground myself. Just to be sure this isn't some sick joke he's playing on us."

Julia went a little pale and reached for her beer. "It's going to be a closed casket," she said. "Remember?"

She stared at the television, at the commercials playing between innings, lost in thought. I sat there beside her, staring at my palms, embarrassed for the cruel jokes I'd made. I could feel the angry heat radiating off her skin.

Waiting for her to cool down, I wondered how the Mets had gotten out of the inning, if there'd been any further damage before the third out, and about what Waters had told me. Were there things he wasn't telling me? He'd been a cop forever; he must've had more gruesome conversations than ours. Yet he'd seemed unnerved by it. They'd found the murder weapon, but Waters still said there wasn't much that was useful at the scene. I wasn't a cop, but I knew there were all kinds of things a gun could reveal. What could be more useful to a murder investigation than the murder weapon? Why did I care?

I tried to think of something else, something useful and kind to say to Julia. She was as stubborn a person as I knew, and, despite her comments about needing me there, if she wanted services, they were going to happen, with or without me. She would do it all herself if she had to. She had so far and was already maybe keeping score against me for leaving her alone with it. I took a deep breath.

"What do you need from me?" I asked.

"First, I want you to take me to the Mall tomorrow," she said. "I need clothes for this. The wake, the Mass."

"The Mall," I groaned. "You're a painter and you're short on black clothes? I hate the fucking Mall. It's everything . . ."

Julia silenced me with a glare. "You're coming with me. I'll buy you lunch. I can't argue about this anymore." She stood and headed for the stairs.

"Where are you going?"

She stopped at the foot of the stairs. "I'm exhausted. I'm going upstairs to read for a while and then I'm going to bed."

"It's barely six o'clock," I said. "You need to eat something. Let me take you to the diner."

Julia looked at me, and then up the stairs, rubbing her hand up and down the banister. "I need some time alone."

I got up off the couch and went halfway to her. "I'm sorry I'm such a jerk. I'll buy you a salad and we can start this conversation over."

She shook her head, held her hand up for me not to come closer. "I want to get an early start on tomorrow. We have a lot to do."

I returned to the couch, my beer, and the game. After a while, I realized Julia was still standing there. I ignored her for about thirty seconds. Then my skin started to itch. "What?"

"You might want to start thinking about the eulogy," she said.

I stared at her for a long time. "You're kidding."

"Who else is there?" she asked. "You're the oldest son. It's your job." I was speechless. Had my sister lost her mind? "Don't look at me like that," she said. "You know I'm right. We'll talk more about it later. Maybe you can talk to Jimmy about it." She walked up the stairs.

I stretched out on the couch, one leg thrown over the back, one foot on the floor, trying to relax into my first real moments of peace and quiet since Purvis had come to my door.

When I woke up, it was dark out and the game was in extra innings. Carlos Beltran, the Mets' All-Star center fielder, stood on second base, clapping his hands, infield dirt staining his uniform from his knees to his number. The cameras panned the ecstatic Shea Stadium crowd. Beltran had tied the game in the bottom of the eleventh with a two-out, two-run double. I was pleased, but my knowledge of the inevitable muted my enthusiasm. I knew Beltran would be stranded at second base. He would never make it home, and the Mets would find a way to lose the game, rendering Beltran's big hit only a pretty but meaningless highlight in what was ultimately a losing effort.

The Mets held on through the twelfth, but I couldn't get back into the game. Instead of getting caught up in the excitement of extra innings, I found myself wishing they'd hurry up and get it over with. The commercials before the thirteenth seemed interminable. Unable to sit still, I stood and stretched. My legs and back ached from the long weekend hours behind the bar. I felt short of breath and the house suddenly seemed claustrophobic. The walls seemed too close, the ceiling too low. Though I knew Julia slept heavily, I couldn't help feeling that my every movement disturbed her. What I needed, I decided, was to get the hell out of the house. And it didn't much matter where I went.

I found house keys hanging on a wall rack in the kitchen. The keys dangled from a Farrell High School key ring, a maroon and gold rubber lion's head. There were tooth marks, mine, around the edges. I slid the ring over my finger and studied the keys in my palm. I'd made a big show of leaving them behind when I moved out, one semester into my three-semester college career. I'd never had another set of keys to my parents' house. I'd never needed them.

I slipped them into my pocket and looked around the kitchen, debating whether or not I should leave Julia a note. Just in case she woke up in the middle of the night and felt compelled to come looking for me. I didn't want her thinking I'd broken my promise to stay with her and gone back to my apartment. I found a pen in a kitchen drawer and scrawled a quick note on a piece of paper towel. Just that I was out, but I'd be back.

When I tossed the note on the table, I noticed Julia had left one picture out, propped up against the cardboard box. A photo of my father at a banquet table, wearing a tuxedo. He raised a pitcher of beer with one hand and held a full glass in the other. Next to him, his elbow on my father's shoulder, sat a blond guy, about my father's age, holding up a beer glass, the bow-tie on his tux undone. I had no idea who he was. Both men were laughing like fools at something only they could see. The photo was dated four years before I was born, the year of my parents' wedding. Something I couldn't put my finger on convinced me I was looking at their wedding reception.

I looked at my father's hands, searching for a wedding ring, but I couldn't see his fingers. The beer was in the way. No matter how hard I tried, I couldn't place the blond guy. And it bothered me. I did have some vague memories of my parents with other adults, or at least of adult voices floating up from downstairs while I was in bed. But I couldn't put his face with any of the voices.

My parents did go out at night, my father pacing as my mother scrambled to feed us dinner and get herself together. I remembered Julia and me being left alone at night when we were little, sometimes until very late. I'd wait up until the headlights turned into the driveway and then I'd bolt upstairs, jump into bed, holding my breath until his voice told me his mood. Sometimes I heard only the muffled voices of my parents, barely distinguishable from each other, discussing what I figured to be all the fun they'd had out in the mysterious adult world of the night. Other times, I could hear my father yelling about something she'd done, or hadn't done, or said, or hadn't said. On those nights, I didn't hear my mother's voice at all. But for hours after the yelling was over, I could hear Julia sniffling in the room next door.

Maybe this blond guy had been a part of my parents' nights out. He'd been with them that one night in the photo, at least. More than that was impossible to know. I figured the tux made him for the best man, or maybe an usher. Or maybe I had it wrong and my father was the best man and the blond guy was the groom. As hard as it was to think of my father as a groom, it was even harder to imagine him as anybody's best man. But there it was, in fading color. I studied the photo, searching for my mother, a blur in white, somewhere in the background, but she wasn't there. It occurred to me that maybe she had taken the picture.

That I could see, my mother bent at the waist, wearing a wedding dress, long blond hair falling, the camera to her eye, waving at my father to smile for her. I could almost hear the sarcastic cut on my mother that my father whispered to his friend. It was probably what they were laughing at in the photo. Something really witty, like they could see down her dress, or that she better use two hands to work the camera. I found myself hoping that both men had suffered through king-hell hangovers the next morning.

I wondered if my mother had known that blond guy well. What had my father done to drive that guy out of his life? There must've been something, because my father eventually did that to everybody. Before I even finished grammar school, not long after the "accidents" started, people stopped coming over, and my folks had stopped going out before that.

Julia wouldn't know who the guy was, either. That was probably why she'd left the picture out, to remind her to ask me about it. There was nothing for me to tell her. It occurred to me, standing there in that empty kitchen, that there was no one left but me to ask. It was a shame. I didn't have any answers. I put the photo back into the box, burying it under a pile of the others. I switched off the kitchen light, grabbed my jacket, and headed out the front door.

I decided to forgo the car and its busted taillight and its expired registration. Minus my few pleasant hours passed out next to Molly, I'd pretty much been drinking for twenty-four hours or so and I'd seen enough cops for one day. So I walked, head down, hands in my jacket pockets, the few blocks along Richmond Avenue down to Joyce's Tavern.

THE PLACE WAS NEARLY EMPTY when I walked in, just two old drunks at the end of the bar and one couple leaning close together at a side table. Old Joyce himself stood behind the bar, white apron stretched across his plump belly, the soft colors of the Christmas lights over the liquor shelves shining on his bald head. He watched me, digging fingers into his black beard, as I took a seat at the bar under the TV. Then he whispered something to the drunks.

They looked at me, the watery eyes of the old men dark in the dim light of the bar. I stared back at the three of them. Joyce was either trying to recognize me, or already had, and was debating whether or not to throw me out. One of the drunks said, "Sanders's kid," to him and he nodded some more. Like it was on the rest of the island, "Sanders's kid" was a strong indictment at Joyce's.

For half a year or so my father had been a regular, picking this joint after he'd worn out his welcome somewhere else. I'm surprised it took him so long to get here. It was the bar closest to the house and literally on the way home from the Eltingville train station. My father had walked right past Joyce's Tavern on his way home from work every weekday for years. It would be his last stop, his last regular bar. His reputation preceded him, but my father paid his tab and didn't misbehave any more than the other regulars, so Joyce gave him a chance. But my old man had a special talent for getting under someone's skin, for picking the one thing that drove them craziest and latching on to it like a pit bull. For Joyce, that thing was Northern Ireland.

Born on the Catholic side of Belfast, Joyce finished high school there before joining his older brother on Staten Island, taking over the bar when his brother died years later. All in all, Joyce had adjusted to the island well enough. He lived with the traffic, the frantic pace, the pollution, and the smell of the Dump in summer. All of it was easier to take, I guess, than riots and kneecapping. One thing he always hated, however, was drunken spouting about "the Troubles." He once smacked a guy right in the mouth for ordering an Irish Car Bomb.

The "barstool Irish" Joyce called them, the Irish-Americans, three or four generations removed from Ireland, who'd never even been to the Republic, never mind the North, but who loved to get shamrock tattoos, shout about getting the Brits out of Ireland, and ask him how to send money to the IRA. Of course, barstool Irish were also the lifeblood of the tavern's business; Staten Island was loaded with them and my father could've been their king. I had the pleasure of being there when, after my mother's funeral, my father wore out Joyce's patience and his reign came to an end.

My father was three-sheets and on his soapbox. The early negotiations for what became the Good Friday Accord had already begun, but it wasn't like my father to learn anything about what he chose to pontificate about. And that day he was eager to make noise about anything other than my mother being dead, to do anything that deflected the accusing stares that followed him.

He stood on the bar rail, waving his wallet in the air, hollering that he would match any donations to the "beloved boyos fighting for the union of the motherland." I sat two stools away, my face in my hands. Julia stormed out. Joyce had already asked the old man three times to sit down and shut up, only to be told to fuck off. Joyce finally got my father's attention by walking away with his whiskey.

When my father jumped down from the rail and protested, stumbling over his own feet, Joyce barreled out from behind the bar. He leaned right into my father's face, demanding to know when the righteous Mr. Sanders would be flying off to Ulster to join the fight.

My father blinked at him, silent for a long moment. "Ulster?" he finally said. "What the fuck's gotten into you, Joyce? I'm talking about Ireland. Where the fuck is Ulster?"

Joyce went right for his throat. It took me and three other guys to pull them apart. My father was banned for life from Joyce's Tavern. I started hanging out there more often.

As he studied on me from the far end of the bar, I wondered if Joyce would remember that I'd helped drag my father off him and out the door. From the look on his face, the jury was still out as he headed my way.

"Harp," I said. He didn't move. Okay, I thought, be that way. I tossed my cigarettes on the bar, took one out and lit it. I thought about spitting on the floor. If he was gonna eighty-six me, it was gonna be for something *I* did. Joyce didn't say a word. He set an ashtray on the bar then went off to pour my beer. I laid a twenty on the bar.

"Who's gonna check on a Sunday night?" he said. He jerked a thumb over his shoulder. "Won't catch those two complaining." He took my money, pouring fresh drafts for the drunks before he made my change.

"I got theirs, too. Keep the change." He did, dropping two fives into his tip jar. The drunks raised their empties in my direction as Joyce set the full glasses in front of them. There. Now everyone was happy. We could all relax.

"I'm sorry about your father," one of the drunks said. "It's a terrible thing."

I turned my back and looked up at the TV. Inning fifteen. Each team had scored one in the fourteenth. This game might never end. Joyce brought me a full beer when mine was empty.

"How come I hardly see you anymore except when someone dies?" he asked.

"I moved to the North Shore, up by the Boat," I said, "a while ago."

"Your old man's at Scalia's then?"

"He will be."

Scalia's brought Joyce a lot of business. We'd waked my mother there, waked her parents not long before her. It was where we'd waked my friend Mike after he flipped his car, where we waked Molly's brother, what they found of him, after 9-11.

"How's Julia doing?" Joyce asked.

"Fine," I said, surprised he remembered my sister's name. "You know, as well as she can, considering. She'll be in this week with me, I'm sure."

Joyce stared at me, grinding his jaw. "Good. I'm glad she's doing all right." He glanced at the drunks, then back at me. "She looked like hell this afternoon."

"She was in here?"

"Briefly," Joyce said. "Talking to that big-nosed detective. Purvis. The one you used to know. He bought her a glass or two of wine."

I turned, looked at the front door, wiped a hand down my face. Well, shit. Halfway between Joyce's and Scalia's was the Optimo deli where my father liked to buy his beer and cigars, the place where he'd been shot. I straightened on the stool. That deli was practically next door. Only the pharmacy and the hair salon stood between it and Joyce's. What was Purvis doing, bringing her to the crime scene? I wanted to strangle him. I thought maybe I would next time I saw him, which explained why Julia hadn't told me much about it.

"What did she see?" I asked. "What was out there when they came by?"

Joyce hemmed and hawed. "Probably not much. Of course, he

was long gone, your father, by then. The meat wag—ambulance—came right away. There was nothin' left but a bunch of cops, some police tape." He shrugged. "I don't know what to tell you."

"Had she been there? To the corner? Did Purvis take her there?"

"I dunno," Joyce said. "I didn't talk to her. I recognized her, you know, of course, but what do you say?" He rubbed some stray ashes into the bar. "They came in and they left together. I poured her drinks. I didn't know what else to do."

"Fair enough." I drained the last of my Harp and asked for another, with a shot of Jameson on the side. Joyce hesitated. "Please. I'm not gonna wreck the place. I'm not my old man. I don't give a shit about Ulster."

Joyce raised his eyebrows at me.

"What?" I said. "Both sides have been throwing bombs at each other so long, they probably don't even remember what for. It's fucking pointless."

He looked at me for a long time. "Seems they've been getting somewhere in the past few years. No one's thrown any bombs in a while. Sure, there's been Omagh, the murder, the robbery. But even Paisley finally retired. People are trying."

"Trust me," I said. "It'll never end. Not there, not with the Arabs and the Jews, not with the Sunnis and the Shiites. People love to hate each other. It's too easy."

He set the beer down in front of me and next to it an empty rocks glass. "It'll end. Either they'll work something out, or they'll just get tired of fighting." He tilted the whiskey over the glass, pouring me what was easily a double shot. "One way or another, every fight eventually ends."

I started to say something else but thought better of it and reached for my wallet. This time, Joyce wouldn't take my money.

He walked over to the drunks. A rerun of *M*A*S*H* played silently on the television over my head. I wondered who had lost the ball game.

At closing time, outside the bar, I shoved my hands in my jacket pockets and looked down the street. I shivered. The weather had changed. Heavy clouds blocked the stars and moon. The wind blew hard and steady, and way too cold for May, even at half past midnight. I could smell the rain on it, and a hint of the Dump.

When he turned from locking the door, Joyce caught me staring at the torn yellow police tape that cordoned off the corner. Loose ends snapped in the wind.

"You all right?" he asked, taking my elbow.

I jerked my arm free, my eyes locked on the corner. "Fine. I hadn't really thought about it being so close." I turned to him; he had backed a few steps away. "What did you see?"

"Nothing," he said, his fingertips worrying his beard. "I was still at Mass when it happened. The cops were already here when I came to open up."

"You see him carted off?"

"Nah. Who wants to watch something like that?"

I thought Joyce might make his escape but he just stood there. "What did you hear?" I asked. He looked away. "C'mon, Joyce. Your bar was full of cops and people from the neighborhood all day. People who knew my father. I wanna know what they're saying."

He sighed through his nose. "It happened real fast. Car screeched up to the curb. Guy got out, hit your father twice in the back of the head, drove away. There were people around, but everybody ducked at the shots. Nobody even saw the gun till it was spinnin' on the sidewalk and your dad was down. The car was long gone." He held out his hands. "Nobody could've done a thing for him."

"Anybody get a good look at the guy?"

Joyce shook his head. "He was white, big. That was the best anybody could do."

I tossed my cigarette in the street and stepped up to Joyce. To his credit, he just set his shoulders and tilted his chin up at me. "All night I sit in your bar and you never think to tell me any of this?"

"It's my job?" Joyce said. "What about the cops? You talked to them. You talked to Julia. I figured they'd told you."

I backed off. "You know any names? Anybody who saw something?" We stared each other down awhile, then I saw the question move across his eyes. I was asking myself the same thing. Why was I asking? "Because I want to know what happened," I said. "I'm thinking I might want to talk to people."

"Not that I know anything anyway," Joyce said, "but I don't think that's a good idea. It ain't healthy. That's what the cops are for."

"Look," I said. "I'm not looking to make trouble. I just want some answers. You know? For my sister."

Joyce squinted up at me, his mouth turned down at the corners. He didn't believe a word I was saying. "It's not always easy with you, Junior. Who can tell how you'll react to things? That way, you're just like your father."

I lit another smoke. My father got drunk and hit things. That was how he reacted. What was unpredictable about that?

Joyce offered me a lift home. When I declined, he patted my shoulder, told me to take it easy the next few days, and asked me to extend his condolences to my sister. I said I would, but I didn't move from the doorway. He looked at me over the roof of his car.

"Go home, Junior," he said. "Leave it alone. Take care of your sister."

He drove away, leaving me in the doorway, smoking and trying to decide what to do next. Richmond Avenue stretched before me so empty, so quiet, that I could hear the traffic light at the intersection changing colors. I heard the echoes of a train in the distance, but I couldn't tell if it was coming closer or heading away, the wind confusing things. I wasn't ready to go home. I was hammered, but felt like I couldn't possibly sleep, like I might never sleep again. I felt more restless than I had when I'd left the house.

Down the street, a late-night train rattled into the Eltingville station. It had been coming this way after all, had been closer than I'd thought. I watched as it creaked to a stop, the silver cars shimmering under the amber lights of the station. All the cars looked empty. The doors hissed open. After a few moments the two-note warning bell sounded, the doors closed, and the train groaned into motion. More than a few nights, when I was younger and still living with my folks, it had carried me home from some bar, or from the ferry terminal at the north end of the line, the only rider in my car, and in the cars on either end of mine.

Then I heard footsteps echoing from the station. Someone coming down the stairs. A slightly inebriated gait. A young woman, short-haired, pulling a denim jacket tight around her, emerged from the shadows at the foot of the station. She paused at the corner, pulled a pack from her jeans and lit a cigarette. She looked familiar, the way she cocked her hips as she flicked the lighter, but I knew it was only a trick of the shadows and streetlights. I didn't know a soul down this end of the island anymore.

She stepped into the street, heading my way, then stopped dead in her tracks. I thought maybe she had spotted me in the doorway and taken me for a mugger, or worse, but when I backed farther into the darkness, she didn't react at all. She was staring at the corner in front of her, at the broken police tape. She turned and disappeared into the shadows of the side street, her steps quick and steady now, gravel crunching beneath her boots. When she was gone, I walked to the corner. I wished I had packed a flask.

A streetlight hung over my father's murder scene, glaring down on it like a spotlight. Strands of tape blew in the wind like the tails of cheap yellow kites. I caught a tail in my hand, pulled it free, and wound it around my fist. I stared down at the concrete. The chalk outline of his body was already smudged, fading away. At the head, someone had tried washing the blood off the sidewalk. They'd done a poor job, the dark stain still a shadow on the concrete. A rusty, graffiti-covered security shutter guarded the front of the store, and I wondered how much of my father's blood and brains had splattered against the building. Joyce's whiskey lurched in my belly.

I passed through the tape, squatted down beside the chalk and the stains, arms draped over my knees, cigarette burned down to the filter, burned out, between my knuckles. I could still smell the bleach. A headache rose behind my eyes and I tried to breathe shallow. My leather jacket creaked at the shoulders when I reached out and rubbed my fingers in the stains on the sidewalk. My fingertips came away clean. I wondered how much longer the outline and the stains would last. The deli would open in the morning, and people would walk right over the bleach and the chalk and the blood, rushing for their coffee and bagels and their *Daily News* before they caught the train.

The chalk would fade away under their footsteps. Whatever tape lasted the night would be stuffed in the trash. In a couple of days the blood would look only like so much spilled coffee.

I don't know how long I'd been there when the rain started, but my knees cracked and my thighs ached when I stood. I dropped my cigarette butt, crushing it under my boot out of habit. I stomped my feet, shook my legs, forcing my blood to get moving again. Another empty train rattled into the station. I turned my back and walked away, a little unsteady on my feet, a yellow kite tail stuffed in my pocket. I got as far as the other corner and the pay phone by the traffic light. I had a bad idea.

I dug through the hole in my jacket pocket and fished out all the loose change I could find. I wiped the rain off my face and stacked the coins on top of the phone. Then I laughed at myself. Like there was any chance the phone would work. I lifted the receiver. The dial tone hummed in my ear. I should be back at the house, dry and warm in my parents' den, drinking my father's whiskey.

When a voice from the phone told me what I should do if I'd like to make a call, I realized the receiver was still in my hand. I set it back in the cradle. I didn't know Molly's phone number. She'd never given it to me. I wasn't allowed to call her. I could call information. I picked up the receiver again, set it back down. I stared at the pile of coins. Yeah, that'd be a big hit, a drunken phone call in the middle of the night. On a school night, no less. What would I tell her, even if she answered? What am I up to? Oh, nothing much, just heading home from hanging around my father's murder scene in the pouring rain. So, I could ask, you alone? I could catch a train.

I tossed the coins into the street. There was a slight chance, between the booze and the rain and the hour, I wasn't thinking straight. The walk home would help me calm down. If I still wanted to make that call, I could make it from the house. I knew I wouldn't, but the thought got my feet moving again. I'd go back to the deli, in the daylight, when there was someone there to talk to and I could find out some things. It took me three blocks to light a cigarette in the rain.

I TRIED TO BE AS QUIET as possible coming in the front door, but the locks gave me trouble. Swearing, I finally got them open, shoving the door so hard it banged against the wall. I stood there awhile, listening. No sound came from upstairs.

I grabbed my bag from the hall and stripped and changed into a T-shirt and boxers in the den. I dried my hair with a kitchen towel, then headed into the living room to raid the liquor cabinet. My father hadn't left a will, but I knew he had left the cabinet well stocked. There they were, the unopened bottles of Jameson, when I opened the door. Beside the bottles was a set of dusty, seventies era rocks glasses. I'd seen them before; I'd been raiding the liquor cabinet since I was fifteen. The glasses, like the rack of poker chips and the cork coasters on the shelf below the whiskey, were holdovers from the days when my folks entertained. It was just like my mother to never get rid of them, just like my father to forget they were there.

I blew the dust out of a rocks glass, fingering the raised brown and gold designs. I cracked open the bottle, the spiced wood smell of the whiskey rising to my nose as I poured. I downed the shot, and immediately felt better. I squeezed my temples in the fingers of my free hand. I was damn glad I hadn't broken down and called Molly.

I poured another drink and settled on the couch. I put my glass on the coffee table and studied my trembling hands. It wasn't that long a walk home but the rain had chilled me bad. I downed half the drink, trying to coax the warmth it put in my belly out through the rest of me, and resolved to forget what I'd done on the corner. I couldn't understand it, and I didn't want to hear Julia's theories on what it might mean. It didn't mean anything, other than I was drunk and restless, uselessly curious about an event that changed my life not at all.

I draped my arm over my eyes, rested my drink on my belly. I wanted to think about things that had nothing to do with the house, with my father. His death or his life. I tried to think about Molly, but I couldn't hold the visions I wanted. Nothing sexual. Molly resting her chin in her palm. Molly turning her cigarette against the edge of the ashtray, her eyes down as she listened to me talk. Grown-up Molly. Something recent. I wanted what was waiting for me at the end of this long, stupid week.

But every time I searched for the Molly of the past three months, I couldn't find her. The Molly of our high school romance shoved her out of the picture every time. I couldn't look away from seventeen-year-old Molly. Her, walking ahead of me down New Dorp Lane, talking a mile a minute over her shoulder. A punk's bright red streak dyed in her hair, a woman's hips straining at her secondhand blue jeans, a girl's arms swinging from her brother's newly sleeveless red hockey jersey. The same butterflies came to me on the couch that came to me that day on the street.

I saw Molly dancing to U2 at a party in the candlelit living room of a friend's house, her Keds abandoned in the corner, her black T-shirt rising over her pale stomach, arms entwined over her head, a perfect picture of "Party Girl." Molly, outside that house later that night, crossing the wet grass of the backyard toward me, her feet still bare.

I saw Molly in the backseat of my father's Cadillac, after he'd picked us up from the party. Her reflection in the window, her streak was blue by then, a curl at the corner of her mouth. Her hand creeping up past my knee. Molly pulling her hand off my thigh when my father's suspicious eyes appeared in the rearview mirror. I'd hated him more in that moment than I had ever in my life. My stomach hurt as bad as it did then.

I stared down into my drink. I'd wanted a few quiet pictures of what was happening now. Just something to ease my mind. But all I'd come up with was a list of lost moments, a sequence of images that had somehow morphed into a trail back to my father. I felt as pissed as I had that night in the car, the way he hung, even freshly dead, over everything. I closed my eyes, ran my palms over my thighs. I was worse than my sister with her photographs. I swallowed the last of the whiskey, pressed the empty glass against my forehead. Young Molly came to me one more time.

She knelt on her parents' kitchen floor, looking up at me. A red bandanna held her hair back from her pale face. Rage danced in her eyes. Muscles bulged at the corners of her jaw, as if she were chewing on curses and swallowing them as they rose from her throat. Bloody paper towels littered the floor around her. Blood smeared the plastic bag of ice in her hand. She pushed my sweaty hair from my eyes and said something about my riding the train in my condition. She asked if anyone had even offered to help me. I shook my head.

She reached up and pressed the bag to my mouth, inching closer to me. Her other hand palmed my cheek, holding my head steady when I flinched at the ice. My eyes flitted from her face to my hands, curled in my lap. I was afraid to touch her and too exhausted to move. She said something about stitches. She said something about her brother's latest hockey game. A joke. I tried to talk and she moved the bag away. Nothing came out. Droplets of blood, from the bag, from my mouth, peppered the floor between my feet. It seemed they'd never stop falling.

I turned out the lights and curled up on the couch. That day in the kitchen wasn't the only time Molly took care of me after one of my father's rages. I often found my way to her after a beating. Sometimes, like that day, I just appeared at her parents' door. Who knows what they thought? Other times, I'd call from a pay phone and we'd meet somewhere. I bloodied more than a few of her bandannas. She never seemed to mind, and I knew I could always steal new ones for her.

Her anger sometimes rivaled mine, it seemed, the way her eyes and hands trembled. She went electric with fury. I could hear it crackling in her voice no matter how soothing she tried to sound. More than once, I half-expected to find her at my parents' front door, calling my father out into the driveway. Sometimes, after she'd helped patch me up and calm me down, I wondered if she was angry at me, for letting it continue and for not finding a way out. More often, I was just ashamed of myself and my family. These things didn't happen in Molly's house.

For a long time she asked about the beatings, asked about my father. Sometimes she asked when the wounds were still fresh. Sometimes she asked after the cuts and bruises had healed. She asked why. She wanted reasons, wanted answers. Then one day, she stopped asking.

Maybe she accepted the only explanation I had, the one I spat out over and over. My father was a violent, raging man and he hated me. Maybe she finally believed me. She'd certainly seen plenty of evidence. Maybe she just got sick of hearing it. Whatever the reason, I was glad when she stopped asking for answers.

I wanted them, too, but by then more for her than for myself. Not having them for her only made everything more humiliating.

We hadn't said a word about him this time around until Purvis had shown up at the door. There was no talk of my father, no talk of Eddie. What was the point? She and I aren't like we were then, wrapped up in each other's lives, needy for each other's teenage drama. We weren't in love anymore. We'd grown up and streamlined. Like good adults, we kept our scars to ourselves. It was just as well. All these years down the road I didn't have any better answers, about either my father or her brother.

Five years ago, after she first moved to Boston for grad school, Julia used to call me with her psychobabble bullshit. Usually, it was right after she'd been to see her therapist, when she was just brimming with insight and hundred-dollar-an-hour wisdom. My father was afraid of his family, she said. And the fear he didn't even know possessed him tore its way out of him masked as anger. This is what my sister told me, that my father kicked the shit out of my mother and me because he was afraid of us. Whatever.

I indulged my sister her theories. I made noncommittal noises into the phone as she talked, wondering who she was really trying to convince of their veracity, me or herself. I didn't much care what she believed or whether it was true or not. It didn't change anything, and if it brought her some comfort, I felt she was welcome to it. I had no right to disabuse her of her illusions. But I didn't believe a word of what she said. I was the one who got hit, who saw his eyes, blind and blank with rage, like the doll-eyes of a shark. I had all the *real* evidence writ in black and blue all over my body, and it all added up to one clear, simple fact. My father was mad as hell.

There weren't any hidden emotions, any identity crises, behind it. There was no mystery. My father was flat-out, full-on pissed off, at the world and everything and everyone in it. For all I knew he was born that way. Or maybe it started when the stadium lights went dark and he was left with nothing but real life. Maybe, in his eyes, he was an improvement over his own father—a hard man from the Irish coast who, drowning in bad debts, a cinder block in his embrace, stepped off a Staten Island pier a dozen years before I was born. That was one thing about my father—for better or worse he was always there.

What I did know was that when he hit the boiling point, when he realized the world wasn't going to crumple at his feet like a second-string running back, my father lashed out at whatever was closest. Sometimes it was Mom, sometimes it was me. He couldn't hit his boss, he couldn't hit all the people crushed up against him on the train, couldn't hit the bank, or the car, or the government. So he hit us. And he kept hitting us. Because, no matter how many bruises I had across my back, the boss kept nagging, the train stayed crowded, and the bills kept coming. Despite all the bone-crushing tackles he'd handed out, despite all the plates he could stack onto the barbell, even into his fifties, my father couldn't bury the dirty little secret that he wasn't tough enough for the life of a middle-class husband and father of two.

That's the way I saw it in high school, when I was with Molly. I still see it that way. I didn't think this way when I was a kid. Kids need reasons for things, the simpler the better. Kids live in the present, not the past. As a kid, I knew he hit me because I had done something wrong. Why else was I being punished? Most times I couldn't tell you, for the life of me, what I had done, but I must've done something. Parents don't punish their kids, don't smack them in the face then punch them in the back when they duck when they're eight years old. Not unless that kid has done something very wrong.

In the dark, I'd sit on the edge of my bed, trying to stifle my sobs, my T-shirt pulled up to the bridge of my nose. I sure as hell didn't want anything to cry about. I'd squint my eyes and clench my little fists, maybe do a little hitting on myself, and try to remember every moment of that day. What had I done? There must have been something. If I could find it, I could not do it again. There are lots of things you can find at eight. Did I come right when he called? Were all my shoes in the closet? Had I left my books on the kitchen table? Did he know my teacher took my baseball cards away during the math test? Was I stupid? Ugly? If I could find it, I could fix it.

I never found it, though, because whatever it was, I kept doing it. I must have kept doing it. I kept getting hit. All that deep thinking ever got me was another handful of broken crayons, another pile of shredded baseball cards, to hide in the bottom of the wastebasket.

Then, when I was ten and Julia was six, things clarified for me.

We were all in the kitchen, the whole happy family. Julia was drying the dishes that Mom was washing. It was Julia's favorite thing to do with Mom, the dishes. To this day, she does the dishes when she's depressed. Even if they aren't dirty. She'll pull them out of the cabinet and wash them for the hell of it. It still works, she says. And my sister tells me I have coping problems.

That day, Julia dropped a glass and it shattered at her feet. My father erupted from his chair at the kitchen table, spilling his coffee and whiskey, and belted my sister across the kitchen, splitting her lip in two places. It was the first and last time he ever hit her. Faster than I had ever seen even my father move, my mother had her nails at his eyes. One of the scratches on his cheek left a scar. And the screaming. She screamed at him over and over, "Not my baby doll, not my baby doll." I crawled out from under the table and dragged Julia back under it with me, hiding her as best I could, her lip bleeding deep into my shirt.

My father dragged my mother into the den by her hair, as if he could hide from us what he was going to do. They had a bad accident, and a few more things got broken. I thought it was the end of the world. It was only later that night, as I lay in bed, that my mother's words meant anything to me. I doubt I thought the words, but I had the realization that my mother had given up on me. She had surrendered me to my father's rage. Not your baby doll, sure. I didn't want that bastard kicking the crap out of Julia, either. But where, over the years, had been the words *not my son*? Why had she never unsheathed those claws for me? That night in bed I discovered the reason. It was the only one, and as clear as the full moon outside my window. I was that bad a kid. Had to be. One parent hated me and the other had given up on me. Parents didn't do things like that unless you gave them a reason. All the time I had spent looking for the things I had done wrong was wasted. *I* was wrong. Whatever a good kid was supposed to be, I wasn't it.

I remember looking at my classmates in the days following that night, studying Purvis and all the other ones who had seemed the most like me. Whatever secrets they had, they weren't revealing them to me. I watched my sister, but I couldn't see the difference between her and me. Our grades were the same. We kept our rooms just as neat. For all I knew, though I never looked, she could've had broken toys under her bed.

All I learned was that I was, for reasons beyond my obviously limited capacities, different. Less than. My classmates knew it, my parents knew it, and my teachers knew it. My sister had to know it, though she never gave it away. I was the last to know. It was proof of how stupid I was.

After that night in the kitchen, things were never the same between my sister and me. She grew wide-eyed and wary around me. She watched me like I was a sickly stray dog that maybe carried a dangerous contagion. I half-believed she was right, and wondered if I'd infect her. I was tempted to bite her. The difference hung, like gauze, between us. I hated myself for pulling her under the table, and hated myself over again for even thinking that way. I hated myself most of all for not getting her under the table before she got hit. Maybe that was why she treated me different, because I'd been too slow. I vowed not to make that mistake again.

I sat up on the edge of the couch, my head down between my knees. The room wouldn't stop spinning. My thoughts spun even more wildly. I wondered if Julia and I could still fit under the kitchen table. I wondered if, that night long ago, we could've fit my mother under there with us. Why hadn't I reached for her, too, that night? My gut boiled. I hadn't been sick from drink in a long time, years. I did remember it well enough to know it wasn't a sure thing just yet. I still had a choice. I could stagger down the hallway to the bathroom and get it over with, or I could fight it. I wasn't in the mood to move, so I dug in for the fight, taking deep breaths and trying to focus on the floor.

The first time I drank myself sick I was at a Halloween party my senior year. At Jimmy's house. Molly'd left me by then, so she wasn't in the car, thank God. She'd brought a date to that party, in fact, a contributing factor to my going overboard. My father had come to pick me up early, just to fuck with my good time.

Jimmy'd already switched me to ice water, but my father's early arrival had totally thrown off my recovery timing. Before we were halfway home, I got sick all over the side of the Cadillac.

My father laughed at me, called me names, lurching the car all over the road while cheap vodka and Orange Julius lurched out of me. He didn't say shit about the car. He'd probably been half loaded himself. If I hadn't locked myself in the bathroom when we got home, he'd have probably knocked me around for breaking my mother's rule about drinking at parties.

Now, perched on the edge of the couch, I could hear him mocking me again, calling me a lightweight, a momma's boy, a faggot, and a fool. No wonder Molly had thrown me over for a college boy, he said.

I decided I'd puke in my lap before I'd lock myself in the bathroom. I told myself I had nothing to hide from anymore. I gagged, tasting vodka though there was only whiskey and beer in my belly. God, how old are you now? I asked myself. Get over it. Just refuse it. Beat it back. I started sweating, realized I hadn't eaten a thing all day. I told myself I wouldn't feel as bad tomorrow if I let it go tonight. But I didn't get up. At least I figured I hadn't when I woke up in the morning on the floor beside the couch.

FOUR

JULIA COVERED HER MOUTH, TRYING NOT TO LAUGH, WHEN I bumped my head on the coffee table. I just glared at her and rubbed my head. She wore pressed jeans and a snug sweater, her face and hair already done up for the day. She sat on the coffee table. I hauled my wounded self up onto the couch.

"Good morning, sunshine," she said.

I nodded. It hurt.

"I made coffee for you," she said. "It's still hot."

She'd made coffee. I loved her so much at that moment I thought I'd cry.

She stood. "But you gotta get it yourself." She walked into the kitchen.

I didn't know if I could stand. I willed myself to forget every-thing I felt, to focus on only the thirty seconds it would take me to swallow that first sip. If I could just block everything out for half a minute, the railroad spike through my head, the molten iron in my stomach, the Brillo pad I'd been chewing in my sleep, if I could forget those things for only a few moments, I could make it. I thought of those people who walk on hot coals, who lift cars off their children. If they could do that, I could get to the coffeepot. I almost collapsed against the kitchen counter, but I made it. When the first mouthful of coffee hit me, I felt like the leper who'd touched Jesus' robe. Halfway through my first cup, I thought I might enjoy a cigarette. I told my sister such.

"Chemically dependent much?" she asked. "Jimmy McGrath called again this morning. You should call him back." She started whisking pancake batter in a big glass bowl.

I decided I wasn't ready to watch that just yet. I waddled into the living room and found my cigarettes. I returned to the kitchen table and lit up. My chest burned and I coughed. I felt light-headed. I took another drag and then I felt perfectly normal.

"So Saint Jimmy's coming down from on high for little ol' John Jr.," I said.

"Don't be like that," Julia said. "You have his number?"

"Back at the apartment," I said.

She handed me a Post-it note with a phone number on it. "I thought that might be your excuse. He really wants you to call him. Have you talked to him since you and Virginia broke up?"

I slapped the note back on the wall beside the phone and held up my hand. "Later. He's at work now anyway."

Julia set the mixing bowl down, turning to continue the lecture. Something in her eyes went soft when she looked at me. "God, you look like death." Her mouth tightened when she realized what she'd said.

I waved away the faux pas. "Thanks for taking the message. I've felt better. I went out last night." I waited for her to ask where. She didn't. "Down to Joyce's."

She turned away to pour the batter into a frying pan. "I went to the store this morning," she said. "The fridge is stocked for the week." She refilled my coffee cup while the pancakes sizzled in the pan. My stomach kicked but my mouth watered at the smell of them. "I didn't get a paper. For obvious reasons."

"Joyce extends his condolences," I said. "He and I talked for a while last night."

For the second time, she didn't rise to the bait. She just stood at the stove, flipping the pancakes.

"So you were there with Purvis," I said. "You two discuss anything I should know about?"

She set a plate of half a dozen enormous pancakes in front of me, put butter and syrup on the table. "Eat." She sat across the table, half an apple in her hand. "I ate my share before you got up."

I polished off half the stack before I spoke again. "Joyce told me some things. About the shooting. About the man, the car."

"And?"

"And nothing," I said. "It is what it is. I just wanted you to know that I know." I swallowed the last of my coffee, got up for some more. "Not much for Waters and Dickhead to go on."

Julia was quiet for a long time. "I wanted to see it. The corner."

I crossed my arms, resting the warm coffee mug in the crook of my elbow. "Why?"

"I don't know," she said. She wouldn't look at me. "I just wanted to. It was so . . ." She picked the seeds from the apple core, dropping them one by one on the kitchen table. "It was so ordinary." She pressed each apple seed under her thumb, turning her hand until it cracked. "Where were you all night? Looking for a man in a car?"

She'd heard me banging the door open. I leaned back against the counter. "Maybe I should've been, but no, I wasn't."

She leaned back in her seat, crossed her arms over her chest. "Joyce stays open till after four now?"

"I took my time coming home."

"Promise me," she said, "promise me you won't do anything stupid over this." She spread her hands on the table, stared down at her fingers. "Waters is convinced you're going to make a mess." She grinned. "I don't think he likes you much." The grin disappeared. "I know he doesn't trust you."

"Fuck Waters," I said. "He doesn't know the first thing about me. I'm no fan of his, or his moron partner, either. The only reason I'm around at all is because of you."

"I know that," Julia said. "So promise me."

"Anything stupid is a real broad category," I said, returning to my seat.

She crossed her arms again, waiting.

"Okay, okay," I said. It wasn't an easy promise to make. Her asking for it annoyed me. Why was everybody so worried about me? All I wanted was to get the week over with. I noticed she was staring at me again. What? She wanted more?

"Messing with Purvis qualifies," she said. "Forget about your history with him for the week."

"He's the one with the history problem. I'm over it; I've been over it. Remember? I won."

"That's not what I mean," she said. "I'm talking about me, not Molly."

I pointed my fork at her. "Messing with you qualifies him for an attitude adjustment, cop or not. Just like last time. He's already gotten his first warning."

Julia stood to clear the table. First thing she did was take my fork away. "That's the kind of thing I'm talking about. Leave him alone." She leaned over me, kissed my cheek. "I can handle Purvis on my own." She laughed as she loaded the dishwasher. "Is he really still pissed at you over Molly?"

"It's more like again," I said. I couldn't help it. Maybe I wasn't as over it as I thought. I couldn't pass any chance to one-up him.

Julia swung around to look at me, dirty frying pan in her hand. "You're not. Tell me you're not. You told me she was practically married."

Oops. Not somewhere I wanted to go right then. I glanced at my bare wrist. "Hey, look at the time. I thought you wanted to go to the Mall."

The Mall was someplace else I didn't want to go, but even that was better than sitting through my sister's cross-examination. "I'll go get ready," I said, pushing up out of my seat. "Be back in a flash."

I left Julia in the kitchen, still frozen with shock. I grabbed some fresh jeans from my bag and headed upstairs to shower.

"WHEN I GET TO THE White House and get my finger on the button," I told my sister as I pulled a clean T-shirt over my head, "the first thing I do is nuke the Mall."

She stared at the TV, flipping channels with the remote.

"Day after Thanksgiving, crack of dawn," I said. "Maybe earlier. I'm not looking to hurt anyone." I sat next to her on the couch, pulled on my boots. "Let them impeach me, I'll be smiling Tricky Dick–style all the way to the chopper. I wouldn't serve a day in jail, either. The neo-hippies and trustafarians would flood in from Boulder and Seattle, spring me and make me the granola king. Dave Matthews would play the coronation and I'd get laid like crazy."

Julia clicked off the tube. "So now you're gonna be president?"

"Why not? Why let the rich boys have all the fun?" I tightened my belt. I was down to the last notch. "A couple more election cycles and I'll be old enough. I'd be an awesome president. I don't like anybody and I don't owe anybody. We'd have a truly independent man in the Oval Office for a change." I looked around the den. "Growing up in this house, I understand oppression and tyranny. I could operate with only the best interests of the little people at heart."

She turned to me. "But the little people like their malls. Your sister likes her malls."

"Ah," I said, wagging a finger, "but is that in their best interests?"

Julia tossed my car keys in my lap. "I don't think your past would hold up under scrutiny. And I don't think Molly'd appreciate *Dateline* camped outside her door."

"Molly needs a little more excitement in her life," I said, standing, putting on my jacket. "We going or not? I want to get this over with."

"I'll tell you what I'm excited about," she said, throwing her arm over my shoulder as we walked down the hall. "Spending some quality time with you."

"Quality time?" I said. "At the Mall?"

She smiled at me as I locked the front door behind us, letting me know I was free to talk but she was going to ignore what I said. She looked at my car. "I can't believe this old beast is still running," she said. "It's older than you."

I studied my car, a gold Galaxie I'd bought for a couple grand half a dozen years ago. I'd earned the money washing dishes. She looked rough, dings and dents here and there from Staten Island potholes and drunken kisses at guardrails. Under the hood, though, all her parts were in order. Never stalled, always started on the first turn, even in cold weather. I'd never learned shit about cars and she'd cost me a fortune over the years. It was worth it though. When I was a kid, I'd wanted a convertible, something long and sleek, but when I went looking, long and sleek was way out of my price range.

Then I'd seen the Galaxie, parked on a North Shore side street, "For Sale" written in soap across the cracked windshield. It charmed me. I hadn't seen an awful lot of them around Staten Island, for one, where the IROC and the Monte Carlo reigned as princes to the mighty King Cadillac. A week later I was paying for it, the retiring firefighter who was parting with it looking askance at the paper-clipped piles of twenties I dropped on his kitchen table. "Dishwashing," I'd said. He'd nodded. "Tip-outs," I'd said. "Uh-huh," he'd said, still not looking at me, pulling the clips off and counting each stack to five hundred. I was about to tell him to keep his goddamn car if he didn't like where the money came from, but then he handed me the keys.

Now, looking at her six years later, I realized that except for my leather jacket, I'd hung on to that car longer than anything else I'd ever had.

"She's a beauty," I said. "Never lets me down. Though the gas mileage stinks. It'd cost me a fortune if I ever drove it any-where."

"You love the old gal so much," Julia said, "do her a favor and give her a bath."

I pointed down the block and a half to Richmond Avenue. "Bus stops right there. Runs to the Mall all day, every day. I'll be here waiting for you."

"And miss my quality mall time with my brother?" she said. "Never."

"That's a cute expression, by the way," I said. "'Quality time.'

Back in therapy? What are we going to talk about next? 'Closure'? Maybe we'll 'make amends' and 'turn it over' while we're at it."

"Careful, big brother, your twelve steps are showing," Julia teased. "That was your gig, remember?"

I walked around the car and unlocked the passenger-side door. I'd taken a shot at AA after I dropped out of college. I told my sister, and no one else. The way she reacted, you'd have thought I was Christ back from the dead. But I'd had all the Jesus I could handle in high school and had heard enough about what a loser I was at home. It didn't take. Julia took it hard when I dropped out. I felt bad about it, but not bad enough, I realized, to go back to the meetings.

"Yeah, I remember," I said. "Get in."

Julia slid past me into her seat. I closed her door too hard. She jumped. Great. Great start to your quality time, I thought.

The night's rain had cleared and the bright sunshine in my eyes revived my headache. The royal treatment at breakfast and the long hot shower had done wonders for my mood. Now, I could feel it turning black again. I slipped on my shades as I climbed behind the wheel. Julia had a pile of paperbacks on her lap, retrieved from the floor of the car. She read the authors' names to me.

"Dennis Lehane, James Ellroy, Dashiell Hammett. Oh, a classic, Edgar Allan Poe. I remember him from what? When you were in the eighth grade?"

I said nothing. Just started the car and backed out of the driveway.

She opened the cover of the Poe. "Aww, look. Look what it says. John Sanders, Junior. Homeroom 8-203."

"This is quality time?" I asked. "Breaking my balls?"

Her smile vanished; she turned away to look out the window.

For the second time in three minutes, I felt like a complete dick. I fought my mood. I wanted Julia to have at least one afternoon of peace before the real shit started.

"Sorry," I said. "Tim, from work, wanted to borrow those. The Poe is for his kid. He's gotta do a paper on him for school."

"That's sweet of you," she said.

"Tim's covered a lot of shifts for me," I said, "and he's got a smart kid."

She looked at the books one more time then tossed them into the backseat. "I thought maybe you were writing again. Remember those cop stories you wrote in high school?"

"Unfortunately. God, they were awful. Too much time watching *Hill Street Blues*."

I'd spent hours locked in my room writing those stories. I thought they were brilliant. They were terrible, and all were minor variations on the same theme: the handsome rogue cop forced by a damsel in distress into bucking the captain's orders one more time, his badge, his heart, and his life on the line. There was much kicking in of doors, much tumbling down staircases in cheap motels. Corny one-liners flew faster than bullets. Just the memory pained me.

"I can't believe I ever showed those to anybody," I said.

"They weren't so bad," Julia said. "I mean, you were fifteen, sixteen? They were good for your age. They were exciting. Lots of action. You should've stuck with it. Every time I watch reruns of *NYPD Blue* or *CSI*, I think of you and those stories. All that tough-guy talk, always a pretty girl in there somewhere." She smiled. "Mom liked them, except for the curse words."

"Mom was biased," I said, "and too generous. She wanted to throw a party if we passed a spelling test."

"True," Julia said. "Dad ever read them?"

"Fuck, no," I said. "I don't think he could read anything that wasn't written in X's and O's. Except for maybe box scores."

"Ever ask him to?"

I frowned. "Please. By then, I knew better."

"Ever show them to Molly?"

"She thought they were okay. Thought the girls always looked like her."

"We all knew that," Julia said. She turned in her seat. "She told me once, when she was over at the house for something, that you wrote her the most beautiful love letters."

"Christ," I said. "She told you that?"

My throat caught. I had written Molly love letters. Piles of them. Because it wasn't enough we saw each other all the time, that we talked every day on the phone. Forget cop stories, I could've been in the CIA, the way I snuck those letters out of the house and into the mail around my father. I caught myself reciting her parents' address under my breath. "Overwrought teenage bullshit," I finally said. "Full of criminally bad poetry. I pray to God she burned them."

"*I* thought it was the most romantic thing I'd ever heard," Julia said.

"You overestimate me."

Julia turned in her seat, her hands pressed to her chest. Her eyes were big with the memory. "C'mon, Junior. Imagine being a fourteen-year-old girl and hearing your big brother was a closet romantic, a poet."

"A normal fourteen-year-old would think it's gross," I said.

"Even then I knew I wasn't normal." Her face lit up again. "I was so flattered Molly would tell me that. God, I thought she was the coolest girl I'd ever met. I thought if I could be like her, someone would write me love letters." She paused. "I'd love to see her again. Tell her that."

"They were syrupy crap," I said.

"What did Molly think?" she asked. "Then?"

I hesitated. She always wrote me back, in black ink on pink stationery, paper that she bought just for me. Pages numbered, little hearts drawn around the numerals. I couldn't remember the last time I'd thought of those letters. It seemed like forever ago. But as I drove, I could feel the fiber in the paper underneath my fingers. I could smell the scent of her skin, of her hands, rising to me as I unfolded the pages, soft, sweet, clean. Vanilla. Strawberries. Did she still smell like that? I hadn't noticed.

I could feel Julia's eyes on me. I knew my face had betrayed me, broadcast every thought. She thought she had me. I waited. I knew what was coming, knew Julia couldn't resist.

"So what's going on with you two now?" she asked.

I glanced at her across the car. "A fling."

"Liar," she said. "You have flings with the waitresses at work whose last names you can't remember. This is Molly Francis, your first real girlfriend. Your first love." She poked my ribs with her finger. "Give."

I lit a cigarette and rolled the window the rest of the way down. We were getting close. I could smell the Dump. "Nope, no way," I said. "The first rule of Molly and John is we don't talk about Molly and John. Not with each other, not to anybody else."

"My therapist would have a field day with this," Julia said.

"So you are back in therapy," I said, making a break for a change of topic. Quid pro quo, sis. I know where to poke, too. "Same woman? I remember you liked her."

"Yeah, I'm back in therapy," Julia said, sighing, dragging out the confession like a smoker admitting to lighting up again. She scrunched down in her seat. "I went back after Cindy left me again. Different therapist. Dr. Evans moved to Colorado. Something about her husband's job. It still helps, though. Like it did the last time."

"I didn't know Cindy's leaving fucked you up that bad," I said. We sat at the intersection of Richmond Avenue and Arthur Kill Road, waiting for the light to change.

"You'd know these things if . . ."

"If I called you more often, yeah, I know that."

"I want to hear from you more often," Julia said. "Is that so bad?"

I glared at her across the car as we crossed the intersection and she agreed to drop the subject. I knew I hadn't heard the end of it.

"I didn't think it got to me that bad, either," she said. "At the beginning, I was so pissed she was leaving again, and I guess I thought she'd come back like she had the other times. But then she told me about moving to California. I guess I never really believed it was over until she packed her car. For a week, I could barely get out of bed."

"I can barely get out of bed every day of my life," I said.

"I wasn't drunk every night," she said. Ouch. Apparently, my stab at levity had been ill timed.

"The next two weeks weren't much better," she said. "I missed classes, started smoking again. When one of my classmates offered some pills, some cheap speed, I really thought about taking them. So that's how I knew it was time to find a doctor."

I pulled on my cigarette. When someone offered me pills, I thought about taking them, too. And usually, I did. But I didn't think about running after some shrink over it. I got depressed, too. Who doesn't? My sister amazed me. The whole 'I'm broken, maybe someone can help fix me' mentality was lost on me. I knew mixing Jameson, speed, and cigarettes probably wasn't a superior alternative, but at least I wasn't paying the note on some geek's Benz.

"I never knew what you saw in that bit—woman," I said, as we waited at another red light for the opportunity to crawl beside a thousand other cars a thousand feet to the next red light. "Cindy was good-looking, and she must've had some brains and talent to be in that school."

"You're answering your own question," Julia teased.

"Yeah, but she'd already cheated on you once when you asked her to move in," I said. "Then she left you twice while you were living together. The second time she wouldn't even tell you where she'd been."

"I know these things, Junior. I was there," Julia snapped. "But I loved her."

She was there, all right, no matter what that crazy bitch did to her. I couldn't blame her for getting pissy. She didn't need me counting her mistakes back to her. She had a therapist for that.

"She wasn't good enough for you," I said. "She treated you like shit."

"At times, yeah, she did. But you never really know what goes on behind closed doors."

The light changed and we ebbed forward.

"She kept beating up on you and you kept taking her back. Why?"

"Love."

My eyebrows jumped up my forehead. "Fuck love, then."

"Don't you think that's a little extreme, Junior?"

"It's an attitude that's served me well, thank you. Mom and Dad were in love. You and Cindy were in love. Virginia and I were in love. Yeah, love is grand."

Julia pouted, crossing her arms across her chest.

"I'm not trying to hurt you," I continued. "I just want to understand how someone like you could get so broken up over being ditched by a fucking loser."

"There's your answer," she said. "Cindy's such a loser, what does that say about me?"

The lightbulb flickered and I nodded. "So you're off that love shit now, right?" I asked.

"Junior, we all need love."

I slid the car deftly across two lanes of traffic, toward the entrance to the Mall. "Not me. I don't need shit."

FIVE

DIRECTLY ACROSS RICHMOND AVENUE FROM THE MALL SQUATS Staten Island's other great contribution to modern American society, the Fresh Kills Landfill. It covers more than twenty thousand acres, taking up over ten percent of Staten Island's total area. For nearly fifty years, all the household waste from all five boroughs of New York City was deposited at Fresh Kills. Back when I was in high school that was three hundred thousand tons a day. It's the largest garbage dump on the planet, and one of only three man-made objects, along with the Egyptian Pyramids and the Great Wall of China, visible from outer space.

The Dump, we call it. That's how we do on Staten Island. Staten Island Rapid Transit System? It's the Train. The Staten Island Ferry? It's the Boat. The Verrazano-Narrows Bridge? You got it, the Bridge. Imaginative bunch, Staten Islanders. I'm just as guilty. I didn't go to Monsignor Farrell Catholic High School for Boys. I went to Farrell. C'mon.

The rest of the boroughs? The Bronx has Yankee Stadium; Manhattan has Harlem, Wall Street, Central Park, and Madison Square Garden, among a thousand other things. Queens has Shea Stadium and two international airports. It hosted the World's

Fair. Brooklyn? It's Brooklyn, that's more than enough. Staten Island? We got the Mall and the Dump.

They try to hide it, wall it off with dirt mounds covered in scraggly greenery. They try to ignore it, running the West Shore Expressway right through the middle of it. They brag about herons and egrets nesting in the waterways behind it. They hunt the rats every night. But you can't hide it. How can you hide millions upon millions of tons of fucking garbage? Because that's what it is. Millions and millions of tons, acres upon acres, of fucking garbage.

Every day of the year, you can see thousands of gulls circling over it, hovering like a noxious cloud. A vermin halo staring down beady-eyed and ravenous for some guy's month-old Chinese food from over in Bensonhurst. You can hear them fighting, screeching and squawking, clawing and snapping at dead dogs from the Upper East Side. In August, when the hot sun returns after a good, hard rain, and cooks up the Dump real good, there's nowhere on the island you can't smell it. It reeks to high heaven of waste, of all things thrown away and buried, things that have reached the end of the chain and no longer have a single use left to them. Things stuffed into black plastic bags and metal cans and hauled away by huge, rumbling, stinking trucks at the crack of dawn.

But on Staten Island? Those thrown-away things? They live here forever, baby. And they stink. It's the stench of Eternal Life. Old diapers never die, they just move to Staten Island. All these thrown-away things, they come back, like a fat, farting, rancid ghost that sits its fat, dead self right on top of the island, and lingers long enough for all of us to breathe it in. And what do Staten Islanders do? They make some empty noise about how they're not gonna take it anymore, and then they build a giant mall right across the street from it. And then they build subdivisions up against it. And then they buy them and move in. They exalt Saint Giuliani when he finally closes it, like it's suddenly gonna go away then, suddenly stop rotting and seeping and polluting. Then they curse the Jersey smog that drifts over from Bayonne, and flip open the paper and read about how Staten Island has the highest per-capita cancer rate, more kinds more often, than any other place in the world. Then they remember they have to go to work tomorrow and they forget everything else. They close the window and turn on *The Sopranos*. Or they hop in the car and careen down Richmond Avenue to the Mall, dropping the trash in the can on their way to the car.

Now here I was myself, I thought, as we cruised through the parking lot at the Mall. And I hadn't even taken out the trash. You'd have thought they were giving away money, whiskey, and porn the way the parking lot was crowded. After one sweep past the main entrance, and one heart attack over a four-year-old nearly darting out in front of the car, I eased us into a spot out on the far edge of the parking lot.

"Sure we're far enough away?" Julia asked as we walked.

"I want as much distance between me and these mall rats as possible." I jerked my thumb over my shoulder, back at the car. "Parking back there? That's not about convenience, that's active disdain. I hate them, I hate this temple to the dollar, and I still can't believe you talked me into this."

"One thing I have to say on your behalf, Junior. The world *always* knows how you feel about it."

I put my arm around her shoulder. "Fuckin'-A, right."

A blast of climate-controlled air hit me as we walked through the doors. Immediately, I wanted to lie down on one of the benches near the entrance and take a nap. When I told Julia this, she grabbed me by the sleeve and pulled me forward. I dragged my feet like a ten-year-old, like when my mother used to haul us out here for the few new school clothes my father would let her buy: Toughskins for me, Garanimals for my sister—the best Sears had to offer.

Sears. Staten Island middle-class common ground. Whenever Mom took us out there, I'd always spy at least one classmate through the racks. I'd try to sneak over and commiserate in shared misery. About the sixth grade. About how scratchy new Toughskins were. Unless it was a girl. In that case I'd simply try to will myself invisible, trying to hide from her without getting too close to my mother.

My mother always ran into someone she knew, too. Some other woman I never recognized, trailing two or three kids about the same age as Julia and me. There were never any fathers around. Just little kids and their moms. I always wondered how my mother had met these women, if there was some way women could meet on the phone. Because my mother was always on the phone, but it seemed to me she never left the house without the two of us in tow.

I bumped into Julia when she stopped us at a kiosk that offered color-coded maps of the Mall. "I need two dresses," she said, studying the map. "And at least one new lipstick."

I had a feeling she wouldn't be getting them at Sears. I pulled out my wallet and counted my cash. Everything I'd made over the weekend was still there, minus the few dollars I'd dropped at Joyce's. I handed her four fifties.

"What's this?" she asked.

"For the dresses. Take it. I know you're on a student's budget."

"Put it away," she said.

"I can make it back no problem," I said. "Take it."

"I appreciate it," she said, patting her purse, "but I've got plenty of plastic."

We stared each other down. I pocketed the cash, deciding I'd just stick the money in her purse later that night when she wasn't looking. She turned back to the map, pointing to the blue rectangle marking the food court.

"Why don't you meet me there in a couple of hours?" she said. "I don't have the heart to drag you through two hours of browsing."

Two hours? I checked my cigarette pack. Had I enough left to kill two hours sitting in the car, chain-smoking? I looked over her shoulder, searching the map for the arcade. I couldn't find it. Didn't anyone leave home to play video games anymore? It didn't much matter, I decided. Even if there was an arcade, chances were the Centipede and Tempest machines were long gone.

"That all right with you?" Julia asked.

"Yeah, sure." I did spot an Applebee's and a T.G.I. Friday's on the map. I could grab a beer. Though that would mean being in one of those places: bright lights, pathologically friendly service, kids running amok. No smoking. Seemed too high a price.

Julia slipped her arm through mine, led me away from the map and forward into the stream of shoppers. I backed away from the crowd passing in front of us, positioning myself against the wall. The smell of processed fruit hit me. As I glanced up at the sign for Bath & Body Works, a baby stroller ran into my foot. I jerked my foot away, muttering an apology. The woman pushing the stroller glared at me like I'd tried to kick her kid. Two toddlers straggled along behind her. The one with chocolate all over her face stuck her tongue out at me. Her mother called her along without turning around. Julia joined me against the wall.

"So I'll meet you at the food court?" she said.

I couldn't imagine I'd have much of an appetite, but I knew Julia was afraid she'd find me still pinned to that wall in two hours. "I guess. I'll stay with you if you want," I said. "You know, for the quality time. I'll behave."

"I'll be all right," she said. "Besides, I couldn't relax with you pacing outside the store." She kissed my cheek. "Go hide in the music store. You know, like you used to."

Julia squeezed my hand before drifting away into the current of passersby. I watched her ride the escalator to the second floor. She looked calm, relaxed, her eyes scanning the names of the stores. Seeing her like that made me feel better. When she was gone, I pulled myself off the wall, turning left against the flow of traffic, trying to remember what end of the Mall the Sam Goody was on.

Meandering along, people pushing past me on both sides, I remembered the music store was next to the barber where I got my hair cut. Where was that? The other end? Should I double back the other way? I stopped and looked around. I realized I'd managed to go several years without setting foot in this place. None of the stores around me looked familiar. I read the names: Abercrombie & Fitch, Banana Republic, Kenneth Cole. Their lesser cousins and clones stretched as far as I could see in either direction. An enormous Saks anchored that wing of the Mall.

I couldn't recall having set foot in any of those stores, here or anywhere else. I'd absorbed the names, I guessed, from ads and other people's clothes, other people's lives; I didn't live in a cave. But nothing around me interested me. I didn't wear those clothes, or walk around with those logos splashed across my chest. I realized I'd stopped in front of a Verizon Wireless store. I peered through my reflection in the store windows into the display.

I had no use for those silver gadgets behind the glass, couldn't even name them, never mind use them. I could barely operate the remote for my stereo, really still hadn't figured out the satellite TV we had at work. It was a running joke there, and I wore my dinosaur status as a badge of honor. Standing there in the Mall, I felt vaguely proud of my ignorance of fashion and technology, and a lot like I'd been dropped off in the middle of Beijing.

Several members of Team Verizon, in their matching red shirts and black pants, stared at me, pained grins on their faces. One of them touched some plastic gizmo in his ear. I waved. Gizmo waved back. I felt like I was about to be shoved into a white van and whisked away for reprogramming, or like I was at the zoo, on the wrong side of the glass in the reptile house. I thought for a moment about asking one of them where a music store was, sure both the Sam Goody and the barbershop were long gone. But I couldn't bring myself to walk into the store. Those guys gave me the creeps.

I got moving again, took my time, watched the girls go by. Once you got out of Sears, it wasn't just middle-aged women with kids anymore. I ducked outside for a cigarette. A gaggle of college-aged girls clicked by in high heels and short skirts, headed for their cars, shopping bags brushing their bare knees. The skin, sunshine, and nicotine made me feel better. I decided against checking the map by the doors when I went back inside. I was having an adventure, why ruin it? There had to be a Virgin or a Tower in here somewhere. Maybe there was still a bookstore. I'd find something to kill the time eventually. I was in no hurry, I thought, pulling the door open and stepping back into the AC. I laughed to myself, at myself, lost and clueless at the Mall. It was hard to believe I'd once spent so much time here that I'd memorized the layout.

Like a lot of other guys at Farrell, my first job was at the Mall.

Unlike the other guys, it wasn't at the McDonald's. I worked at a bakery, some chain with a fake French name. Of course, the stuff we sold was all prefab, like everything else in a Mall. Everything came to us premade and frozen in big, color-coded boxes. Bagels had blue stickers, cookies had red, bread had yellow. No matter what color the stickers were, though, all the dough was always the same color: beige.

My job on weekdays after school was hauling the boxes out of the freezer, laying the next morning's bake on metal trays, sliding the trays into the baking racks, and rolling the racks into the cooler, where the dough would defrost by the next morning. Every Friday I'd put on a hat and gloves and organize the freezer by color. It was monkey work, but it made me money, and it kept me out of the house.

When the summer came, I took over the baking, if you could call it that. All I did was roll the racks out of the cooler and into the oven, set the timer, and drink a pot or two of coffee. Maybe give the poor schmuck who took over for me a head start on laying out the next day's bake. I got grief for it, for being a baker, from my friends. It wasn't sexy, or tough, but I didn't care. It wasn't flipping burgers. And while they jumped from one fast-food joint, or grocery store, or gas station, to another, bored or fired or both, I held on to that same job. By the end of my tenure there, I had my own keys to the place.

The only difficult part was the hours. To have everything ready by the time we opened at ten, I had to be in by four-thirty in the morning—five at the latest. But I got used to it. And starting so early had its perks. Hours of solitude, for one. No one else came in until nine. I liked slipping into the Mall before sunrise. It was clean and dark and quiet. No sunlight yet through the skylights, the escalators still, acres of pristine, faux-marble floors, freshly scraped of gum. There was something pure about the stillness, the silence, the half-light. I hated when the people, all noise and demands and complaints, came and ruined it.

During the summer, I made sure my mother never knew exactly what time I got off work, so there were never too many questions about where I was. If I brought home enough cinnamon buns, she forgot to ask questions altogether. My father always worked until deep in the evening. But I always made sure Molly knew when my workday ended. So the job also bought me a lot of hours with Molly.

The Mall was our default date. When we'd seen all the movies we wanted to see, couldn't stand another trip to the comic book shops, the Fantastic Store at the train station by her house, Jim Hanley's Universe at the train station by mine, there was always the Mall. I was already there. It was a short bus ride from her house. It was just a place to do what we liked best, be together.

We wandered its confines for hours, arm in arm, me smelling like French bread, muffin batter under my fingertips, her smelling like vanilla soap and strawberry shampoo. We spent a small fortune, one quarter at a time, in the arcade, typing our initials into the middle regions of the high-score list, me making sure my name was always under hers.

We bought each other peace-symbol pins for our knapsacks and denim jackets, bargain bin cassettes for our omnipresent Walkmen. I bought her posters for her room. She always had them up on her walls by the next time her parents were out and I came over.

It meant something to me seeing those posters on the wall, even if they were pictures of men I knew I would never be. And it wasn't just that Molly was sitting under them, flush in the face and half undressed, though I'm sure that didn't hurt. I liked having cash in my pocket and liked having earned it. I loved being with someone who made me want to be generous. And, of course, I loved Molly like crazy, like only a teenage boy can love.

On the rare weekend days I wasn't with Molly, I made Mall excursions with Jimmy McGrath, stealing all the same things I bought when I was with Molly. I stole things for her, though I never told her the gifts were stolen. I replaced every bandanna I bloodied three times over. I enjoyed taking on her behalf almost as much as I liked giving to her. Taking risks for her felt romantic and rebellious. Knowing I could give to her, whatever I had to do, made me feel like a man.

I was a good thief. Fearless. Jimmy tried to keep up, but he lacked, at least in those days, my nerve and my skill. Of course, I had certain advantages over him, experience being the main one. I'd started stealing back in junior high, as soon as my sister fell in love with drawing. Paper, markers, colored pencils, charcoal—I thieved whatever I could get from the art classroom. I had other experience to build on, too.

Compared to my father, what were underpaid clerks and overweight rent-a-cops gonna do to me? Living with my father, I'd learned when I was being watched, and when I wasn't. And what was one more beating if I got caught? There was always one coming down the pipe at me anyway, I figured. But I never did get caught.

When we weren't stealing, Jimmy and I leaned against the wall in the black light glow of the arcade, waiting for a machine to open up or just modeling our weekend uniforms, our dress code as strict as the one we despised at school. Tight jeans. Black T-shirts advertising bands that had broken up before we were old enough to buy their albums. Denim jackets emblazoned with the logos of our more contemporary heroes: Van Halen and Iron

Maiden, Def Leppard and Rush. We taunted the preppies and the guidos, deriding their uniforms, their turned-up collars, or their gold chains. We were rookie tough guys in training, a pair of sheltered puppies pretending to be strays, itching for a fight we were grateful never materialized. We laughed, a lot.

Walking around the same but different Mall fifteen years later, I realized I probably wasn't the thief I thought I was back then. I couldn't remember taking anything that made me worth chasing. I did wonder if I could still get away with it. Not that it mattered. I didn't see anything worth buying, never mind stealing. I wondered whatever happened to the bakery chain with the fake French name, if it had gone out of business. A Starbucks probably replaced it. I decided I'd look for it when I went up to the second floor. I needed another cup of coffee, even if it had to be Starbucks.

When I smelled the Bath & Body Works, I realized I'd made a complete circuit of the first floor. I slipped on my sunglasses and wandered outside for another cigarette before tackling the second floor. As I lit up, a kid, about fifteen, sixteen, big diamonds in his ears, his shorts and his T-shirt both four sizes too big, stepped up to me. He asked for, no, demanded, a cigarette. I tucked the lighter into the pack and the pack into my jacket, next to my wallet.

"Fuck off," I said.

He took half a step closer to me. I closed the distance by half again, stepping into a fog of cologne. I took an exaggerated drag on my smoke, realizing I'd love nothing more than to put it out in this kid's eye. I looked over his shoulder at his friends. Four of them plus the tough guy made five. I wished there were more of them. I got a sour taste in my mouth. My palms itched. I could do this. I could wipe the fucking floor with these guys. I needed it. I thought of my arcade days. I wasn't a puppy anymore. I held up my lit cigarette in front of his face.

"You want a cigarette," I said, "take this one."

I switched it to my left hand and put it back in my mouth. I hoped he'd try. I realized that I'd wanted to pound the shit out of someone since Purvis had delivered his news. I hadn't been in a good fight for years. Something told me that if I did this, I could sleep through the night. All I wanted was a reason to swing first.

"Fuck you, motherfucker," the kid said.

"Creative," I said. But not enough. I wanted to fucking snap, to come unhinged, not just swing for the hell of it.

I watched his eyes as he breathed stale French fries into my face. I wondered if he was high, but his eyes were clear, intense. I was disappointed. Hopped up on something, he'd take that much longer to put down. He had the beginnings of a mustache on his lip. In another six months he could start shaving. He wore braces. They'd tear his mouth and my knuckles apart if we started swinging.

I took another drag and let the smoke float out of my mouth and into his face. One of his eyes twitched and I relaxed my shoulders, set my weight forward on my toes.

One of his friends walked up behind him, his eyes on me, and put a hand on his shoulder. Tough Guy snapped around. "Wha'?"

"Cab's here, dawg."

Tough Guy backed away, his arms loose at his sides, easing back into the group. Together, they drifted toward the cab, watching me. At least two were afraid. The cabbie leaned on his horn.

"You a lucky motherfucker," Tough Guy finally said from the curb.

He lifted his T-shirt, just enough for me to see the handle of the gun tucked in his shorts. My blood went hot, rushed to my heart. Too late. I was pissed, furious he hadn't done that thirty seconds ago.

They all stared at me through the back window as the cab drove away, two of them flipping me the bird. I watched the cab until it disappeared into the Richmond Avenue traffic.

Waiting for the adrenaline to recede, I watched the gulls circle the Dump across the street. I couldn't shake the feeling that somehow that little prick had managed to steal something from me. My hands shook. Sweat trickled down my rib cage.

I needed to figure out how much longer I had before I met Julia, but I couldn't get my head straight. It'd upset her to see me all jacked up. If I didn't take some time, some air, to calm down, she'd read it right off my face. I decided to circle the Mall from the outside, afraid that if I went inside, I'd hit the first person who bumped into me.

The sun baked the back of my jacket, but I didn't want to take it off. I walked fast, like I knew where I was going. A security truck slowed as it rolled up behind me. It followed me for a while, making sure I wasn't casing the cars in the lot. I stopped, turning my head far enough for me to see him but not far enough for him to see my face. I told myself that if he wanted to talk, I'd do my civic duty and tell him about the kid with the gun. Unless he gave me attitude, in which case I might have to drag him from the truck by his plastic badge. The truck idled for a moment then turned away and cruised deeper into the lot. Apparently, I still wasn't worth the hassle for a few bucks an hour.

Walking on, I thought about the kid with the gun. Seeing it hadn't frightened me. If he'd meant to use it, he would've made a move for it right away. He'd only flashed it to impress his friends, to save face. It was probably his big brother's gun. He'd stash it back under the bed when he got home, before his brother realized it was gone and whipped his ass for taking it. That kid, he was armed, but he was really no different than I was at fifteen. He'd rather brag about the fight that almost was than shed his blood over the real thing.

A real predator didn't stare you in the face, didn't wait for someone else to make the first move. He materialized out of thin air, moved with quickness and efficiency. Decisiveness. Authority. He didn't weigh consequences. A real killer didn't give you a chance to finish your sentence or light your cigar, never mind swing first, or fight back, or run.

A real killer stepped out of a car, shot you dead, and disappeared before anybody saw his face. He left a corpse at the feet of half a dozen dipshit witnesses who couldn't do any better than "big and white." Left an old man's blood and brains splattered on shop windows. Left the cops drawing on the sidewalk. Left a big, empty house where someone's daughter, where my sister, wept over pictures of people and places she didn't remember, asking her brother questions he couldn't answer. A killer left my sister, my baby sister, buying fucking funeral dresses at the fucking Mall. And all I could do about it was pace the parking lot looking for a fight, which, I decided, wasn't nearly enough.

I walked up to another entrance. I pulled the door open hard, but I let it go when the cold air hit me. The walk had done me no good. I watched my reflection appear in the glass as the door closed. The sunlight stung when I pulled my sunglasses off. I closed my eyes, pinched the bridge of my nose. My eyes burned. The pain got worse when I rubbed them. I couldn't breathe, my throat dry, my lungs constricted.

I thought of my sister in a store, standing at the register, a black dress on a plastic hanger tossed on the counter. I could see her digging through her purse for her credit card, telling the salesperson why she'd spent so long in the dressing room, why her eyes were red and puffy. Telling a complete stranger her father was dead. Not even noticing, or caring, that the salesperson wasn't even looking at her. I could feel Julia's chest heaving as the words rushed out of her, clearing space for the cool air that'd make her lighter for a while. Light enough at least to get to the next store and the next dress.

I'd told Molly I was happy someone had shot my father. I'd said something stupid like that. I thought of her sitting silent on the edge of my bed, staring at the wall. I tried to see myself going to her, saying something to her, anything, that I didn't punctuate with a chuckle and a smirk. But all I could see was her getting up as I sat down. I tried to picture myself with a black suit tossed on a counter in front of me. Tried to imagine handing over the cash, telling someone the suit was for my father's funeral. Just saying it, waiting for the air to rush into my chest. But I couldn't see it, couldn't feel it. The only place I could see myself was in a dark alley, beating some big, white guy's head against the pavement.

I forced a deep breath, trying to shake the alleyway from my head. I thought about another smoke, but there wasn't much point. I knew I couldn't relax no matter how long I stalked the parking lot or how many cigarettes I smoked. I chewed the inside of my cheek, biting down until it hurt, and tried to clear my head but I kept seeing my sister, this time as a tiny, happy, innocent girl in a bright yellow dress, riding a carousel pony with her father. What the fuck was I doing out here, holding my dick in a parking lot?

I figured I still had close to an hour. I could get there and back and still meet Julia for lunch without her ever knowing the difference.

———

I PARKED THE CAR across the street from the deli and ducked into Joyce's for a quick double Jameson. The bartender, thankfully not Joyce, shook his head as I slammed the shot back, slammed my money down, and walked back out the door. The whiskey went down hard. I lit a cigarette and laid hot smoke over the whiskey-burn in my throat. My head cleared and my nerves stilled. I slipped my shades over my eyes and jogged across the street through a break in the traffic.

I sat in the car for a while, drumming my fingers on the steering wheel, trying to work out how to play it inside the deli. As a teenager, I'd been in that deli almost every day. Buying a paper and coffee before school, maybe cigarettes, playing video games after. Buying beer with a pathetic fake ID on weekend nights. Just another one of the neighborhood kids. But that was years ago; nobody in there would know me now. If I was going to do any better than Waters and Purvis, I would have to come strong. Strong enough that whoever I turned up would tell me what they knew.

I was out of the car and waiting to cross the street when a tall, skinny kid, maybe eighteen or nineteen, greasy black hair down to his shoulders, backed out of the deli's front door. He held a bucket heavy with water in one hand and clutched a long-handled brush in the other. Tucked under one arm was a bottle of bleach. I knew he was out there to finish the job he'd begun the day before. I started across the street but the blare of a car horn backed me up against my car. A sharp pain in my chest shortened my breath as my heart punched my rib cage. That was new.

Pinned against my car, waiting for a break in the traffic, I watched the kid set everything down and rummage through his

apron pockets. He pulled out a cell phone and a pack of cigarettes. He lit up and started a call, leaning against the storefront,
constantly glancing at the door while he talked, hitting the cigarette often, in quick, nervous puffs. After a few minutes, he closed
the phone and dropped it back in his apron. Grinning, he tossed
his smoke daintily into the middle of the sidewalk in front of
him. The light on the corner turned red and the traffic slowed in
front of me. The kid stepped forward and crushed out his cigarette in my father's blood.

I darted through the cars, trying to remember what I'd come
there to do. The kid bent to pick up the bottle of bleach. I was
on him before he got the cap off, my toes almost meeting his, my
heels in my father's blood. He dropped the bottle. It hit the concrete with a dull thump, rolled to the corner, off the curb, and
settled in the gutter.

I pushed past him, bumping him with my shoulder, and walked
to the corner, turning once to make sure he didn't bolt for the
door. With him watching, I picked up the bottle, unscrewed the
cap, and poured the bleach into the gutter, the scent of it stinging
my nose as it rose from the street. The sting turned up the humming behind my eyes.

"Yo," he finally said, "what the fuck?"

I spiked the bottle in the street and walked back over to him.
His eyes danced as they searched my face, looking for a reason
for my behavior. I felt disinclined to give him one. I stood as close
as I could to him without us touching.

"Pick that up," I said, pointing at the cigarette butt but staring
at him.

"What are you? Some kind of fucking clean freak?" He waved
a hand over the dozens of crushed-out butts on the sidewalk and
in the street. He backed up a step. "What's the difference? You

got a problem with it, you pick it up. Get the rest of 'em while you're at it. Save me some work." He turned to pick up his brush. "Fucking weirdo."

I shoved him into the storefront window. The glass boomed and shook on impact. He yelled and his hands flew up in front of his face. I smacked them out of the way and grabbed fistfuls of his shirt.

"What's that stain on the sidewalk, shithead?" I asked, breathing in his face. "You work yesterday? What is it? Tell me what it is."

He wouldn't look at me, but I saw the recognition, the pieces start to come together in his face. "Blood."

A young girl, a plumper, prettier version of the guy I was about to throttle, stuck her head out the door. "Vito, what's goin' on out here?" She gave me a hard stare. I let Vito go. "Everything all right?" the girl asked. "I need to call somebody?"

Vito nodded. "Yeah, yeah, Angie. I mean no, no, I'm fine, don't call nobody."

"What'd you do now, Vito?" Angie asked.

"Nothin'," he said. "Go the fuck back inside, Angie. Now."

She did, swearing in Italian, at me or at Vito or at both of us, under her breath.

"That your sister?" I asked.

"Yeah," he said. "Fucking *puttana* busybody."

I smacked his face. "Don't ever talk to or about your sister like that ever again." Vito stared at me, utterly confused. I raised my hand, as if to hit him again. "Capeesh?"

"Yeah, whatever. Who the fuck are you?"

"Whose blood is that?" I asked. I took out my cigarettes, shook out one for each of us. I felt completely relaxed.

"Some guy," he said. "Some guy got shot out here yesterday."

"What was his name?"

"I don't know, man," he whined. "I wasn't even here yesterday. My old man just told me to clean it up today, after the rush. He didn't tell me nothin' else about it. Just that a guy got shot."

"You ask about it?"

The kid shrugged, lighting the smoke I'd given him. "No. I mean, I didn't think to—"

I smacked the cigarette out of his mouth.

"Jesus. Fuck." His hand came away from his mouth with a little blood on his fingertips. "Whadda you fucking want?! Jesus." People walked past us without hesitation. No one looked over from their cars, just a few feet away.

"So somebody gets shot in front of your store," I said, sliding my arm across Vito's shoulders, "and you don't ask any questions? Somebody *dies* out here, and you're crushing out your cigarettes in his blood the next fucking day like it's fucking nothin'? And you never even ask his name?"

"I'm sorry, I just . . . it's just habit, with the cigarette. I didn't mean nothing—"

"Anybody here today who worked yesterday?" I asked, my lips close to his ear. "Your old man inside?"

"No. He left a while ago. He ain't coming back today." Vito squirmed under my arm, but he didn't try slipping away. "I don't know who worked yesterday. I ain't here on weekends."

I bent down and picked up Vito's still-burning cigarette. I handed it to him. "That guy who got shot? He's got a beautiful daughter with a broken heart, prick that he was. Maybe you should show some respect. Maybe you should find out who worked yesterday. Maybe you should ask your old man some questions." I backed away a few steps. "I'm comin' back to talk to you again."

"Why don't you just talk to the cops?" Vito asked. "Whatta you buggin' me for? I don't know nothing."

Turning, I stepped between two parked cars. As I waited for a break in the traffic, I felt Vito walk up behind me. I didn't turn around. "Who are you?" he asked. "You a collector?"

"Fuck, no," I said.

"You that girl's boyfriend or something?"

"I'm her brother."

Sick of waiting, I walked out into the street, cars in both directions slamming on their brakes.

WHEN I GOT BACK INTO the Mall, I headed straight for the escalator. I stared at my feet on the way up, taking deep breaths, hoping I hadn't kept Julia waiting. There wasn't any need, I thought, for her to know where I'd been or what I'd been doing. It wouldn't do anything but upset her, and I hadn't learned anything she'd want to know.

I spied a coffee stand as I approached the food court. Some cheap imitation of a Starbucks with a pimpled kid in a blue apron behind the counter. He poured my coffee and made my change without a single word. I took the lid off and sipped, burning my tongue. It hurt but the coffee felt great going down. I needed a cigarette and a shot of whiskey to get the maximum benefit, but I felt myself settling down, felt like maybe I could eat. I spotted an empty table next to a plastic tree and sat down to wait for Julia. I was halfway through the coffee when she appeared, shopping bags swinging from her fingers.

"I must look horrible," she said as she sat. "The way you're looking at me." Most of her makeup was gone and her eyes were swollen.

"Not horrible," I said. "It's just, I can tell you've been crying."

She looked around, shrugged her shoulders. "Oh well. Like I've never been caught crying in public before."

"I should've stayed with you," I said.

"So you could hand me tissues?" she asked. "I did most of it in the dressing room anyway. Nah. It did me good, just walking around, taking care of some business. It helped, just knowing you'd be waiting for me." She checked out our choices for lunch. "Whadda you think? Chinese? Pizza? Mickey D's?"

"Whatever," I said. Maybe I'd just have another cup of coffee.

"I'm feeling Chinese," she said.

"Funny, you don't look Chinese," I said. Julia smiled at me. "Works for me," I said. "Surprise me. I trust your judgment."

She came back with a plate of shrimp lo mein and two egg rolls for me, two tiny spring rolls for her. I knew she'd only eat one, but I didn't say anything about it. I'd let her eat my fortune cookie.

I had polished off my lo mein and half an egg roll when my sister kicked me under the table. I ignored her. She kicked me again and finally I looked up. The shock on her face made my heart skip. She pointed across the Mall, through the crowd. It took me a minute. I didn't know what I was looking for. But then I spotted her. Tall, long red hair, black T-shirt with the sleeves cut off. Leather pants, right arm sleeved down to the wrist with an elaborate tattoo. She sure held my attention. For all kinds of reasons.

"Is that who I think it is?" Julia finally said.

I stood and watched the redhead walk. There was the right kind of sway to her hips. She stopped to look in a store window, turned to talk to a friend. It was her, all right. I stared, my heart doing flips and my stomach at my knees, hoping she wouldn't glance over and see me. I sat back down, still staring in the direction she'd disappeared.

"Virginia." I looked down at my half-eaten egg roll. I'd lost my appetite.

"I thought so," Julia said, laughing. "Junior, the look on your face was priceless. I wish I had a picture of that face to show all your friends down at the tough-guy club."

Julia surprised me by biting into her second spring roll. "Talked to her lately?"

"Who?"

"Virginia, duh."

"I haven't talked to her in months," I said. "Haven't had anything to do with her since we split." I rolled my egg roll in a puddle of duck sauce. It was almost the truth.

"You're a liar, Junior."

"What're you talking about?" I asked.

"Wasn't her birthday not long ago?" Julia asked. She was pushing me now and it was about to make me irritable. Which she knew. And she was doing it anyway.

"Yeah. March."

"What'd you do for it?"

"Nothin'."

"You're lying again."

I started to protest but then it hit me. I remembered. It was probably true that I should call my sister more often. It was definitely true that I had to stop calling her when I was drunk. When I did that, I talked too much. I strained to remember how much I'd given up. Probably everything.

"So I sent her some roses," I said. "Big deal."

Julia set her plastic fork down on her plastic plate. I couldn't tell if she was shocked, pleased, or pissed. Shit. She hadn't known.

"Not bad," she said. "To her house?"

"No," I said. Virginia had never bothered to tell me where she went after she moved out. "I sent them to her shop. I even had them put my name on the card."

"And she accepted them?"

"I'm not sure."

"I'm confused," Julia said. "She didn't call you? Say thanks?"

"She called when she knew I'd be at work. She mentioned that she didn't work at the tattoo parlor anymore."

I took a deep breath and blew it out. It wasn't big fun explaining it. It was embarrassing, in fact, revealing how Virginia and I had yet again, even apart, turned a simple gesture into a duel of hidden agendas. I guess it didn't help that I knew damn well she didn't like roses.

"She never specifically said anything about the flowers," I said, "but I figured with the timing of the call, she at least heard about them."

"Where's she working now?" Julia asked.

"She didn't say."

Julia picked apart her spring roll, separating the contents into tiny piles. "You told me she loved that shop, that she was going to buy into it for good."

"I guess the way she felt didn't last," I said, growing irritated with lingering on the subject. "It's been known to happen with her."

My sister looked away and then back at me. Christ, I thought she was gonna cry.

"The flowers, it was no big deal," I said. "Just a spur-of-the-moment thing. It was her thirtieth, only happens once in your life. The phone call was more than I expected. Overall, it was probably a bad idea. It certainly didn't accomplish anything."

That was the truth. My intentions hadn't been entirely honorable when I sent the flowers. I did care about her birthday, but I had sent the flowers, at least in part, to prove I missed her so little I could do such things casually, with utter disregard for any implications. In return, she'd let me know she'd gotten them, just to make sure I knew she didn't care, either. And to remind me she could find me, but that I couldn't find her. The whole dumb exchange was Virginia and me in a nutshell. We'd gotten so close we could lie to each other without even speaking.

"None of it's a big deal," I said. "The flowers, the breakup, none of it. I'm over it, all of it."

"I'll never understand you," Julia said. "You don't make any sense."

"Yeah," I said, "but you love me anyway."

Julia stood and gathered her packages. "That I do."

I searched my jacket pockets for my cigarettes. "Wish you could've taught that to Virginia."

WE WERE HALFWAY TO the car when Julia started in again.

"I always liked her," she said.

"Of course you did. She was gorgeous, and she was a switch-hitter."

Julia punched my shoulder. Hard. I shoulda let her carry her own goddamn bags.

"That had nothing to do with it," Julia said, "and you know it."

"I know. I liked her, too."

I threw Julia's bags in the backseat and started the car.

"You were together for what? Three years?" she asked.

Two years, eight months, and three weeks. "Something like that. Give or take." I backed the car out of the space.

Julia turned in her seat to face me, bending a long leg up on the seat. "I thought she was gonna be the one."

I glared at her. "Can we drop this?"

Julia dropped her leg with a thump. "I really thought you two would make it." She sat quiet for a long time, picking at her fingernails. "How did you two do it?" she finally asked. "How do you write someone out of your life like that? Just go on like nothing ever happened."

I changed lanes. I didn't have an answer and I wasn't much interested in coming up with one then and there. It was just the way it turned out. Some women I've dated, I'm still on good terms with them. It's no big deal if we bump into each other. A couple still buy me drinks. I've got one coming home with me on a semi-regular basis. Virginia was just different. In the six months since we'd split, I'd tried not to think too much about why.

Anything I found of hers in the first week after we broke up— old T-shirts she slept in, CDs, pictures of us—I boxed up and dropped off at the tattoo parlor. Whatever else of hers I found after that went in the trash. She never called looking for anything. Nothing of mine came back to me. I'm sure she threw it all out. I knew there were things I'd lost, but I couldn't recall anything I missed.

"Seems to me it would shrink you," Julia said. "Letting someone disappear with big parts of you in their heart."

"She didn't disappear, she left," I said. It came out harder than I'd wanted.

Julia stared straight ahead through the windshield, thinking her own thoughts. I got a little peeved. Suddenly, I wanted her to be listening to me.

"Look, it's better this way," I said. "All we were doing at the end was brawling or screwing. Most of the whole last year was like that. She got sick of it first and I don't blame her. And I don't hate her, either. Anything but. But we're best out of each other's way." I stole a glance at Julia. "What about you and Cindy? You two gonna be old pals?"

"Not anytime soon," Julia said from a distance. "But the facts are I loved her and she loved me. I can't see us being out of each other's lives forever. We shared too much, taught each other too much. Someday we'll be friends."

"Yeah, she taught you how to get hurt and come back for more," I said. "Why even give her the slightest chance at hurting you again, letting you down again?"

Julia frowned at me, knowing I was at that very moment wishing I could take that back. I rolled my shoulders, squinting with the sun in my eyes.

"See, to me," I said, "what you're talking about? That's settling." I paused, stuck for the next thing to say. Against my better judgment, my sister had me thinking. My head started to hurt. I struggled on.

"Like, for example, Virginia and I should have lunch once a month because we used to be a couple? So we could stare at each other like idiots and talk bullshit? What's the point?

"You know, I see exes together at work all the time. It's painful. Both of them look like they're gonna fucking die. I wanna walk over and shoot the both of them, just to end the misery. The woman never eats and the guy always drinks too much. It's play-acting, some junior-high slow dance based on denial of what's really there."

"I don't think of it that way at all," Julia said. "Yeah, things are never what they once were, but that doesn't mean they can't still be good, and valuable. There are limitations. It's tough to readjust, it hurts, but love changes colors; it's flexible. You keep what works and live on that."

I shook my head, but didn't have an argument. Honestly, I was sick of the subject. What point was there in not letting go? People came and went and there was nothing for it. Even I knew life had some rules you just didn't argue with. Someone at that table would always be left longing for something—another chance, another night in the dark, an admission of guilt or fault or love or regret that would never come, to remember something, or to forget something else. Virginia and I had been smart enough to see all that, to avoid it. We'd already said everything we'd ever have to say to each other. Yelled it. Screamed it. At least, in the end, we'd been able to agree on that. That's what I told myself, anyway.

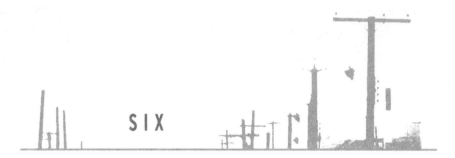

SIX

A COP CAR WAS PARKED IN FRONT OF THE HOUSE WHEN WE GOT
home. Purvis waited for us on the front porch. It was strange, and
disturbing, having him around the house again. I didn't like it. It
reminded me of our dying days as friends, when he would loiter
on the porch, trying to talk to my sister while waiting for me to
get home from swimming practice. He'd see me walking up the
street and just stand there, watching me, until I got to the house.
Then he'd make some stupid joke, and I'd give him some lame
excuse about why I couldn't hang out. I could never figure out
why he never took the hint, why he hung on so long. I didn't
know what he had to prove.

"Whadda ya want?" I asked, climbing out of the car.

"Hey, Julia," he said, walking over to us. Standing beside me,
he tapped the driver's side of the windshield. "Expired." He
walked around the back of the car, locking his thumbs in his belt.
His fingertips tapped at the badge next to his belt buckle. "And
you've got a taillight out."

"Hello, Carlo," Julia said, grabbing her bags from the
backseat.

Purvis rocked back on his heels, tilting his chin up as Julia walked away from him. "John, I need to talk to you a moment," he said, watching her back as he spoke to me. "Just a few little things that need clearing up."

I put myself between them. "Write me a fucking ticket, you got problems with the car."

He finally looked at me. "I can let the car problems go," he said. "I know grief can be disorienting. That it's distracting. That maybe you've mixed up your priorities right now."

Julia stopped at the front door, turning toward us. "You want to come in?" she asked, glancing back and forth between Purvis and me. She didn't want him in the house any more than I did. The invite was to prevent Purvis and me from being alone, and to hopefully find out what he had to say about my "priorities."

"We're fine out here," I said.

Her eyes settled on me. She stared me down hard, her cheeks red with anger and confusion. I had a bad feeling there was guilt all over my face, but she ground her teeth on her questions, breathed deep through her nose.

"I'm sure my brother knows what he needs to do these days," Julia said. She turned to Purvis. "He's been a huge help to me. I don't know what I'd do without him." She disappeared into the house. She left the door open as she walked away.

"We won't be long," I said.

Purvis leaned around me to look into the hall. "You're not," I said, stepping into his line of sight. "You're not checking out my sister while I'm standing right here."

"What? No. Of course not. I could go for a cup of coffee, though."

"So you can talk more cryptic shit in front of Julia? Make me look like an asshole? You're outta your mind. That badge has made you crazy." I walked away from him, out onto the lawn.

Purvis followed. "You got something to tell me," I said, "get it over with."

"First of all, Waters wanted to update you on the investigation. I hate to show up always bearing bad news, but I have to tell you, we haven't got much. We're looking again at the store's security tapes, reinterviewing potential witnesses. We've got people canvassing the other shop owners on the block, but we're not expecting anything new from them."

"The gun?" I asked.

"Useless," Purvis said. "So far, at least. No prints, no serial number."

I didn't believe him. He'd lie to me just because he could. I knew I should be the one trying to trace that gun.

"So you came all the way over here to tell me you've got nothing to tell me," I said. "Bullshit."

"Waters and I want you guys to know we're working hard. We can still get somebody for this."

"Waters forgot how to use a phone? He couldn't call to tell us this?"

He tossed his head. "Mr. Fontana, down on the corner, he was there, at the deli. I had to come over and talk to him so I figured I'd save Waters the trouble, handle it myself."

"What'd Fontana tell you?" I asked.

"He asked when the funeral was."

"That's nothing you need to know."

"Well, I thought I might—"

"Forget it," I said. "Fucking forget about that." I walked away, to the sidewalk. He was smart enough to wait for me to come back to him. "Look, if you're using my father's murder to get near my sister, I'm gonna knock your fucking teeth out. Again."

Purvis looked at me like I'd slapped him, but he recovered

quickly and didn't back down. "It's not like that. Jesus. You don't like me, that's fine, but you gotta treat me with respect now. I'm not your punching bag anymore." He paused, straightening his tie. "This isn't just another case to me. I know Waters knew your dad. Julia and I were friends. We were friends once, you and me." He stopped again, licked sweat off his top lip. "Look, I always felt bad about how your father gave you . . . such a hard time."

"We don't need any favors from you, thanks," I said. "Forget all that 'used to be' shit. It doesn't count for a fucking thing. After today, you don't need to come to the house. Don't come to Scalia's. Julia doesn't need the stress. Waters can call. It won't hurt our feelings. I can meet him somewhere if he needs to talk in person."

"Waters and I will decide the best way to handle things," Purvis said, hitching his thumbs in his belt again and straightening his shoulders, back to playing the badge-toting tough guy. "You don't get a say."

"The hell I don't. Tell me this, does Waters know about you and Julia? Is he weighing that in his decisions?"

Purvis blanched. "He knows."

"Did he ask why I told him to keep you away from Julia?"

Purvis feigned a yawn, but he knew I had him. "So what if he did? I told him the truth, that she and I had a history. That we dated when we were younger." He paused, took off his sunglasses. "That it didn't end well and maybe you were still pissed about it."

"So you left out the fact you kicked her out of your car in the middle of the night? That I had to pick her up at a pay phone on the edge of the projects?"

I waited. He didn't say anything. He just looked sick.

"She was fucking sixteen and you left her alone in a crack-infested ghetto because she wouldn't put out," I said. "And then you went and told everybody she did anyway. In graphic detail."

"For chrissakes," Purvis said, "that was years ago."

"She was hysterical when I found her. Her lip was bleeding. Her blouse was torn."

Purvis looked away from me, rubbing his palms on his cheeks.

"I was stupid," he said. "That stuff was accidental; I was just clumsy." He studied the streetlights along the block. "It was a bad night. I felt bad about it. I told her I was sorry. I left her alone after that."

"After I beat your ass all over your front yard," I said.

"You want me to apologize again? Let me in the house," he said. "Or tell her for me that I'm still sorry. It was stupid. Mean. I guess I was still pissed about Molly."

"Julia had nothing to do with that."

"I know," he snapped. "Molly was my first girlfriend. You took her from me. That can fuck a guy up for a while, you know?" He rubbed his hands on his shirt. "I don't care about that now, you know, but then, it made me a little crazy."

"Please, we barely hung out by the time we got to high school," I said. "I heard all this a long time ago."

"I know, but my point is, look, maybe now I'm trying to make something up to Julia," Purvis said. "Get her some justice. You ever think about that?"

"You're a fuckin' hero. You wanna do her some good? Stay away from her. She's got enough to deal with this week."

"Fine. Whatever," he said. "We'll see how it plays out. God, there is no fucking talking to you. And you know what else? There never was." He put his sunglasses back on; he was a cop again. I knew he regretted trying to talk to me like a human being. I might've even felt bad for him, but I had Julia to think about. Fuck him if he couldn't understand that.

"When I was down at the deli, doing my follow-up," he said, "Vito told me about your visit."

"So?"

"So you can't do that shit," Purvis said. "You scared him half to death."

"Good."

"He had nothing to do with your father's murder," Purvis said. "You're lucky I'm not arresting you."

"Please. I'd like to see you try."

"Get a grip, John," he said. "What would that do for Julia's stress level? She really needs her brother in jail while her father's in the morgue?"

"You let me worry about my sister."

"I wish you would," Purvis said. He rested one hand on his hip and leaned forward, actually pointing a finger at my chest with the other. "Stay away from the deli. And don't let us hear you've been near Fontana."

I stared down at his finger. He stepped back and crossed his arms.

"My father was shot in the middle of the sidewalk in the light of day," I said. "On a crowded corner, outside a busy store, and you and Fat Nat can't buy a clue. This is New York, there's people everywhere all the time." It was my turn to point the finger. "Either the two of you are bumbling idiots, or you're full of shit about what's really going on. Neither one sits well with me."

"Gimme a break," Purvis said. "And get your finger out of my face. I've been a cop for ten years while you've been pulling your tap all over town. Waters has been a detective longer than you or I have been alive. What the fuck do you know about investigating anything other than the bottom of a bottle? I got news for you. Nobody gives a fuck what sits well with you and what doesn't. The sooner you learn that, the better it'll be for everybody."

"You're about to learn," I said, "how it feels to be in traction."

Purvis backed up a few steps. "I'd say you're about to learn what the inside of a jail cell looks like, but you already know." He folded his arms again. This time, though, one hand reached inside his suit jacket. It rested on his gun, I was sure.

I probably should have been frightened, or at least chastened. Twice already that day, my mouth had made somebody reach for a gun. Somewhere in the back of my mind, a little voice told me that was a bad thing. It wasn't hard to ignore; I'd had plenty of practice. Anyway, I couldn't imagine Purvis drawing down on me, never mind shooting me, any more than I could that kid outside the Mall. Instead, my head filled with images of me and Purvis back in the schoolyard at P.S. 42, each threatening the other with our respective powers: physical violence for me, a main line to authority for him. All that was left was for us to tough-talk our way to a face-saving truce.

Purvis seemed to be thinking something similar. He threw his hands in the air and walked away back up the lawn. My father would've thrown both of us in the street for parading all over his grass like this.

"You're not worth the paperwork," he said.

"Who helps you with the big words?"

"Waters probably will be calling you," Purvis said, almost smiling, slipping his hands into his pockets. "He's got some questions, routine shit about your father's habits. I was supposed to ask you, but I don't think now is the time."

"My father went to work every day. Nights and weekends, he got drunk and hit people," I said. "Those were his habits."

Purvis sucked his teeth, looking like he was debating what to say next. "We'll keep you posted." He headed for his car. He stopped after he opened the door and leaned his elbows on the roof. "I see David, Molly's David, down at the courthouse every now and then."

"Go for it," I said. "See what it gets you."

"Do everyone a favor," Purvis said. "Stay home, like a good boy. Stay outta trouble."

"Do everyone a favor," I said. "Kill yourself."

Purvis smiled his little shit-eater's grin, the one that hadn't changed since grade school. "Stay away from the crime scene. Stay away from any and all potential witnesses. Interference in a police investigation is a crime. This is your first, and only, official warning."

"Shove your warning up your ass. I'll do whatever I damn well please."

"Go for it," Purvis said. "See what it gets you."

I flipped him off as he drove away.

I FOLLOWED THE WHISTLE OF the tea kettle into the kitchen. Julia stood over the stove, watching the steam rising from the spout. After a moment, I walked over and turned down the heat. Julia didn't move. She just blinked at me and then the warbling kettle. I patted her shoulder then reached into the cabinet for a mug. When I held it out to her, she seemed to come around. I went over to the fridge for a beer while she made her tea.

"What did Carlo have to say?" Julia finally asked, moving over to the table.

"A whole lot of nothing," I said, popping the cap and tossing it into the sink.

"They're not getting anywhere. They'll never catch who did it, will they?"

"At least not yet," I said. "It's only been a day." I wanted to ask her what difference it would make, why she even cared, but had she asked me the same questions, I wouldn't be able to answer them, either.

Julia sipped from her mug, staring over the top of it. "You were out there awhile, to be talking about nothing. Why was Carlo talking about your priorities?"

I realized she'd taken to sitting where our mother used to, at the head of the table. My father had liked to sit where he could reach me. I leaned against the counter. "He was just fucking with me, being a dick. We caught up a bit. Talked about old times."

"You promised," she said. "I know you're up to something. Just don't let it interfere with what we have to do this week. Don't let it come back on me or this house."

"Relax," I said. "He and I had a few things to clear up." I drank my beer, watching birds in the yard through the kitchen window. "Nothing to worry about."

She pointed at the phone. "There are messages for you."

I was surprised. I didn't know who had my parents' number. I downed half my beer and pressed the button on the answering machine, leaning on the doorway as I listened.

"Holy shit, John, it's Brian from the Cargo," the first one began. "For fuck's sake, you've worked for me for how long and I gotta read about your father in the paper? You can't call a brother with news like that?" Shit, I thought. Work. I hadn't given it a second thought. "You need anything, call or swing by the bar," Brian went on. "Swing by anyway. We're all keeping a thought for you. I got your shifts covered." There was a pause.

"Don't let me find out about the arrangements in the paper, okay? Okay. Stop by."

I probably wouldn't. I liked the people I worked with well enough, I just didn't want to be around any of them right now. It would just be awkward. They knew I hated my father. Why force them to act sorry about a guy they never even knew? But I'd call Brian, thank him for covering my ass. Tell him my sister needed me here.

The next message was from Molly.

"Hey, it's me. We had a half-day and I was in the Cargo this afternoon for lunch." A pause. "With Rachel, from school. So Brian was there and he asked me for this number." She was whispering. I didn't know why. David had to still be at work. "I hope it's okay I gave it to him. He was kind of frantic." There was a long pause. "I can't believe I remembered it." I looked at Julia. She was staring into her tea, pretending not to listen. Like she hadn't heard it all already. "Anyway. I gotta go," Molly said. "Maybe you could call me at school. Tomorrow, or whatever. I'm free most days from one to one-thirty. You know, if you needed to." Another pause. "I mean, if you wanted to."

I turned the machine off and raised a finger in Julia's direction, not looking at her. "Not a word," I said. "Not a word from you."

"What've you been doing to that poor woman?" Julia asked. "You've got her stammering like she's eighteen again. It's adorable."

"It's not adorable. It's guilt. She's stammering because she's calling the guy she's cheating on her boyfriend with."

Julia blew on her tea. "There's one more message."

When did I get so popular? I'd gotten more calls today, at my parents' number, than I got in a week at my apartment. "Who?" I asked Julia. She just nodded at the phone. Probably Brian again. He could be a little intense. Most likely it was Jimmy McGrath.

I skipped the messages I'd already heard, went straight to the last one. Whoever called waited a long time to start talking. I finished my beer while I waited.

"John," she said, "it's Virginia. I saw what happened to your father in the paper. I know how you felt about him, but it's still a terrible thing. I'm sorry." Her voice sounded different, older. "I'm sure you don't want to talk to me about that and there is . . . there is something else I've been meaning to call you about. I think, well, there's something we need to talk about. Something I need to tell you. In person." She told me her work number. It wasn't the tattoo parlor. "Call me here, soon. I know you've got a lot happening, but time is an issue for me. We can get together. Thanks. I saw you at the Mall today with your sister. It was a cute picture. I mean that."

The answering machine clicked off. Julia was silent, holding her breath. I grabbed another beer from the fridge.

"Nothing ever changes," I said. "Nothing ever fucking changes." The beer went down hard and I felt vaguely sick. "She did that shit to me all the time. We need to talk, but not now, not here. I've got something on my mind, but we'll talk about it later. God, I hated that. I'd be sick to my stomach for hours, waiting."

"Will you call her?"

"Hell, no," I said. "I don't give a shit what she has to say. I don't owe her a thing." I paced the kitchen, caught myself and stopped. I leaned back against the counter and studied my beer bottle. "This is so like her. God forbid something comes along that distracts me from missing her. She can't have it both ways. She can't walk out of my life and still want to be the most important thing in it." I looked at Julia. "That's what she wants, you know."

"You really think that?" Julia asked. "When's the last time you slept with her? Maybe she's pregnant. Maybe something bad has happened to her. Wouldn't you want to know that? She'd have wanted to know about Dad from you. I'd want Cindy to call me, if something like this happened to her."

I sat at the table, scratched at the label on the beer bottle. I raised the bottle to take a drink, decided I didn't really want it, and set the bottle back on the table.

My sister was probably right. Why, after six months, would Virginia start playing head games again? That kind of bullshit was what she'd gotten sick of, or so she said. I'd made her that way, she'd said. Manipulative. Made her do things she hated doing, made her into someone she didn't like. It was the only way to get me to talk about anything meaningful, she'd said. Did she miss the challenge? It was possible. I must've given her something she needed, if she stuck around so long. Had I misread the thing with the flowers entirely? Was all the mystery an invitation to go looking for her? Was she telling me she wanted to be found?

If it was an opening, I didn't know if I was up for it. One ex-girlfriend back in my head was enough. Still, she'd made me curious. She'd always gotten to me so easily. It was hard not to hate her for it.

"She'll keep calling, if it's something important," Julia said. "Or she won't, and you'll never know what it was about. Why not get it over with? Besides, it might make you feel better, having an adult conversation with her."

"Who said I was feeling bad about anything? And believe me, I'd have no problem never knowing. Hell, I'd probably prefer it." I took a hit off my beer. It was warm. "But maybe you're right. I don't want her to keep calling. Maybe I should just get done with it." I got up, poured the beer down the sink.

"Just meet her in public," Julia said. "To avoid any, you know, potential pitfalls. Meet her for lunch. If she doesn't eat, you know to head for the door."

I stared at the empty beer bottle, wishing I hadn't poured it out but not wanting to get another. I opened the cabinet, grabbed a coffee mug, then put it back. The morning coffee was long cold by now. I didn't really want coffee anyway. I rubbed my eyes, hard, until I saw sparks. I didn't know what I wanted. I wanted Virginia to not have called, wanted for her to not have left me, wanted to have never met her. I wanted to be home in bed, or even at work, a nice buzz on, making money, talking baseball, watching the door for Molly. I wanted my father not to be dead, to not be going through this. I wanted not to care about any of it. The pain in my chest came back.

"Junior," I heard Julia say. "You all right?"

My hands were on my head, fists clenched in my hair. "Yeah. I'm fine." I told my hands to let go, but they wouldn't.

"Why don't you go lie down for a while? Somewhere other than the couch. There's still a bed in your old room."

"Jimmy hasn't called again, has he?" I asked.

"No," Julia said. "Can you blame him?"

My hands finally relaxed. I wiped them down my face. My knuckles ached. I walked to the phone. Julia asked me who I was calling, but I didn't answer. I plucked Waters's card off the refrigerator. I got his voice mail.

"Waters, it's Junior. Deputy Dog said you wanted to talk to me. I'll be at the Golden Dove around seven. Meet me there, or not."

"That was productive," Julia said as I hung up.

"I'm not feeling very goddamn productive right now."

"I'm taking a nap," Julia said, rising from the table. "I recommend it." She walked out of the kitchen and headed up the stairs.

I got another beer and headed out into the backyard. I dragged an old, rusty lawn chair into a spot of sun and settled into it, slouching. I pulled off my shirt and slid on my shades. The beer sat untouched at my side. I lit a cigarette.

There had to be a way to get through these next few days without losing my grip. Outside Joyce's and the Mall and then in the kitchen, I'd come too close. That wasn't the way it should be. Hadn't I, in some way, won? My father was gone. My lifelong battle with him had ended the only way it could, with one of us dead.

I'd always figured that when he died I'd feel some satisfaction, or at least some relief. I thought I'd feel a thousand pounds lighter. I'd grow six inches taller, walk different, breathe different. All this space would open up in the world just from knowing he wasn't in it anymore. It'd feel like letting go of that breath you hold when you pull open the closet door looking for monsters. Like when you wake from a nightmare and not only realize that it wasn't true, but you can feel yourself forgetting it with every breath.

Sitting there in the yard, I didn't feel any of that. All I felt was the same things I'd felt for twenty years when I thought of him, like there was something hard inside me, pushing up against my lungs. Like a fist clutched the muscles in my back. Like I was loading a weapon, waiting for my enemies.

But the enemies had passed me by and left me in the dust of their horses, their gun smoke in my nose and their bullets in my father. They'd left me standing with a jagged rock in my hand and no one to throw it at. With a body to bury and a family to console, a family of one.

Why wasn't there any relief? Was it that the war had ended a couple of decades before I'd ever thought it would? That someone else had ended it for us? That my war had ended without me? Before I was ready? Ready for what?

For most of my life, even after I'd grown old enough to understand just how dishonest the imagination can be, I'd harbored secret fantasies of deathbed confessions in some indistinct future. I saw my father, laid low and wasted by some vindictive disease, crippled in a hospital bed, his handsome face yellowed and cracked with age, his powerful hands curled from atrophy. I stood at his bedside, younger than I could possibly be with him so old. I'd be taller and more broad-shouldered than I ever was in real life, my shadow falling over him. Him, spending his last breaths recounting his sins, fear settled deep behind watery eyes that pleaded for forgiveness. Me, denying him with my silence. Me, for once, pressing the fear deeper into him. Me, for once, taking the heart out of him. Him, turning away from me, dying. Me, walking away from him, finally alive.

But somehow, by dying the way he did, by surprise, he'd outmaneuvered me. As if I'd gone to that imaginary hospital bed and found it empty, curtains blowing in the open window, a rope of knotted sheets hanging to the ground. At the same time, he still wasn't gone. By disappearing, he was suddenly everywhere. I felt as if he'd caught me hard by the arm and pulled me close to him. Just so he could smother me with his size, his strength again. So I wouldn't forget who was faster, stronger. And there was nothing I could do to stop it. Here I was, under his roof again. Trapped here, surrounded by him, and fighting him off. Grinding my teeth until I could escape again. Not winning, not losing, just enduring.

I stood up, stuffed my hands in my back pockets. This was the last time, I told myself. No more. Never again. I leaned back, looked up at the sky, stared into the sun. You hear me, old man? This is the last fucking time. After this week, you get nothing more from me. I will never set foot in your house again. I will never say your name. Ever.

I closed my eyes tight and watched a flock of suns scatter across my eyelids. I waited for him to shout me down, to laugh at me. Nothing came. I wondered if he heard me. And if he'd heard, did he believe? Probably not. I struggled to believe it myself, that I could put myself beyond his reach. I looked down at my feet. I'd told him it was the last time a million times. Told myself that a million more. And I'd never been right.

SEVEN

DONNIE FONTANA STARED AT ME FOR A LONG TIME BEFORE HE stepped out his front door and pulled it closed behind him. Though a good fifteen years older, he'd been the closest thing to a friend my father'd had on the block. They'd worked across the street from each other in Manhattan, my father a contracts manager for a construction firm, Fontana an accountant for an insurance company. Two desk jockeys riding the same train nearly every morning for twenty years, until Fontana retired. As far as I knew, Fontana had never been inside our house, and my father had never been inside his. If their wives had ever met, I never heard about it.

Fontana had a bad back and so throughout junior high and high school my father shoved me out the door to mow his lawn in the summer and shovel his sidewalk in the winter. Five bucks every time. I hadn't laid eyes on him in years. He was stooped; his long arms hung thin and limp from his short sleeves. A cigar poked out of his shirt pocket.

"Mr. Fontana," I said. "I need to know what you saw when my father was killed."

Fontana looked away from me, up the block. "I don't know

nothing. There was nothing to see." He bent down, groaning, and snatched up a gum wrapper that had blown onto his lawn. I wondered who cut it for him these days. "It was so fast," he said. "I never saw a gun, nothing." He stuffed the wrapper in his pocket.

"What about the car? The man who got out of it?"

"It was too fast," he said. "Cars, they drive like crazy there all the time. Screeching up, guys jumping out. Everybody always in a hurry. Why look?"

I wiped a hand down my face. "So you were outside the store when it happened. Anybody say anything when the car pulled up? When it drove away?"

"Junior, the cops asked me all this already," he said. "I'm telling you what I told them. I didn't see anything. I didn't hear anything . . . other than the shots. Your father was there talking to me." He looked down at the sidewalk, a grimace on his face. "The next minute he was . . . he was gone." He put a hand on his back. "It's a terrible, terrible thing. I don't know why someone would do that." He shook his head. "I'm sorry. Please let me know when the services are. I'd like to pay my respects."

I looked at him. His crooked back, the slippers on his feet. There was no car parked in front of the house. "Mr. Fontana, if you don't mind, how'd you get down to the store on Sunday?"

"Same as always," he said. "Your father and I walked down there together."

I blinked at him, stunned. I couldn't figure out why. It was the answer I had anticipated. I thought maybe it was the "same as always" part. I'd always assumed my father took his Sunday walks alone. That was their point, to get him away from everyone else. I struggled so hard to see the two of them together, I squinted at Fontana, blurring him. I could imagine them, as if seeing them from a few blocks behind—my father inching down Richmond Avenue, cars speeding by, Fontana shuffling along beside him, a hand resting on my father's arm. Did they talk? What the hell about?

It was such a strange image I wanted to remind Fontana who he was talking to, and about. A lot of boys and their fathers had come and gone on this block. But Fontana was looking at me like I was the one gone senile. I just stood there embarrassed, feeling exposed. I fought to remember if my mother had ever mentioned this, if I had ever been invited on those walks. It didn't much matter. I wouldn't have gone.

"Every Sunday?" I finally asked.

"When the weather and my back would let us," Fontana said, pulling the cigar from his pocket. "You got a match?" I dug my lighter from my pocket and lit his cigar. "While I'm outside anyway," he said. He waved a hand toward the door. "The wife."

"So you were there most of the time," I said. "My father have any problems down there? Guys he didn't get along with?"

Fontana sighed. "Far as I knew, he only talked to me down there. He didn't like most people, your father."

I waited again, but Fontana just puffed on his cigar.

"So nothing, you know, the cops might take issue with, goes on there," I said. "Nothing of a financial nature that anybody might not want talked about."

Fontana leaned over, releasing a long gob of brown spit onto his lawn. "Junior, I don't understand what you're saying."

"Look, Mr. F, you and I both know what my father's murder looked like," I said. "People who die like that, they usually owe somebody something."

"I was your father's friend," Fontana said, "not his babysitter. He was a grown man. I wouldn't poke my nose in his business even if he let me. I can tell you this, your father hated owing people, and he hated losing." He grinned, tapping his finger on his forehead. "I heard the stories so often; I know every play of every football game he lost in college." He puffed on his cigar and leaned closer to me. "I would tell you anything I knew, even about financial things or whatever, even stuff I wouldn't tell the cops. But I don't know nothing. I don't know anything more than you.

"It's hard, I know. So senseless." He reached out and patted my arm. "He was a nice man, your father. It's a shame you two weren't closer. He talked about you a lot." He grimaced again. "I'm sorry, I have to go in and sit. You'll let me know? The services?" He patted my arm again and turned to go back inside.

He stopped in the doorway and stood there awhile. From somewhere inside the house, Fontana's wife called his name. He called me to him. I went. He settled his old, brown hands on my shoulders. He waited until he had my eyes before he spoke.

"Junior, we all die owing somebody something. Who knows what debts your father left behind? Who knows what I will, or what you'll leave behind? It's best to let go of the dead and their secrets." With that, he went back inside.

I stood there for a while, looking at his front door, his lawn. I heard the TV from inside. So now I knew some of what they talked about, at least. It wasn't all football. Part of it was me. But what was there to discuss? How far back did these walks go? My father and I barely saw each other in the five years since Fontana retired. When we did, it was accidental, the meeting always short and violent. I couldn't imagine Fontana wanting to hear stories about father-son fistfights.

I thought about what he'd said about my father, again wondering if he'd confused me with some other kid. I tapped my fingertip on the doorbell, not hard enough to ring it, feeling like there were questions I'd forgotten to ask. But I couldn't remember what they were. I felt like I knew less than before he'd answered the door. Still, it didn't seem worth getting Fontana out of his chair again. He'd already said he'd told me all he knew. I stepped back from the door. I'd come back when I had something to tell him, about the services.

I took my time walking back up the block. It occurred to me that none of the neighbors had called or stopped by the house. Not to ask about the funeral, not to check on me and Julia. My sister would've mentioned it.

I stopped and looked at the houses on our side of the street. Five exactly the same model as ours, one old brick number, and another six exactly the same after that. Across the street, another half dozen just like ours, and another six in a third model. I wondered if I could still name all the families, then realized I never knew all the names to begin with.

But I remembered some of them, more than I thought I would. Fontana, Rizzo, and Riordan. Hopkins. Carlucci, Norris, Balaban, Ellis, and Grabowski. Ruth Balaban had a crush on me in junior high. Mr. Rizzo wore blue running shorts and a white T-shirt every day of his life. Rumors went around that he slapped his wife senseless after she backed the Caddy into a mailbox. Mr. Ellis ran off with Mrs. Grabowski. Well, ran as far as next door. Ellis's oldest son had done some time. The middle Grabowski girl was pregnant by nineteen. Maybe the Sanderses weren't the screwiest family on the block after all. I wondered what rumors circulated about us. I never heard them, but no one ever hears their own worst rumors. Maybe there weren't any. Maybe we hid things better. That was what I always told myself, anyway.

The old block looked the same to me as it always had, but all those kids, the kids my age, were grown now. And a lot of the parents were grandparents by now. Some must've moved to Jersey. These houses were big for two people. They were built for families. Except for Fontana, there might be no one I knew left on the block. I laughed at myself, offering excuses for the neighbors, old and new, ignoring my father's murder.

Could I blame them? I didn't want any part of it myself. But they'd show up. For the wake, if not the big day. They'd see it in the paper, or hear about it at Mass, or in line at the grocery store. Word would make its way around, the way those rumors used to. Husbands would float the idea past wives at the dinner table, wives would float the idea to their husbands over the ironing board. They'd talk about the right thing to do. They'd agree to think about it, to look into it, but they'd never talk about it again. They'd just find themselves dressing for it when the day came. Maybe getting a belt at Joyce's beforehand.

I knew most would go because they didn't want to admit, as they would by staying home, that they couldn't care less that a man who'd been married with kids, who lived two doors down, who they saw every evening walking home from work, was shot dead on the street. They'd go out of fear of being found out. Of getting caught not going by someone who went. Out of fear of rumors and whispers that they didn't go to John Sanders's funeral, when he'd lived practically next door for ten whole years. Of someone saying, *I* barely knew him, and *I* went. Or worse. They feared running into me, or Julia, and that we'd hold their absence against them. That it would matter so much to us that *they* weren't there.

And they'd go because they knew, somewhere deep inside, he was one of them. They'd never admit it, but that grainy fact made them afraid for their own exit. And showing up for his funeral would prove, at least to them, at least for a day, that they were still alive. And it would reassure them that if they showed up for him, someone would show up for them.

Well, fuck 'em all, I thought, heading up the walk to the house. I'd rather the neighbors didn't show up. I sure as hell didn't want to see them at Joyce's, whispering over their glasses, their staring faces shadowed in the dim light. Julia was forcing me to pretend I cared about the services. I wasn't going to pretend I cared about seeing slimy old Mr. Ellis. And I wasn't going to help him pretend he cared about seeing me. I'd make sure Fontana knew dates and times; the rest of them could go to hell. Their fears and guilt were their problems, not mine.

I CHECKED THE ANSWERING MACHINE when I got home. Jimmy hadn't called, but Waters had, agreeing to meet me. He told us not to give up hope, told us that something could break at any time. He asked us to call him when we set the schedule for the services, and to let him know if we needed anything. That was a surprise. There was no love lost between Waters and my father. Or Waters and me. As Julia dutifully copied down his home number, I voiced my confusion over Waters's sudden concern for what was left of our family.

Julia smiled at me. "C'mon, Junior. You know he always had a thing for Mom. This is probably just his way of doing right by her. He kept an eye out for us after she died, too."

"News to me," I said.

"I'm not surprised," Julia answered. "You were drunk for, what? A month after the funeral?"

It wasn't a shot, just a statement of fact. I took no offense. A month seemed about right.

"He called me every week at school for two months. More often than someone else I know," she said. That was a shot. "Who do you think lost the paperwork on that brawl you started at the Loft after the funeral? And had your car towed when you wouldn't quit driving around drunk."

I vaguely remembered the incidents she described. "I always suspected your hand in the car."

"Wish I'd thought of it. But that was all Waters."

"Weird way to play guardian angel," I said.

"The Lord works in mysterious ways, she does," Julia said.

My sister went upstairs to try on her new dresses, again. When she didn't come back downstairs to ask me how she looked in them, again, I knew she was calling Cindy. Fine with me. I cracked open a beer and plopped down on the couch. I flipped on ESPN, realizing I'd never gotten the score of the game from the night before. As realistic as I tried to be, that last glimmer of hope for a win wouldn't fade until I knew the final score.

I still hadn't gotten it, but I was all caught up on my golf and NASCAR when Julia came back downstairs. She was in sweats, her eyes wet. She sat next to me on the couch. I sat up and slung my arm around her shoulders.

"Y'all right, sis?"

"I feel so much better," she said. She blew her nose. "She always was a good listener."

"Long as you weren't asking where she's been all night," I said.

"Not funny," Julia said.

I apologized, and decided not to mention that she hadn't disagreed with me. Cindy was in California, the relationship didn't need my help being over. I squeezed her closer to me.

"You wanna come to the Dove with me? It's about that time," I said. "Talk to Waters? You gotta have dinner anyway."

"No, that's all right."

"Want me to bring you something back?"

She shook her head. "My stomach can't do greasy spoon like it used to." She grinned. "Too many years of too many meds." She sat up straight and tried to pull herself together. "Or something like that. I'll fix something here."

"Promise?"

She patted my knee and stood. "I promise. You going out after you talk to Waters?"

"Probably."

She walked into the kitchen and peered into the fridge, disappearing behind the door. "Joyce's?"

"Probably. Want me to swing back here and get you first? Might do you some good to get out."

She looked at me over the door.

"I know," I said, "might do me some good to stay in." I looked around at the walls. "This house is killing me."

"I know it's hard for you being here," she said. "It's tough on both of us." She let the fridge door swing closed. She hadn't taken anything out of it. "But I appreciate you being here. I'm grateful for the effort."

"No problem," I said. "I might be late."

"I know," Julia said.

I grabbed my jacket off the arm of the couch.

"Is Waters gonna tell us anything useful?" she asked.

"Doubt it," I said. "Nothing that's gonna change the facts."

EIGHT

WATERS, AWASH IN BLUE NEON AND SMOKING A CIGARETTE, STOOD outside the diner as I turned the corner out of the parking lot.

"Didn't know you still did that," I said.

"Every now and again," he said, "when the night tour bores me silly." He offered me one. I declined and lit one of my own. He checked his watch. "You're early. Didn't know you did that ever."

"I like to throw the world a curve every now and again," I said. "When it bores me silly."

I turned and looked at the fountain out in front of the diner—three leaping metallic silver dolphins, brightly spotlit. It was a horrendous contraption, but it matched the building, which was silver plated and piped with blue neon. The Golden Dove. It made perfect sense, in a Staten Island kind of way. "That new? The fountain?"

"Relatively," Waters said. "Year or two." He flicked his cigarette into the street. "I just chased away a gang of kids thieving the change out of it. Their parents yelled at me like I was beating the little punks."

"Well, they probably couldn't see your badge," I said.

He laughed. "Yeah, that was it. C'mon, let's eat."

I looked through the windows; the place was packed. I could hear the screaming kids from outside. One smeared chocolate pudding on the window. "We can do this out here. I got plenty of smokes. It's a mess in there."

"Relax," Waters said. "Owners'll give us a quiet booth. My treat."

That raised my eyebrows. "Generous."

"Purvis really does not like you," he said, heading up the stairs in front of me. "You're probably all right."

WATERS WOULDN'T ANSWER a single question about my father until after we ate. He demolished a chicken-fried steak and two slices of apple pie before I got halfway through my Reuben. I found myself wishing Julia would eat like he did. She'd probably be close to his size, but I'd worry less about too much than I would about hardly at all. He ordered two cups of coffee as the waitress carried off our plates. I wasn't done eating, but Waters seemed to be in a hurry.

"Where's the Boy Wonder?" I asked.

"Running errands. I don't wanna get any on my shoes while you two are pissing on each other. And another thing, I heard about your performance down at the deli. No more of that shit."

"Yeah, Purvis gave me the message," I said.

"I want you to hear it from me. Any more bullshit like that and I cut you out of the loop."

I blew on my coffee. "Whatcha got?"

"We understand each other?"

"All right," I said.

"Tell me we understand each other," he said.

"We understand each other. Now, what've you got?"

He raised his hands in caution. "Nothing huge, but something. I gotta ask you some questions first. I want answers, real answers, no 'I hate Daddy' bullshit." He stared at me, I guess to prove he was serious. "Be an adult."

"Okay," I said. "I can behave."

"Did your father's interest in sports extend beyond football?"

He was trying to lead me, but I knew where he was going. I'd taken the same thoughts and basically the same question to Fontana's doorstep only hours before. Unfortunately, Waters would get as much info from me as I'd gotten from Fontana.

"As far as I know, he never bet on games," I said. "He watched football religiously. Jets and Giants. Believe me, I know. I had to sit there right beside him every Sunday until I was in high school. Mass in the morning, football all afternoon. One hour for God, six for the NFL. He knew a hell of a lot about the game, like a freakishly large amount, even for an ex-player, but he was just a fan. Why?"

"Maybe too close to home," Waters said, more to himself than to me. "Was he into anything else? Basketball? Hockey?"

"Basketball, a little bit," I said. "I can remember the Knicks being on every now and then. Him yelling at the TV. But my mom wasn't wild about him watching the games. His commentary had, let's say, racial overtones my mom didn't like."

The hockey question made me think. Molly had been a huge hockey fan, and so, naturally, I became one. I remembered, suddenly, that in a brief experiment, I'd tried to win my father over to hockey, thinking there was enough hitting and fighting to satisfy him. And that my interest in that hitting might get him to lay off me a little bit, even if I had come to the sport by way of a girl.

We made it through a few weeks of the season, watching the

Rangers on TV. He let me teach him the rules. We might've even talked about going to the Garden for a game. He liked the violence and the speed, but ultimately couldn't take to a sport dominated by Canadians and Europeans. Their names were too difficult to yell at the television. "Hockey had too many foreigners for him," I told Waters. "Even if they are white."

"Anything else? College ball? Baseball?"

"Nah. He never watched college anything. My father hated baseball, said it was too slow. That it wasn't a real sport, I guess because there was no violence in it. Wasn't manly enough for him. He never understood it, though, that was the problem. The precision, the strategy, the way the possibilities of the game were always shifting." I stopped, realizing I was drifting. I had fifteen examples to make my case at the ready and caught myself hoping Waters would want me to continue.

"You're a fan, I take it," Waters said.

"Big time," I said.

"That's nice. Let's stick to the subject."

"Fine," I said, irked that he cut me off. He was the one who kept asking questions when I'd already answered the important one. So I answered it again. "My father wasn't a gambler. He had all the normal debts a guy has, and he hated those. No way he'd risk a debt with some bookie, or some loan shark."

Waters sighed. I could tell from the look on his face that I was telling him things he already knew. But I respected the effort.

"Like you said, he knew a lot about the game," Waters said. "Don't forget, I played with him. He'd change the coaches' plays on the field. Nine times out of ten, he was right." He paused. "I always thought he'd have made a good coach, if it wasn't for that temper of his."

"A lot might be different," I said, "if not for that temper."

"Your father never did let go of his football career," Waters said, his tone apologetic. "I thought maybe he found a way to stay in it. A lot of ex-athletes, they can never let go of that adrenaline and develop some bad habits trying to hang on to it. Your mother's gone; you and Julia are out of the house. He had a lot of voids to fill. Your grandfather was a gambler."

I thought of Waters, and his career, maybe a few bad habits developed in the decades he'd spent wearing a uniform and playing defense for the City of New York. He had his own voids to fill. Weird that my father, the selfish bastard, got the family with the nice house, and Waters, who seemed on the whole a pretty all right guy, ended up with nothing. It just seemed to be the way things had always gone with them.

"Sorry," I said. Waters pushed because he wanted whatever ideas he had to match the facts. Here he was trying hard to prove my father was a degenerate gambler, and all I felt was guilty for disappointing him. I raised my empty hands. "My father was a big-time drunk. That one bad habit took up all his time. He knew what gambling did to his old man."

"Let's finish this outside," Waters said. He threw some money on the table.

I reached for my wallet. He tried to talk me out of it, but I threw a ten on the table anyway. "Toward the tip. Karma."

We stopped at the counter for coffee to go.

"Give," I said, when we got back to the street.

"We found a witness. Guy called us today."

"You got someone there who actually saw it?" I asked.

"Saw a little bit," Waters said. "Seems there was a line inside the store that morning. This guy was at the end of it as a particularly attractive member of the female persuasion walked by, heading toward the train station. He was leaning back, looking out the door at her when the car pulled up. He got a pretty good look at the car, caught a glimpse of the guy. We got partial descriptions of both."

"That's not a whole lot," I said. "The girl?" She would've turned at the shot, had a view of the license plate.

"Disappeared," Waters said. "But, listen, any particulars help. We got build, race, and clothing on the guy. Last night, we picked up the car."

That caught my attention. "Where?"

"South Beach parking lot. It was stolen. Couple of kids called in a torch job. There was enough left to give us a pretty solid ID on the vehicle." He stopped, looked down at his shoes.

"But?"

Waters sighed, rubbed his temples. "But not enough to get us closer to who was driving it." He looked at me. "Not yet, anyway."

I took a hard drag on my cigarette, a long drink of coffee. I was pissed, and disappointed. The coffee was awful, and cold. After all that suspense, despite his warning, I really thought Waters had news about an arrest, or at least a warrant. Something solid. I wanted the whole picture and all I kept getting were bits and pieces. Nobody, it seemed, including people who were there and people paid to find out, knew much more about my father's demise than I did.

"You wanna tell me about the car?" I asked. "The kids who called it in?"

"I don't think so."

"You've got the murder weapon," I said.

"This ain't TV," Waters said. "The gun doesn't necessarily mean anything."

"But it could if you could trace it," I said. "Learn its history."

"Stop it, Junior."

"Tell me about the girl," I said. "I might have better luck than you digging her up."

Waters snorted. "Yeah, right. Why don't I give you a little tin badge and your gun back? That'd work out great. You showed some real skill at the deli."

"Well, it is my gun," I said.

"Just stop," Waters said. "Stay out of it. You said we understood each other."

"Forget I asked," I said, waving my free hand in the air. "I don't even know why I'm here."

"You're sure?" Waters asked. "About the gambling?" He laced his fingers together in front of his face. "I know there was no love lost, but blood does funny things."

"Positive," I said. "My father didn't like owing anyone. Learned it from his father. Debt made him crazy. My mother explained it to me often. I had no idea they were even making book out of that place, and I'm sure he didn't, either."

"We never thought so," Waters said. "But we were gonna start looking, if your father had been gambling there." He shook his head. "I knew it was bullshit. Who does hits in their own front yard?"

Waters glanced over my shoulder. I turned and spotted Purvis's car idling at a red light a couple of blocks away. I wondered if he'd ever worked up the nerve to tell Waters the whole truth about him and Julia. Maybe I should take care of it myself, I thought. Just to be sure. It was probably best to do it with all three of us together.

"You know, Purvis was at the house this afternoon," I said. "Preening and posing on the front lawn for Julia, making like there'd been a big break in the case. But he didn't tell me any of this." I turned to Waters. "I'm telling you, he's fucking with the wrong guy. He keeps trying to be a hero for my sister and it's getting on my nerves."

"Relax," Waters said. "The badge gets to his head sometimes, and good-looking women always do, but he doesn't know anything I just told you. I sent him to Fontana's while I checked out the other witness, speed things up. He didn't even know I was meeting you here."

"I don't want him around us," I said, trying to sound casual about it. "He's too interested in other things. Julia, Molly."

"He's working the case with me," Waters said. "Julia's the daughter of the victim. Molly's your alibi. It's professional."

"The hell it is. He likes to play games with what he thinks he knows."

We watched Purvis pull the car to the curb. He came in too hard, scraping the hubcaps on the concrete. Purvis swore inside the car. I laughed. Waters just stared down into his coffee. "Every time," he said.

Purvis sat with his hands on the wheel, trying to mask his embarrassment with a scowl. Waters rapped on the window with his knuckle. "Unlock the door, Carlo," he said. Purvis jumped and hit the button. Waters turned to me before he reached for the door. "You give Carlo too much credit." He opened the door and piled his bulk into the passenger seat.

I grabbed the door before Waters could close it. Waters raised his eyebrows at me, but I leaned into the car anyway. "Purvis," I said, "you tell your boss what we talked about this afternoon?"

Purvis swallowed. "My conversations with my partner are none of your business."

Waters turned. I knew he was giving Purvis the eyebrows now.

"You tell him you abandoned my sister to the fates in Crack Town?" I asked. "And maybe that's why I have a problem with you."

Purvis looked at Waters. "It's a long story."

Waters just stretched his arms out, gripping the dashboard and flexing his arms. He wouldn't look at either of us.

"It was back in high school," Purvis told him.

Waters blew out a long breath that clouded the windshield. He turned to Purvis. "Carlo and I will discuss it," he said. He turned to me, glaring at my face, and then at my hand on the door. I let go and backed up. "As for you, Junior? Maybe you should think about how long and how hard you need to hold grudges. They only get heavier with time." He slammed the car door but he rolled down the window. "I'll stay in touch."

"One more thing," I said.

Waters leaned his elbow out the window. "What?"

I meant to ask him about his own grudges, about how often he took his own advice, but the look on his face told me he was about out of patience. "You know who won the Met game last night?"

"The Mets," Waters said. "Delgado hit a walk-off. You still follow those jokers?"

"Not really," I said. "But I had a bill riding on the game."

Waters just waved as they pulled out into traffic. I watched them drive away, then walked back to my car.

An extra-inning, walk-off home run. A thing of beauty, that was. My anger at Purvis vanished. The win, and the way it happened, made me feel better than I had in days, even if I had missed it. Even if the Mets were still mired in second as the Braves ran away with the division again. What mattered was that it had happened. I stood by my car, keys in my hand, just thinking about it.

I'd seen enough of Delgado's moon shots to imagine it well enough. The ball an aspirin-sized dot in the night sky, unstoppable, unalterable, soaring over the field, the fence, the stands, and out into the parking lot. Sheer bedlam at Shea. Ecstatic teammates leaping up the dugout steps. Delgado oblivious to it all, his cool conqueror's glare fixed on the ball the whole way, as if the hit not only won the night's game, but exacted some kind of primordial, private vengeance he'd sworn to reap. He hit home runs the way they ought to be hit. High and far and long, leaving no question. He took someone else's best shot and beat a perfect, pure, victorious moment out of it, a moment when everything went right.

I unlocked the car, cheered more than any grown man with dead parents had a right to be by a day-old baseball game. I wondered if I really was losing my mind, and how much further I had to go before I got it over with. I thought maybe I was such a fan of Carlos Delgado and his team because we all took the game of baseball way too seriously.

I DROVE TO JOYCE'S, EAGER for a shot and a pint and a spot in front of the night's Met game. Feeling a twinge of guilt for my wavering faith yesterday, I resolved to stay planted in front of the TV until the last out, regardless of the score or the time. I circled the block looking for a parking space. The first pitch was only a few minutes away. I found a spot next to the train station. I stepped out of the car and found myself staring at Scalia's funeral home. In my haste, I'd trapped myself. Getting to the bar from here meant walking past Scalia's, and through the murder scene. It was either that or walk around the block. Delgado's moon shot vanished into the distant past.

I stepped into the street in front of Scalia's. The place was dark, except for a dim light burning in the back, its glow bleeding out into the parking lot. I wondered what room it was, if it was the room my father was in. It couldn't be. No way a room like that had windows. He'd be in the basement, underground, already down in a hole. As I stood there in the street, I envisioned my father's huge form prone on the slab, still and silent beneath a sheet. If I knocked at the door, would the Scalias let me in? Let me see that he was really dead. Really gone.

I dragged my hands down my face. Who was I trying to kid? I wanted no part of that room or anything that happened in there. My mouth went dry and I tried to spit in the street anyway. I lit a cigarette and it made me sick. A trickle of sweat ran past my ear. I stood there, waiting.

Maybe if I stood there long enough my father would walk out that door, down the steps and meet me in the street, playing out the sick joke to the bitter end. He'd be laughing at me all the way, rolling his shoulders to loosen them up, cracking his knuckles, eyes sparking with violence. We could settle things once and for all. I cracked my knuckles, rolled my shoulders, breathed shallow.

What if the guy who helped Fontana down to the corner store every Sunday walked out, the quick-minded guy who would've made a great coach. The man who rode carousels with his daughter.

What would I do then? Because him I didn't know. Him, I'd never even met. And I wanted to. I had some things to say to him.

I felt sicker. My hand shook against my forehead. I licked my lips, swallowed hard. Something stuck in my throat. Something hard that had risen up from my gut. I felt badly confused, off-balance. I wanted to ask my father something, but I didn't know what. Or which version of my father to ask. Should I ask *Where the hell ya been*? Should I ask if the Jets would make the playoffs? Which man would answer? Which one did I want to talk to me? I didn't know what answers I wanted.

Then the light in the back of the funeral home went out and I was alone in the dark. Sick and sweating and afraid.

And I remembered, as a train rolled into the station, that my father wasn't walking out any doors, wasn't picking fights or talking football with anyone anymore, no matter how long I waited. I felt a hole open inside me so wide I thought I'd disappear. It swallowed the hard thing I couldn't swallow myself as it moved up my throat and it hurt like hell and I welcomed it. I closed my eyes and held my breath, waiting for it, wishing for it to happen. But it didn't, because I lit up in the headlights of the car that turned the corner and screeched to a stop three feet short of where I stood.

I think I screamed. The adrenaline charge sucked me right back into my boots. I stumbled away from the car and tripped over the curb, nearly toppling the makeshift 9-11 shrine by the sidewalk. The driver put her cell phone down long enough to shout a few choice curses at me as she drove away. I was too confused to answer. I rubbed the sweat on my forehead back into my hair and tried to catch my breath.

Standing alone under the streetlights and stars, shaking in my boots, I watched a stray dog sniff around the trash can on the corner where my father died. I looked around at my feet for something to throw at it, but found nothing. The dog watched me as it lifted its leg on the can before trotting away out of sight.

I turned to the memorial and righted the pictures and candles I'd knocked over. When I'd fixed things up as best I could, I lit a candle underneath a fading picture of a dead police officer. He was Eddie Francis, NYPD, age thirty-six years, father of two. Beloved brother. I'd known him well when we were both younger, different men. He'd always thought his sister and I made a good match.

I hustled through the murder scene with my eyes closed and headed for Joyce's to drink all the whiskey the Republic had to offer.

NINE

I EDGED OVER AS SOMEONE TOOK THE BAR STOOL NEXT TO ME, keeping my eyes fixed on my pint of Harp, well on my way to seeing double. There was no ball game. The home stand had ended and the Mets were traveling to Houston. I still felt better, more solid in my skin, sitting in Joyce's, wrapped in a warm crowd of strangers, even without the distraction of a ball game. Each shot of Jameson blurred my thoughts of Scalia's a little more. I worried they'd come looking for me again when I hit the couch that night, but what was there to do about that?

The gathering pile of coins before me on the bar was enough to call Molly three times over. But with each drink, the bubble around me solidified, the gravity in my bar stool got stronger, and the hour got later.

The voice next to me caught my ear when he ordered a double Jameson, neat. Then he told Joyce to back me up, and I turned to look. Jimmy McGrath, Jimmy the Saint, grinned back at me. It was a night for ghosts, and there was no getting away from it. "'Tis himself," Jimmy said, settling back in beside me.

Joyce brought over the shots. Jimmy raised his glass and I met it with mine. *"Sláinte,"* he said, and we drank. "Julia said you'd be down here." He grinned again and half-stood, fishing for his wallet.

Back in high school, Jimmy was the only close friend I'd had. Right off the bat, our freshman year, Jimmy and I bonded in the back of the detention hall. We learned quick that we frustrated the dean much better as a duo than we did individually. We were greater than the sum of our parts, bolder and more confident. It made all the difference to me, having someone share both the commission and the consequences of my minor crimes. I thought *I* didn't care about anything? There was nothing and no one Jimmy wouldn't laugh at. I admired the hell out of him and sometimes, when he was at his most dismissive of the world, burned with envy.

I'd hung the nickname Jimmy the Saint on him our senior year. In the midst of a U2 fixation he took up Jesus, Causes, and black clothes, morphing from a mischievous teen into an insufferable little Bono right before my eyes. We didn't see each other in detention anymore, though for different reasons. Jimmy straightened up and stopped getting sent. Bored there without him, I simply stopped going. I didn't graduate from Farrell as much as I was shoved out the door.

Jimmy went away to college in Florida, where he traded Jesus and Causes for keg beer and older women. I enrolled at the College of Staten Island, even pulling decent grades my first semester. On his holiday breaks, we'd get together and tie one on, but there wasn't much to talk about. I didn't know the people he knew down in Florida, didn't do the things he did.

We got some of the old magic back the summer of '99, after he graduated. For a couple of sweet months, it was like those four years apart had never happened. We were eighteen again, running the same streets. We went out to Shea and the Garden together, played softball and darts for the same bars. We chased women and caught bands in Manhattan, riding back on the empty ferry at the crack of dawn, Bud tall boys in paper bags between our knees, Jimmy in a black leather jacket and wraparound shades.

I didn't know it then but that summer wasn't a reunion; it was a last hurrah. He was gone again in the fall, this time to graduate school upstate. He didn't come back to the island for three years. I blamed school for taking Jimmy from me. It made a good excuse to drop out of CSI after my third semester. Just when I figured I'd never see him again, he came back for a teaching position at Tottenville High, working like crazy to learn the ropes of a job he discovered he loved. I didn't see much more of him than I did when he was upstate. Then, in December of his third year teaching, he met Rose Murphy. It wasn't long before he discovered he loved her, too. He moved in with Rose the next summer, way down at the southern end of the island, near his school. They never answered the phone after ten.

I called him every few months. Rose hung up on me if I was drunk. If Jimmy answered, he just apologized and talked about breaks from school. But those breaks always came and went without us getting together. We'd have a drink now and then if he could steal an hour to swing by whatever pub I worked in. We could never decide between resuming the old conversation and starting a new one. Sometimes it was months between visits, and as each year went by, we each sank deeper into our different worlds.

In truth, I let myself be seduced by the action and steady cash of the bar business. I met Virginia over the bar. A tattoo artist in the East Village, she stopped in every night for a double Maker's on her way home from the ferry. She was wilder, funnier, and more exciting than any girl I'd met at CSI. She had no use for school, either. She was, like me, into getting about the business of living. Her appetite for sex was monstrous and insatiable. I took Virginia as proof I made the right choice in leaving both school and daylight behind. We made the nights a lot less lonely for each other and every now and then, for someone else. For my thirtieth birthday, she gave me my first tattoo, inking my right shoulder with an elaborate mesh of Celtic tribal patterns and symbols. It covered my switchblade scars from high school.

I thought being coupled-up might get me back in Jimmy's good graces, but it never worked out. We squeezed in two late, rushed, uncomfortable dinners. Virginia rambled on endlessly about her various schemes for the future, as Rose just stared thin-lipped at her tattoos all night. Both times, Jimmy and I got way too drunk. I was disappointed, but Virginia filled my social schedule and slowly seeped, like ink, into the spaces of my heart. She made me laugh. She got me into trouble. We asked very little of each other. I didn't worry about Saint Jimmy anymore. Three years went by like one long, slow day. Jimmy and I kept things barely alive with sporadic phone calls. Until Virginia walked out on me six months ago. I think Julia sent him to me then, too.

He just appeared at my door the night Virginia moved out. The cavalry, with a case of beer in one hand and a copy of *Braveheart* in the other. He stayed the weekend, drinking beer, watching hockey and violent, profane movies with me. I can't remember a single thing he said to me that weekend, only that on Monday morning Jimmy was gone back to his world and I'd somehow managed a tether-hold on mine. I was able to clean the house and Monday night I was back at work, my life somehow moving again.

With me back on my feet, Jimmy went back to his grown-up world on the southern end of the island and I held a small orbit around the bars at the northern end. Until he sidled up to me at Joyce's, I hadn't seen him since that weekend.

"Bit of a shock," I said. "Seeing you out on a school night with a drink in your hand."

"Extenuating circumstances," Jimmy said. He covered the glass with his hand. "Just this one, though." He picked up his drink and knocked it back. "Okay. Maybe one more." He called for Joyce.

"Rose'll be mad," I said.

Jimmy shrugged.

"You married yet?" I asked.

Jimmy studied his left hand. "Nope, not yet. Maybe soon. We'll see. It's an odd thing, the continued success of our relationship argues both for and against matrimony."

"Rose buys that bullshit?"

"Not at all," Jimmy said. "She's not big into paradox."

"So whenever she says it's time?"

"It's time," he said, laughing. He shook a finger at me. "Not that long ago, you were whipped as I am." We laughed. It was true. I wondered for a moment if he was talking about Virginia or Molly. Jimmy had a way of making time disappear.

"You doin' all right?" Jimmy asked. "It's a lot, you and Virginia and now this."

"I'm fine," I said. "I just wanna get it all over with."

Jimmy looked at me. He knew there was more to it than that, but he had too much class to call me a liar to my face.

"This powwow is overdue," he said. "What happened to us?" He shook his head, took a tiny sip of whiskey. "Shit like this makes you think."

"Forget it," I said. "Lord knows I could've tried harder.

We're all busy; life goes on. We grow up, or at least you did. You and Rose came to my mom's funeral; you came by when Virginia split. "

"No, it's not cool. That's what I'm talking about," Jimmy said. "I don't want to be one of those people, paying my respects when tragedy strikes then disappearing back into the ether." He paused. "We joke about Rose, but it's not her fault."

"Look, I haven't come looking for you much, either," I said. "You and I both know I wouldn't have called you this week. It goes both ways. And I know it ain't Rose. She was good to me when Mom died."

"She's always liked you," Jimmy said.

"Oh, I don't know about that," I said.

"No, really," he said. "She sent me down here tonight. I was just going to call you in the morning. She's always rooted for you. She's just, you know, protective."

"Rooted for me to do what?" I asked. "You need protection from me?"

Jimmy grimaced, realizing he'd talked himself into a corner. "She wants you to, you know, find a girl, settle down. She just pulls for you to . . ."

"Grow up?"

Jimmy stalled. "Mellow out, maybe."

"Virginia and I lived together. I tried to settle down. She left me. Rose just never liked her."

"Believe me, I know," Jimmy said. "Virginia was wild. And not exactly stable."

"Gimme a break," I said. "What's a couple tattoos? A nose ring?"

"And a belly ring," Jimmy said. "And a tongue ring."

"And a nipple ring," I said, "and a . . ."

Jimmy waved away the rest of my sentence. "Enough." He laughed. "It's a wonder she didn't jingle when she walked."

We sat silent for a while, until Jimmy reached his arm across my shoulder. He leaned in close. "Look, lad, it wasn't some catty thing. Rose never thought she was good enough for you, but it really had nothing to do with Virginia's . . . accoutrements. Admit it, man. She tortured you. She's going to Europe then she's not. She's going to Japan then she's not. She's going away to grad school in Bali or whatever fucking country half the world away, buying language tapes and everything, then she's not."

"She had an adventurous spirit," I said. "I admired it. I hoped it might take me somewhere, too."

Jimmy scoffed. "And now that she's been liberated from the burden of you, where has she gone? Nowhere. Face it, she was a fake."

"She was like me," I said. "She wanted more than this stupid island has to offer."

"Japan? Bali? The City's a twenty-five-minute boat ride away. Answer me this, you ever get an invitation to these locales?"

I had, sort of. Meet her there when she got settled, that kind of thing. We never got further than that. I knew she was being careful, wanting to be sure she was more to me than a ticket off the island. "Nobody's perfect. It went both ways," I said. "I wasn't easy to live with, either."

"Who is?" Jimmy said. "I never knew how you lived so long with it. Her, always with one foot out the door."

"I held on hard to the one I had," I said. I smiled. "Till she chewed it off." We laughed, and I relaxed. Then Jimmy shone his troublemaker's grin at me. The one I used to get before Bono happened, the one I used to get right before we got Saturday detention. "Now, Molly she likes a lot."

I blinked at him, startled. How in the hell did Rose know about Molly and me? Jimmy must've read the question off my face.

"Tottenville held an in-service, about a month ago," Jimmy said. "Molly was there. Bunch of us went out for drinks after and Rose met up with us. I introduced them. I didn't know about you and Molly, your current situation, yet. Shit, I hadn't seen Molly in forever. We told Rose how we knew each other, started talking about you, high school. Poor Molly, it just popped out of her." He grinned. "Like she'd been just dying to tell." He waved a hand. "Don't worry. Rose can keep a secret. And me, you know I never see anybody but Rose."

"I don't know how much of a secret it is, anymore," I said. Jimmy and Rose knew. Waters and Purvis knew. Julia knew. I tried to relax. None of them were big talkers. Except for maybe Purvis, but he was *all* talk. And what did I care? I wasn't the one with something, someone, to lose. Though who knew what Molly would do if David found out?

"For the record, I don't blame you," Jimmy said. "The years have been more than kind to our Ms. Francis. Rose spent three days talking about her legs. You don't know how hard it was pretending I hadn't noticed them, or the rest of her."

"I'm glad you approve," I said. I thought of Jimmy checking out Molly, noticing the shape of her from behind, the rise of her breasts, and realized I felt uncomfortable with it, almost offended. Possessive. I pushed the thoughts away. What would David think, as if I cared, about what I was doing with Molly? If anyone was violating someone else's space, it was me.

"Just so you know," Jimmy said, leaning close again, like a

conspirator, "Molly didn't say anything explicit, but Rose got the distinct impression that she might be up for a little more than . . . well, what you've got going on right now."

"You can say 'just fucking,' " I said. "Nobody's feelings will be hurt."

Jimmy raised his hands. "It is what it is. I'm just saying, in case you were wondering." He put his hand over his heart. "As for me, I, too, must come out in favor of such an arrangement. And I think I can speak Rose's approval."

"It's getting David's okay that'll be a problem," I said.

"Fuck him," Jimmy said. "You and I both know he was a rebound after nine-eleven, after she lost her brother. Hell, I wouldn't want to be alone through all that, either. You remember that first year. Bad relationships spread like herpes all across New York." He shook his head. "Use the brains God gave you, boy. Separate apartments and no ring after five years? Trust me on this, David ain't nothing but habit at this point. Don't use him as an excuse. I know we were young and naive in high school, but you had hope when you were with Molly. You talked about the future instead of the past. Think about that."

I knew I would think about it. But I wasn't telling Jimmy that.

"Molly's got a tattoo, you know," I said, looking down into my lap, "right above her—"

Jimmy waved away the information again. Joyce mistook it for a signal and came over to us. Jimmy ordered another round. "Don't you smoke anymore?"

"Of course."

"Then let's indulge," he said, grabbing the drinks from Joyce and standing. "I'll blame the smell on you, like I will the second and third drink. And Rose, good sport that she is, will pretend to believe me." He laughed. "We oughta hang out more often."

I rocked a little as I stood, and took my time following Jimmy to the door.

Outside, I gave Jimmy a smoke and lit it for him. Against my better judgment, I itched to know more of what Molly had said about us, how Rose had gotten the impression she had. Just because, I told myself, it didn't make any sense. Her throwing away a stable, steady thing, for what? Me?

Sure, she'd been full of romantic fantasies when we were teenagers. I had, too. But we were kids. We were supposed to think that way. Then. Surely she'd given up all that and grown up. Wasn't a teaching career and a big apartment proof of that? Wasn't three-piece, big-briefcase, big-income David living proof of that? But she'd been coming, more and more often, to my small apartment. She lingered longer the morning after. I saw the tattoo before David did, patted away the blood after she slid down her underwear and lifted the bandage. Took care with my hands, entered her gently, slowly, in case she was sore. What did any of that prove? That we weren't "just fucking" anymore? I could go on calling it that if I wanted, same as I could go on calling Virginia's restlessness and indecision an adventurous spirit. But calling something a name didn't make it so. I'd called John Sanders, Sr., "Dad" my whole life.

I tried not to think about Molly and I being together, out in the open, but it was hard not to. I imagined making love to Molly in her bed. I imagined meeting her parents again after so many years and the death of their son. I saw Molly and me at dinner with Jimmy and Rose. As each picture appeared, I pushed it away. But a stubborn thought kept pushing back.

I'd always assumed we didn't talk about David because it made her feel guilty. Or that it was a way of protecting him. But what if she was ashamed of being with him? Of not having the guts to leave when she knew the relationship was long over. They'd met at a 9-11 fundraiser, only months after that day, when her mourning for Eddie was at its deepest. David chased her for a year. I could understand her hanging on to him. Letting go of him would be like letting go of another piece of Eddie. Why hadn't I seen this sooner? She could be here. Now. The thought made my skin hum.

"So," Jimmy said. "The elephant in the corner."

"What's that?" I asked.

"Oh, I don't know, the one thing we haven't talked about. Your father."

"What about him?" I asked, almost relieved he'd brought it up. Anything to get my thoughts of Molly away from the dangerous territory they'd wandered into.

"He's dead," Jimmy said. "Somebody murdered him."

"See?" I said. "The facts are out. What's to talk about?"

"C'mon, John, this is me, Saint Jimmy, you're talking to. I was there when we were younger. I know what it was like."

"No," I said. "I don't think you do."

"This the same magic you worked on Virginia?" he asked.

"Fuck you, Saint," I said. "That was cheap."

Jimmy just laughed. "That's it, hurt my feelings to keep me distracted. You gonna smack at me till I walk away, too? Then cry about how I deserted you?" He polished off his shot, then dropped the empty glass into my jacket pocket. He pulled out the scrap of police tape. His eyes narrowed. "No, fuck you, Sanders. You can't run this bullshit on me." He jabbed his finger into my chest, the tape dangling from his hand. "I know you." He held up the tape. "I don't need this to know you're a fucking mess."

"You of all people know that ain't nothing new."

"You're breaking my heart," Jimmy said. "You really are."

I grabbed the tape and stuffed it back in my pocket. I had nothing to say.

"Why are you here?" Jimmy asked. "Why are you down here at Joyce's, all by yourself, all fucked up on a Monday night?" He jerked his thumb over his shoulder. "Why'd you go . . . there? To the corner? Why aren't you back on the North Shore, or at work, or rolling around with Molly?"

"I promised Julia," I said. My voice cracked. I didn't want Jimmy to make me talk anymore. "I promised Julia I'd stay with her this week. Help her out."

"Then why are you here?" Jimmy asked again, quietly this time. "Why aren't you home with her?"

My head hurt so bad I thought I might go blind. Pain crackled in my chest, dancing from rib to rib. I raised my glass to my lips. It was empty. "I can't stand it there. I can't breathe in that house. I knew it was a bad promise when I made it, but I couldn't tell Julia anything else. I just hoped I could pull it off. But I don't think I can." I pulled my cigarette pack from my jacket. It was empty. "I offered to bring her down here. Tried to get her to come to the diner, but she wouldn't go. All she wants to do is stay home and try on her funeral dresses and look through old pictures and call old girlfriends on the phone." The words poured out of me now. "She just wallows in it and talks about the funeral arrangements and how I have to give the eulogy." I turned to Jimmy. "I'm just fucking drowning in it."

Jimmy studied the tops of his shoes while I wiped my eyes. "It's called mourning," he finally said. "That drowning feeling? That's grief. It keeps bubbling up and you keep swallowing it. No wonder you're fucking drowning."

"You smoking crack?" I asked. I couldn't believe what he was telling me. "Mourning? Grief? For my father? What'd he ever *give* me but grief? He beat the *shit* out of me till I was almost nineteen years old, Jimmy. You know this. You saw it all the time. He beat up my mother for years. You ask me, he put her in her fucking grave.

"And what'd he do with himself after she was gone? Not a fucking thing. He never went to my mother's grave. My poor sister wrote and called him all the time, and he never fucking answered. He was a coward. He cared for nothing and no one but himself. He was a fucking *animal*. Now I'm supposed to *mourn* him? Are you insane?"

Jimmy just raised his eyebrows. "I'm not the one staggering around the sidewalk, screaming."

I could've fucking killed him. Anyone, anyone but Jimmy'd be swallowing teeth for a crack like that. "I'll piss on his fucking grave."

"He was your father," Jimmy said.

I lunged at him, grabbed fistfuls of his shirt, growled in his face. "Then he should've fucking acted like it. He wasn't any kind of father. Why should I care that he's dead? What did he ever give me that was worth a damn?"

Jimmy pushed away from me. "You're pretty hysterical for someone who doesn't care."

"It's you, it's Julia, that makes me hysterical," I said. "It's Waters, it's Purvis. It's Fontana. It's all these people, in my space, in my head. It's *him*." I shook my head. "He can't have anything more from me. No grief, no mourning, nothing. It's not fair. It's not right.

"He owes me, McGrath. He owes my sister. His whole life, he obsessed about his bills, his debts, about what he owed to complete strangers. How'd he manage to forget what he owed his kids? His wife? He owed us a decent life where we didn't have to be afraid all the time in our own house. He was supposed to protect us from harm, not dish it out. He died a failure, all his bills paid and still deeper in debt than his old man ever was. I'm sick of me and my sister paying the price."

Jimmy smoothed his shirt and stood his ground. "Then stop it here. Make your peace with this."

"I been running from him since I could walk," I said. "How do I make peace with that?"

"He ain't chasing you no more, Sanders," Jimmy said. "Don't pick up his body and put it on your back. Don't run from the rest of us, especially Julia, because of it." He stepped closer to me. "Catch your breath. You gotta make your peace with this."

"Please," I said, frowning, backing away as if his words released a stench. "You don't know what you're asking. This ain't Dr. fucking Phil."

"You bet your life it's not. This is real life, and you better find a way to fucking deal."

"I've been facing it," I said. "Dealing with Julia, the cops. I'm standing here talking to you. I face him every time I close my eyes. In more ways than you know."

"Try keeping them open," Jimmy said.

Fucking Jimmy. An answer for everything. For my father. For what was wrong with Virginia, for what's right with Molly. All this wisdom, way too late. A lot of help he was. Here I am, lost in a flood, just trying to stay afloat, and he keeps pushing me under. Fuck him and his sage advice, I thought. What did he fucking know?

I circled him, leaning toward him. "You enjoying this, Saint? Been a while since you've been in the pulpit, has it?"

"I'm not enjoying it at all," Jimmy said. "Breaks my heart, actually. Watching you flail like this. I feel like I'm at the fights, watching some bloody, punch-drunk fool who doesn't know when to plant his ass in the corner. You say you wanna get it over with, but you won't let it even begin to end."

"Sorry to let you down. You did your good deed. Ain't nothing keeping you here."

"Nothing but sixteen years," Jimmy said.

I waited. Waited to see what those sixteen years were worth to him. Waited for him to walk away. To go home to his goddamn beautiful girl and his goddamn warm bed and get a good night's sleep for his great fucking job. It's what I would've done if I were him. But Jimmy just stood there.

"Everything's different now, Saint," I said, quietly. "We're not those kids anymore."

"Doesn't mean we never were."

I was exasperated, exhausted. He was relentless. I threw up my hands, wanting really just to collapse on my ass on the sidewalk. I could barely breathe anymore.

"Whadda you want from me, Jimmy? There's not a thing I can do about any of it. Nothing I do is gonna make anything any different."

"Talk to Molly," he said.

Her name made me even more tired. "Molly? What're you talking about? What's Molly got to do with any of this?"

"You gotta try to be that thick," he said. "Molly buried her brother." He licked his lips. "Eddie was murdered sure as your father was. Left the house one day and never came back."

"I know," I said. "I can't. We never talk about that."

"When was the last time you asked? Maybe it's time. Eddie died seven years ago."

I rubbed my eyes with my fingertips. "Molly made that rule herself, back at the beginning."

"Since when do you care about rules?"

I wondered what I'd ask her about; it wasn't like I hadn't been there.

Molly had buried her brother, and she'd done it with more class than I'd ever display in all my years added together. I'd gone to the funeral. I stood in the back of the church and watched her speak strong and elegant in front of hundreds of people, most of them strangers, about her brother, a police officer who'd gone running to the Trade Center when everyone else was running away.

Molly's eulogy for her brother had been an act of pure magic and courage, borderline supernatural. She conjured her brother out of thin air and filled the church, filled all of us, with him, his life. With only the music of her voice, she sang to him. And yet, at the same time, as she spoke, I felt as though she and I were back at a train station and that she was speaking just to me, her cheek on my shoulder, her voice in my ear. Through it all, you'd never have known the casket held only a spare police uniform and a class ring. That morning, Molly carried her brother home from Ground Zero all by herself.

By the end, I felt as if Eddie Francis was more alive than the rest of us. I'd never been more proud to have loved her, or to have been loved by her. I left the church without saying a word to her, missing her more than I had in years, and believing Molly Francis was the toughest person I'd ever known.

"Molly's not exactly accessible," I said.

"I bet you could find her if you wanted. Do a little work. Meet her halfway."

"Molly's different," I said. I couldn't do anything like what Molly had done. I wasn't that brave. "Molly loved her brother. They were best friends, they knew each other. *That* was grief.

That was mourning. I couldn't speak like that about my father. I refuse to."

"You don't have to," he said. "Just say something. Just stand up there and say something. Let Julia help you."

"I got a couple days," I said, "a couple days before he goes in the ground. What the hell am I gonna say? How do I make peace for thirty years in a couple days?"

"You don't," Jimmy said, "but you can start."

"And when does it end? When is it over?"

"That, I don't have an answer for," Jimmy said. "Maybe it never is. But it can be different. If you can let him go." He checked his watch. "Shit. You feeling all right? You gonna make it through the night in one piece?"

"I will," I said. I let go of a long, long breath. "Thanks for tonight."

"You're welcome. Please call me tomorrow. You got a rough couple of days ahead of you. I hate to cut us short, but pumpkin time is coming soon. Man, only a couple of years ago, we'd just be getting warmed up."

"Things change."

"Yeah, they do," Jimmy said. There was real regret in his voice. "It ain't so bad, once you get used to it."

I didn't want to believe him. I didn't like the idea of getting used to anything.

He pulled out his cell phone, rolling his eyes. "This call will not be a surprise to her."

I stepped to him, closed the phone in his hand. "Before you do that, let me ask you a question."

"Let's hear it."

"Just how short is this leash you're on?"

"Depends," Jimmy said, "on how bad I'm willing to choke myself on the end of it. Why?"

"I need a favor. There's something I need you to help me do."

Jimmy tapped his cell phone on his thigh, his eyes shining in the glare of the streetlight. He looked like he'd been waiting to hear me say that for a long time. He looked, for a moment, like he was seventeen again. "We're not picking out a suit for the funeral, are we?"

"Not exactly," I said. "It does involve my father, though. I'm going looking for an answer or two. It's nothing crazy, but I could use a little help."

He looked at his phone, then at me. I knew he was in.

"One hour," I said. "I'll drop you back here in one hour. Make your call."

Jimmy dropped his phone in his pocket. "Why wake her up? Rose saw this coming when I walked out the door. Where'd you park?"

IT FELT GREAT BEING in a car with Jimmy again, racing down the Staten Island Expressway in the middle of the night. It felt like maybe the first right thing I'd done since I found out about my old man. I wished, not for the first time in my life, that there were many more miles for the two of us to drive. I wished there was something better waiting for us at the end of this highway. That we were really going somewhere, and that I wasn't just sucking Jimmy into the mess I was quickly making of what I called a life.

I tried to take comfort in the fact that Jimmy knew full well what he was doing, that he'd always been up for a little trouble, and that maybe this was a little payback for all the times he'd dragged me in almost over my head. But I knew the time for that had long passed, and that no matter how much he looked seventeen when mischief flashed in his eyes, he wasn't anymore. Neither of us was.

We had options other than the one I'd chosen. A quick change of direction could put us in Brooklyn, and then Manhattan if we wanted, or we could go another way and head down to the Jersey Shore, get drunk on the beach till the sun came up. Jimmy hadn't believed my promise to bring him back in an hour when I made it; I knew he wouldn't hold me to it. He wouldn't question anything I did, anywhere I took him. He'd just go along for the ride. But while I knew the options, I also knew we wouldn't leave Staten Island. I knew I wouldn't change course. I couldn't. Not then. I had things I had to do.

First thing we did after I pulled off the expressway was stop for more cigarettes and a couple of tall boy six-packs. Jimmy let me spring for them. He cracked two beers open as I turned out of the parking lot.

"Shame they don't sell pony bottles of Bud anymore," Jimmy said, handing me a beer. "Then this would really be a trip down memory lane."

"All my Mötley Crüe tapes are back at the apartment," I said.

I made a right at the light and turned us onto Willowbrook Road. We sped along the dark Atlantic coast of the island, not talking, just smoking cigarettes, drinking beer. Every other streetlight was out, and the road was dark and quiet. There were no other cars. As we ran one red light after another, a silver sliver of beach and the cold, black ocean flew by on our left. Rows of run-

down, abandoned bungalows littered the roadside on our right—
fossils of the island's long-lost heyday as a beach resort. More
than a few now stood charred by amateur arsonists, or addicts
careless with the pipe. The rest leaned at odd angles, exhausted
and distant, like homeless drunks slumped in a doorway.

As we neared South Beach, the partial silhouettes of swing sets
and softball backstops materialized in the darkness between the
road and the beach. After another couple of miles they gave way
to the shadowy remnants of the crumbling, tumbledown boardwalk. It ran along between us and the sea like a long, black Stone-
henge. A thin mist drifted inland off the sea. The low rumble of
the waves on the beach made strange echoes. Up ahead, the gauzy
glow of headlights in the South Beach parking lot.

"What a shithole," Jimmy said. "I can't believe how much
time we used to spend here." He took several long swallows of
beer. "You'll know these guys when you see them?"

I tightened my grip on the steering wheel. "Well, no. We'll have
to ask around a little."

"You sure they'll be here?" Jimmy asked.

"It's Staten Island, McGrath. Whatever they were doing last
night, that's what they're doing tonight."

Jimmy drank more beer and bummed another smoke off me.

I eased into the parking lot, staring past Jimmy at the disembodied heads that turned in our direction. A few dozen teenagers,
mostly boys, milled around in close proximity to their cars, late-
model SUVs almost to a one. I wheeled the Galaxie around and
parked it facing the crowd, catching them in my headlights. A few
of the kids shielded their eyes. A few more flipped us off. Silver
beer cans glinted in their hands. I left the lights on and the engine
running as Jimmy and I got out of the car. We circled around the

front of the car. Standing in the glare of the headlights, we cast huge, deformed shadows across the asphalt.

"I guess driving the folks' old station wagon has gone out of style," Jimmy said.

I could barely hear Jimmy speak. What I'd took for the rumbling of waves was really the thumping of discordant, bone-rattling bass coming from the SUVs. Each crew had their stereo turned way up in an attempt to drown out the others. All I heard from where we stood was a lot of aggravating fucking noise. A salty stink blew in on the ocean breeze. Low tide. I leaned closer to Jimmy.

"You still up for this, Saint?"

"Why not?" he said. "What could possibly go wrong?"

I stuck my hands deep in the pockets of my leather jacket and led us across the foggy parking lot. Two guys met us halfway.

They could've been brothers, twins almost, in their blond buzz cuts, white T-shirts, and gold bracelets. They were seventeen or eighteen, lean and hard from weight lifting for football, one slightly taller than the other. Both were half in the bag from Coors Light and Crown Royal. In unison, they shifted their varsity jackets off their shoulders and spread their feet. I tried real hard not to feel old.

"The fag section," the short one said, tilting up his chin, "is back toward the bridge."

Jimmy glanced at his watch. "You two better hurry up, then. You'll be late for the circle jerk." He surprised me almost as much as he surprised them. I hoped I hadn't let it show. We were off to a flying start.

The boys glanced at each other then stepped closer to us. "Fuck you, motherfucker," the short one growled at Jimmy.

"Get in the car," Jimmy said, jerking his thumb over his shoulder. "We'll go see the bridge." He wiggled his eyebrows and grinned.

The boys held their stares, trying to hide their growing fear. Jimmy and I were old, outnumbered, and out of place. That we weren't afraid confused them. They were wondering, I knew, what secret, pedophilic black magic we might know and whether we might use it to drag them, terrified, under the Verrazano. They were wondering whether or not they'd fucked up and picked a fight with two cops. I liked it that way. I saw no reason to dispel their imaginings. The tall one finally broke his stare and glanced over his shoulder for the cavalry. I reached out and grabbed his forearm. He jerked it back like he'd been stung.

"Ladies," I said. "We need to talk to you and your, uh, homies over there. Let's just get down to business."

I started toward the cars. The twins followed, Jimmy close behind them. The music got turned down. Someone in the passenger seat of the nearest Escalade hid something under the seat. They were hedging their bets, figuring we might be cops. And not the usual cops that hit the lights and sat in their patrol car until the parking lot cleared out. We were cops who wanted something, or knew something.

I walked over to the Escalade. "You wanna give me that?"

A big-eyed girl, not more than fifteen and buried in makeup, stared down at me. She smelled like pot. "Give you what?"

"Whatever it is you just jammed under the seat."

Her eyes searched the boys around her. "What? I don't know what—"

"Just fuckin' give it to him, Gina," someone shouted.

"Move your feet," I said, tapping Gina's bare calf. She snapped her legs up underneath her. Under the seat I found a bottle of Crown. I stepped back from the car and took a long pull, then tossed the bottle to Jimmy. He did the same.

"Fucking Canadian pisswater," Jimmy said. He lobbed the bottle to Gina but she didn't catch it. It smashed on the pavement. A groan went up in the crowd. "Fuckin' Gina," someone said.

"Gimme a break," I said. "You got plenty more stashed around here."

I turned to face the gathered crowd. "Last night, some fuckhead burned a car out here. I wanna talk to whoever called it in."

A murmur went through the crowd. Heads shook. Whispers passed from lips to ears. Nobody had anything to say.

"Don't give me this shit," I said. "You spoiled-ass motherfuckers are out here every night. Somebody saw something. Give it up."

"Cops been here about that already," the tall twin said. "Talk to them."

"I did already. That conversation is why I'm here. Who'd they talk to?"

The tall twin stepped forward. "What, your cop friends didn't tell you, big man?" Maybe he wasn't as dumb as he looked. So I smacked his beer out of his hand and shoved him hard against the Escalade. "Abuse," someone shouted from the back of the crowd. "I got a camera phone," shouted someone else.

"You'll fucking eat it," Jimmy shouted back. A couple people jumped. He'd been so quiet they'd forgotten he was there.

I closed in on the tall twin, close enough to let him smell my whiskey breath. Close enough for him to think maybe I wasn't a cop after all, maybe I was something worse. He flattened his back against the car.

"You know, I fucking hated football players when I was a kid," I said. "Really fucking hated them."

"Why?"

"I had my reasons. Sometimes it still keeps me up at night. You gonna tell us about that phone call?"

"I don't know nothin'," he said. "We talked to the cops when they got here, but me and Sean and Gina got here after the fire was out. Nobody I know called nobody."

A short, fat girl in a red sweatshirt, hair piled high, jaws furiously punishing her gum, shoved her way forward through the crowd. "Fuck this shit. I was here last night. Talk to those faggots across the lot." She turned and pointed a plump, diamond-ringed finger into the darkness. "Down by the boardwalk. The two greasy faggots in the shitmobile. Cops talked to them a long time. Betcha those are your boys."

I looked at Jimmy. He acted bored, slouching, running his hand through his hair, but his eyes burned bright and wary. I took a deep breath and backed away from the scared kid in front of me. His friends parted as I made my way over to Jimmy. We stepped away from the murmuring crowd.

"Whadda ya think?" I asked him. "You know teenagers better than me."

"Either those are our guys in the other car," he said, "or these punks will try and bail soon as we walk away. If they don't scatter, we'll know they were telling the truth."

"Fuck it," I said. "Let's see what the other two have to say." As we headed across the lot, the music in the SUVs behind us got louder. I took it as a good sign.

When we got closer, I recognized the car as a Gremlin. The hatchback was open and two pairs of denim-clad legs dangled down to the bumper. System of a Down spun out of the car on a cloud of marijuana smoke. Crushed, empty cans of Milwaukee's Best were piled on the asphalt, where they'd been tossed from the back of the Gremlin. I felt like I'd traveled back in time. I could tell from the grin on Jimmy's face he was feeling the same way.

"Maybe we can go easier on these guys," Jimmy said.

"That's up to them," I said. I rapped on the windshield. "Sit up straight, children. The grown-ups are here."

A long "Awwwww-maaaaan" drawled out of the car as they turned down the music, slid out of the back, and stood up at the bumper. One was tall and chubby, with an explosion of wiry black hair. He wore a black long-sleeved shirt with a big white bat signal on it. He shoved his hands in his pockets and threw a dejected glance at his buddy, a short, skinny kid in a penta-grammed hoodie. His hair was already thinning. He shoved a pair of John Lennon glasses on his face and blinked at me and Jimmy. "I guess you guys want the weed," he said, reaching into his sweatshirt pocket.

"No, we don't," Jimmy said. "What're your names?" His voice was calm and quiet, but the kids only looked more afraid. These guys didn't have an ounce of violence in them. "Ronnie," the fat one said. "Mike," said the other.

"One of you," I said, "called in that car fire last night."

"Who told you that?" Ronnie asked.

"The honor society across the lot," I said.

Ronnie and Mike grinned and glanced at each other. "You mean the nightly 'my new haircut' convention?" Mike asked.

"Whatever," I said. Their grins vanished. We weren't here to make friends. "Is it true?"

"I guess," Ronnie said.

"You guess or you know?" I shouted. Ronnie jumped back and I stepped into the space. I was getting tired of dicking around with these fucking arrogant kids. It's not like I was asking com-plicated questions.

"Yeah, yeah, I know," Ronnie said. "We called it in on Mikey's phone."

"For sure. It was totally me," Mike said, desperate to get me out of Ronnie's face. "It was my phone. I called nine-one-one."

"What did you see?" I asked.

"A car on fire," Ronnie said.

"Jesus fucking Christ," I said. "I fucking know *that*." Still, I backed off, gave Ronnie a little breathing room. "It was burning when you got here?"

"No," Ronnie said. He clammed up, looked over at Mike.

"Well?" I asked. "What happened then?"

Ronnie shook his head. Mike shrugged. I snatched fistfuls of Mike's sweatshirt. When he grabbed my wrists, I threw him down. He fixed his glasses before he tried getting up. I put my boot on his chest and pushed him back down. "Those fucks killed someone, shot him in the fucking head. What did they look like?"

Jimmy walked up next to me. We stood shoulder to shoulder. I handed him a cigarette. My palms started to itch. Mike scrambled to his feet and Ronnie didn't move.

"You miserable little fucks," Jimmy said, tapping the cigarette against his wrist. "This exciting for you? Jerking our chains about a dead man? What'd you get? Fifty bucks? A dime bag?" He rocked back on his heels, blowing smoke out of his nose. "You little shits burned that car and that's bad news. It was a real important car."

Something barked in my chest at Jimmy's suggestion, something under my heart. It took my breath away. I knew he was right. Lights flashed in front of my eyes, my brain spun. I grabbed Ronnie by his fat cheeks. He cried out, knees buckling. I bent his head back. I screamed in his face.

"You burn that fucking car? Did you?" Finally, I was gonna get an answer. "Who drove it in here? Who told you to?" The man I was looking for was in there, just beyond Ronnie's terrified eyes. I knew it for sure. His name, his face, his throat, were just beyond my reach, just the other side of this kid's skull. I could see him behind my own reflection in Ronnie's eyes. I bent and twisted Ronnie's head to get a better look. I couldn't let him get away, even if I had to smash this kid's skull to get at him.

When Ronnie's legs gave out, Mike grabbed one of my arms. I smacked him aside. He plopped onto the bumper, his hand over his mouth. I shoved Ronnie into the back of the Gremlin, crawling in over him. I caught his throat in one hand, dug into my jacket pocket with the other. A million miles away I heard Jimmy shouting my name. Ronnie struggled weakly underneath me. I jammed my lighter under his chin and lit the flame. "You like to burn shit?" He jumped and screamed, wriggling away from the fire.

"Tell me everything," I shouted. "Who was that fucking guy? What's he look like?" I shoved the lighter under his chin again, unlit. "Every fucking detail."

Ronnie just babbled incoherently, crying. Somebody grabbed the back of my jacket and hauled me out of the car, slamming my head on the hatchback. I wheeled around and threw a wild punch that Jimmy sidestepped easily. He shoved me away from the car. "For fuck's sake, John. Calm down."

"I'm gonna find out what I wanna know," I said, glaring at Mike as he inched away from me. "You run," I told him, "I'll chase you down and fucking kill you."

"They didn't do it," Jimmy said. "Jesus, where's your head? I just blamed them to scare them."

"We didn't burn it. We swear," Mike said. "We just watched from over here."

"Tell him what happened," Jimmy said.

"Two cars parked across the lot, way over there, by where all the lights are busted out. One guy got out of each," Mike said. He couldn't talk fast enough. "One car was a Corvette and the other was boxy, like an old Monte Carlo, or a Cadillac. They torched the old car and took off in the 'Vette."

I turned to Ronnie, who was up on his elbows, holding a cold can of beer to his chin. "That true?"

He nodded and wiped his nose.

"What color was the 'Vette?" I asked.

"Dark, like blue or black or something," Mike said. "It was dark over there."

"What about the guys?" I asked. "What did they look like?"

"Guineas," Ronnie said. "For sure."

"Yeah, yeah," Mike said. "For sure. I figured it was some Mob shit. That's why I waited to call the fire in."

I glanced back and forth between Mike and Ronnie, not sure which one I wanted to strangle first. "I don't give a *fuck* about the fire. What about the fucking guys?"

Ronnie eased out of the car. "They were both wearing those tracksuits, you know the ones with the stripes? They were both kind of big."

I clenched my fists and dug them into my eyes. "Like a thousand other guys on this fucking island. Did you see anything specific? You hear any names?"

"No names. They had dark hair, I think," Ronnie shouted. "Kind of had bellies, um, um, big white sneakers, I think." He was practically jumping up and down, desperately searching his memory, or his imagination, for something to tell me. "It was dark, man, and the fire made them all shadowy and shit."

I felt Jimmy beside me. He put his arm around my shoulder and led me a few feet away from the boys.

"They don't know anything," he said. "Give 'em a break."

"This is impossible," I said. I spat. "Murder in broad daylight, arson in a crowded parking lot." I looked over at Ronnie and Mike, huddled by the back of the car. "And nobody knows a fucking thing. It's bullshit."

"I don't know what to tell you, John," Jimmy said, his hands in the air. "This isn't getting anywhere." He looked at his watch. "Shit it's late. I'm gonna be hurting tomorrow."

Jimmy was right. This excursion had been pointless. I suddenly felt empty and stupid, marooned out on this desolate stretch of island. I felt guilty for asking Jimmy along. I didn't know if I ever believed we'd get any answers. I'd never even considered what I'd do if I did learn something. I had thought that at least we'd have some fun.

"Mr. McGrath?" somebody called from the darkness. Jimmy and I snapped around to look.

"Oh, shit," Jimmy whispered.

A boy stepped away from the two on either side of him. "Mr. McGrath? You all right?"

"Yeah, Matthew," Jimmy said. "We're fine."

The kid tugged at the strings of his Tottenville sweatshirt, the same school where Jimmy taught English. I tried as hard as I could not to laugh.

"What're you doing out here?" Matthew asked, a hint of curious insinuation in his voice.

Jimmy wiped his mouth. He glanced over his shoulder at Mike

and Ronnie, sitting cross-armed on the bumper, glaring at us hatefully. "Over there," he said, pointing over his shoulder at the Gremlin. "They promised me reports by last Friday. How's your report coming, Matthew?"

I lit a cigarette to hide my face. Jimmy was some piece of work. I loved that guy.

Matthew swallowed hard. "It's good, Mr. McGrath. It's almost done."

"I expect it *on time*," Jimmy said in his best teacher's voice, rocking back on his heels.

"Yeah," Matthew said.

Jimmy touched a finger to his ear. "Excuse me?"

"Yes, Mr. McGrath," Matthew said.

"Matt, man," one of his friends said, "I gotta fuckin' piss."

Matt gave us a weak wave and backed away. The boys turned and ran for the boardwalk.

"Jesus, Jimmy," I said, laughing, "I am so fucking sorry."

"Are you kidding?" Jimmy said. "When this gets around the building, my street cred will skyrocket. I won't have discipline problems for a month." He looked over at Mike and Ronnie. Their music was roaring louder than before. "We done with those two?"

"For sure. Fuck it." I stuffed my hands in my pockets and drifted toward the boardwalk.

Underneath it, crack vials and hypos crunched under my feet. Behind me, I heard Jimmy swear as he wiped God-knows-what, probably a used condom, off his shoe. The whole place stank of piss and rutting and puke and stale beer. Fifty yards from the sea and I couldn't catch a whiff of it through the filth. At least I could hear the waves. I unzipped my jeans by a piling and, settling my eyes on the dark ocean, made my contribution to the ambience, like I had countless times in high school, just like the kids here tonight.

When I was done, I heard Jimmy walk up beside me. "I know," I said. "We gotta get you home."

"How many hours you think we spent in this parking lot?" he asked. "I can't believe kids still hang out here."

"I can't count that high."

"It's funny," Jimmy said. "This one time, around when your mother died, I was telling Rose stories about us and I told her about this place."

"What did she say?"

"She couldn't believe we drove all the way down to this huge stretch of beach and stood around in the parking lot. All those nights, I never set one foot on that sand."

"She's got a good point," I said.

"I know. It never occurred to me until she said it." He took a deep breath and grimaced. "Weird."

I toed the sand, uncovering more broken glass and bottle caps with each swipe of my boot. Nobody walked on this ruined beach anymore, day or night. I couldn't remember a time in my life when anyone had. I'd heard the Mob left bodies out here. Didn't even bury them, just tossed them in the sand for the tide and crabs and the gulls.

"This beach is a wreck," I said. "Who'd wanna hang out in a litter box? Glass, needles, oil slicks. You couldn't walk knee-deep in that water without your skin burning off."

"Still," Jimmy said. "We were kids back then. We didn't give a shit about any of that. I just remember being scared of what was happening in these shadows under the boardwalk."

I patted him on the shoulder. "Now we know. Ain't nothing happening. Let's get outta here."

WALKING PAST MIKE AND RONNIE, I thought about stopping to offer an apology. But they were engrossed in some heated debate, probably about which Green Lantern was the coolest, if people still argued about things like that. I didn't want to bother them again. And I didn't want to feel any worse about pushing them around, as I knew I would when they told me to go fuck myself. We cut a wide arc around the kids in the SUVs. There were a few shouts, probably insults, but we couldn't decipher them over the bass. I was pleased to see the Galaxie sitting where I'd left it, engine humming. Jimmy and I made sure we kicked away the empty bottles that had been hidden behind my tires.

I climbed into the driver's seat, but Jimmy didn't get in. He just stood in the open passenger-side door, leaning on the roof. I got out of the car and assumed the same posture.

"More nostalgia, Saint?" I asked.

"Nah. Look, I was happy to come out here with you tonight. I understand why it seemed necessary. I don't like what we did, but . . ." He stopped, squinting off into the night.

"All right," I said. "Good to know."

"But this, this thing has to end here," he said. "You could have really hurt that kid."

"I know. It was an accident; I didn't mean for it to go that far. I won't come out here again."

"I'm not talking about here, about tonight," Jimmy said. "I know where this is heading, and it's someplace bad."

"I don't know what you're talking about."

"Don't insult me. I know you. You're already looking for the next eye to poke. What's next? You gonna go cruising for black Corvettes?"

"Maybe." We stared at each other for a long time. I was thinking about the .38 that had gunned down my father. I had some ideas about it.

"You gonna go crack skulls at the deli?" he asked.

"Been there already."

Jimmy threw his hands in the air. "I knew it. And what'd you get?"

"Nothin'."

"See what I'm talking about?" Jimmy asked. "Your father just got killed, you're drinking like a fish. You're beating up on teenagers. You look fucking awful. Maybe you're not thinking so straight."

"Don't worry," I said. "I won't drag you along on any more adventures. I know you got responsibilities."

"Yeah, I do. And I'd forget just about any of them if I thought it would help you out. But this bad-ass Don Quixote shit is no good for you." He drummed his fingers on the car. "Never mind that what we just did was probably criminal. You got responsibilities, too. Julia, your mother's memory, your father. Molly. This does not qualify as making your peace with anything. It's not what I had in mind. Finding the murderer is the cops' responsibility."

"If they'd get on with it," I said, "I wouldn't have to be out here."

"Yeah, this is where you need to be. Riddle me this, Caped Crusader," Jimmy said. "What'd Julia think of you coming out here?"

"She doesn't know," I said. I pointed a finger at him. "And she's not gonna know. And neither is Molly."

"Why not?"

"It'd upset both of them. Julia'd freak out, in fact. She's upset enough."

"Then why even take a chance on making it worse?" Jimmy asked. "Or say by some miracle, you find this guy. What if those two really had known something? What if you find someone who does? Then what? A citizen's arrest? What if he's not in the mood to pay his debt to society? You gonna drill him like he did your dad? That's a lot bigger than knocking scared kids around."

My eyes started to sting. They felt swollen. I rubbed my fingertips into them until it hurt, a lot. I wished Jimmy would just shut up and get in the car. "Gimme a break, Saint. I'm exhausted."

"You're a tough guy," Jimmy said, "but are you a killer, John? You got that in you? He'll kill you, too, if you don't."

"I don't know what I got in me anymore," I said.

Whatever I was carrying, I'd planned on getting a little lighter by leaving some of it in this parking lot, but that hadn't happened. I'd thought the rot in my throat, in my nose, was from breathing in this filthy beach. Suddenly, I wasn't so sure. My guts swelled and churned more than ever. Did I *really* need to kill the man who killed my father? Given the chance, the choice, to do that, what would I do? I couldn't answer. But still, I was choking on something. I could feel it pulsing in my throat, every minute of every day. I couldn't breathe again until I got rid of it.

I laced my fingers on the roof, dropped my forehead onto my knuckles. I started feeling sick from the booze and the hour. Everything I did made me feel better while it was happening, but ultimately left me feeling worse than when I started. This trip to the beach was playing out true to form.

"Let's bail," Jimmy said. "I'm not trying to browbeat you. Just ease back on the throttle some. I'm not looking to bury you, too."

I looked up at him. "Kill the drama. Nobody's burying me. Not anytime soon."

Jimmy held up his hands. "I just want you to think about things, lad. Before you act."

"All I do, McGrath, is think about things. I'm trying to stop."

"How's that working out for you?"

I stared at him a long time. "Get in the fucking car, Jimmy."

I GOT THROUGH THE FRONT DOOR without making too much noise this time. The dark, silent house told me Julia was asleep. I got a beer from the kitchen and sat on the couch. I left the lights off.

There in the dark, my conversations with Jimmy swirled in my head, and I found myself clinging to pieces of them. I couldn't shrug off anymore that things were getting to me. I'd pretty much lost my shit in the street four times in one day. Every time I gathered my trash back to me, in the parking lot, in the yard, in Joyce's, it seemed, I spilled it back out again. I reached into my pocket and pulled out the tape. I wound it around my fist.

Molly, Virginia, Julia, I couldn't chase them out of my head right now any more than I could get them out of my life. And now, Jimmy had worked his way in. I studied my fist. Even with the lights out, I could see half the word "caution" stretched in black letters across my knuckles. I had tried so hard the last few times I saw my father alive not to cower from him, to meet him on his own terms. I had grown so sick of running from him.

But what had I been doing for two days *but* running from him, from who he'd been, whatever that was? Wasn't I cowering from what had happened to him, no matter what I told Jimmy, or myself? I felt sick, embarrassed for myself. For how easily he'd made me a frightened child again. For my complicity in the transformation. But what, I asked myself, was I going to do about it now?

That was what my father had always wanted to know. The bigger kids at school were picking on me. What was I gonna do about it? My locker had been broken into, I'd failed a test, the train had made me late for school. What was I gonna do about it? Molly had left me for a college kid who took her out in Manhattan every weekend, instead of to the same movie theater and the Mall. I had told myself I was running after the killer, but now I thought maybe I was just running away from my father. So what was I gonna do about it?

I put my feet up on the coffee table, cradling my beer to my belly. When I shifted my feet, to press myself deeper into the couch, I knocked something off the table. My head spun for a moment when I bent down to look. Julia's pictures. I held my beer between my knees and collected the photos back into the box, glad I'd left the lights off. I set the box back on the table, but it just fell again, dumping its cargo again and this time taking a notebook with it. Cursing, I turned on the light and gathered up the photos. I picked up the cloth-covered notebook in my hands. It was obviously my sister's. The spine cracked as I opened it; it was new, maybe another purchase from the Mall. I was reading what she'd written before I realized I shouldn't be.

The first two pages were just Cindy's name, and my mother's and my father's, drawn over and over again in large letters. In some places names blotted out parts of other names, in others the letters connected. Pages of neat, detailed notes followed the names, notes on what Julia had eaten every day and how she felt before and after each meal. She'd marked each meal she'd thrown up. There'd been two, the two she'd forced down after I'd gone out for the night. My heart stopped. I set the book on my knees and covered my face with my hands. I remembered Jimmy asking me why I wasn't home, instead of at the bar. I wanted to crawl in a hole. What was I going to do about this? Could I force a grown woman to eat? Babysit her until she digested it? I would if I had to. I'd find a way.

I looked back at the book and my heart started up. Shame washed through me again. Julia had written out all her meals for the rest of the week, each one a little more substantial than the one before it. She'd drawn a smiley face next to each meal. She'd covered the pages with encouraging stickers, the kind a grade-school teacher puts atop a perfect spelling test. The kind our mother used to hide in our school lunches. At the top of each page were phone numbers—home, office, and cell—for her therapist. I didn't need to do a damn thing for my sister, except maybe not make an already difficult week harder. She was doing all right on her own. Not perfect, but all right. Better than me.

Her eating disorder developed late for that kind of problem, when Julia was already in her early twenties, not long before Mom died. It got worse after the death, but Julia bounced back quick and conquered it, or so I'd thought. She'd called me with regular updates, putting almost all her weight back on, slowly but steadily. Cindy's departure, I guessed, had brought the problem back. And now this with our father. But instead of letting it get worse, she was fixing it again. Again with no help from me. For the first time, I thought about the burden of something as basic, as essential, as normal as eating, being so difficult. I could barely imagine it, facing those demons, all the time. I set my beer on the end table and walked upstairs. I stood for a while outside Julia's bedroom door, leaning close to it, listening for her breathing.

She slept, as she had the night before, in her old room. She'd kept the door closed since she'd been back at the house, but I imagined the room looked much like it did when she moved out to go to graduate school. Tall bookshelves, splashed and spotted with paint, a tiny bed, old newspapers and garage sale rugs covering the floor. Her desk from when she was younger, white with gold around the edges. No mirrors. An easel propped against one wall, where she sat and painted with her back to the lone window. I couldn't imagine my father had done a thing with that room; it contained two things he feared—artists' tools and girl stuff. I'm sure he had no use for it, anyway, just like most of the house.

Beside Julia's bedroom was my old room. The door was half-open but I couldn't see anything inside. Not that I needed to. I already knew most of what there'd been of me in there was gone. Julia had told me all about it. With a new bed, new carpet, paint, and curtains, my parents had declared it the guest room, though we hadn't had overnight guests, as best as I could recall, ever. I moved away from Julia's door toward mine. I opened the door the rest of the way and turned on the light.

My bookshelves remained, still stocked with my books, un-opened for years. I walked over, running my finger along the creased, dusty spines. Dozens of boy-and-his-horse and boy-and-his-dog adventures from junior high. *Lord of the Rings*. *Chronicles of Narnia*. All the required reading from high school I pretended I never read. Chandler, Hammett, and Poe I'd stolen from Waldenbooks at the Mall. A Bible. My desk was still there, too. I pushed the blotter aside, revealing the deep, angry scars and scratches I'd cut into the wood.

I sat down at the desk, ran my hand over the cuts. My mother discovered them while dusting one day, as I probably knew she would when I did it. But she never said a word. That surprised me. My father never let us forget how much those shelves and desk had cost. My mother had been so proud of that furniture when it was delivered. Her penchant for polishing it made hiding Molly's letters a serious challenge. I only knew she'd found the cuts when I came home from school one day and found an expansive blotter placed over the gouges. I kept carving, but always under the cardboard and plastic bandage my mother had laid down. I finally stopped when she threatened to take my typewriter away. The typewriter was gone now. I slid the blotter back into place and pushed up out of the chair.

I looked around the room, wondering what would happen to this stuff now. Julia would probably pack up the books and donate them to some orphanage or school somewhere. The other stuff was bound for the Dump, I figured. I'd never come back for any of it, never even thought about it. It couldn't mean that much to me. I certainly had no room for it in my apartment. I sat down on the bed. Julia had made it up with fresh sheets. What was the harm? Why spend another night on the couch while a perfectly useful bed went empty? It was just a bed.

I lay down on my side and spied a dusty paperback on the nightstand. Curious, I picked it up: *The Black Stallion*, by Walter Farley. I smiled. I'd read it a dozen times. The pages were yellowed at the edges. When I flipped through them, a slip of paper fluttered out, landing on my chest. The print was faded, but I could still read it. A receipt from the grocery store, dated the year my mother died.

I stood, tossing the book on the nightstand. Wiping my hands on my T-shirt, I looked back at the bed then around the room. Suddenly, everything seemed foreign. Like I'd fallen asleep in my room and awoken in someone else's. Things I hadn't noticed just moments ago jumped out at me. The soft, feminine colors of the drapes and the carpet. Prints of flowers on the walls. The flow-ered comforter. After I'd left, had this become my mother's room? Maybe she'd finally carved out a space of her own in the house. A shelter from my father's relentless snoring? Maybe, I thought, a shelter from something else? Something worse. I shoved my hands in my pockets, afraid to touch anything. I wished I'd found a way to move out at ten and give my mother that many more hours of peace. When had she taken them? When he was at work? Late in the night, when he was asleep? Should I even be in here?

I could picture her, curled up at the top of the bed, dressed in stretch pants and a sweatshirt, holding the book under the lamplight. Holding it in one hand, her nail polish chipped and worn. Her other hand tucked under her chin. Her reading glasses on, her blond hair crushed under a bandanna. The steady frown she always wore when she read, bags under her eyes, her bottom lip pushed out. I studied the nightstand, searching for the telltale rings of a beer glass or a coffee mug. Of course I didn't find any. She would've always used a coaster, still protecting the furniture.

What would she have thought about my father's murder? When she died, Julia and I agreed it was best she had gone first. As cruel as he was, my mother was devoted to my father. His death alone, never mind his murder, would've destroyed her. Her heartbreak would've been unbearable—for all of us. But I couldn't help wishing that she had outlived him. Maybe she would've found a way through it. She'd survived all those years of marriage with him. At least she would've had a shot at some time, maybe a lot of time, free of him, much more time than she'd stolen in this little room. But she'd never have thought of it that way. For her, his absence would've been a prison, not a lib-eration. I could almost see her in the room with me, looking up at me from the paperback, her eyes bright but sad, agreeing with me with a silent nod of her head.

I rubbed my eyes, wondering at the time. I stared down at the empty bed before me. I pulled the covers up, tucked them neatly under the pillows, smoothed the comforter with my hands. Julia turned over in bed, talking to someone in her sleep. I slipped the receipt back in the book and returned it to its place on the shelf. There was nobody left in the house with time for schoolboy adventure stories. I turned out the light, closing the door behind me as I left the room.

TEN

"COFFINS," JULIA SAID, SHOVING THE BROCHURES INTO MY HANDS.

I set my coffee on the kitchen table and slid into the booth. "They make brochures for coffins?" It was way too early in the morning for this. I turned them over in my hands. "Sick."

"Necessary," she said, sitting across the table from me, wrapping her hands around her mug of tea. "I went to Scalia's this morning. We gotta get moving on this. There's only so much more I can take."

I thought of her notebook, if there was a check mark beside her breakfast. "I understand."

As weird, and unprepared, as I felt, I wanted to give her a serious answer about the coffin. I frowned at the brochures, trying to look like I was wrestling with a decision. I had no idea what I was doing. What should I be looking for? Style? Durability? Comfort? I checked out every brochure, hoping she had circled or starred a couple of samples to give me some guidance. Nothing. Finally, frustrated, I tossed them on the table.

"Something simple," I said. "White's out. Gray, too. Glossy black seems too flashy." I squeezed my forehead in my hand. I sounded like I was picking a limo for the prom. "A deep hard-wood. Basic but classy?"

Julia snatched up a brochure from the pile, opening to a specific selection. She tapped her finger on a photo, but I couldn't see which one. "Exactly what I was thinking," she said. I felt like I'd just won fifty grand on *Jeopardy!*

"So that's done," she said, tucking the brochure into a bag at her feet. She pulled out a newspaper, slid it across the table toward me. I didn't pick it up. "The obit ran in today's paper," she said. "I did it over the phone with Joe Jr. yesterday. We stuck to the basics. He was very sweet about it. The wake is tomorrow night from seven-thirty to nine-thirty. The funeral is Thursday morning."

"Um, okay."

She straightened in her chair, sliding her mug to one side and folding her hands on the table. "You're entitled to get through this however you choose. That's what I keep telling myself. You had issues with Dad I never did. I know I pushed you the past couple of days, to walk through this with me." She chuckled. "And then went out and did everything myself anyway." She held her breath then blew it out in a long sigh. "It's just, I worry that if I ask too much of you, I'll end up with nothing at all."

She stared at me, waiting for me to contradict her. I did want to tell her that her worries were unfounded, that I would do anything for her, that I could take whatever she dished out. But I didn't believe it when I thought it and she'd never believe it if I said it. So I just lit a cigarette and said nothing at all. When had I gotten so soft? So fragile that my baby sister had to shield me from burying my father? I had come here on Sunday mostly for her, intent on protecting her, from Purvis, if from nothing else. Now I was the one getting the kid gloves. Suddenly, I felt silly for trying to pick the right coffin. I got the distinct impression it had been ordered already, and I'd been handed those brochures only so I wouldn't feel left out. "What about the eulogy?" I asked.

"That's up to you," Julia said. "I'm sure you haven't given it much thought. You'd only have a day and a half, really, to write it."

"Well, Jimmy and I did talk about it."

"Really?"

"Yeah, we were talking about things, you know, and I mentioned I might be doing it. If you still want me to." I looked down at my hands. Two days ago, I'd nearly pitched a fit over delivering the eulogy, now here I was talking Julia into letting me do it. I looked up at her, impressed. She'd learned a few things, apparently, spending all that time with psychiatrists.

"Of course I do," she said. "If you feel up for it. What did Jimmy say?"

I drew circles on the tabletop with my finger, not looking at her. "He thought it might be a good idea. And it is my responsibility as the oldest son. I thought I could talk to Molly about it." I looked up at Julia. She was trying not to smile. "She did the same thing for her brother."

"I think that's a great idea," she said. "Let's do this: I'll sketch something out, in case you don't feel up to it. If that happens, I can say a little something, just to fill the void. It's just to take some of the pressure off of you." She stood and slung her bag over her shoulder. "But if you feel capable, it's your show."

"That sounds fair," I said. "Where're you headed?"

"Back to the funeral home," she said. "I need to finalize the coffin. Joe wants me to firm up some flowers. Pick a room for the wake."

I leaned back in my seat, crossed my arms. "You like it there."

She blushed. "It's quiet. Calm. Everyone there is just so . . . peaceful about everything."

"That's 'cause everybody's dead," I said.

"I meant the Scalias," she said, laughing. "And all their helpers and stuff."

"It's weird," I said. I stood. "But look, I'll go with you this time."

She looked at her watch. "It's almost noon."

"So?"

"Almost lunchtime."

"So? I can wait," I said. "We'll eat after."

She glared at me, hands on her hips. "Call Virginia. I've got our business under control, handle yours." She dashed off, her admonition hanging in the air.

When the door closed behind her, I turned and looked at the phone. Now that someone had told me to do it, calling Virginia was going to be that much harder. When the phone rang, I nearly jumped out of my skin. But it was Waters calling, not Virginia. My throat closed up when I heard his voice. My brain scrambled to figure out how he could've found out about my trip to the beach.

"Junior? You there?" he asked.

"Yeah, yeah. Tell me you caught somebody."

"Not yet," he said, "but the trail's warming up. Sunday night we had shit. Now we have a little more."

"Enough?"

"I don't need much," Waters said. "I been doing this a long time. But that's not what I called about." He cleared his throat. "You and Julia finalized anything?"

"Wake tomorrow at seven-thirty," I said. "Mass Thursday morning."

"All right," he said. I could tell he was writing it down. "I'll see you there, one or the other, most likely."

"Suit yourself."

"Sit tight. Look after your sister," he said. "We get a break, I'll bring it to you." He hung up.

I had trouble sharing Waters's optimism. But it did feel good that Waters believed something was happening. I liked the idea of a net closing around someone, the image of some meathead bragging to his buddies, oblivious as the shadows crept closer to his door. More than likely, Waters had hunted killers longer than this guy had been killing. He'd certainly been doing it longer than I had.

The shooter had stepped out of that car and dumped another world of hurt on my sister. I thought of what he would've done to my mother, if she was still alive. He'd stepped into my life uninvited and fucked it up. All morning I'd nursed the feeling that going back to the life I had before the murder wasn't an option. I could tell myself all I wanted that my father got what he had coming to him, for what he'd done to me, to my mother, my family. But the shooter didn't know that. I was struck again, and sickened, by his utter disregard for my family. He knew we existed, in one form or another, and just didn't care. Who was he, no matter what shape my family was in, to walk into it and blow it apart? Fucked up or not, our lives were ours, my father's included, and he had no right to them.

I pressed my head against the freezer door, squeezing the phone in my fist. My short-lived humility before Waters's investigative experience died a quick death. I didn't want any cops in between me and that murdering son of a bitch. I was my parents' oldest, only son. I was now the senior member of my family. I had responsibilities beyond the eulogy. Somebody other than the Sanders family was paying the price this time.

The fucker who'd blown up my family had something ugly coming to him and I wanted more than to see him get it. I wanted to deliver it myself. I wanted a look at him after he got it, after I told him where it came from. I started hoping Waters would call again soon. My mind raced through ways I could con or cajole info out of him, bully or maybe even beat it out of Purvis.

It didn't look good. Maybe if the cops had been strangers. If they hadn't already taken a gun off me, hadn't been watching my temper burn out of control my whole life. I was smarter, and tougher, than Purvis. But he did wear that fucking badge, a complication for sure. I wasn't stronger or smarter than Waters. I had nothing to bargain with. I couldn't think of any bullshit or con that he'd fall for. Nothing coming from me, anyway. But what about Julia? They both had a soft spot for her. She could get something. I laughed at myself, disgusted. That's it, pimp out your sister for info even you know you're better off without. Like she would give it to me if she got it. Like it or not, I was on my own.

I tossed the phone on the table and took a hit of coffee. Hell of a way to start the day. A hangover, coffins, and cops. Fuck it. I appreciated Jimmy's warnings from the night before but I had business to attend to; I had responsibilities. I needed to be in motion. There were people who needed to hear from me, to deal with me. I needed to take something, someone on, and better now that I was fired up. I dialed Virginia's number.

It rang twice before someone answered. I couldn't believe my stomach could hurt so bad so fast. "Silverdale and Green, attorneys-at-law," a woman who wasn't Virginia said. Attorneys? Had I called the right number?

"Virginia Ostertag, please," I said. One moment, I was told, and I was switched over to Pachelbel's Canon. Suddenly, I wasn't so fired up anymore. It just wasn't fair.

"This is Virginia," she said.

"And where did you go to law school, Ms. Ostertag?" I asked.

"John?" She had a laugh in her voice, despite herself. She killed it quick. "I appreciate the return call."

"You said it was important."

"It is, but I know you're dealing with a lot right now. How are you? It's so awful, what happened. I'm so sorry."

"I'm hanging in," I said. "Julia's doing okay, too. We're dealing."

"Good, I'm glad to hear that. Tell her I said hello."

"I will," I said. I had to stay focused. "So, you said you had something important to discuss. I'm all ears."

"I can't really talk right now," she said. "I've got a lot of stuff here to wrap up, before . . . before we talk."

No good, I thought. Deliver the ultimatum. We talk right now, or not at all. "Um, okay. So I should call you later? At home?" Nice. Nice reaction. Lay off the curve, I knew this. But there I was on my ass in the dirt.

"That's no good," she said. "My phone's not working."

"Sure it's not," I said. Here we go. I should just hang up right now. Don't play it her way. "Why am I talking to you?" I asked, her or me, I didn't know. "You wanted me to call, so I called, because you had something so fucking important to tell me that now you can't tell me." I paced the kitchen. "We quit this game, remember? You quit this game."

"I'm not f-ing playing games," she said, the professional sheen off her voice. "I'm in an office full of people."

I could picture her glancing around the office. Good. At least

I was getting a rise out of her, evening the count. "You don't get to do this to me anymore, Virginia. Tell me what you want."

"I'm not trying to do anything to you," she said, whispering now. "I'm trying to extend you some courtesy, show you some respect. What I have to tell you is important, more than the kind of thing you discuss over the phone at work."

There she was throwing the Uncle Charlie again. I saw the hook, but I flailed at it anyway. She just made me so tired and impatient so fast. "What do you want to do?"

"I'm about to duck out to lunch," she said. "Can you meet me? How about the Four Corners, over by the Cargo? It's close to the office."

Defend the strike zone, I thought. Foul her off. "Can't do it. I have plans." She paused, wondering, I knew, what I could have planned that was more important than her big fucking news. "How about Club Forest, on Clove. It's halfway between you and me."

"What about the park?" she said. "Clove Lakes?"

Okay. She wanted to stay out of a bar. Fair enough. Booze in both of us might complicate things. "The park it is, then," I said. "By the bridge. Five? Six?"

"Three," she said. "I'm leaving early today. Lots of errands."

"Three works. See you there," I said, but she had already hung up.

I plopped down on the bench, drummed my fingers on the table. I got up from the table, walked over to the sink. I leaned over it, looking out the window into the backyard, grinding my teeth. Standing around, brooding about her, accomplished nothing. I badly needed something to do. Booze was out. Virginia expected me to show up a drunken wreck. I wouldn't give her the satisfaction. But I needed a distraction. I picked up the phone and called work. Brian answered.

"Yo, Bri, it's John."

"Hey, man," he said. "How're you doing? We've been waiting to hear from you."

"I'm hanging in," I said. "I'll be back by the weekend."

"Don't worry about that," Brian said. "Take as much time as you need. You're dealing with family. This is only a bar."

"I appreciate that. I got a quick question. Theo been in at all?"

There was a long pause. "I ain't exactly a role model," Brian said, "but you really think pills are what you need right now?"

"It's not about that," I said. "I've just got a question for him." It was true Theo sold pills. And it was true that I often bought them from him. But Theo also sold guns. "Have you seen him?"

"Not lately," Brian said.

"He get picked up again?"

"If he has," Brian said, "I haven't heard about it. You're making me nervous."

"Don't worry about it. You see him," I said, "tell him I'm looking for him. Give him this number. It's important. Keep me on the schedule. I'll be in on Friday."

Brian started in again with words of caution. I hung up on him and took the car down to the deli.

Vito glanced over at me when I walked in then dropped his eyes to the cash register. Fluorescent lights flickering overhead, I walked the aisles checking for other customers. There were only two, both in the back at the deli. Vito's father, Big Sal Costanza, sliced pastrami behind the counter, a bloodstained apron over his belly, an unlit cigar in the corner of his mouth. Johnny Mathis played on a radio beside him. Big Sal sang along. Squatting, Angela stocked Cokes into the coolers. If she recognized me, she didn't give it away. The Costanzas: one not so big but happy family working away the last few hours of a quiet Tuesday morning. Me? I felt like a bomb.

I poured steaming hot coffee into a foam cup. As I sugared and stirred it, I watched Vito's head turn back and forth between the back of the store and the front door, begging with his eyes for a customer. I walked over to the counter.

"How ya doin', Vito?" I put a twenty down.

"Fine," he said, not looking at me. "A buck fifty. For the coffee."

"Throw in a *Daily News*." I leaned forward on the counter. I laid down another twenty and shoved the forty toward him. "You talk to your father?"

He stared at the money, but he didn't reach for it. His hands didn't move from his sides. "No. Haven't had a chance," he said. "Two and a quarter."

"Throw in two packs of Camel Filters." Two more twenties went down. "You heard him talking about it? Anything at all that might help me out?" I put down the last twenty I had with me. "You remember who worked that day?"

"Look," he finally said, "the cops told me not to talk about it to anyone. I don't want any trouble with them." He looked down at the money, pinched his forefinger and thumb at his lips. "I can't afford it. Feel me?"

"I feel you." I took the top off my coffee and sipped it. It was so hot I gagged. My eyes watered. I crushed the plastic top in my fist. I tried to smile at Vito. "But what the cops don't know can't hurt either of us. Right?"

"Sorry," Vito said, snatching up a twenty and ringing me up in a hurry. "I can't help."

"Correction," I said, leaning close to him, speaking quietly. "You won't help. There's a difference." My palms had started to sweat. I wiped them dry on my jeans. I picked up the rest of the money. He hadn't gotten me my cigarettes. I looked around the store. There was no one in sight. "Can I have my fucking smokes at least? Can you do that for me?"

"Yeah, sure. Anything to make you happy." He was talking like a smart-ass now, but his hand shook as he reached over his head for the cigarettes.

I lunged at him, grabbing Vito's arm and yanking him hard against the counter. Hot coffee splashed all over both of us. I snatched his throat in my other hand. Gagging, Vito grabbed my wrist with one hand. His other hand darted under the counter, searching for the bat or pipe or whatever weapon he kept there. I pulled him closer to me.

"I fucking told you I'd be back," I said. "But you did nothing for me. You useless piece of shit. Where's your sense of civic responsibility?"

Vito's answer couldn't make it through my fingers at his throat. Both our heads snapped around when a tiny lady in a black coat screamed, her hands flapping in the air, her fresh cold cuts at her feet. I released my hold on Vito. He grabbed a baseball bat from under the counter and held it out in front of him, shaking it at me. Angela appeared at the end of the soda aisle as Big Sal came rumbling up the aisle. "What? What? What?" he shouted.

"Pop!" Vito yelled. "This is the psycho I was telling you about. The one all crazy about the dead guy."

Big Sal looked at me. The panic disappeared from his face. Sadness replaced it. "Junior, I had a feeling my son was talking about you the other day," he said. "Put the bat down, Vito."

Vito shook the bat at his father, then back at me, then at his father again. "Pop, this guy is dangerous."

Big Sal frowned at his son. "Dangerous? I known this kid since he was a little nothing." He looked back at me. "Upset maybe, but dangerous? I don't think so. Right?"

I nodded, looking helplessly at the spilled coffee then back at Big Sal.

"Let me finish up something in the back," Big Sal said. "Vito, clean up that coffee. Junior, you wait right there for me. Don't do nothin', don't say nothin', just wait." He looked at his daughter. "Angie, sweetheart, you keep an eye on these two knuckleheads and make sure they do what I told 'em."

Everybody did what Big Sal told them. None of us said a word.

Big Sal *had* known me since I was a little kid, since my father used to walk me down to his store so I could rifle through comic books and packs of baseball cards while he shot the shit with Big Sal and his brothers. It was the highlight of my weekend, hanging around the corner store with big, smoking, swearing, laughing men. Sal would always pat me on the head when I jumped in the conversation. My father would put his hands on my shoulders and redirect me back to the comic books. It seemed like a fine time, and I felt lucky to be part of it.

God, I hadn't thought about that in years. Those trips to the store had ended twenty years ago, long before my father took up with Fontana. Both of Sal's older brothers were dead.

To my surprise, there was still a black wire rack full of comics at the end of the counter. I could see my younger self straining to reach the top, could hear the squeak of the rack as I turned it while trying to eavesdrop on my father and the Costanza brothers. I remembered staring at the packs of baseball cards, trying to guess which one hid the Dave Kingman card I coveted, terrified of making the wrong choice. I remembered the brothers' sudden silences when my father snapped at me to make up my goddamn mind already.

It was always either-or with my father. No matter how hard I argued, or bargained, he would never buy me both comics and cards, though each cost less than a dollar. As I watched Vito, muttering to Angela as he cleaned up and she rang up the terrified old lady, I recalled my father talking about life lessons, about being forced to make hard choices. I never learned that lesson. I insisted on what I wanted, forgetting or ignoring that I'd never gotten it in the past.

Usually, I left Sal's store empty-handed and impossibly frustrated, unable to make up my mind. My father would drag me home by the arm, alternately laughing and swearing at me, promising to never bring me back, though the next weekend, he always did and I was always glad for it.

Finally, during one walk home he made his threat and I surprised both of us by telling him that would be fine with me. I told him that one day I would have my own money and I would get things for myself. I fully expected to get belted. But he didn't hit me. He just squeezed my shoulder hard enough to hurt, and told me I was finally learning something. I had no idea what he meant.

Big Sal made his way back up front. He poured two cups of coffee, dropped ice cubes into each one to cool them off. "Let's go outside," he said. I followed him through the door and around the side of the building. Sal lit his cigar stub before he spoke.

"Normally, I wouldn't let someone behave like that in my store," he said. "Never mind toward my children." He puffed. "It's not something I'll overlook again."

"I understand."

He looked at me through his cigar smoke.

"I'm sorry," I said. "I wasn't trying to offend or disrespect you. I was just trying to—"

"I know what you were trying to do," he said. "I know it was your father that got killed out there. I feel for you, kid. I really do. I knew the man for over twenty years. It happened in front of my store. How do you think that makes me feel? And I know what it looks like, with the way he died. That shit has never, ever gone on in my store."

I just stared at him. He'd tell me that whether it was true or not.

"This vendetta shit won't work," Big Sal said. "I can tell from the state of you that it's not making you feel any better."

"I'm not after some vendetta," I said. "And I don't care how I look. I've got everything under control. I'm not the problem. Nobody'll tell me a damn thing about what happened. That's the problem with this situation."

"You blame 'em?" Sal said. "The way you been acting?"

"I refuse to accept this, Sal," I said. "It was broad fucking daylight."

"This is New York City," Sal said. "You know how much shit happens in broad daylight that no one has an explanation for? Where's your head, kid? Why should you be special?"

"Because it was my father." The words were out before I realized how foolish they sounded.

"I know, I know," Sal said. "I feel for you. I do."

"So what do I do?" I asked. "Shit happens? That's what you're telling me?"

"I know it ain't that simple," Sal said. "Gimme some credit."

"If it was you that got shot like that," I said, "what would you want Vito to do? Just let it go? Or would you want some kind of justice?"

"Justice? Junior, you're smarter than this. What's justice got to do with real life? I know how your father treated you. I tried talking to him about it all the time but he wouldn't listen. Where's the justice in that?" He plucked his cigar from his mouth, picked some tobacco off his lip. "Listen, who was that pretty Irish girl you used to bring around here in high school? Meagan?"

"Molly," I said.

Sal clapped his hands. "Molly. Right. Molly Francis. She was a looker. Listen, you think Molly doesn't want justice for her brother? You think she's ever gonna get it? You think she doesn't wonder, that we all don't wonder, how that coulda happened?"

"How should I know?" I said.

"You asked me what I'd want Vito to do," Sal said. "It's hard to even think about; I wouldn't wish the hurt you're feeling on my worst enemy. But I'd want Vito to do what a man is supposed to do. I'd want him to take care of his family."

"You think Julia doesn't want to know who did this?"

"I'm sure she does," Sal said. "But I bet she wants her brother more. When I had my bypass, I missed my brothers like hell."

"All due respect," I said, "but your brothers weren't murdered."

"They weren't. They died a little young, but they went fat and happy. But they're still gone, and I'd give anything to have them around, the fat bastards."

A coughing, filthy delivery truck pulled up beside us. The driver tossed his McDonald's bag out the window.

"That's my fish," Sal said, waving away the acrid exhaust. "I gotta send Angie to the bank and there's no way Vito doesn't fuck this up if I leave him with it. I gotta go back in. I'm gonna send Angie over to the house with some things. Some sausage, a good red gravy, some fresh bread. You like fish?"

I was going to protest. I wasn't going to be there long enough to eat the stuff and who knew what Julia'd do with it, but I figured there was no point in arguing. I felt utterly defeated. I'd come down to the store hunting a killer and I was walking away with flounder and some red gravy. Pathetic. I'd turned out to be a complete dud.

"I'm telling you this as advice, not as an insult," Sal said, tossing his dead cigar into the gutter. "Stop being so fucking selfish. It's your choice as much as hers how you and Julia get through this."

I wiped my lips with my fingers. "Thanks, Sal." What else was there to say?

"You're welcome," he said. "You need anything else, call or stop by. I'll tell Vito I got your word about no more trouble."

"All right."

"I do have your word on that, right? You won't make me a liar to my son?"

"Yeah, yeah," I said. "You got my word." It was an easy promise to make. The deli was another dead end for me and I knew it.

Big Sal left me standing there on the street, the delivery driver keeping a close eye on me as he unlocked the back of his truck. I never had gotten my smokes, or my change. Without either, I walked back to my car. I had more people to see before the day was out.

IF SEAVIEW HIGH SCHOOL had a parking lot for guests, I couldn't find it. The faculty spaces were all taken, so I parked among the students' cars. I slipped on my shades as I crossed the lot. Back at my apartment, I'd showered, shaved, and put on fresh clothes: a black, collared shirt, matching pants, my old black suit jacket. I was shooting for gracefully aging rock star, but I knew I still looked, despite the cleanup, like a bartender. At least I looked fine-dining instead of local watering hole. It would have to do.

The sheer enormity of the school, its multiple, multistoried brick buildings with only a few, dark windows, made me nervous. I wondered if I could even get inside. I guess they called it a campus, but as I crossed from asphalt to concrete, "compound" struck me as a better word. Seaview dwarfed the private school I'd attended, and looking up at the buildings, I had serious fears about getting lost, even if I did get in. I stopped at the foot of the main entrance steps, trying to plot a course of action.

Maybe I'd be better off ducking in a side entrance. I could surprise Molly in her classroom. If I walked through the front door, someone might make me check in at the office. They would call her down to see me, probably over the intercom. I'd have to give my name, and maybe she wouldn't come. There'd be questions about who I was. But I had answers for that. I was just an old friend. I'd come to tell her about the wake and the funeral, though, I suddenly remembered, she hadn't asked. I was in the neighborhood, figured I'd just stop by. Then again, what did it matter what I told some secretary? I'd felt no special obligation to the truth when I was attending school. Why feel one now, when I was only visiting?

I told myself I looked respectable, if not professional. Last night's liquor was off my breath by now. Besides, Molly had said I could call her at school. What was the difference, really, between a call and a quick visit? They're pretty much the same. Besides, I had honest intentions. There was no reason at all for me to sneak in the back door. I crushed out my cigarette at the foot of the stairs, hoping, as I trotted up, that no one had seen me do it.

I made it through the metal detectors on the second try. A security guard escorted me to the main office, where I signed in on a clipboard. After slipping a piece of hard candy into her mouth, the secretary slid the bowl across the counter toward me. I took one and ate it. "One moment," she said, turning back to her computer. I sucked on my candy, hands in my pockets, shifting my weight from foot to foot.

Two kids, two boys about fifteen or sixteen, sat close to each other on a nearby bench. One had the beginnings of a shiner. I'd been there. It was gonna be ugly when it filled out, all yellow and green. The other held a blood-soaked rag full of half-melted ice to his mouth. Been there, too. His lips would sting like hell every time they touched hot food for two weeks.

The boys slouched, legs stretched out, trying to say with their bodies how little the violence meant to them. Just another day at the office. But they both stared at me hard, fear and defiance fighting for prominence in their eyes. It wasn't either boy's first fight, but I could tell just by looking at them that it was the first time either of them had shed, or drawn, blood.

Shiner tilted his chin back and refixed his stare on me. Mouth imitated him. They were trying to figure out who I was, whether or not I had come for them. Should they be relieved, or more afraid, that I didn't wear a badge and a uniform? I realized I still wore my sunglasses.

"You're here to see Ms. Francis?" the secretary asked.

I turned back to her. She stared at me, her face stern behind her bifocals.

I nodded and slipped off the shades. I wondered if the boys, now armed with that information, grew more or less interested in me.

"What's the nature of your visit?" Losing the glasses had done nothing to improve her attitude toward me.

"Personal," I said. The lady sat like a statue. Not the right answer. "Ms. Francis and I are old friends. I have a personal message for her." I tried to smile. She still stared. I started to sweat. I decided that saying I'd come to fuck Ms. Francis in the broom closet wouldn't have sounded any worse to this woman than what I'd already said. I glanced around for the security guard. I wondered if David got the third degree like this. If he ever came to visit her, that was.

I leaned my elbows on the counter. "Ma'am, my name is John Sanders. My father . . . passed away this weekend. Molly"—I paused, cleared my throat—"Ms. Francis is an old friend of mine, she knew my father, and she asked that I let her know about the services. I was in the neighborhood, on an errand, and figured I'd tell her personally."

I panicked, realizing I'd just given the dragon lady the old "death in the family" excuse. I was standing outside the principal's office, trying to sneak my girl out of class. I was fucking doomed.

But the secretary's gaze softened and she held up a finger. My being twice as old as most of the student body must've bought me some credence. She clicked away on her computer. "Ms. Francis has a free period right now. I'll call over and see if she's in her office." When someone answered, the secretary turned away from me in her chair. She spoke too low for me to hear. "Ms. Francis will be with you momentarily."

A small, round man appeared through a door at the end of the counter. He focused a hard stare on me. Maybe Molly hadn't been called, after all. But after a moment, he turned and crooked his finger at the boys. They rose, their defiance replaced by an imitation of remorse. Without looking back at me, they followed the man through the door. I took their place on the bench. The

secretary smiled at me over the counter and tossed me a second
piece of candy.

Molly looked tense, her jaw set, when she opened the office
door and waved me out. Her eyes were elsewhere, like she hadn't
even recognized me. She held the office door open with one arm
as I walked through, passing close enough to her to smell her
shampoo. I followed her silently around the metal detectors and
out the front door, which I jumped to hold for her. She got halfway down the steps, her boots loud on the concrete, before she
stopped and waited for me.

I took a moment to enjoy looking at her as I approached; I'd
never seen her in school clothes. Her burgundy skirt had chalk
dust at the pockets. Her hair, looking desperate to escape, was
wound on the back of her head, a pen stuck through it. Looking
at me, she straightened her blouse. It was a reflex, I figured, born
of years of schoolboys trying to peek down it. On her feet were
brown cowboy boots, well worn. I recognized them. I'd heard
them hit my bedroom floor many times. When I reached her, it
was all I could do not to kiss her. I held out my arms.

"Surprised?" I asked.

With a nod of her head, she told me to follow her. She led me
around the building, to the side of the gym, where the windows
were high on the wall. It wasn't at all what I had come to see her
for, and she obviously wasn't in the mood, but all I wanted was
to kiss her, to make out behind the gym. The thought made me
giddy. She read my mind and put a little distance between us. I
remembered just what a flagrant violation of our rules I was really committing.

"Gimme a cigarette," she said.

I did. "So, I just thought I'd check in," I said. Her eyes flitted over the parking lot. What would be worse? Getting caught with me, or with the cigarette? I'd made a poor choice coming here, but she hadn't chased me away. She was willing to let me redeem myself. "This was a bad idea," I said. "I'm sorry."

Her eyes met mine for the first time. "It's fine," she said, waving her hand through our cigarette smoke. "It really is. You just caught me off guard." She smiled, and her face relaxed. "It's good to see you, in the daylight." She tucked a few stray locks of hair away, dragging hard on her cigarette. "It's been a long day already."

"Kids outta control?"

She scrunched her nose. "Not that. Discipline's never been a problem for me. I just get sick of running into the same problems, apathy, attitude, short attention spans, over and over again." She blew stray strands of hair off her cheek. "And that's just the parents. That's what I was doing, calling parents. Then I wonder why I can't get through to the kids. All part of the job, I guess. They're the same age every year, and I keep getting older."

"Sounds aggravating."

"Today it is," she said. "I'll get over it. I always do. They're just being teenagers, poor things. The best thing about them is also the worst. If you don't like who they are, give 'em a day, an hour, and they'll be someone else. Today, they're thick as bricks, tomorrow they'll be my confused little angels again." She fiddled with the buttons on her blouse. "Anyway, I'm sure my bitching isn't what you're here for."

I didn't want to talk. She'd just told me more about her job in half a cigarette than she had in three months of staying the night. I loved hearing it; I didn't want her to stop. I wished that I'd come to talk about something else, or about nothing at all. I wished I'd come to hear her bitching, or her joy, over her job. I wanted to make plans for dinner. It was scary out here, but I liked this daylight thing.

But looking up at the high, brick walls of the buildings that surrounded us, that cast us in their shadows, I knew we weren't standing in daylight at all. Molly was hiding us. I understood it, understood her reasons that had nothing to do with her being at school. I understood my place, but, for the first time, I hated it. I wanted out of it.

Molly wiggled her fingers in front of my face. "Speaking of short attention spans."

"Sorry. I've got a lot on my mind. It wanders a lot these days."

"I know," she said, "and here I am babbling about mundane shit."

"It's all right. I could use some mundane shit in my life."

"How's it going?" Molly asked. "Your life?" Like we hadn't seen each other in months, not less than two days. But it did feel like months had passed since Sunday afternoon.

"Okay, I guess." I ran my hands through my hair. "How do you measure progress in a thing like this? We've got the casket. We've got the times. Julia's finalizing the flowers and meeting with the priest today." I looked away from her, out over the parking lot. "I've been keeping myself occupied."

"It's good things are moving along. Good to stay busy. But that's not what I meant. How're *you* doing?"

"Oh, well, up and down," I said. I looked at her. Better now. I took a deep breath. "Maybe not so good overall. Or maybe all right. Julia hasn't thrown me out. No one's locked me up. You're still talking to me." I shrugged. "I don't know what to judge it against."

Her eyes got distant again. "Sounds about right. The up and

down, the confusion." She tried to smile. "That'll go on for a while, I'm afraid. I got so sick of fucking crying. Sometimes I still do." She stopped and looked away, biting her cheek.

When? I wondered. When did she still cry, and what for? For Eddie? For herself? And who was there with her, if anyone.

"You'll get through it," she finally said. She checked her watch. My window was closing. I remembered that, like always, we had limited time.

I shuffled my feet. I'd wanted to ease into this better. I'd come to ask a lot, more than I realized.

"So, I told Julia I'd give the eulogy," I said. I was having trouble with the words, putting them together, getting them out. "The wake is tomorrow night, at seven-thirty." I swallowed hard. My mind went totally blank. "So, can you make it?"

Molly cocked her head at me. Nice. Like it was a friggin' cocktail party. I'd been smoother when I was fifteen. I wiped my hand across my forehead. Do better than that.

"Mol, it'd do a lot for me, mean a lot to me, if you would be there. If you helped me through."

She pinched her bottom lip, her head still tilted to one side. I couldn't read her face. I couldn't tell if I was losing her, or if I'd just shocked the shit out of her. Hell, I'd shocked myself. When she didn't respond, I babbled, trying to get both my feet back on the wire. "Not for the whole time, naturally. I wouldn't ask that. But, you know, maybe for a while? A little while? Julia'd be thrilled and Jimmy McGrath will be there with Rose." First, I couldn't talk, now I couldn't shut up. I was realizing, too late, how much her being there would mean to me.

"I don't know," Molly said, crossing her arms, but stepping closer to me, looking down at her boots, then up at my face. "It's at Scalia's, right?"

"We'll be right by Joyce's," I said, trying to get the focus off of Scalia's. "The wake ends at nine-thirty. Come by late. We could get a drink after."

"I'd like to," she said, sighing, "but I don't think I can. Not for the drink, or anything else. I'm sorry. I really am."

I could tell she really was, and that she was torn, that her decision might not be absolute. I tried to shake her loose, before her decision solidified, before she closed completely to me. "Look, David would understand," I said. "To hell with it, bring him."

"Yeah, right. Like he would come." She looked up at me, so close now all I could see were her eyes. "And even if he did, I don't think I could stand the both of you in the same room. I couldn't not give myself away." I felt her hand on my arm. "It's not David. And it's not you."

"It's Eddie," I said. Of course. I couldn't push her on that. It was a part of her I wasn't allowed to touch.

"I can't go back to Scalia's. Shit, I still have to ride in the back of the ferry. All that empty sky. I still can't stand it." She slipped her arms around me and my knees almost gave way. But my hands hung at my sides. "I'm sorry, John," she said. "I want to see you. I've picked up and put down the phone a hundred times since Sunday. I'll come see you this weekend. You'll be back at work?"

"Molly," I said, my throat suddenly dry, "it's been seven years since Eddie died. I know it's hard but, please, do this for me."

She blinked up at me, her eyes wet. "I'm confused. I thought I just heard *you* telling *me* to get over what happened years ago. But that couldn't be true. I must've misheard."

My stomach went sick. I wanted to crawl under the gym and never come out. "No, no, no. I'm not saying you should be over it, or forget it, I'm just saying . . ." I stopped, stuck, dead in the water. "I don't know what I'm saying."

She put her fingertips to my mouth, rescuing me from my own stupidity. "It's all right. I'm sorry. I know it took a lot for you to come here and talk to me. It means a lot, it really does. But I can't come to the wake. I just can't."

I let my hands rise to her hips. This weekend wasn't enough, not nearly enough. But I knew it was all I was going to get. I should've known that all along. She kissed my temple. I was glad I hadn't asked for her help with the eulogy. That only would've made it harder for her to say no, and made it hurt more to hear it.

"Don't hate me for this," she said.

Hate you? I pulled her closer. I couldn't if I tried. There was too much in the way. I couldn't hate you. Just the opposite, if anything, if you really want to know the truth. But it seemed I couldn't do that, either. There was too much in the way for that, too.

I slid a hand to the small of her back. "It's all right, Mol," I said, breathing her in as deep as I could. Vanilla. Strawberries. "I understand. This weekend sounds great."

My own voice sounded dead in my ears and cold flooded my insides. I knew she felt it happening. I was terrified I wouldn't see her this weekend, or any weekend after that. And I'd always worried she'd be the one to ruin things with silly ideas, to wreck our careful arrangement by breaking the rules or asking too much. It's hard, I thought, after fancying yourself the flame, finding out that you're really just the moth.

She stepped out of our embrace, looked at her watch. "I really have to get back inside. My last class starts in five minutes."

"Right," I said. "See you later."

She kissed my cheek, whispering, "Saturday night" into my ear as she swept past me, hurrying to the stairs. She waved without looking back as she ascended. I watched the hem of her skirt slip through the door just before it closed behind her. I stared at the empty space she'd left before the door. If I waited long enough, would I see her come back through it? But what would happen then? My waiting wouldn't change anything.

I walked out to the edge of the parking lot, where the asphalt ended at Miller Field, a windy old airstrip the city had transformed into a public space decades ago. The tips of my boots stopped just short of the grass. The field was empty, but after school let out, the playgrounds, soccer fields, and ill-kept softball diamonds would fill with laughing, running kids and their frustrated, yelling coaches and babysitters. I put one foot up on the concrete block that marked the end of a parking space.

Molly had taken a job close to home. To my left, hundreds of yards away, a chain-link fence, obscured by hedges, marked the northern edge of the field. There was a hole in that fence that opened onto Carter Street, where Molly had grown up, where I'd gone to see her when her parents weren't home. I'd ride the train to the New Dorp Station, walk down New Dorp Lane, across the field, and duck through the hole in the fence.

In the winter, snow and ice covered the field and the wind ripped across it like it was the frozen edge of the Earth. The field was always barren. Going to see Molly then had felt like such an adventure, a journey across the wasteland. I never wished I had a car, never wished getting there was any easier. I'd be plenty warm when I reached her.

Going to see her then, I ran across that snow waiting to fly. When I crossed that field, navigating the snow and ice and the wind in my black denim jacket, jeans, and black Chuck Taylor high tops, U2's *Unforgettable Fire* on my Walkman, I was a warrior. I *loved* that girl. When I was sixteen, crossing that field in the winter was the most romantic thing in the world. Standing there in the sun fifteen years later, that snowbound field felt impossibly distant. That romantic journey felt like forever ago. Or worse, like someone else's memory.

Meet her halfway. Fuck you, Jimmy, I thought. But I knew he hadn't fooled me, and neither had Molly. I knew full well I'd fooled myself into being there, had fooled myself into a lot more than that. Molly and I weren't just old friends anymore, hadn't been since we'd started this affair, if we'd ever been. But I wondered now, for the first time, if the affair hadn't made us something less, instead of something more. I wondered if the privileges I'd been granted weren't a poor substitute for the ones she withheld.

Straight ahead, far away from me, Miller Field ended at the beach, and when I took a deep breath, I could smell the ocean on the wind. I heard the buses and the traffic behind me on New Dorp Lane. If I listened hard enough, I knew eventually I'd hear the train. With all the traffic and people and stores and the stink of the Dump, it was tough, almost impossible, to remember that we all lived on an island. It was times like this that reminded me.

Walking back to the car, I thought about how I had seemed so brilliant to myself when I'd left the deli. After that defeat, my plan had been to fortify myself on Molly's affection before joining into one last battle with Virginia. But talking to Molly had left me feeling like the walking wounded. The thought of Virginia made me ill, another ex standing within arm's reach, checking her watch until she could get rid of me. Astonishing. Not many men could put that together in one day.

I could just not show, I thought, starting the car, just stand her up. What would she do about it, leave me? I didn't owe her anything. But I dismissed the idea. That move wouldn't surprise Virginia at all. She was probably thinking that very thing right at this moment. No, I'd show up and endure whatever fiasco she had in store for us. I couldn't think of any alternative that I could live with.

I pulled the car out onto New Dorp Lane. Exhaust filled the car when I rolled down the windows. It stung my eyes. It was a miracle anyone on this island could breathe at all past the age of twenty. I lit a cigarette and with the first drag came the shooting pain in my ribs. Maybe I was finally getting the cancer. About time.

I slouched in the driver's seat. The lights in front of me, tail and traffic alike, were red as far as I could see. I was going nowhere fast. It was probably best to head straight for Clove Lakes. If I did, I'd have time to legally park the car and grab a cup of coffee, maybe walk the track around the lake. Get my mind right before I met Virginia. But, on the other hand, if I hurried, if I bagged New Dorp Lane and took a couple of shortcuts, I might catch up to Theo. I hit a tight U-turn that had ten drivers in either direction swearing at me. I was gonna get something done that day if it killed me.

Only a few blocks from work, not far from my apartment, I turned right on Jersey Street, at the same corner where Purvis had abandoned my sister years ago, and headed into the Park Hill projects, Staten Island's very own miniature imitation of the worst of Harlem. Black faces of all ages stared me down as I eased along in the Galaxie, trying to remember which of the hollowed-out, brown brick buildings Theo lived in. I wished I'd gotten my gun back from Waters, and immediately felt guilty about the thought. I hadn't been to see Theo at home in a few years, but I'd never had a problem in this neighborhood. Back in the day, I'd never wished for a gun. I also knew that since then things around here had gotten a lot fucking worse.

Theo and I met washing dishes and busing tables at an Italian joint on Richmond Terrace. It was on the North Shore, not far from the ferry terminal and right by the water. Both of us were fresh out of high school. We used to smoke cigarettes, and the occasional joint, out back by the loading door where we could see the shining castles and towers of Manhattan, just a short stretch of gray water away. We never socialized except at work in those days. He made me laugh like crazy. He was the only person I would've named as a friend had someone asked me. By then, Jimmy and Molly were both gone.

Theo was the first one to bail on the job, going into business for himself on a stake from his older brother, Val. About six months later I left for a bar-backing job on Forest Avenue. But we kept in touch. It wasn't hard; I was one of Theo's first clients. We both started with cocaine, doing sloppy lines of shitty product off CD cases in the Park Hill apartment he shared with Val. I never saw their parents, and never asked. They never offered any information. It was as if Theo and Val had just sprung to life there in Park Hill, independent of anyone but each other.

I lost my taste for cocaine quickly. The high made me violent, and the lows, the morning-after depressions, were intolerable. I didn't need any help, even back then, a time I considered myself relatively happy, stoking my temper or climbing into a black hole. Theo's kick with coke didn't last, either, at least as a user. We both had the same problem with it, coming down made it too hard to go to work. And we were both all about working then.

I found pills much more manageable. Theo used to joke he

started slinging them just for me, so I wouldn't have to mess with someone untrustworthy. Maybe he was telling the truth; he never did make much money off me. By the time I went to work at the Cargo, he'd made a name for himself, supposedly killed a man, expanded his business dealings, been busted twice, shot once, and certainly didn't need me and my fifty-dollar-a-week semi-habit. Sometimes I think he only keeps me in the loop out of nostalgia; I'm like that worn-out first dollar shopkeepers pin to their wall.

From my car, I spotted his building. Number six. The one with the fire escape that stopped at the fourth floor. A cop car prowled by in the opposite direction, moving even slower than I was, the cops looking at me hard. I thought, not for the first time, that Theo might not appreciate the attention I drew. I told myself I'd be cool, and I'd be quick. The way my day was going, I wasn't real optimistic about learning anything useful. But the gun was the last remaining link I had to my father's death. I couldn't let it go just yet.

I parked and locked the car, stuffing anything that might look tempting under the passenger seat. By the doorway to Theo's building, a couple of kids were on their knees in the dirt, poking sticks at a stray cat they'd trapped under a bush. They giggled every time it hissed at them. They ignored me as I walked by them and into the building. The cops were nowhere in sight. I knew the elevators hadn't worked since I first started visiting Theo. The dealers wrecked them so the cops couldn't surprise anyone. I made right for the stairs.

Someone stood at the foot of the stairwell, his back against the wall, the hood of his black sweatshirt hiding his face, his camouflage pants bunched at the top of his Timberlands. He cleared his throat, took a toothpick from his mouth, and spat on the floor as I approached. One hand went into the pocket of his sweatshirt. He stuck one foot out just enough to get in my way. His hand moved in his pocket.

I'd played this game since he was in diapers. I stopped next to him and reached into my jacket. He smelled like weed and sweat and fabric softener. I could feel his breath on my cheek and neck. The hallway smelled like piss and fast food and stale menthol cigarettes. I took out my Camels and lit one. Then I stepped over his foot and headed, slowly, casually, up the stairs, listening for footsteps behind me.

Sentry number two met me on the third-floor landing, one floor short of where I needed to be. His gun was in plain view, tucked into the front of his jeans. He wore short twists tied up in multicolored threads and one of those oversized baseball jackets covered with Negro League patches. Big diamond earrings. A huge diamond nameplate that said *Skinny* though he was anything but. I wanted to ask him what he knew about Josh Gibson. Less than I did, I figured.

"My goodness," he said, "a white man." He hitched his thumbs in his belt like an imitation cowboy and did a little shuffle. It made me think of Purvis. He put his whole body in my way. I stared at a spot on the wall over his shoulder.

"Theo's waiting for me," I said.

"I don't know no Theo."

"One day, when you move up in the world, maybe you will."

"Oh, a funny man," Skinny said. "Here's a riddle for you, funny man. If there was a Theo, what the fuck he want with a ghost like you?"

"So what you're telling me," I said, "is that Theo needs your permission to do his business. I can't see him being real thrilled with that attitude."

"It was him. I wanna find the guy who did it. For my sister. For my mother." I couldn't believe it, but I was begging. "Every lead I had has gone dry. This is the last one I got."

"Bad idea, bro. Bad, bad idea," he said. "Once you start this shit, it never stops. Believe me, I know. You think Skinny and Kenny are out there 'cause they love the hallway?"

"I gotta follow through on this," I said. "I gotta get this done. I can't breathe."

"I know the feeling." Val just looked at his hands. "The cops have the gun, don't they?"

I swallowed hard. "Yeah, they do."

"You got to go, bro," he said, standing. He wrapped a slice in wax paper and handed it to me. "I can't do nothin' for you."

"Can't you call Theo?" I stood as well. "If I could just get a description of the guy who bought it, I can take it from there. No one'll ever know you guys were involved."

"Nigga, please, you've already been seen here." Val shook his head. "And even if Theo did sell that gun, which I doubt, highly, he can't ever give up a client."

"Ain't this bigger than business?"

"No doubt," Val said. "Protecting clients is about more than business, ya heard me? Now you gotta go." He put his hand on my shoulder and turned me toward the door. He followed me to it.

I stood there in the hallway, holding my pizza, staring up at Val's face. It told me the subject was more than closed. There'd be consequences for staying on it. Even if I gambled with Val's patience, there was no way I'd reach Theo before he did. The last door had been slammed shut on me. I was done pursuing the murder weapon. At the end of the day, it really was all about business. I should've known better.

"You still got that classy whip?" Val asked.

"Yeah, I do."

"Drive her home," he said. "And give both of you a rest."

He closed the door in my face. I stood there listening to the locks tumble into place. Neither Skinny nor Kenny said anything to me as I walked down the stairs. I had to chase the kids out front off the hood of my car. Their sneaker prints were all over the hood, and the windshield, and the roof. I gave a little girl in pink barrettes my slice. There was no sign of the cat.

AT PRECISELY THREE, VIRGINIA materialized on the paved jogging trail that circled the lake. It was the sound of her heels on the pavement, echoing in the trees and over the lake that caught my attention. She'd always walked like a soldier, her steps falling hard and sure. I watched her sweep around a heavy woman pushing a double stroller. If not for her gait, and my utter, complete familiarity with the shape of her body, I might not have recognized her, and it wasn't just the huge dark sunglasses.

She wore a black suit, skirt below the knees, a midnight blue blouse buttoned to the neck. I leaned back against the stone bridge and crossed my arms, awed more than stunned. I'd never seen her in a suit before, nothing even close. She'd been a leather pants and sleeveless T-shirt girl when we were together. That was part of the attraction for me. Between the leather and the tats and the jewelry, it'd been like dating a rock star. She turned heads like one everywhere we went. She kept me in a constant state of arousal, especially after I learned what happened when the leather pants came off. Her looks had also aroused more than a little envy in me.

I wasn't ugly. I knew I was nearly as handsome as my father.

But I wasn't the type to blow people off their bar stools; she was. And I'd always hoped some of her force-of-nature vibe would rub off on me. It should've been enough of an ego boost that she voluntarily slept with me, sober, often, and enthusiastically, but it never was. Seeing her look that good in a suit brought the envy back in force, and a lot of other things.

I reminded myself, while watching her bear down on me, that Virginia had punished me for months before finally breaking my heart, bending it back and forth in her hands like a bad credit card until it cracked. I *knew* this. In time with her steps, I ticked off the list of offenses, of half-truths, and baits and switches, and lies of omission, but when she got within ten feet of me, the humming under my skin drowned out everything else. All that stuff was in the past, and for now she was right in front of me.

Our time together hadn't always been like it was at the end. We lasted three years. We must've satisfied something in each other. Then I thought of what Jimmy had said about David, about someone becoming a habit. Had it been that shallow and she just woke up and kicked it before I did? I hoped it wasn't that simple. It didn't do enough to explain why her leaving me had hurt so badly.

There had been more to it, though I don't know if it was any less shallow. I realized Virginia made me feel like I'd caught up to Jimmy. She and I did the same things he and Rose did, we shared one bed and one kitchen. We paid the rent together. And not only did we do the normal things, we did better and more exciting things. We knew all the coolest dives in Manhattan, where we bought drinks all night for actors and models. At the night's end, we crashed at artists' lofts in the Village or on sailboats down by Battery Park, riding the ferry home in the morning, watching the rest of the island heading in the opposite direction on their way to work. For a while at least, Virginia seemed to be just like me. She sought out the edges, the fringe. She seemed to enjoy having me as her partner in crime. And then she didn't, and I never knew why. She got closer to the bridge, smiled at me, and I got the feeling I was about to find out.

I steeled myself for that conversation, trying to anticipate what she'd say. Then I noticed her hair. It was gone, most of it anyway. The change unnerved me.

From the first night I met her at the bar, until the moment she'd walked out the front door of my apartment, she'd sported long, flaming red hair that reached her tailbone. It announced her arrival in a room like angels' trumpets or a brimstone cloud. Just the other day in the Mall, it had been that red hair that caught my eye.

She stopped in front of me and stuck out her hand. I reached for her head. "Your hair," I said. Brilliant.

She backed away, raised her sunglasses into her hair. It was cut short and straight, barely reaching her jawline. She'd colored it a modest brown, dark, pretty, but unremarkable considering what it replaced. She put out her hand again, I took it.

"Good to see you," she said.

"Good to see you, too." I turned her wrist. The flaming nostrils of a dragon peeked out from beneath the cuff of her silk sleeve.

"You look well," she said. "Black always suited you. Though you've lost some weight. You never had much to spare."

"I'm surviving."

I noticed her nose ring was gone, though the tiny hole where it had once been remained. I wondered if those holes ever closed. I figured she'd done away with the tongue ring, but I couldn't be sure without staring at her mouth, which, I figured, was a bad idea. Her jacket was buttoned, leaving me to speculate about other things, as well. "Let's walk," I said. That way I don't have to look right at you.

We walked around the lake, my slower pace throwing off her determined stride.

She asked a lot of questions about my job and the people she knew there. She asked about my sister. I played along. I knew this drill; it was the necessary prelude to serious conversation. These test questions told her how to approach me, how obscure a path to take to the heart of the matter. I kept my answers short and quiet. I did my best to appear calm, and cool. She moved on to the subject of my father, and I made her lean in a couple times to hear me.

"I take it," she said, "nothing changed between you and him since I last saw you."

"Not at all."

"It must be hard," Virginia said, "letting him go with so much unfinished."

"It's been a tough couple of days. But things between him and me were finished a long time ago. All this stuff, the wake, the funeral, it's all formality. I'm just going through the motions."

"The police know anything?"

"Not really," I said.

The conversation, such as it was, died for a while and we walked on in silence. I wanted her to ask real questions, personal questions. I hadn't talked to her since we split. I wanted her to ask if I slept at night. Was I angry? Was there anyone consoling me in my time of need? I wanted her to need to know what was going on inside me, like she used to. I wanted her to feel a void, to feel left out. But I had a feeling she didn't want in to begin with. We passed the bridge again.

"So, you seeing anyone?" she asked.

I didn't answer right away. I'd been looking for ways to work Molly into the conversation, let Virginia know there was someone more than happy to fill her empty space in my bed, and perhaps elsewhere—at considerable risk to herself.

"Adding them up?" Virginia asked, when I still hadn't answered.

I looked at her, gazing back at me with a decent impression of cautious anticipation on her face. I considered how much of Molly and me to reveal, whether to play it up and dig the needle in deeper, or play it down and let Virginia's own imagination do my dirty work for me. Then I noticed that old sparkle in her eye, the false bemusement that hid the killer instinct. I knew her asking about my love life was only baiting the snare. She was hoping I'd say yes. She was counting on it.

She'd tell me how happy she was for me, how healthy it was, how glad she was that someone was helping me through this difficult time. She'd ask all kinds of questions about this mystery woman that she had no interest in knowing about. There'd be the fake jealousy questions: *Is she prettier than me, smarter than me.* Loyalty-testing questions where she'd tell herself yes was a lie and no assuaged any twinge she felt in her ego.

But then, and this was what it was really all about, this meeting, this stupid fucking conversation, she'd tell me about the fabulous new man she was with. And her questions would give her license to tell me all about him, all kinds of things she knew I wouldn't want to know, all the things she knew would hurt the most. She'd watch me like a hawk for any revealing flinch or any flare of temper that would tell her she'd hit the mark. She didn't want to get me back; she just wanted to make sure she could. She just wanted now what she'd wanted when we compared scars and tattoos. The same thing she wanted when she went down on me to get me hard for the third time at four in the morning. She wanted what she thought she'd lost when she couldn't endure the brutal collision of ecstasy and agony our life together had become. She just wanted to show she was tougher than me.

She was, but I wouldn't give it up easy.

"No," I said. "I'm actually enjoying being single."

She set her jaw. "That's good. I feel better about this knowing we're both moving on."

"Better about what?" I asked, though I knew the question should've been "better about who?" I steeled myself.

"I'm leaving town," she said, and my spine turned to water. I knew she'd seen it happen and I hated myself for letting it show. My face went hot; I felt like a complete fool.

"Manhattan?" I asked.

"West," she said.

I drew away from her, horrified. "Jersey?"

She rolled her eyes. "Texas. Austin."

I stopped walking. We stood at a bend in the trail, at the end of the lake. Across the water, I could see the bridge. A couple jogged by with their dog, huffing at us for being in their way. I wanted to run them down and break their legs. It wasn't a big dog, I could take it. I took a deep breath, figured I might as well go right for the heart of it.

"Who with?" I asked.

"Sandra. She's been there six months already, getting things ready."

"Sandra Castronova?" I asked. "From the tattoo shop?"

"The very one."

I should've fucking known. They always were touchy with each other. I'd seen more than a few mysterious glances cross the room between them. Well, and there was that time Sandra was spending the night at the apartment and we invited her into the bedroom . . . Well, it was best not to think about that now. I'd always felt I was more in the way that night than anything else.

"You two should be very happy together," I said.

"God, will you ever grow up? Sandra's down there with her fiancée. They've been apartment hunting for me for two weeks."

"Well, fuck, what for? I mean, fucking *Texas*? What the fuck is there in Texas?"

"A coffee shop. It's—"

"Coffee? Whadda you know about coffee?" I looked at the cup in my hand, threw it into the lake. "You're moving halfway across the country to serve fucking coffee?"

I was furious, absolutely enraged, that there wasn't another man in this somewhere. That she was moving half a country away from me over coffee. It wasn't a good enough reason. I had no fucking clue why I cared about the reason at all.

"If you'd let me finish talking," she said. She waited for another outburst, but I didn't have one ready just yet. "It's our coffee shop. Mine and Sandra's and Devin's. I'm part owner and I'm going to be handling the books, just like in the City. Sandra's been planning this for a year. She knows plenty about coffee, and about owning a business. And she's going to teach me."

"And Devin's daddy has plenty of money," I said. "Just like in the City."

"Maybe he does," Virginia said. "But Sandra owns twenty percent, and I own twenty."

I wasn't buying it. "Six months. You'll last six months out there."

"Thanks for the vote of confidence," she said. "I should've known you'd be a prick about this."

"I'm being realistic," I said. "What happened to playing law-yer? There's better money in decaf lattes? What happens when that gets boring, too?"

She stepped between me and the briefcase. "They're a firm specializing in small business, I'll have you know. I took some temp work there. I thought I might learn a few things. In fact, I did." She crossed her arms. "Learn any new drink recipes in the past six months?"

"You cut your hair for temp work?"

She ran her hand through it. I don't think she even knew she was doing it. It may have been the only unself-conscious move I'd ever seen her make. "I cut my hair because I felt like it."

"It was beautiful. I loved it."

"It was in the way."

We started walking again, a guarded distance between us. My temper subsided, and a few things started to add up. "We broke up six months ago." I looked at her. "Which would be when San-dra left. Where *did* you get the money to buy into a business?"

"I'd been saving it," she said, "for a while."

"While we were living together?"

"Yes," she said. She stopped walking.

I continued a few steps ahead then stopped, hands in my pock-ets. I could feel her eyes on my back. Fuck the walk. We should've gone down to the dock by the bridge, rented one of those little rowboats, and rowed out through the beer cans and oil swirls to the middle of that fake little lake. Then, when we got to this point in the conversation, I could've just slipped over the side and down to the lightless bottom. Could've just disappeared. I could do that now. I should just keep walking, through the trees. That wouldn't work, though. I'd pop out onto the hospital parking lot in five minutes. Still, it had to be better than this. Then I heard her say my name. She was closer to me.

"You started this coffee shop shit before you and I ever even broke up," I said.

I felt like such a dope. When she'd suddenly started letting me pick up the tab all the time, when she let me pick up a larger slice of the utilities, let me work extra shifts to do it, about a year before the end, I'd taken it to mean she was settling in, letting me look after her. Shit, I'd never looked after anyone but myself before her, and I'd considered the change progress. "How long before?" I asked.

"About a year."

I turned on her. "What the fuck, Virginia? You were planning on leaving for a year and you didn't have the spine to tell me? I'm not rich, it's not much of an apartment." I held out my hands, just in case she wanted to drop an answer into them.

"Exactly," she said. "It wasn't money, it wasn't the apartment. I probably could've saved more, faster, on my own." She blushed. She actually fucking blushed. "Without having to hide it from you."

"You apparently had no fucking problem hiding things from me," I said. "Did you, at any point, have any intention of asking me to go with you?"

"All the time. But something always held me back."

"What?"

"The same thing that kept me there. The same thing that kept me from doing anything, going anywhere I talked about. You."

"Me? I could've helped you," I said, throwing my hands up. "Fuck, I did help you. I would've gone with you. I would've followed you anywhere."

"Exactly."

I took a step toward her. If she said that one more time, I was gonna lose my shit. Nothing about this was exact, no matter how neat and clean she had it all added up and justified in her head. It was a big fucking mess.

"You would've followed me," she said, "eventually, maybe. If I did all the work, found the apartment, set it up, scoped out places for you to work. How often did we talk about getting a new apartment? How many times did you say you were sick of bartending? How often did we talk about getting married? And what happened? Nothing."

"So I was supposed to do everything?" I asked. "You talked as much as I did. Things come up. We just never found the time. You gave up before we did."

"I gave up," she said, "because we were never going to find the time. I know I didn't do anything, either. I know I never followed through. There was always something else to do. Another shift to work, another party to go to, another bunch of friends to catch up to. For a long time, that was enough. I never thought I'd find a man that could keep up with me. We always had so much fun. But we weren't going anywhere together, we were just getting older."

"Austin would've been different."

"For a month," she said. "If you ever got there. Think about it realistically. You would've just picked up and moved with me? No, you'd have to give Brian your two weeks, which would've turned into two months, then six months. I would've been stuck waiting for you, either here or there. I was sick of waiting."

"So I'm loyal. You run out on me because I'm loyal?"

"You're stuck," she said. "There's a difference."

"You did this whole thing behind my back, for a whole year," I said. "You never gave me a chance."

"I gave you a year's worth of chances. A year to start coming home from work before dawn. To save some money. A year to call your sister and treat her like a brother should. Did you know, at one point, you didn't fuck me sober for three months? Three goddamn months. What do you think that was like?"

"I wouldn't know," I said, "because you never told me. That's so you, Virginia. You'd always rather keep score than speak up. You'd rather win than be happy. How can I know you're unhappy if you don't tell me?"

"If you loved me, really loved me like you said you did, you would've known."

"That's bullshit. How can I know what you're feeling when you're always hiding it? You put me through a test I didn't even know I was taking, and then you leave me when I fail. It's fucking cruel. It's fucking cruel like this conversation. Why do I need to know all this? You could've told me yesterday on the phone you got a job in Austin. And I would've said good luck and that would've been that. But no, the whole world always has to know what Virginia feels, unless it might actually serve some fucking purpose."

"I never told you the truth about why I left you," she said.

"I figured that out."

"I thought you might want to know," she said. "I thought you might want to know that it wasn't because I didn't love you. In a way, I always will."

"That's rich. So this is all some big sacrifice for you. Is that how I'm supposed to feel about it now?" I snapped my fingers. "Just like that. Just because you say so. I should give you a big hug and wish you well and send you a Christmas card every year? Fuck that. Fuck you. You love me but you're gonna do fuck all about it. What good does that do me?"

She tilted her head back in defiance but it didn't hold. Her mouth worked on words, but they didn't come out. Her head dropped and her shoulders shook with her refusal to cry. Even now, with absolutely nothing at stake, she held back. She seemed small, like a girl playing dress-up in mommy's clothes. She looked like just another girl. I realized I'd gotten what I'd always wanted. I'd won, but all I felt was sick and ashamed. For me, for her. I would rather have lost. What did winning get me? She was still going. She had still left me behind, and conspired to do it. She'd go on to Austin and I'd still be here, here with all the rest of the trash.

She looked up at me, and I hated her. Hated her for losing. For not being tougher. I hated her for not staying the girl I remembered, for falling from the pedestal before I could push her off.

I stepped to her, took her chin in my hand. With all I had boiling inside me, I still couldn't resist the urge to finish her off. "Austin's not far enough. You'll never be far enough away from me."

Then I walked away, completing the circle around the lake, heading for the bridge and the exit from the park, leaving her where she stood.

ELEVEN

I POINTED THE CAR INTO TRAFFIC AND FOLLOWED THE FLOW, drifting away from the park, from the high school, away from my parents' house. I just floated wherever the green lights took me. I finally stopped when I hit the intersection of Elm and Bay Terrace, the northern edge of the island, and parked under a tree on the corner. Through the chain-link fence across the street separating the road and the docks, across the slate expanse of the bay, I could see the skyscrapers of Manhattan. I lit a cigarette, watched two dirty orange Staten Island ferry boats, squat and square, chug past each other through the water. Molly's empty sky loomed over the southern tip of Manhattan.

I'd hardly thought about the Towers when they were there. Just the tallest among a faraway horizon of tall things looming in the distance, they were always just part of the larger picture. Now, in their absence, the Towers seemed more prominent than ever. Before that day, getting off the ferry, it had always been easy to separate the tourists from the New Yorkers. The tourists stopped and looked up as they left the terminal. The locals looked down, at their newspapers, their watches, their cell phones. I wondered how many New Yorkers snuck glances up at the sky now, at the hole in it, as if they couldn't yet believe that what had stood there so large and so long was really gone. I wondered how many looked down at whatever was in their hands simply to still the impulse to look up. Either way, I figured they reacted more to the void left by the fall of the Towers than they ever had to their presence. I couldn't remember if I had looked up or down the last time I crossed the water. It had been a long time.

And now, those Towers were nothing but remains and rubble scattered, of all places, across the Fresh Kills landfill. I couldn't think of a more modest resting place for them. Fresh Kills was where the dump trucks went as The Pile was hauled away, in buckets at first, by hand. It was where cops and firemen searched the debris for identifiable scraps of bodies and lives. It was the final resting place for an uncounted number of people. Fresh Kills was where someone found Molly's brother's class ring. In a weird but very real way, the world's largest landfill had become hallowed ground.

Shifting in my seat and staring up at that space over Manhattan, I thought of my conversations that afternoon, of how much went on unseen, unknown in a given day. Virginia and her elaborate plans to move halfway across the country. Molly's secret, ongoing mourning for her brother. Her continuing life of deception with David. She had met the man she would eventually leave me for at a party I had taken her to. I thought of my mother's secret hideout, of my father and Mr. Fontana. My sister's notebook and her struggle with food. My parents' whole fucking marriage.

I realized nobody knew where I was, or what I was doing at that very moment. There were any number of things I could do on that corner that no one would ever see. If I had a gun in the car I could take potshots at passing traffic and drive away and I'd

never be caught. I could get out of the car and drop my lit cigarette in my gas tank—just immolate myself along with everything in a hundred-foot radius. In the thirty seconds it would take
to complete the act, four or five cars would speed down Bay Terrace, and not one driver would remember seeing a thing. Hell,
someone shot my father in front of multiple witnesses, and no
one could recall a single telling detail about it. Just yesterday, that
had seemed so impossible to me. Sitting there in the car, staring
across the water at the air left in place of three thousand lives, it
made perfect sense to me now. I felt utterly stupid for ever thinking any different.

Someone had taken the time to plan my father's murder. To
pick the day and the time, to get the gun and the car, to load the
gun. Did he sit and contemplate which gun in his arsenal to use?
Did he get one just for this task? Did he gas up the car on the way
to the deli? Go through the drive-thru at Burger King? Did anyone other than the guy planning it know it was about to happen?
How many people had seen the guy, a murderer, on his way to the
deli? Was someone sitting in a secret room somewhere, waiting
for news the deed had been done? The murder had started happening hours, maybe days, before the fatal shots were actually
fired, right in front of God only knows how many people and no
one had known, or even suspected, a thing. I marveled that Waters had uncovered any leads at all.

I'd always considered myself a smart man. Street smart and
well read, at least, if not overly educated. I'd always figured my
years in the service industry, years spent woven into its elaborate
fabric of people and personalities, had taught me more than most
about both, and about life. What did a bartender do but educate
the masses? What did he do but spin webs out of accumulated
wisdom with a dirty rag tucked in his belt? I spat out the car

window. It was all bullshit. If I'd spun anything, it was a cocoon of elaborate lies around myself that let me look in the mirror. Two days ago, I'd been pretty damn happy in that cocoon. Now everyone and everything around me pulled at the threads, letting the daylight in and burning my eyes. And it stung so bad, pissed me off so much, that I snapped and bit at everything around me, at every hand that reached in. And when they stopped reaching, when they got tired of the effort or sick from the poison, I'd be twice as angry.

When the patrol car parked behind me, its red-and-white lamps muted in the fading daylight, I set my hands at ten and two on the steering wheel. Someone had ratted me out, gotten sick of my shit—one of the kids from South Beach, one of the Costanzas, maybe even Val or Theo. Those sharp pains darted across my chest again. I squeezed so hard on the steering wheel my knuckles turned white. I hoped it was Purvis walking up to my car. Maybe then I could bully my way out of a night in jail. Then I thought maybe a cell, preferably one with padded walls, was just what I needed.

It wasn't Purvis approaching; it was just some guy in a uniform. He tapped on the passenger-side window. I leaned across the seat and rolled it down.

"License, registration, and proof of insurance," he said.

I handed everything over and waited while he frowned at my paperwork.

"This registration is expired," he said.

"I've been real busy lately."

He raised his eyebrows at me. "I can see that. Remove your sunglasses, please."

I did. His frown got more dire. I guess I looked as bad as I felt. He handed me back my papers. "It expired six months ago."

"I'm sorry," I said. "I just keep putting it off, and the time got away from me." Cops love the truth; they hear it so rarely.

"Sir, step out of the car, please."

I did.

"You can't park here," he said.

I looked around for the sign.

"You're blocking a fire hydrant."

I took his word for it. I hadn't seen it when I pulled over.

"Anything in the car I should know about?" he asked.

"Not at all," I said. "Old books, empty packs of cigarettes."

He jerked his flashlight out of his belt. "Mind if I take a look?"

Of course I minded. "Go right ahead," I said. It wasn't like I had anywhere to be.

I reached into my jacket for my cigarettes. His face tightened. "Don't reach into your pockets," he snapped. So I put my hands over my head.

The cop pulled open all the doors, giving the inside of the car a cursory sweep with the flashlight. I was sure it was the mess of trash that deterred a closer inspection. I knew I looked too exhausted to really be up to no good. He hitched his flashlight back on his belt when he was done.

"Get the registration legal," he said, "and move along, please." He walked back to his car, switched off the lights, and drove away.

I stood there, aggravated that he'd hassled me, relieved he'd not said a word about my recent adventures, or even written me a ticket. I was grateful that after two straight days of driving drunk, the only time I'd run into a cop I was stone-cold sober. Once again I was reminded that I attracted much less attention than I liked to believe. I did what he asked; I moved along.

A couple of blocks later, where Bay Terrace turned into Bay

Street, I pulled over at a gas station that had a pay phone. I needed to call Julia and let her know I wasn't going to be back until late, very late, in fact. Even though I knew it was the better idea, there was no way I was going back across the island to sit in that empty house with my failures.

After leaving Julia a message, I tooled down Bay Street, looking for somewhere to fuse my ass to a bar stool. I'd done my time for the day, faced up to enough. There would be more to deal with in the morning, and I would face it then. I'd spent all day keeping my composure. All I wanted with the night was to blow off some steam and disappear.

On Bay Street, I had my choice of watering holes. Among them was the Cargo Café, where I worked, but that didn't seem like too good a place to be a stranger. I felt like drinking, not talking. I'd talked enough to last me the rest of my life. I kept driving past the Cargo and hooked a left onto Cross Street where I parked across the street from the Choir Loft.

It was a popular bar; I'd spent a lot of time there in my late teens and early twenties. It had a good happy hour that attracted a boisterous after-work crowd. It was early enough that I could get a seat at the bar, but enough people would eventually materialize for me to fade into the background. I praised my choice as I crossed the street. Only it wasn't the Choir Loft anymore, as the sign above the door told me. Now it was the Crossroads Tavern.

The place was nearly empty. The dartboards by the front door were gone, replaced by pen-and-ink sketches of sailing ships. There were now flat-screen televisions in every corner of the ceiling. The old Mets jerseys, Koosman and Seaver from '69, Wilson and Knight from '86, no longer hung behind the bar. Now it was blasphemous pinstripes: Jeter and Williams and O'Neill. They hung among fake sailing artifacts: drift nets and telescopes and captains' wheels. I was willing to wager number 4407 on the jukebox wasn't "The Fly" anymore. My old watering hole looked like some bizarre sailors' sports bar. Well, I thought, settling on a bar stool, any port in a storm.

I drank my beers, scratching at the labels with my thumb, trying to look like a guy waiting on his friends and not like a guy who didn't have any. I stepped outside and chain-smoked three cigarettes. I backed up my fourth Brooklyn Lager with a shot of Jack Daniel's. I thought of the night Jimmy and I shot JD from his shoe at a New Year's Eve party. I thought about calling him, but decided against it. He'd have to come all the way across the island on a school night. It seemed a lot to ask. I'd see him at the wake.

I ordered a second shot, dropped a big tip when it arrived, and tried to make small talk with the bartender. I asked about the old bartenders I'd known, when the place was still the Choir Loft. None of their names rang any bells for him. I asked him who was playing at the Dock of the Bay, a blues and R&B club a few blocks away. Jimmy and I, Virginia and I, we'd spent hundreds of hours in that place. Darker and louder than the Crossroads, the Dock seemed a better place to be shit-faced, which I would certainly be by showtime. I knew the exact corner table in the back where I would sit. Live music suddenly sounded like a great idea; the noise would be that much more for me to hide behind. But the bartender just looked at me funny.

"Nobody plays there anymore," he said. "Place changed hands. It's some late-night hip-hop club now." I felt like somebody had told me an old friend had died. The bartender just walked off down the bar.

———

BY NINE O'CLOCK the bartender had moved the Jack Daniel's bottle to my end of the bar. I drained another Brooklyn and tried to figure out how I could make a bathroom run without losing my seat. I was dying for a smoke. The place had filled up around me, suddenly it seemed, and I'd chased a couple of vultures away already. I hunched over my drinks, crowded on all sides by backs and shoulders. Name change or not, this was my bar. We had a history. I'd logged more hours there than these kids surrounding me had put into college. They figure you can't last forever. But I can. I can hold a bar stool till it rots out from underneath me. But, then again, as territorial as I was feeling, I didn't feel like pissing on the floor. Leaving my cigarettes was an option but I couldn't trust any of these motherfuckers not to rip them off while I was gone. Same with my money. Then I remembered another rule of drinking alone—it makes people afraid of you.

I made a big production of standing and stretching. Anyone with an eye on my seat had seen the shot glasses and beer bottles come and go. I tucked a cigarette behind my ear and left the pack and two twenties on the bar. I peeled off my leather and hung it on the back of the stool. Fuck all you motherfuckers. A fight wasn't on the agenda, but there was always room in my game plan for improvisation.

When I got back from the bathroom, the jacket, the money, and the cigarettes were where I had left them. And Carlo Purvis was sitting in my seat.

I pushed my way up to him. "Purvis, ya mind?"

He swayed as he stood. I wasn't the only one who'd started hitting it hard early.

"Just keepin' it warm for ya," he said. "I knew it was you. I recognized the jacket." He tipped his beer bottle at my empty bottle and glass. "Getting a start on the old-fashioned Irish wake?" I noticed he was alone.

I raised an eyebrow at him. He conformed well to the standard for a slick Staten Island guinea—hair gel, fog of Drakkar cologne, open collar, gold chain with Christ's head adangle. Not quite seventies mafioso, but attire as subtle as, say, a kilt, or yarmulkes and a black hat. I always figured he overdid it to compensate for his mom marrying a Polack, the only one of six daughters not to marry another Italian. Hard-core as he was about proclaiming his Italian heritage, Purvis had been fascinated by my "Irishness" since we were kids.

"I wouldn't drink to the old man," I said, sitting, "if you were buying. Thanks for holding my seat." I turned to him. "See you around."

"C'mon," he said. "Lighten up." He slapped his palm on the bar and waved his empty beer bottle at the bartender.

"I've had a long couple days," I said. "I'd rather be alone."

"We've known each other for years, least I can do is buy you a drink. One drink. Let's do a shot. I'm buying." He breathed cheap light beer in my face. "We used to hang out all the time, right? And I'm sorry about the other day at your folks' house. C'mon. We're both men now. It's about time we had a drink together."

He stared at me, his face way too close to mine, waiting for an answer, for permission. His drunken brain had locked on to buying me a drink. I knew there was nothing in the world more important to him at the moment. There'd be no shutting him up about it, no getting rid of him until it happened.

I figured I could tolerate one drink, one shot, with him. Maybe it could be a start toward making my peace with things, like Jimmy had said. Spending five cordial minutes with Purvis would show some kind of progress. When the bartender came over, he ignored Purvis, looking at me.

"Two Jamesons," I said. Purvis grinned at me stupidly. Let's see what he's really made of, I thought. "Make 'em doubles. And a Brooklyn for me. Coors Light for him, I guess."

"On me," Purvis blurted, leaning way over the bar.

Purvis made a weak move for his wallet when the drinks arrived, but the bartender waved him off. Despite the freebie, Purvis didn't tip. I slid a ten across the bar.

"So much for you buying," I said. "That's twenty-five dollars' worth of drinks. When'd you get that kind of weight around here?"

Purvis pulled from his bottle of Coors Light, glancing nervously at his shot. "September twelfth. I can't pay for a drink anywhere anyone knows I'm a cop since the Trade Center."

And I'm sure, I thought, they know you're a cop everywhere you go. And then I winced, glad I hadn't said that aloud. I was trying to make progress here. Besides, it was a hell of a thing to accuse even Purvis of, capitalizing on something like the Trade Center. At the Cargo, we never charged the guys from the firehouse around the corner. Sure, I told myself, Purvis was a prick, and we had our differences, but this was 9-11 we were talking about.

"Know anyone?" I asked.

"A few. You?"

"No," I said. "I'm not in touch, but I checked the lists."

We drank our beers in silence.

"You down there?" I finally asked.

"When the second tower came down," he said, looking at his feet. "Never seen nothing like it. Nowhere. Ever. The fucking sound of it, you wouldn't believe."

Suddenly, I got the feeling he was lying to me. His eyes worked the edges of my face, flitting to my forehead, my chin, over my shoulder, looking everywhere but right at me. I didn't believe he'd been there. The little prick was lying. My mouth fell open. He hadn't set one leather-clad toe on Ground Zero that day and was desperate for everyone not to know it, still. Wrapping himself in stolen, bastardized bravery. Using the deaths of his brothers and fellow citizens as a pass for free drinks. I didn't know what stunned me more, that he was lying or that I had actually believed him for even a few seconds.

I was angry, but more than that, I thought he was pathetic. Like it was a crime not to have been there, to have been doing some other normal thing on what started as so normal a morning. I would've slept through the whole disaster if Julia hadn't called after the second plane hit. Maybe it was a cop thing for him. He couldn't say he was lucky enough to be home in bed while so many others, like Molly's brother, took the ultimate loss for their city. It was Purvis but I wanted to give him credit for something. I wanted his lie to have noble roots. I wanted him to be capable, somewhere inside himself, of shame. If he had that capability, I wouldn't have to feel sick and hateful. I had come down here to relax, not to wallow in yet another filthy little secret. I couldn't stand it. I needed a way to break the moment, to change the subject. I pulled my smoke out from behind my ear.

"I need a cigarette," I said.

Purvis looked at the shots, still sitting on the bar.

"You're right," I said. "We better knock those off first."

I picked up mine and handed him his. He was terrified, but he lifted his glass.

"To Julia," he said. "And Molly."

I let it go and touched my glass to his. "To Eddie Francis. *Sláinte*." I threw back my shot.

Purvis looked at his glass, up at me, then back at his drink. I waved the cigarette before his eyes. Suddenly, I was enjoying myself. Purvis swallowed most of the whiskey. His face contorted, and one leg jerked up at the knee. He drank the rest and gagged, turning red and then a light shade of green. I patted him on the shoulder and, grabbing my jacket, headed for the door. I thought he'd make a break for the men's room, but he followed me outside.

As I lit up, Purvis bent over with his hands on his knees, taking slow, deep breaths. I waited for him to recover. Wounded as he was, he kept the whiskey down. He straightened, exhaled long and loud, rubbed his palms on his shirt, and asked me for a cigarette.

"You don't smoke," I said. "You never did."

"I do sometimes, lately," he said. "It's the job."

I pulled one from the pack and held it out to him. "You better smoke the whole fucking thing. I hate wasting cigarettes on social smokers."

"Relax," he said, his badge and booze-induced bravado returning. "I finished the whiskey, didn't I?"

"It almost finished you," I said, but I lit his smoke.

He laughed, resting his elbow in the opposite palm, holding the cigarette inches from his lips. "True." He sighed. "Man, you drink that shit all the time?" I nodded. He shook his head. "You learned something from your pop." He took a tiny puff. "Don't tell me Julia drinks like you and your father."

"Not at all."

"Roger that," he said.

His eyes narrowed in thought. Don't, I thought. Don't stay on the subject of my sister. But a grin tickled the corners of his mouth. The booze had settled in him heavy. He was hitting the next stage, where he wouldn't stumble or slur but his mouth would get way too bold. I'd seen it happen at work thousands of times. It never ended well.

"How is that hottie sister of yours?" he asked. He glanced at me, still grinning, like he was scoring points with me by declaring her hot. "She seeing anyone? She ever moves back from Boston, I'm way available. Cops are at a premium these days."

I studied my cigarette. What did it take to get through to this guy? Maybe he thought, mistakenly, that we'd cleared the air somehow on my parents' lawn, or that we'd bonded during our brief 9-11 conversation. I decided there were two ways to handle him. One was to smack the grin off his face. I'd threatened him so many times, not hitting him would be like breaking a promise. But he was a cop. I decided to at least start down the high road, and let him decide how far along it I'd get. I thought of a way I could bring some truth into Detective Purvis's life and have some fun doing it, without punching him in the mouth.

"What is it you do again, Purvis?" I asked.

He frowned at me. "I'm a detective. You know that. I'm on your dad's case, for chrissakes." He dropped his jaw and wiggled his head. "Duh."

"So let me see if I have this right," I said. "Not to get too Scooby-Doo, but your job is to assemble clues and solve mysteries. You gotta be logical, perceptive, observant."

"Well put," he said, nodding, puffing again on the very end of his cigarette.

How did he learn to smoke? Watching the starving model channel?

"We have to be all those things," he said. "Much more than your average guy in the street. But it's not just a job, not just my job; it's my life. You live for it. Always thinking, searching, always looking for the way things fit together." He actually sighed. "Keeps me up at night sometimes."

I wanted to laugh. I was getting his pussy-hunting speech, the same routine he ran on every fake-tittied, empty-headed girl he came across.

"Well, Sherlock," I said, "I don't know how you missed it, doing what it is you do, but my sister's gay."

Purvis gagged on his cigarette, covering his mouth with the back of his hand as he coughed. He looked around the street and over his shoulder, as if to make sure that not only no one saw him but that no one had heard me. He leaned close to me, as if we were suddenly exchanging secrets.

"What is it about art school that turns everyone queer?" he said with a weak laugh. He dropped his smoke in the street and slapped me on the back like I was the one who'd been choking. "Don't worry, John. It's a phase, I'm sure. She's finding herself."

"I'm not worried," I said with a genuine smile, "and it's not new and it's not a phase."

He bumped me with his shoulder. Hard. "Hah, you almost had me there, you crazy mick. You sure can sling the blarney. Look, you don't want me to date her, fine. You got your reasons. But you don't hafta go spreading lies about her." He cocked his head at me, eyebrows high, looking at me like he'd caught me stealing hubcaps. "This gets back to her, she's gonna be pissed. Not that I'd ever tell her, but, you know . . ."

"If I remember correctly," I said, my voice rising, "you were the one who got in trouble, got his ass kicked, in fact, by me, for spreading lies about my sister." I poked my finger in his chest. "She came out to me when she was in high school. She's a bona fide lesbian, through and through."

"Fuck, all right." He backed away from me, rubbing his hand on his shirt, as if wiping away a stain. "You gotta be the first guy ever to get pissed 'cause someone said his sister *ain't* a dyke."

"I'm going back inside." I turned away, jumped up the stairs, and pushed through the door.

My seat was taken. I tapped the guy in it on the shoulder, intending only to ask that he hand me my money, but he popped off the stool so fast he almost knocked it over. I thanked him and sat down. I slid a twenty across the bar, ordered another beer, and bought the poor guy's next round. I needed to do something nice to flush out the bitter burn in my gut. Just when I'd started feeling better, Purvis reappeared at my elbow.

"She never looked like a dyke," he said. He wagged a finger in the air. "Although, that would explain what happened in the car."

"I wouldn't bring that up if I were you. For fuck's sake, let it go."

"We got a few on the job," he said. "I know what dykes look like and Julia ain't it."

I snapped around in my seat. "Then what's she look like, Purvis?" The question was out before I realized what a bad idea it would be for him to answer it.

"She looks like, like, I don't know . . . a woman. A gorgeous, feminine woman who would dig a good-looking, successful man. Like, you know, a normal woman."

"A man like you?"

"Shit, you said it, not me." He flagged down the bartender and ordered us another round of shots. Doubles. A bad idea. He was feeling too brave for his own good, and I wasn't feeling much like protecting him from himself.

"Look," I said, "I realize your experience is limited, but gay women *are* normal women. They just pick off a different menu."

"Yeah, our menu." He pulled on his beer. "It's a damn shame. I'm sorry to hear that about Julia. Not that you seem to care."

"What's there to care about?"

"I guess there could be advantages, you know, for a guy like you."

"A guy like me?" I asked. "Advantages?"

He ignored my questions and handed me my shot. This time, he put his down without a wince. "C'mon, Junior. It's no secret you got, what would we call it, alternative tastes. It's no secret Virginia goes both ways. Ever try on any of your sister's leftovers?"

"What?"

"C'mon, don't act all offended," Purvis said. "Lord knows you've always had a special taste for other people's girlfriends."

I dragged my finger across my throat. "Let's eighty-six this conversation right now. Let's call it a night right here." But if Purvis heard me, he ignored me.

"Like Molly. You banged her back in the day when she was my girlfriend. She's David Coyle's girlfriend now and you're banging her again. Not only do you mess with other guys' girls, but it's always the same girl when you do it. That ain't weird to you?"

"What it is to me is my business. So drop the fucking subject. In fact, this whole conversation is over." I started to stand and then eased back down. He stood so close I couldn't get up without bumping into him. I turned my back, but there was little room to move. I had to keep my eyes off him.

"Your mother must've blown a gasket," he said, "when she heard her only daughter was gay. A good Irish Catholic woman like your mother."

I turned back to him, held up my hand. It was imperative that Purvis stop talking. I patted his shirtfront and then tucked my cigarettes in my jacket. If I kept that hand moving maybe it wouldn't end up with a fistful of this stupid cop's collar.

"Don't go there, tough guy," I said, standing in a hurry, bumping him, and a few others. "We're done." People shuffled a step or two away, glaring at me over their shoulders. I collected my possessions and stuffed them into my jacket. I had to get out of there, somebody was going to get hit. But Purvis still stood there, right in fucking front of me. We were practically chest to chest. My heart punched against my ribs like someone beating on a door. Pain crackled in my chest, jumping like electric current from rib to rib.

"Jaysus, don't talk about me dear ol' mum," Purvis said, using a cheap Irish accent.

"Step aside, asshole."

"Me poor sainted mudder." Then, with venom, "What is it about you Irish and your mothers?"

My hands had risen into the small space between us. I could see my pulse beating in my wrist. There was suddenly no air at all in the bar.

Purvis lifted his beer bottle to his mouth and kept it there, draining it. His eyes smiled at me over the bottle. Sure he was asking for it. He couldn't still think this was guy talk, that this was harmless fun. What was it about? When I beat him up? Was it about Molly? Julia? Or something else that had happened fifteen years ago that I couldn't even remember? I felt my weight settle on the balls of my feet, my shoulders go loose. The reaction was unthinking, automatic, like sex, like that last second when orgasm can still be caught by the ankles, if everything just freezes where it is. But of course, it didn't. Purvis had more to say.

"Your poor mother. A drunk, loser husband, a drunk, loser son, and a fuckin' dyke daughter," he said. "No wonder she fuckin' dropped dead."

TWELVE

LIKE WITH AN ORGASM, I DECIDED IF I COULDN'T STOP THE PUNCH, I might as well make it count. I had the advantage. I knew Purvis couldn't even imagine me hitting a hero cop. I knew he was counting on that fact.

I made the fist on the way up and busted Purvis right in that big, stupid mouth of his. My middle knuckle tore open and his top lip split clean up to his nose. I felt the blood, his and mine, burst across the back of my hand. His knees buckled and he half-collapsed against the bar, clawing at it like a drowning man going under. I felt liquid and enormous, all-powerful, like I could throw lightning, with either hand. I feigned another right and dropped a left into his cheek like a fucking safe, like thunder. My arm snapped back beautifully; my fist reset like a machine. So I hit him again, this one coming all the way from my hips. I hit him fucking hard. Hard as I'd ever hit anyone, as hard, maybe, as anyone had ever hit me. His head bounced off the bar before he hit the floor. Face down, he didn't move.

Arms locked around me as a bouncer and two other guys pulled me back against the jukebox. Sweat and tears slicked my face. They released me when I started throwing elbows, forming a semicircle around me. I wiped one leather sleeve across my eyes, paced the three-foot space I'd been given. The cop's eyes fluttered open.

Purvis got to his elbows and knees. He puked on his hands. Spitting blood and booze and vomit, he staggered to his feet, putting his weight on the bar, not his legs. No one helped him up. He had his hand over his mouth but I could see the blood dripping off his chin onto his shirt. His right cheek and eye were already swelling. Good. He'd be wearing this one for a while. His eyes watered as he scanned the bar, looking for me. Someone slid a chair over behind him. He kicked back at it but couldn't even knock it over.

Sluggish, hunched over, his eyes finding me, he reached behind his back. Don't do that, I thought. Don't be drunk and embarrassed enough to pull your gun. Please don't be that stupid. What if you miss?

He brought his hand back around. His badge. I winced for him. I'd just dropped him, easily, in a crowded bar. Was now really the time to announce you're a cop?

"You're fucking in it now, Junior," he yelled. "This ain't kid shit no more! You're fucked. Assaulting a cop? A detective? You're fucked!"

He was beyond furious, but his threats rang out like high-volume whining. He may as well have been screaming, "I'm telling!" Just like he did when we were fucking kids. Several onlookers, witnesses now, I guess, had to cover smiles.

"Keep him here," Purvis told the bartender. "He's leaving in cuffs!"

The bartender offered to call him an ambulance. Purvis told him to fuck off. A cab to the emergency room? Purvis spat at him. He just glared at me over his shoulder as he pushed out the door.

The bouncer locked it behind him. I got the feeling it was more to keep Purvis out than to keep me in. The bartender called me over. I had all the room I wanted at the bar. He set a shot glass on the bar in front of me and filled it.

"With me," he said. "Long time coming, you ask me. Nobody 'round here likes that creepy bastard. Waves his badge around like it's a ten-inch dick." He refilled my glass. "That being said, I do have to keep you here until they come for you." He tilted the bottle in his hand toward me. "Consider this a real casual citizen's arrest. You ain't gonna make it problematic, are you?"

I downed the shot. I'd spent the afternoon degrading myself in front of the two women I'd loved in my life, and, for happy hour, beat up a cop. No, I wasn't going to make anything problematic. What was left for me to do? Start a fire for an encore? Even if I talked, or fought, my way out of the bar, they'd just come to the house. I'd done the only thing dumber than punching a cop. I'd punched a cop who knew where I lived. What was I gonna do then? Hide behind my sister? I thought about calling her, but why wake her up? What could she do? Nope. I wasn't going anywhere. Except to the bathroom.

I ducked into a stall and locked the door behind me. I pissed, flushed, put the lid down on the toilet and sat. Elbows on my knees, I settled my head in my hands. The adrenaline hangover kicked in and my hands trembled against my sweaty forehead. I barely felt strong enough to hold my cigarette. Any omnipotence I'd felt beating on Purvis was gone. I knew if he came back, Purvis could wipe the floor with me. But he wouldn't come back for me, even with backup. Maybe I'd get a ride to jail from the cop I'd met that afternoon.

I'd started the day begging to participate in my father's funeral. I'd made a commitment to my sister; I'd joined what was left of the family. I'd taken my best friend's advice on matters of death and the heart and gone to see Molly. Tried to have an adult conversation with my most recent ex. Tried to smooth over a falling-out with an old friend. I'd tried all day to be a grown-up. And where had all that landed me? Fucking jail. I figured I didn't have to worry about what to say at the funeral. I'd be locked up in a cell when they put him in the ground. Maybe Purvis and Waters should've taken me in the afternoon of the shooting. It would've saved all of us a lot of trouble.

I'd been in jail once before. For trying to kill my father. Destroyed half the kitchen swinging at him with a tire iron. Broke his wrist. He broke mine in two places with his bare hands. And a couple of ribs. Waters only took me to the hospital after I started coughing blood onto the holding cell floor.

No one, not Waters, not Julia, not even my father, really believed I was trying to kill him. But I was. I wanted to kill him, but I couldn't take him. That's the shameful truth of it. They didn't charge me with anything. My father wouldn't press any charges. He told Waters he'd already taught me as good a lesson as jail ever would. It was a father-son matter that'd been settled between father and son, in the house, in the family kitchen—not ten feet from where he'd found my mother's dead body.

TWO YEARS AFTER JULIA left for graduate school, my father came home from work and found my mother sprawled on the couch, looking for all intents and purposes like she was taking a nap. But she was dead.

My father called Julia. My sister called me just moments before she broke down so completely she had to be carried to the campus infirmary. I was headed south on the expressway at ninety miles an hour probably before Julia even dropped the phone. I'd already drunk a half a pint of Jack Daniel's that evening and I finished the rest on the way. I had a three-item agenda: kill my father, console my sister, bury my mother. The agenda was to be executed in that order, as swiftly and efficiently as possible. I ended up going one-for-three, but there was no lack of effort on my part.

I pulled into the driveway, ripped to the gills, and got the tire iron out of the trunk. The front door was unlocked.

My father sat at the kitchen table, half a bottle of Irish whiskey in front of him, the other half in his belly. He was smiling. I thought at the time I'd surprised him but I know now he let me have the first shot. Maybe he knew he had it coming. I swung for his head but then instinct and history took over and he blocked it with his arm. That was how I broke his wrist. Weapon and dead mother not withstanding, it was the same old situation.

Once he got the tire iron away from me, my father pretty much took me apart. The beating only stopped when the cops showed up. A neighbor had seen me careen into the driveway and enter the house with a weapon. I was cuffed and facedown in the front yard when Waters showed up. Ranking officer, he took control of the scene. The uniforms were only too happy to give it, and me, to him. I heard him joking with the other cops as he stuffed me into the back of his car.

"Put 'blunt instrument' down for the assault weapon," Waters said. "On second thought, put that where it says 'name.' "

My father stumbled up next to him, his wrist wrapped in a dish towel filled with ice. "Just put 'pussy.' "

Waters stood toe-to-toe with my father. "For fuck's sake, Sanders, quit breathing whiskey all over the neighborhood and get back in the fuckin' house." Then Waters took me to jail.

Julia didn't make it to New York until the next day and by then I'd moved from jail to the hospital. She told me the broken ribs were a great chance to quit smoking. Then she slipped two packs of Camels into the leather jacket hanging on the end of my bed. She was obviously on sedatives, something strong to keep her upright. She pulled a chair to the edge of the bed and sat. She laced her fingers through mine and stared at our hands. Her eyes got wet and she told me, slurring a little, what the doctor had told her about our mother's death.

My mother had lived for years with astronomically high blood pressure, undiagnosed, untreated, and unchecked. Eventually, one of the weaker, more badly stressed blood vessels in her brain just burst, like a pipe under too much pressure. Her heart killed her; her blood drowned her brain.

I asked Julia what the doctor had said about the cause of the hypertension. He hadn't gone into that, but Julia guessed that it began around the time my grandfather, my mother's father, got sick. He died slow, devoured from the inside out by a hideously patient stomach cancer, and my mother, her own mother having died only two years before, nursed her father through the final months of his life.

That was the first time she ever spoke of her sister, a woman named Kate. Not long after the wedding, Kate declared she wouldn't speak to my mother until she got rid of her husband. They never spoke in person again. My mother sent Kate cards every year for her birthday and Christmas, until Kate moved and left no forwarding address. Julia and I saw Aunt Kate only once, right after my mother died, when she stuck around just long enough after the burial to spit in my father's face. She never even introduced herself to us. My father told us who she was. I was so drunk at the burial, I thought I'd imagined the whole thing.

Laid out in a hospital bed and whacked on meds myself, I listened as best I could as Julia talked. She knew what I wanted and I knew she wasn't going to give it to me. I wanted the accusations against him to come. I wanted the anger I knew had to be schooling somewhere in my sister to finally break the surface. I watched the side of her pretty face for shadows, for ripples, for anything. I waited, wanting the trial of John Sanders, Sr., in the court of Julia Sanders to finally, after all these years, begin. It never did. Instead, I got the long and elaborate defense of Susan Sanders, the gospel of St. Susan's martyrdom, complete with Sister Kate as Judas. When Julia paused to wipe her eyes, I offered her my glass of ice water.

Whatever Julia wanted to believe about our mother was fine with me, but there was no way she could harbor illusions about the old man. She had *seen* him beat our mother, beat me. She had heard the same screaming, the same threats and curses that I heard. Unlike my mother, there was no pretense, no veils, to my father, no feigned smiles and dismissive sighs and thin excuses in which to root illusions. He was a demon, but he was an obvious demon.

As Julia lied to both of us, I forgave the lies in the same instant that she told them. My sister's pain over our mother's death was so severe, and I knew would get so much worse, it was impossible for me to hold anything against her. The fear that Julia and I were headed down the same path as Kate and Susan cut through my drug-induced fog just enough for me to keep my mouth shut. But I knew, and I knew Julia knew, my mother's "anxiety" did not begin with the death of her last parent. It began long before Julia and I were ever born. It began with my father. It began the first time he yelled at her, his spit flying into her face, and she stood there only breathing, her eyes pinching back her tears. It got worse the first time he slapped her face and she stood there frozen, her cool palm held against the red swelling of her cheek. It started the first time he poured his venom into her and got worse every day until the day she died.

My father killed my mother and there was no other logical way to see it. He poisoned her, plain and simple. In doses big and small. So what if it happened over time, in small enough increments to hide it from the outside world. He may as well have reached into her and torn open that vein with his own hands. And I'd never done a thing about it, not when it was happening, not after it was done.

And neither had she. She had taken it and taken it, swallowed every dose. Swallowing and cooking him dinner. Swallowing and ironing his shirts. Swallowing and crawling into bed beside him. For what? Did she do it, like Julia had said, for love? Because she'd promised God she would? For us? A lot of good it had done. Julia wouldn't look twice at a girl who wouldn't walk all over her. Me? I walked around like a junkie, boiling with his poison every day of my life. I was polluted with it. And I couldn't live without it.

In the bathroom stall, I stuck my cigarette in my mouth and stretched out my arms, pushing at the walls of the stall, trying to still my shakes. I dug my nails into the paint, clutching for fistfuls of the cheap metal. I let the cigarette smoke curl up into my face and burn my eyes. I wanted to kill the old man all over again. I didn't care about anything Waters or Fontana had told me. None of it mattered. None of it was sufficient defense against what he had done. How dare he fucking die. I was so angry at him for dying I wanted to scream. I hung my head between my knees, locked my fingers together behind my head.

I couldn't do this. I couldn't live without him. I needed him to be the reason for the way I was, for the things I did. I needed him to blame. I needed his arms to run from. I needed his weight to crawl out from under. Without him I had nothing but what I wished for, nothing but the end of the war. With him out there to fight, I couldn't be him. Without him, I was left standing in the field, alone, beating my chest for no one. As long as he was out there, I could tell myself he wasn't where I least wanted him to be—inside me.

But trapped in that stall, my father was all I could feel. Crawling and oozing around inside me. Soaking into my bones. Curling into my fingerprints. I realized his invasion of me was nothing new. It had started my first day, my first hour alive. It had started the moment he gave his name as my name. I knew it had been happening my whole life, like ink falling onto paper, one drop at a time, building a stain. Like blood, falling one drop at a time, from a child's mouth onto his cheap Sears T-shirt. Like blood falling one drop at a time from the mouth of a boy in love onto a kitchen floor. Falling and falling until the little drops disappeared and the stain they made was all you could see. Look at the stain, Junior, and tell me what you see.

How could I undo it? There was no way left to me. Could I cut him out? Bleed him out? Spit, puke, piss, curse, or scream him out? Hadn't I been trying those things already for years and years and years? And I'd washed nothing away. All I'd done was make mess and noise. It was way too fucking late for any of it. My father was in the snot running from my nose. He was in the sour whiskey breath that clouded the stall. He was in the stink floating from my armpits. I was tattooed and stained, infected with him, forever.

There was no resolving any of it, no making peace with anything. Something had to give and I thought it might be my heart. I thought it might be the skin stretching across my stomach. I thought I would split open, spill my insides onto the tile floor. I hoped for it. Maybe he would pour out with them. And I could kick him, kick both of us, out under the door. I wished he had killed me. I wondered if he still might.

Someone beat on the door of the stall.

"Your ride's here," the bartender said.

I took a deep breath, dropped my cigarette and crushed it out beneath my boot. I pushed out of the stall and out of the bathroom, unsure of whose legs I was really walking on, or where they were taking me.

WATERS WAS EXPRESSIONLESS AS he waited for me by the door. The crowd parted as I approached him. He said nothing when I got there. He just pushed the door open with one hand and shoved me hard out the door with the other. I regained my footing at the top of the steps outside, but another shove from Waters sent me stumbling down to the sidewalk.

I turned to face him. Waters didn't like Purvis any more than I did, but the kid was a fellow cop and his partner. Waters was going to beat me stupid, right in the middle of the street. I was sure of it. I couldn't possibly take him, even under the best of conditions, but I wanted to put up a fight. Just so I could tell myself, while I was curled up on the jailhouse cot, that I had. I rolled my shoulders and tried to prepare.

"Don't be stupid, Junior," Waters said, pointing to the black sedan behind me. "Get in the fucking car."

I stood my ground, debating. Of course. Why do it here, in front of witnesses? Waters was way too savvy for that. He was taking me somewhere he could pound me in private. Somewhere he could really work out on me.

"It's too late to fuck around, kid," he said.

Should I rush him? I didn't have the strength to do anything but run up to him and collapse on him, but taking him on right here might minimize the damage by keeping things public. Puking on his shoes might diffuse the situation, or it might make things worse. There was already a crowd at the bar's front window. Should I bolt? I'd had an awful lot to drink. I didn't know how far I'd get. Maybe to the corner.

Waters stepped right up to me, breathing coffee in my face. He smacked me so hard across the mouth I saw stars as I sprawled on the pavement. My ears rang but I could hear laughter from inside the bar, and Waters's heavy, impatient breathing. I raised myself to my hands and knees, a thin trail of blood and spittle dropping from my mouth to the street. I could feel Waters standing over me.

"Is that what you were worried about?" he asked. "It's over, quit worrying."

I sat in the street, my knees drawn to my chest, and squinted up at him, the streetlights shining over his shoulders.

"Pathetic," Waters sighed. "Some kinda tough guy you are." He reached down and pulled me up by my jacket. I turned my head and spat blood in the street.

"At least your asshole father had some pride. Get in the fucking car, Junior."

He pulled open the rear door and handed me a handkerchief. I climbed into the backseat. I tossed the handkerchief on the floor and wiped the blood from my mouth with my sleeve.

"I'm glad your sister turned out halfway decent," Waters said, climbing into the car. "Your mother deserves a better legacy than you."

THIRTEEN

WATERS DROVE WITH A BEEFY ARM STRETCHED ACROSS THE BACK
of the seat, holding an empty foam coffee cup between his fingers. Any second now, I figured he would drop it among the
dozen or so others at my feet. I wondered where he was when he
got the call, what he was doing. I could see him in a diner, maybe
the Golden Dove, eating a late dinner alone, flirting feebly with
the waitress. Not wanting to be home alone in his empty house.

"You always this difficult when someone tries doing you a
favor?" he asked.

I stared out the window and said nothing.

"You gonna pout all the way home?" Waters asked.

I turned and looked at the back of his head. Home? "Purvis
isn't pressing charges?"

"He's not," Waters answered. "He can't. Right after he called
me, he plowed his car into a mailbox and then ran over a fire
hydrant."

"Jesus. Don't tell me . . ."

"He's fine," Waters said. "A little worse for wear, banged up
pretty good. How much from the accident"—his eyes met mine
in the rearview mirror—"and how much from other things,

there's no telling." He sighed. "But he'll be up and around in a couple days."

I swallowed hard. I told myself the accident wasn't my fault, that Purvis was drunk and otherwise impaired when he got behind the wheel. The bartender had offered him a cab and an ambulance. The crash, and any trouble that came with it for him, was on Purvis. I had a feeling Waters saw it the same way.

"You got anything to say about this?" Waters asked. "Purvis said it was unprovoked. That you suckered him." We stopped at a red light and Waters turned around. "Doesn't seem like your style, and the bartender told me different." The light went green and Waters faced front again, dropping the coffee cup. "I figure, as usual, the truth is somewhere in the middle."

I leaned my head against the cool glass of the window, drunk and exhausted. My jaw throbbed where Waters had hit me. "Purvis took his mouth somewhere it shouldn't have gone."

"I don't doubt it. The kid, he's got an attitude problem. He don't know when to stop pushing. Makes people crazy. It works with suspects, he's actually not a bad little cop, but he can't seem to turn it off." Waters raised his shoulders, holding the shrug as he drove. He talked like he was trying to explain Purvis more to himself than to me. "So he gets on everybody's nerves—mine, the lieu, the guys at the station." He yawned. "Yours. For what it's worth, I told him to stay away from you, but, as usual, he didn't listen. I'm guessing your sister came up again?"

"That was part of it."

"He crack wise about your old man?"

"Like I'd give a shit about that," I said, straightening up.

"He come at you?"

"Like I'd give a shit about that, either. He came at my sister and my mother."

I saw him smile at me in the rearview mirror. "At least some things are sacred to you, Junior. There's hope for you yet."

"What happens now?"

"Well, as we both know, Carlo's got trouble keeping his mouth shut for his own good. But I'll have a heart-to-heart with him in the morning, when the painkillers wear off. Explain how hard it's gonna be to keep the drunk driving and the accident out of the rest of the story, the possible impact of things on his job. The accident gives him an excuse for the other bruises. I think I can make him see the sense of calling it a wash and we can all get on with our lives."

I watched Hylan Boulevard blow by through the window, the rows of streetlights, mini-mall after mini-mall, their signs dark and their sprawling parking lots empty and at peace for the night. There had to be one store for every person on the island along the boulevard alone. One store and half a parking space. We passed Seaview High School. Rain started falling outside and I looked up at the sky. It had to be late, there were few cars sharing the boulevard with us. Getting on with my life. I was finding it hard to look forward to that.

"About the demise of the aforementioned John Senior," Waters said. "Have you told your sister we're getting somewhere?"

"More or less. I didn't want to get her hopes up. What you told me didn't leave me real optimistic." I breathed on the window and wrote Molly's name in the clouded glass. "I thought the shooter left a pretty cold trail."

"He did. But he left one. That's the important thing. I know a lot of guys. They know a lot more guys. I got guys, outside the department, that owe me favors. That many ears to the ground, things get heard. Of course, there's the more complicated matter of substantiating those things."

We made the right onto Richmond Avenue, turning toward my parents' house. I cracked the window and lit a smoke. Waters reached his hand back and I handed him the one I'd just lit. I lit another for myself. I wished the ride home was longer.

"Any new details?" I asked.

"None that I can discuss."

I exhaled hard. "Well then, why bring it up? What do I tell Julia?"

"Tell her we know some things. More than we thought we would know. We got eyes and ears on it. Purvis's call, in fact, came in the middle of a rather revealing conversation."

"Why? Why are you calling in favors on this? Doing me favors? Why are you out, after hours, working this thing? You hated him. You hate me. You barely know Julia. He was my father, and I just want the whole thing to go away. There have got to be more important cases, more important people, on your list." I decided to push. I leaned forward, resting my arms on the top of the front seat. Unrequited love dies hardest. "Is it because of my mother?"

Waters pulled the car to the curb, tossing me back in my seat, and turned to face me.

"Because someone committed a murder on my watch. He was your father, but he got killed on *my* street corner. Because it's my fucking *job* to catch the guy who killed him. It's what the city pays me to do. Shit, I knew the man. We were friends once. We had a history. I knew his wife longer than he did. I know his kids." He dragged a hand down his face. He turned away from me, staring out the window.

"You wanna pretend you don't care some stranger killed your father for no reason, fuckin'-A fine," he said over his shoulder.

"That's between you and him and the Man Upstairs. But a lot of other people live in the neighborhood and that your father got whacked ain't a secret. Those other people? Their safety, and their fear, is my responsibility. The concerns of good people matter to me." He dragged hard on his smoke, turning again to face me. "And yeah, your mother's memory matters to me. It *oughta* matter to *you*. Someone ought to speak for her, and for Julia, and, yeah, for your father, even if you lack the nerve, or the heart, or both." He stared at me for a long moment. "Someone oughta speak for you, Junior. Someday, you'll be glad somebody did."

He turned and sat staring out the windshield, catching his breath. He tossed his smoke out the window then pulled the car back out onto the avenue. He drove faster.

Neither of us said another word until we pulled up in front of my parents' house. He opened the back door of the car for me.

"Now I'm done with you," he said, leaning against the car as I got out. "I don't have much more faith in you than I have in Carlo, but I'm giving you orders anyway. Somebody has to." He crossed his arms. "Stop spreading your shit around my island. This is the last break you get from me."

I slammed the car door shut. "Thanks for the lift."

Waters's hand snapped out and grabbed the front of my jacket. He yanked me to him, my feet dragging on the pavement. His face was in mine, and I'd never even seen him move. He leaned over me. I dropped my cigarette.

"Look at me. Listen to me," he said. I waited for the slap. "Stop. Stop spreading your garbage all over my island." I hoped he couldn't feel me shaking. "Do something with yourself, Junior. Your father is only half of who you are, if that much."

He pushed me away from him. I adjusted my jacket and

crushed out my burning cigarette under my boot. The rain fell harder. "Thanks for cutting me a break. You can shove your lecture up your ass."

He laughed at me. "Suddenly you're a tough guy again."

I stood in the rain, in the middle of the street, until his car turned back onto Richmond Avenue. Your island, I thought. You can fucking have it.

I made for the kitchen and a beer. I needed something to wash the lingering blood and bile from my mouth. Julia was waiting for me at the kitchen table, in her pajamas, wrapped in a blanket. Like the goddamn ghost of my mother, complete with steaming mug of tea. For a weird instant I was sixteen again. How *had* this night gotten so fucked up?

"Interesting message on the machine," she said. "Phone woke me up but I didn't catch the call. Press the button."

I skipped past my message from earlier. There was a hang-up. Molly, maybe. Possibly Virginia. I decided not to care. The next message was from Waters.

"Julia, sorry to bother you so late. This is Nat Waters. I'll be dropping off your shithead brother in about an hour. He'll have some news for you. You probably won't want to, but let him in anyway. I don't want him out on the streets."

Julia folded her hands. I slumped onto the bench. It was ice cold in that kitchen.

"So I don't know what to ask first," she said. "Let's start with what happened to your face."

I ran my knuckles along my jaw. "Waters tried smacking some sense into me." I sipped my beer. "I got knocked around, I got a stern lecture. It was glorious, like having the old man back for a brief, shining moment."

Julia said nothing. Behind her eyes, I could see her rifling through the files, counting the nights she'd listen to me talk shit while a bruise flushed and colored on my face. But this night was different. Her eyes didn't go soft with sympathy, like they always had in the past. I could tell, just from the set of her shoulders, from the feel of the room, that she'd been loading up for me since she got that phone call. Bad memories weren't going to get me off the hook this time. Waters wasn't the only one getting sick of my shit.

"Did it work?" she asked.

"Did it then?"

"God, you are fucking tiresome sometimes," she said. The words came out slow and heavy. She meant it. "What's the news?"

"Waters said they have some leads. He didn't say so directly, but I think he thinks they're gonna get someone for killing the old man."

Julia's eyes defrosted. She was excited, hopeful, for a moment.

"I'll believe it when I see it," I said.

Julia blew on her tea. "Do I want to know why Waters was smacking you around and driving you home?"

"You might enjoy this," I said. "I decked Purvis at the old Choir Loft."

The color drained from her face. "You fought a police detective in public?"

"I kicked his ass."

"You assaulted a cop?"

She wasn't enjoying it. I went on the defensive.

"He had it coming. You think I'd do something like that without a good reason?"

"You are unbelievable, Junior." She threw her hands up. "I can't believe I'm surprised, but I am."

Christ, what was her problem? She knew firsthand what a little shit he was. I had to drop the big card.

"He was bad-mouthing Mom."

It didn't have the desired effect.

"So what?" she said. "Who cares what he thinks? Or says?"

"I thought you would, of all people. About Mom, at least."

"Me? I knew Mom better than anyone in this crazy family. What do I care what a jerk-off like Carlo says?" She slumped in the chair, covered her face with her hands. "I can't stand it. I really can't." Then she sat back in her chair, slowly wrapping her fingers around her mug. It was like having my mother back from the grave. "The problem isn't Purvis, or Waters, or Dad. The problem is you, Junior."

"Me?"

"Yes, you. You're a bitter, hateful man who doesn't know what to do with himself, beyond get drunk and pick fights with a world that's not interested. I keep waiting for you to grow out of it, but you only get worse, the older you get. And I am fucking fed up." Julia stood, waiting for me to answer. "Look at you. Your father's wake is tomorrow night and you're shit-ass drunk, coming home in the back of a cop car." She pulled the blanket around her and leaned into my face. "You want to run amok through your own life, that's fine, but not through mine. I won't have it. You said you came here for me, and you're making me miserable. It's selfish and it's mean."

I gaped, mouthing at the air like a fish on the bank. "It's not on purpose." That was the best I could do. "Purvis was asking for it. You weren't there."

"Do you do anything on purpose, good or bad? Or is everything just random with you? It sure seems like it. It doesn't matter if I wasn't there. I know you. You just walk around, blowing shit up at random, thinking of excuses for it later. Getting pissed off when people don't understand.

"And who cares about Purvis? What about what I'm asking for, Junior? You got anything coming my way? Any kindness? Compassion? Or is anger all you've got to give anymore?"

"Why not? It's all I ever got," I said. "And now it's all I'm getting from you."

"That's such bullshit, Junior. You know it. You make me furious, but I love you. Mom loved you. Virginia loved you. Molly probably still does. Who knows how long she has? I know you won't believe it, but somewhere inside, Dad did. He could never have been so . . . so violent with you if he didn't.

"You've had your share of the good stuff, Junior, even if you never got it from him, but all you ever do is spit it back in people's faces. You always throw it away. It broke Mom's heart when you stopped coming back here to visit. She blamed herself, and you let her. Why, Junior? Why do people have to pay such a price for loving you? Why is the pain all you'll accept, all you'll remember? Why can't you hold on to anything else?"

I didn't have an answer. But I didn't argue with her, either.

"When does your whole life stop being about Dad? I'm sorry. I am. Even now, mad as I am at you, my heart breaks for what he did to you. I'm sorry I couldn't stop it. I'm sorry Mom didn't stop it. It's horrible. But it's over now, Junior. It's been over for years."

"It's never over," I said. "I want it to be. So bad it hurts." I was crying. She wasn't. "I've tried, Julia. I really have. But it hurts all the time."

"Then try something different," she said, her voice thick with the emotion she'd exiled from her face. "Please. There's nothing I can do but beg you."

"It's too late. I'm too polluted, Julia, and I'll never be clean."
I held out my empty, swollen hands. "What do I do? I don't know
what to do."

"I can't tell you that. It's your life. Yours, Junior. You have to
find it."

I opened my mouth to speak, but she cut me off.

"I'm sorry. I should've known better than to ask for your help,
to ask you to suddenly be the son and the big brother you've
never really wanted to be. It was too much to ask." She was crying now. "I just . . . I just wanted it." She wiped her eyes in the
blanket. "Just go home. It's okay. It's what you wanted from the
beginning. You win."

She dumped her tea in the sink and went to bed.

I went as far as the backyard. The rain had stopped, though
the sky hadn't cleared. Out there, I couldn't hear her crying.

I smoked and drank a beer, and then another. Try something
different, my sister said. I looked across the neighbors' yards, the
flower boxes, the concrete patios, the plastic lawn furniture, the
oblong swimming pools covered with dark blue tarps. The block
was silent; it was too early in the spring for the hum of air con-
ditioners and pool filters. It was too late at night for the mumble
of televisions.

Try something different. Like what? Be like Waters? Wander-
ing all night, a used-up man in a used-up car full of used-up
coffee cups, hollering about what a knight in shining armor I
was? Should I be more like my neighbors? Get me a Sears tie and
a real job. A steady paycheck, benefits, a 401K. I could fight with
the rest of the block over who gets to park the minivan where.
Over whose neglected Christmas puppy barks too much. Is that
what I should do with myself? Live my life on a train schedule, a

bus schedule, a ferry schedule. A school, dentist, and soccer practice schedule? I'd already lived a life on everyone else's schedule;
I'd already been a kid.

I lit another cigarette, easing into an old, rusty lawn chair. I
stared into the burning match, pulled from a Crossroads matchbook. When it burned down, I tossed it aside and lit another,
breathing in the sulfur. I had a bad ache in my chest, different
from the sharp stabs I'd started getting since the shooting. It felt
old, like my busted ribs from years ago hadn't healed right. Yeah,
I was my own man all right. Didn't my beer and my cigarettes,
my afternoon of ex-lovers, my split knuckles, my ride home in
the back of a cop car tell me so? A dozen years out of the house,
shift after shift, bottle after bottle, girl after girl, sunrise after
sunrise, and there I was in my father's yard—drunk, angry, and
alone. I lit another match, watched it burn down.

I'd spent countless nights out here in high school. Sleepless,
restless, for no reason I could figure out, clinging to the ache of
something broken in my chest then, too. I chain-smoked around
the side of the house, pounding down a strong screwdriver full
of Mom's vodka. Through the chain-link fence that bordered the
yard, I stared out at the empty street and wrestled with the urge
to wander the dark and silent neighborhood. I needed to go looking for something. Sometimes I even felt something calling to me.
It wasn't a voice. It was just a hum in the air, like the vibrations
of the metal tracks before the train rolled into the station. But I
knew there was nothing out there to find. I knew I was surrounded on all sides by streets just like mine, full of houses, and
backyards, just like mine. And so I never went anywhere. I stayed
in the yard watching the empty street and listening to the trains
rattling in the distance.

I tossed the matchbook into the grass. I wandered around the side of the house and pissed on the wall. If I was gonna be a disgrace, I might as well go all the way. I wasn't even sure I should be there. My sister had done what even my father never had. She'd thrown me out of the house. Could she do that? Wasn't it my house, too?

I staggered back to the chair and sat. I'd leave in the morning, my house or not, if Julia wanted me to. I had to go get my car, anyway. But I'd go to the wake. I'd give her that, show her something, at least. Maybe I'd even get a suit, if I could find one. I drank the last of my beer and flicked my cigarette butt into the neighbor's yard. I'd had enough of my life for one day, enough of my own head. I wanted to pass out right there in that chair.

So I did.

At sunrise, the daylight chased me inside.

I WOKE UP, IN MY OLD BED, at noon. I couldn't hear Julia in the house. I wondered for a second if maybe she'd had enough of this silly production and had gone back to Boston. I certainly wouldn't have blamed her. When I stumbled into the kitchen, I saw a note on the table. She'd simply gone to the store.

I pulled open the fridge. The sight of beer made me queasy. Disappointed, I remembered everything. The bar, Purvis, my mother, Waters, Julia, the backyard. That made me queasier. As much as I drank the previous night and as bad as I felt that morning, I felt entitled to a blackout. I swallowed a glass of juice, belched half of it back up, and put on a pot of coffee, wondering if Dad had left anything in the liquor cabinet that wasn't too harsh to drop in my coffee. Just to still the shakes.

On my way to the liquor cabinet, I noticed my travel bag sitting on the couch. I unzipped it and pulled out a T-shirt, holding it to my nose. Everything in my bag had been washed and folded, and neatly packed. I got the message, and I agreed. Maybe there was nothing left to talk about. I put the T-shirt on and walked back into the kitchen for my car keys. Then I grabbed my jacket and my bag and headed for the door, leaving the coffeepot gurgling on the kitchen counter.

STANDING ON THE ELEVATED train station on Richmond Avenue, through the scraggly, budding trees, I stared at the corner where my father was murdered. The sun beat down on me hard, and even with my jacket off, I sweat bullets. My fresh T-shirt was soaked and I couldn't smell anything but the stink of sour liquor.

On my way to the station, I'd forced myself into the deli on that corner, for a paper and a cup of coffee. Everyone inside was a stranger, but I felt accused and exposed before their eyes. I tried hating them. I tried glaring at them, but I couldn't lift my eyes to theirs. All I felt was ashamed, like I owed every one of them an apology and an explanation for being alive. The bag I carried gave me away, marked me like Cain. I knew they saw it and knew what it meant. That I'd been sent away, that somewhere I was unwanted and unwelcome.

But I had waited in line, paid for my coffee and *Daily News*, considering the whole experience a minor victory. In front of the store, I tossed away the lid of the coffee and opened the paper to the sports section. There'd been a Met game the night before. They'd gotten killed, 12–3. Gave up eight runs in the first, went through three pitchers before they got three outs. The Yankees had won their fifth game in a row. I saw there was another Met game that afternoon. I stuffed the paper into the trash, picked up my bag, and walked away.

No one else was on the train platform, and I was glad for it. I was feeling bad, bone-deep bad. My sister's words clung to the walls of my skull like bats. I felt too grotesque to be looked at, like every ugly thing I'd thought and felt and said over the past three days had sprouted legs and was crawling around on the outside of my skin. More were popping out into the sun every minute. I felt like soon their weight would crush me to the ground. I'd still be lying there when the sun went down and the evening trains brought the commuters home. They'd step over me on their way to their cars. I turned my back on the corner and leaned my weight on the platform railing, studying Amboy Road.

The Amboy Twin movie theater was gone, replaced by the shrill green-and-white neon of a diner. I remembered sneaking pony bottles of beer into that theater. And the time, during a Godzilla double feature, that Molly knocked over an empty and it rolled, highly audible, under the seats and broke against the wall under the screen. Then Jimmy somehow convinced the usher we weren't responsible, though we were the only people in the theater. Jedi mind trick, Jimmy said.

There was a video store where there used to be something else. The yard of the tire store still swelled with tires but obnoxious purple neon now framed the roof. Next to it sat a Quickie Lube that was formerly a beauty salon. Up and down Amboy it was the same story. The buildings had new proprietors and so they had new signs, new lights, new uniforms for their employees, but the same graceless, boxy shapes; their yards and parking lots still littered with trash and encircled in rolling coils of barbed wire.

So much had changed, but really, from where I stood, the neighborhood didn't look, or feel, any different.

I glanced up and down the tracks. There was no train coming. I knew that you could hear them vibrating the rails before you could see them, but I looked anyway. I knew it might be a while, that the trains ran infrequently during the afternoon and late at night. The line existed mostly for the morning and evening rush hours. Herds of commuters packed it every morning and rode it to the boats that carried them en masse to Manhattan, where they rode the subway to various cubicles, where they sat, like cubes in an ice tray, for the day. Every evening the process was repeated in reverse.

In high school, I rode the train to high school every day, from Eltingville to Oakwood Heights, a miniature of my father in my jacket and tie, going somewhere because I had to, not because I wanted to, and never thinking much about the difference. Sometimes Molly met me at the Oakwood Heights station after school and we would make out on the platform while train after train rattled away beneath out sneakered feet.

After Molly left me, the fall of my senior year, right when I turned eighteen, I took to riding the train, just to ride it. To get out of the house. I'd get on at Eltingville, maybe with a pack of cigarettes, maybe with a beer or two, and ride toward St. George, the ferry stop, the last stop. Then I'd cross the tracks and ride the train all the way back in the other direction. Both ways, all the way up and down the line, I'd gaze through the window at the passing buildings and roads and lights and think. Think about the girl. The end of high school. Where I was going. What I was not going to be. I'd curse the island. Everyone and everything on it. A deep thinker without many deep thoughts to think.

I was going to be bigger, better. I was going to be unique. How that would happen, I never figured out. I never got as far as planning the future, but I had clear snapshots in my head of how it would be. I had sharp clothes and a cool haircut. I raced around Manhattan, always on the move, in and out of the shadows of skyscrapers, flicking half-smoked cigarettes into the gutter as I caught cabs and hustled down train station stairs, gliding from someplace merely impressive to somewhere important. I wasn't rich or famous, but I was Big Time, whatever that meant, another free and fearless, whip-smart prince of the City. One of the many I had never met but knew lived over there just across the water, just beyond my vision, walking through their days with six inches of ether under their Spanish leather shoes, nodding to one another as they passed on Park Avenue. I'd be unassailable and invincible inside the grand castle of concrete, steel, and glass that was Manhattan. I'd be home, and I'd belong there.

I was not, in any way, shape, or form, going to be my father. I wasn't going to be loud, frustrated, or cruel. I had no idea what I was going to be but I knew damn well what I wouldn't be. I defined my future by contrast. I wasn't going to be my friends, my teachers, my enemies. I wasn't going to be middle management. I wasn't going to be like everyone else: a debtor, a pawn, a servant, a lemming. I wasn't going to be bored, lonely, impatient, or angry. I wasn't going to be, I guess, human.

I finally heard a train. I picked up my bag and looked toward the stairs, suddenly deciding my sister was way out of line. She had no right to tell me where to go or what to do, I thought. What I needed to do was go back to the house and tell her so. But I didn't move as the train rolled closer. My anger died and I knew it was because my sister was right about me. Her words rang in my head and I couldn't get rid of them, couldn't shout them down. She had nailed me.

So I stood there at the station, rails humming and lights coming around the corner, black leather jacket, black leather boots, a cup of coffee, a Camel, and the feeling that I was the biggest fool in the world. When I flicked the burning filter of the finished cigarette onto the tracks it landed among hundreds of others tossed there by bored, lonely, frustrated people. When I tossed the empty coffee cup into the trees behind the platform, I saw the others lying in the dirt. Hundreds of them. Nothing special, nothing romantic about any of it.

Had I been there a month ago, a week ago, anytime before my father's murder, I would've felt completely different, leaning against the No Smoking sign while lighting a cigarette. Dirty jeans, dirty habits, bad attitude. Waiting at the station, like a timeless character out of a John Lee Hooker song. Most important, I would've felt different from the people I watched walk and drive along Amboy Road. Now, as the train rattled to a stop in front of me and the doors hissed open, I didn't feel any of that. I felt like what I was, another aimless, restless, self-absorbed, pissed-off dope. A coward, riding out to the edge of town then, reaching the border, turning around and riding right back into what I sought to escape.

As we pulled out of the station, as the streetlight that marked the corner where my father died disappeared around a bend, I thought of his chalk outline, drawn in ghostly white under the No Loitering sign outside the deli. I thought of the family photos full of strangers that Julia had shown me on Sunday. I recalled the ugly shirt my father had worn on the carousel; I wondered what number he had worn on the football team.

I dropped into a window seat, so I could watch the island go by through the bulletproof glass. The train rumbled along the eastern edge of the island, high enough that I could see past the houses and roads and stores and look out over the vast blue sea. Farther down the line, we'd bend west and run along the docks and wharves, toward the end of the line, and the skyline of Manhattan would rise into view.

I reached into my jacket pocket and pulled out the scrap of police tape. I wound it around my scabbing knuckles as I listened to the disembodied voices of the other riders in my car. I was surprised at their number. Baseball scores and the mayor. Friends and enemies. Wives and husbands, sons and daughters, mothers and fathers. I wondered where they were all going, who they were going to. Their conversations comforted me; they didn't seem to care who heard them. It made me feel invisible.

There were certain things I've always prided myself on, I thought. The guys I knew in high school, the poets, the musicians, the outcasts and rebels, they'd become those faceless commuters who nodded off over the *Daily News* on the Boat, drooling on their ties. At work, I pulled their evening drafts as they snuck in a round or two, not talking to me or anyone else, before the wife got suspicious. I'd kept the faith, I told myself. I lived a life where I answered to no one. I'd never made the easy choice.

One day, on our way to detention, I told Jimmy I hated the football players with every fiber of my being. The connection to my father was obvious, but I'd also decided they were the biggest jerks in the school all on their own. Yet they had everything handed to them: A's from the teachers, cars from their parents, headlines from the *Staten Island Advance*, coke from the dealers, pussy from the cheerleaders. They were the young gods, the screaming emblems of everything that was wrong with America.

"Look at us," I'd said to him. "We get detention for fucking leather ties while those fuckers don't wear ties at all."

Jimmy just smiled. "Think of how miserable they'll be when they realize they peaked at seventeen. We still got the rest of our lives."

He had a point. They didn't know that ninety-yard touchdown or that game-saving tackle had put such a charge in their bloodstream they'd not only never get it back, they'd never let it go. Now, years later, when their humanity bubbled to the surface, when they longed for people and places, longed for things that happened instead of things to own, they strapped on those old letter jackets, met their old teammates at the bar and relived the last and maybe only time they ever felt truly alive. I saw it all the time at work, Friday nights especially. And I laughed at them through the wee hours of Saturday morning, as I washed the last of their glasses and counted the tips they left.

As the train rolled on, it was their yards, their flower beds, their pools I looked past to see the ocean. But I wasn't laughing at them now. So what if I put on a leather jacket and went looking for a fuck or a fight, went out looking to play conqueror for a night? So what if hatred was my lightning bolt, the only charge that really made me feel alive? What was the difference? One part of my life, one part of my heart, ruled all the others.

Did I really pace that different a cage than those guys? I saw them as cowards because they had fallen so easily into the trap. In high school, I mocked them because I envied them. I mocked them now because they'd walked into the middle-class cliché without a second thought. But had I done anything different in becoming the angry young man? Different clothes, different schedule, different attitude, same set of blinders. I had been so fearful of becoming certain things that I hadn't become anything at all. I had run so hard from becoming one cliché that I ran right into another. Hadn't my mantra at one point been the complete opposite?

I was an adult, at least chronologically. But by my count, I'd been seventeen for fourteen years. And the past few days had forced me to realize I was fucking tired of being seventeen years old.

FOURTEEN

I SAT NAKED ON THE END OF MY BED, FRESHLY SHOWERED AND shaved, elbows on my knees, listening to the rhythmic clicks of the dog pacing the wood floor in the apartment above me. A cigarette burned in the ashtray at my feet. I watched the smoke spiral and curl though the sunlight up toward the ceiling. The clothes I'd run through the day before, getting ready to visit Molly, lay scattered on the bedroom floor. The late afternoon sun heated my bare back. I could sit here forever, I thought. That was what I wanted. Just to sit. Never answer the phone, never answer the door. Let the mail pile up in the mailbox. Let the world turn, indefinitely, like an empty carousel, without me.

But the cigarette would burn out. The sun would go down. The dog overhead would settle in a comfortable corner somewhere and give up his pacing. These things always happened. The ball game always ended, no matter who won or lost, the bar always closed, whether I had made the rent or not, Molly always went back to David, no matter what we'd done in bed the night before. And in a couple of hours, my sister would drop one of her new black dresses over her head, pull on her heels, sling her purse over her shoulder, and walk down Richmond Avenue to Scalia's funeral home.

All the way home I'd felt well-martyred enough to justify leaving my parents' house. I hadn't abandoned Julia; she had sent me away. I was just doing what she'd told me she wanted. But now, a few miles and a couple hours away from the scene of the crime, I doubted my decision. I didn't doubt her relief at finding me gone, but I realized I'd simply repeated myself. I'd walked away and left her alone with everything.

I thought of her, preparing to spend the evening with our dead father, memories of our dead mother, and a smattering of play-acting strangers. Preparing to spend the evening alone, again. It seemed too much to ask of her, no matter what she said she wanted. It sure as hell wasn't something I'd want to do. I wiggled my toes on the floor, getting restless again already. Hollowed-out as I felt, I didn't know what I had to offer Julia if I went.

I couldn't pretend I'd forgiven our father, or that I'd even begun to understand him. I understood him, and me, and us, less than ever. In fact, I'd started to miss the man I'd leaped the bar over, whiskey bottle in hand. I missed the man who smiled drunkenly at me as I reeled into the family kitchen, a tire iron clutched in my fist. I recognized I had a sick list of father-son moments to look back on, a selection quite different from the photos in Julia's box. But I knew the men frozen in those moments. I understood their reasons and their roles. They were the devils I knew, and losing them destroyed the only compass I had ever used. It left me with only the devil I didn't know. Me. Now.

But Julia wasn't asking for forgiveness or understanding, of me, of her, of our family or anyone in it. She wasn't asking me to plan my future, to tell her who I was, or what I would be. She wasn't asking me not to be hurt, or angry, or confused. All week, she'd really only asked one thing of me. Show up. Be there. She asked me not to be so fucking selfish. To not be so fucking scared. To be brave her way, brave with an unclenched fist.

I knew this was my last chance. The funeral would be too late. And my relationship with my sister, which I cherished and neglected with equal force, which already had been fragile for years, would fracture beyond repair. My family, which I had spent so much time and energy trying to deny and escape, would be gone. And I could never touch this bed, walk in this room, look in any mirror, without knowing I was the one who killed it. There'd be no yellow tape and there would never be an investigation; there wasn't a single witness. But none of that would matter. I would know.

And that might be enough to kill me.

Sitting there on the bed, my thoughts horrified me more than any I'd had about my father coming back from the dead, more than any memory I had of him. I looked up at the ceiling. The dog steps over my head had stopped. I looked down at my feet. My smoke had burned out. I thought again of the empty carousel, only this time it was still, dark, and abandoned. Like that, it wasn't a carousel at all. It was just another piece of junk.

I stood and picked up something off the floor to wear. It didn't matter what; I wasn't headed to the funeral home just yet. First, I had to stop at the Mall and buy a new suit.

WHEN I FOUND THE ROOM, half an hour early, Julia was the only one there. She knelt before the casket, her head bowed. At either end of the casket sat a few modest pots of flowers, roses, lilies, and forsythia, my mother's favorites, on tall wire stands. Underneath the flowers, bunches of shamrocks spilled out of their pots.

Behind the casket exploded an enormous monstrosity of color. My father's company had to be responsible for that. It was certainly nothing my mother or my sister, never mind my father, would produce.

I imagined some guy at an overflowing desk, calling a florist with an order number he knew by heart, then hanging up and unwrapping a sandwich. These were the same people who'd given my father a tie tack for his thirty-year anniversary with the company. A tiny chip of emerald at the center of a New York City manhole cover. At the time I'd been deeply offended on my father's behalf. He'd been thrilled. He'd kept his tie on all the way home from work for two weeks.

I walked halfway up the aisle, then sat waiting for Julia to finish her prayers. Even with her back to me, she looked lovely, her blond hair at rest against her back, her shoulders straight and strong. After a few minutes, she pushed herself up with a sigh and turned. It took her a few steps before she recognized me. Her eyes popped open wide and she slowly laced her fingers together over her stomach. She stopped, and stood there, waiting for me to come to her. When I got up and walked toward her, she smiled.

We held each other for a long time, her cheek pressed against mine, one hand spread open between my shoulders, the other on the back of my head. *Thank you*, she whispered. I told her she was welcome before I let her go. She grabbed my elbows and stepped back from me, looking me up and down. She took another step back and crossed her arms, raising an eyebrow at me.

"You're in a suit and you're early," she said. "Who are you and what'd you do with my brother?"

"You know how Dad used to hit the ceiling if we were late." I straightened my jacket. "I didn't want to cause any more trouble than I already have."

Julia took my hand. "Apology accepted."

We sat, Julia still holding my hand. "So," she said.

"So," I replied. "Here we are."

We sat in silence for several minutes. Eventually, Julia released my hand and nodded at the front of the room. "You have anything to say to him?"

The question was a bit overwhelming. Anything to say? Everything. Nothing. I figured our plan for me to give the eulogy was still in effect. "No. Not now. Tomorrow." I turned to her. "If it's all right with you, I think I'd like to just sit here for a while and be quiet."

She touched my face. "That'd be fine. As long as you'd like."

So we sat there. Me, Julia, our father, and somewhere in the air with us, in the roses and lilies, in Julia's hair, in her profile, in her breathing, was our mother. None of us spoke a word.

In the hall behind us, other mourners from other rooms shuffled past. I heard the pause in their footsteps as they stopped in the doorway. I wondered what they thought about the two of us sitting there in the otherwise empty room. The room hardly seemed empty to me. It felt, in fact, way too small to hold the four of us.

Joe Sr. came in to check on us, to ask if everything was in order. It was, we told him. The flowers? Excellent. The good father was on his way. We were in no hurry, we said. The room was comfortable? It was. He set his hand on my shoulder. There were ashtrays in the courtyard, he said. I should feel free to make use of them. I said I would. Very good, he said and he vanished. I leaned back in the seat and crossed my legs. I started to say something, thought better of it, and stopped.

"What?"

"Nothing," I said. "Forget it."

"Oh, go ahead," Julia said. "Say it."

"Well, you think anyone else will show up?"

Julia patted my knee. "Sure they will. It's early yet. Not that I care. It's enough that you're here. That's what I really wanted."

JULIA WAS RIGHT, MORE people did show up. A few men from the office, none of whom seemed to have known my father very well. They had little to say after introducing themselves, and they huddled around the water cooler in the corner. A few of the neighbors came. They introduced themselves, as well; I had never met a single one of them in my life. They'd all come to the block after I moved out. They had the decency not to ask what we planned to do with the house. Two of Julia's friends from school arrived, a tall, willowy brunette and a short, stumpy redhead.

Mr. Fontana waddled in, his wife by his side. I was happy to see him. His wife, a surprisingly attractive woman with long silver hair, wept copiously and nearly squeezed the breath out of me. She would cook for us tomorrow, we'd be home? I told her we would. I knew we'd eat for days. She couldn't keep her hands off Julia, hugging her, grabbing her hands. Julia seemed to love it. While they chatted, Fontana merely hugged me quick, kissing me on both cheeks. He suggested we duck outside for a smoke. I loved the idea, I told him. I offered him my arm and walked him outside.

After we lit up in the courtyard, I thought, this is the moment I'd been dreading. Now the stories would come, about my father, about what a great man he was, about how much he'd be missed. And I'd have to hold my breath and my tongue. Just clench my teeth and bear it. But Fontana said nothing at all. He just stood there and smoked, content, his eyes roving over the plants in the courtyard. Whatever he was thinking, he didn't seem inclined to share it and that was fine with me.

When I stubbed out my cigarette in the ashtray, he did the same with his cigar. He patted my shoulder before he took my arm again.

"You're a good man," he said.

I nodded and led him inside.

As I eased Fontana down next to his teary-eyed wife, I noticed another group had arrived. Three large men, enormous really, all shoulders and bellies, about my father's age, stood at one end of the casket. There was an entirely different air to them than the other furtive groups huddled around the room. They didn't seem to care how much space they took up. They laughed, and didn't care that their laughter echoed around the room and into the hall, if they were even aware of it. They didn't whisper. They kept hitting one another.

I cast a quizzical glance at Julia, who was across the room with her friends. She caught the question and was on her way to me when the priest walked into the room. Even the big guys went quiet and sat down. Right in the front row, across the aisle from Julia and me. They bowed their heads and folded their hands immediately, as if loath to have been caught doing anything else, though the priest had yet to even reach the front of the room.

The good father went first to Joe Sr., who shook his hand and pointed out my sister and me, alone in the front row. The priest came to us, bending to kiss my sister's cheek, shaking my hand, introducing himself as Father McDonald.

He asked us to bow our heads and he rested a soft hand on each of us, imploring the Lord to look after our young souls in our time of grief and sadness, and reminding us that though we had lost our father and mother in this life, we were still His children. Our parents would be waiting for us with open arms in the Afterlife, he said. I wondered if I would have to take an elevator or the stairs from Heaven to Hell and back again. I pictured my father and the Devil. My father complaining of the heat and Lucifer wondering if God had outsmarted him again by burdening him with this trying soul from Staten Island. My sister must have noticed my grin because she bumped her knee hard against mine.

After the Amen, Father McDonald lifted his hands and went to the front of the room. I watched him as he thumbed through a Bible full of bookmarks. I felt a hand on my shoulder and turned to see Jimmy and Rose taking the seats right behind me and Julia. Rose blew me a kiss, smiled at me, her eyes sad. I twisted in my seat and shook Jimmy's hand. He held on for a while after I was ready to let go.

"Jimmy and Rose," I whispered to my sister as I turned back around. "Friends of mine."

"I know," she said. "I remember Jimmy."

When Father McDonald asked all gathered to bow their heads for the prayers, I felt Jimmy's hand on my shoulder again.

As the prayers went on, I snuck glances around my sister at the trio across the aisle. After a while, she'd had enough. She leaned close to me, speaking in a barely audible whisper.

"Dad's friends," she said.

I stopped looking, but her answer only made me more curious. I'm sure Father McDonald's words were moving and beautiful, and maybe even sincere, but I didn't hear them. I couldn't stop thinking about the men across the aisle from me. When he was done, I did regret not paying more attention. There may have been something worth stealing for my own little speech the next day. But I forgot about that as soon as Father was done and everyone rose from their seats.

Jimmy caught my elbow in the aisle. "Sorry we were late, bud." He tilted his head at Rose. "Herself takes forever getting ready."

"I'm just glad you made it," I said.

"Of course," Rose said. She offered her hand to Julia, ignoring Jimmy. I was guessing she did a lot of that. "Rose Murphy," she said. "Pleased to meet you." She glanced at the coffin. My father's friends were lined up before it, waiting to pay their respects. "I'm terribly sorry. But I know you two will be okay."

"Thank you," Julia said. "We're surviving."

Rose patted Jimmy's arm. "I'm getting in line," she said. "Save you a place?"

"Yeah, definitely," Jimmy said. "But gimme a minute with the bereaved here."

"I'll wait with you, Rose," Julia said. "When we're done, I can tell you embarrassing stories about Jimmy."

"Lovely," said Rose, offering Julia her arm. Julia took it and they made their way to the casket.

"So, how're you doing?" Jimmy asked.

"All right," I said. "Better today."

He looked around the room. "Molly?"

I looked away, shaking my head. I knew he understood to leave it at that, and I loved him for it. I'd tell him everything later, maybe over a few laters: Molly, Virginia, Purvis. But for the time being, I kept my silence, and my eyes away from him, watching my father's friends. The last of the three knelt at the casket while the other two waited off to the side, respects already paid. One of them checked his watch. It made me nervous. I didn't want them getting away from me.

"Who are those guys?" Jimmy asked.

"Friends of my father's," I said.

"Wow."

"I know."

"Talk to them?" Jimmy asked.

"Not yet," I said. The third man was rising to his feet.

Jimmy put his hand on my shoulder. "What're you waiting for, lad?"

"I have no idea."

"Go," Jimmy said, giving me a little push. He walked away, turning before he got in line. Only Julia and Rose remained. "Joyce's after?"

I nodded. He patted his jacket over the inside pocket, telling me he was buying. I shook my head. I was so grateful he'd shown up, he'd never pay for another drink in my presence for the rest of his life. He frowned at me, then smiled and turned away. We both knew we could argue all night, without either of us saying a word.

I shoved my hands in my back pockets and crossed in front of the casket, glancing at it as I passed. My father's friends looked at me, hands in their pockets, the same sad grin on each of their faces. The largest one, a round giant with a red face under a salt-and-pepper crew cut, his pants hitched halfway up his bulging belly, cried silently. The middle one, completely bald with a gray goatee and glasses, bumped the crying man with his shoulder and nodded at me. The crier wiped his eyes, and his nose, on the sleeve of his suit jacket. The third one, the last to pray, stepped toward me, away from the others. He was the smallest, thick in the middle, but not bulging like the others, and his shoulders were almost freakishly broad. His hair was short at the sides, the remaining blond wisps combed over a large, pink bald spot. He held something in his left hand that he shifted behind his back as he extended his right hand. My hand looked like a child's in his.

"George Stanski," he said. He gestured to the bald man. "Arnie Jackson." And then to the crying giant. "Weepy over here is Chuck Dugan."

"John Sanders," I said, "Junior." I shook each man's hand in turn.

"We know," Stanski said. "God, you look just like him."

"Only better-lookin'," Jackson said.

"You could be his brother," Dugan said.

"Anyway," Stanski said, "we played football with your old man, at Wagner. We saw what happened in the papers. It's a god-damn tragedy."

The other two nodded angrily. Dugan blessed himself with the sign of the cross, to cancel out the swear word. Then he gripped my arm. "They'll get that son of a bitch," he whispered. "They'll get him, the rotten mother—"

Stanski grabbed Dugan's arm, pulled it away from mine. "Give the kid a break," he said. Dugan mumbled an apology then blessed himself again.

"We were his line mates," Stanski said. "The four of us, we all started every game together for three years."

"We were tight," Jackson said, crossing his fingers. "Like this."

"So where ya been?" I asked. I couldn't help it. It just popped out. All three blushed and shrugged. I tried to remember if they'd been at my mother's funeral. I couldn't. They looked at one another.

"Jersey, Connecticut," Stanski said. "Your dad was the only one who stayed in New York." He shrugged. "Time passes so quick. We all got wives, kids, careers. Like your dad. We all moved on."

"Stanski here is a dentist," Dugan said. "Can you believe that? From knocking teeth out to putting them back."

"We haven't seen each other, in what," Jackson said, "ten years?"

"Life, you know?" Stanski said. "It takes up a lot of time." He looked at the casket. "It's a shame that it takes something like this."

"But we're here," Jackson said.

"And we brought you this," Stanski said, pulling his hand from behind his back. He held out a photograph in a frame. It was a football team, lined up in three rows. A team picture. And there, in the top row, in the middle, stood George Stanski, Arnie Jackson, Chuck Dugan, and, wearing number 92, John Sanders, Sr. The other three smiled, my father scowled. But I could tell there was a smile hidden behind the scowl. It was in his eyes. My father stood out for more than the scowl, though.

The others, despite the uniforms and the pads, they still looked like boys. Big, fast, powerful boys, the kind of boy I never was, but boys nonetheless. My father, he was closer to a man than a boy. He stood straighter, taller, regal even, like he was posing for more than a picture. My father stood like a king among his knights, one with the others, but different and alone at the same time. His eyes, my eyes, bore into something just off to the side of the camera. I wondered if it was my mother. I could see her there, out on the cold field, wrapped in his letter jacket, her hair in a ponytail, still a girl. I hoped it was her he was looking at. If he looked at her like that, I could begin to understand why she loved him. I could at least understand how it all began, even though I might never understand how it ended.

The photograph was old and faded, but I could see the passion in him, the pride, the defiance, and with the sad, hard knowledge of the decades beyond that photo, I saw the violence into which those things would decay. It frightened me, all of that, there, in that one young man. I got angry, jealous, of his friends. That they had known the man in the photo, and I had known only the monster he became. But the feelings faded almost as soon as they rose. It wasn't their fault, what he had become, how he had changed, what he had lost. What I had gotten from him, in my life, in my blood, and what I had not, and what I had done with my inheritance was mine. No one else carried the weight for it but me.

I looked up at the guys; all three of them were teary-eyed, waiting for me to speak. "Thanks," I said. "I like seeing him like this."

"We figured you didn't have much of him, from back then. He was never big on nostalgia," Stanski said. He chuckled. "He'd probably thrash the three of us for acting like this, all sentimental and bawly."

I stared at Stanski, my eyebrows knit. I looked back at the photograph. It was all there, the blond hair, the mischievous grin. My mouth dropped open.

"I have this picture," I said. "My mom must've saved it. My sister showed it to me the other day. It's my father, in a tux, some blond guy sitting next to him. They're laughing. Looks like a wedding photo."

Stanski laughed. The years fell off him when he did. "It's me. God, you still have that? I was best man at your parents' wedding."

Dugan blew out a long sigh. "Jesus H. Christ. What a night that was. I thought the hangover might kill me."

"Do you remember," I asked Stanski, "what you were laughing at?"

"For sure. Your mom had just made a crack about your father's . . ." He didn't finish; he just blushed. He glanced at the other guys, all of them suppressing smiles. "Let's just say your mom got him good. Your dad was a good sport about it, though. Your mom got away with saying stuff the rest of us would've gotten crippled for."

I smiled, blushing myself, proud of her. "I gotta show this to my sister."

I looked around. Nearly everyone was gone. Jimmy and Rose had left, gone over to the bar, I was sure. Julia was at the door, exchanging hugs with her friends. "Seems this thing is about over," I said. "A couple of us are heading up the block to Joyce's for a drink. Come over with us. I'm buying."

The guys shuffled their feet. Looked at their watches. They were waiting to see who would bow out first and let the other guys off the hook. Stanski spoke first.

"Man, I'd love to," he said. "But I got a long drive back to Trenton, a morning full of appointments."

"Trenton?" Jackson said. "That's nothing. I gotta go all the way back to Fairfield. And be back in the City by eight."

"Boys, we ain't the men we used to be," Dugan said, patting his gut. "It's a goddamn shame."

The three of us waited for Dugan to bless himself yet again, then the four of us headed for the door.

I shook each of their hands on the steps outside Scalia's. I heard them promise each other a happier gathering in the future as they fanned out in different directions to their cars. I hoped to myself they would do it. I liked the thought of the three of them together. Julia appeared at my shoulder.

"They're a great bunch of guys," she said.

"They are."

"They're so . . . I don't know, roly-poly now," she said. "It's hard to imagine them the way they used to be."

"Not so much," I said. I showed her the picture.

"They showed me that when they arrived," she said. "I told them they should give it to you."

"I might take it home."

"I think that's a great idea," Julia said.

Stanski appeared out of the darkness at the bottom of the steps. "Junior? You still write those stories?"

"Not in a long time," I said, surprised he even knew about them. "They were, you know, kid stuff."

"Huh. Well, we all grow up, I guess," Stanski said, looking up at me. "Your old man, he told me about them once. He got a kick out of them. Anyway. Just curious." He waved. "See you around."

Julia and I looked at each other. "Mom," we said to each other.

"The little devil," I said, reaching into my jacket for my smokes. I felt good. I still had no idea what I was going to say at the funeral, but I was too relieved the wake was over to stress about it. "You ready for a drink?"

"Who's that?" Julia asked.

"You," I said. "You ready?"

"No," she said. "Who's *that*?" She was squinting through the darkness, out toward the street.

Out on the sidewalk, a figure wrapped in black stood in front of the 9-11 memorial, candlelight casting shadows on her face. I couldn't believe it. My stomach dropped and my heart swelled, filling in the space. The hair stood on my arms. And there it was, I felt it clear as day, lightning in my veins.

Molly.

"I'll meet you at Joyce's," Julia said. She squeezed my arm then headed down the stairs, cutting across the parking lot to the corner.

I waited until she was out of sight before I made my way over to Molly.

"Whatcha doin'?" I asked, walking up to her. "Out here in the dark."

She looked gorgeous, her dark hair down, spilling around her face and shoulders. Her face was all big green eyes and black lashes. I wondered how long she'd been out there. She tilted her chin at the memorial. I saw that Eddie had a brand-new candle.

"Nice," I said. "It's good to remember him."

"Thanks," she said. "I get him a new one from time to time. Least I can do." She licked her lips. Her eyes trembled. "But I didn't really come here for him." A wave of hair fell across her face, she swept it out of the way. She looked at me. "I wanted to come inside. I really did. I saw Jimmy and Rose walk out, and I felt so bad. But, uh, I just couldn't get to the steps, and I got here so late anyway, and I figured it'd be over soon and I had to do this anyway and . . ."

I put my finger to her lips. I pulled her to me, ran my fingers up through her hair. It was like holding everything in the world.

"It's crazy," she said. "I tried staying home. I really did. But I just couldn't. I couldn't stop thinking about you. And all this. And then I got here and I couldn't get through the door."

I held her face in my hands, my fingers feather-light on her cheeks, and I kissed her. I kissed her right there in the street, out in the open, where anyone passing by could see us. She moved into me, lacing her fingers across the back of my neck. I kissed her gentle and slow, deliberate, and she kissed me back the same way. Our hands didn't move at all. Not like at my apartment, where kissing was just an excuse to tear at each other's clothes. This time, kissing her was quiet and easy, and as natural as falling asleep. Behind me, or maybe just way back in a memory, I heard a train roll into the station.

Molly finally broke the kiss, pulling me even tighter to her, resting her head on my shoulder. Her lips brushed my cheek, my ear. "What am I gonna do about you?"

I felt her breathing against me, savored her body rising and falling against mine, warm and alive, as she clung to me. "You're doing it now."

JIMMY, ROSE, AND JULIA were gathered around a small back table in front of the fireplace, when Molly and I walked into Joyce's. Julia must've said something, because nobody reacted much over Molly being there. Jimmy winked at me when he pulled up a chair for her, and that was the end of it.

Julia and I didn't talk much, content to listen and laugh as the other three traded stories. As the night wore on, I watched Molly carefully, for signs of discomfort, or reluctance to be there, for signs of the old rules. Outside we were alone, but now we sat and talked among people who knew her situation. But Molly seemed entirely at ease. She didn't check the door, or keep an eye on the other patrons like she did when she came to me at work. She leaned into me when I draped my arm over the back of her chair. She grabbed my tie and pulled me to her for a kiss, told me I looked great in a suit when I got up to buy a round of drinks. I couldn't remember the last time I'd felt so relaxed.

Shortly before midnight, as Jimmy returned to the table with a fresh round of drinks, Rose, ever the matchmaker, announced to the group that she had a friend who'd be perfect for Julia.

"As long as she's not the gym teacher," Julia said.

"Not at all," Rose said. "She's a massage therapist. Looks kind of like a redheaded Molly."

Julia arched an eyebrow at me, then at Molly. She dove into her bag for a pen. She scrawled her cell phone number down on a cocktail napkin and slid it across the table to Rose. "Feel free to pass this along," she said. Rose said she would, her next appointment was on Monday.

"Can I borrow that pen?" Molly asked, already reaching for it. I expected her to ask for the therapist's number, but she wrote something on a napkin then slid it over to me. I picked it up. "Just wanted to make sure you had it all," she said. She'd written her own cell phone number, her home number, and her address. "Feel free," she said. She grinned at me. "I will be."

We left Joyce's not long after the exchange of numbers. Jimmy and Rose had taken the next morning off; they would meet us at the church. As I walked Molly to her car she told me that, when she'd left school that afternoon, she hadn't planned on attending the funeral. But if she was still welcome, she said, she could still arrange for a substitute teacher in the early morning. I told her how glad I was she'd changed her mind, and that she was welcome anywhere she wanted to be. See you in the morning, she told me, and she kissed me good night beside her car. I watched her drive away, her hand out the window, waving at me as her taillights disappeared down Richmond Avenue.

When we got home, Julia trotted upstairs to change into sweats. I stripped off my jacket, tie, and dress shirt in the living room and tossed them on the couch. In the kitchen, I opened a beer for each of us, pouring hers into a glass and setting it on the table. I checked the answering machine but there were no messages. I remembered I'd told Brian that I'd call him about the services. I felt guilty about forgetting, though I was sure he'd understand. I called his office at the bar and left the time and location for the funeral Mass on his machine. He'd never get the message in time to let anyone know; he was always headed home to the wife by eleven. It was no big deal. No one from work would've come anyway. I didn't know any of them well enough.

I'd learned years ago that the bar business is a poor place to find friends. You could work beside someone for years, even sleep with them occasionally, and never really get to know them. I'd always liked that about the business. There was no time for anything more than the most superficial of entanglements. Too many people came and went, killing time and making money through the in-between: in between jobs, or marriages, or schools, or moves. It was true of customers and coworkers alike. As much as I liked working at the Cargo, and liked most of my coworkers, it was in that way no different from any other bar.

But I found myself looking forward to going back to work. Maybe I'd even stop in before my next shift. Just to say hello, get any awkward moments out of the way. The Cargo would be a good place to be, familiar territory and familiar faces. Everyone would know enough to give me a little space and sympathy; nobody would know enough to ask any questions I didn't want to answer. The bar might actually be for me what it was supposed to be for the customers, something I hadn't been able to find for what felt like a really long time: a place to catch my breath.

Julia joined me in the kitchen, folding her legs under her on the chair at the head of the table. I moved from the bench to the chair on her left. We sat there for a while, in our parents' old seats at the table, Julia in her pajamas and me in my undershirt and dress pants. Julia ran her finger along the rim of her beer glass. I smoked a cigarette, using her empty bottle for an ashtray.

It occurred to me that this might be the last night we sat together at the kitchen table in our parents' house. I knew she was thinking the same thing. Watching her watch her finger make circles, I could see she was miles away, deep into our past. We hadn't talked yet about what to do with the house we grew up in, but I knew we wouldn't keep it. She'd never expressed any interest in coming back to Staten Island from Boston, when and if she ever graduated. I wasn't going to live here alone. This table, these chairs, they would go somewhere else. Another family would move into the house, bringing their own kitchen table with them. I hoped it'd be a young family with plans to be a big one. There had always been more space than people at our table. I hoped the new family would make enough noise to chase our ghosts away. I hoped they'd have better luck with the place than we did.

"You feeling okay?" Julia asked.

"You gonna miss this place?" I asked.

"Yeah. I am. I can't think of Mom without seeing her here." She looked around. "It's weird, though. We grew up in this house, it's the only one we ever had, but I feel like we weren't here very long. All of us together, you and me, especially. Makes it harder to let it go." She sipped her beer. "Will you miss it?"

"I don't know," I said. "It's hard for me to think of the place without thinking about Dad. But still, I never thought about this house being empty one day. That seems strange."

"I know. I always assumed Dad would live forever."

"Me, too," I said.

Julia finished her beer. She wrapped her fingers around the

empty glass. I wondered if she felt as exhausted as she looked. "You still want to have your say tomorrow?" she asked.

"I do. I told you I'd do it, and I feel like I should. I don't want to wake up one day wishing I had."

"Any ideas?"

"A few," I said, lying. I didn't want her to worry. I had no clue what I'd say. "It'll probably be brief."

"Brief is fine," she said. "I'm proud of you. For finally taking this on, for showing up."

"Sorry I was so late and so much trouble along the way."

"You got here," she said. "That's what matters."

"You should go to bed," I said. "It's late."

She stood. "Don't stay up too much longer." She put her hand on my shoulder and I covered it with mine. "This time tomorrow," she said, "it'll all be over."

I patted her hand. She kissed my cheek and told me she loved me before she left the kitchen. I heard the stairs creak under her footsteps. I realized, as I heard her bedroom door close, that I was now the oldest member of my family.

I SET UP SHOP IN the living room with a short glass of whiskey and several blank sheets of paper on the coffee table in front of me. I propped up the photo of my father's football team, leaning it against Julia's box of photos. I had run out of time to get the eulogy together. Julia's words about the end had been meant as a comfort, but facing the last day of this whole ordeal, facing saying good-bye, frightened me. It was something I thought for a long time I had already done, but I'd been very wrong. Not only had I not said good-bye to my father but now that it was really time, I didn't feel ready at all.

I didn't know where to begin; all my different responsibilities got tangled in my head. I wanted to do right by my sister, by my family, and not sell myself out at the same time. I didn't want to embarrass myself or anybody else. I had no desire for spectacle. But I didn't want to, I refused to, lie. What did that leave me to say about a man who, until a few days ago, I only ever knew well enough to hate and to blame? It was suddenly my job to encapsulate a life I knew very little about. I didn't know how what I knew before and what I had learned fit together. I certainly hadn't forgiven him. I wasn't over it; I didn't feel healed. I couldn't say I ever would. In fact, I resented him for leaving me this task. But I also knew it hadn't been his choice for me to do this. It hadn't been Julia's choice. It had been mine.

I got nowhere for about an hour. I filled one piece of paper with sketches of names: mine, Julia's, my mother's. At one point, I even dug out the family Bible. I flipped through it, regretting again that I hadn't paid more attention to Father McDonald at the wake. I glanced through the prophets, the Gospels, Revelation. But nothing was revealed to me, nothing inspired me. Despite my Catholic school education, the Word of God proved to be foreign and un-navigable territory. I gave up and put the book back atop the liquor cabinet, relieved it hadn't burst into flames in my hands.

I set Julia's box of photos on my lap. I went through them one at a time, separating pictures with my father in them from the rest. I found all the ones Julia had shown me plus a couple of others. One shot was, according to my mother's note, my christening, the after-party at least. I was bundled in blue on the couch, my mother touching my cheek. My father was in the background, Jackson on one side of him, Stanski on the other. They were all laughing. I found only one photo of just my father and me. We were on the ferry, my father standing against the rail, a five-year-old me perched on his shoulders, smiling, my hands in his hair. Manhattan, against a cloudy backdrop, Twin Towers and all, rose in the background. My father and I wore matching New York Mets sweatshirts. I wondered what we'd done that day in the City.

I remembered a field trip I'd taken with school, three or four years after that photo. We'd gone to the Towers. School trips were how I'd seen the few Manhattan landmarks I'd ever visited: the Statue, the Empire State Building, the Museum of Natural History, the Bronx Zoo. On the trip to the Towers, my father had come along as a chaperone. I hadn't thought about that trip in years, even when the Towers came down. That day, like everyone else, I'd been too caught up in real time to think about any history. It was the only one of those school trips he'd taken with me.

I couldn't remember anything about the trip into or back from the City. I couldn't remember the name of the teacher who had taken us. My classmates blurred together into a generic gaggle of schoolchildren. All I could recall was a few moments up on one of the top floors, standing at a wall of windows, looking out at the sprawling world.

I could see Staten Island, all of it, from end to end. It seemed so small, just a gray and green bump of land floating in the blue water, a brown cloud of pollution hovering over it. I wondered if all the people went away, would the cloud? Would the island look any different? I reached up and covered the whole island with one hand, making it disappear. I stared over my hand, at the horizon, wondering how far I was really seeing. Was I looking at New Jersey? Pennsylvania? Beyond? It seemed there was nothing in the way. If I was on the roof, how much more, how much farther could I see? Maybe I would work up at the top of the Towers one day. Then they would let me onto the roof. I would have a pass and permission and I could find out how far I could see.

I asked my father about the building where he worked. It was down there somewhere, he said, among all the others. Look for it. See if you can guess, he said. I leaned against the barrier, pressed my hands and my forehead against the cool glass. I was too warm in my winter coat and the cold felt good. I looked down at a million rooftops, at helicopters flying below us, at countless cars and people. We were so high in the air I couldn't see the foot of the tower. It was like we were floating in the sky. I leaned more of my weight onto the glass. I felt my father gather the back of my coat in his hand and waited for him to pull me back away from the window. But he didn't, he just held onto me. There was nothing, I realized then, between me and falling forever but a few inches of glass. It fascinated me that this was even allowed, that we were permitted so close to the edge. But I wasn't afraid. Even if the glass fell away, I felt, even if it suddenly wasn't there, I still wouldn't be afraid.

But I screamed when my father pounded his fist against the window. I fell away from the window, tumbling against his legs, clutching at his jeans. He just laughed and pulled me to him, gathering me in his arms. He wrapped his big arms around me, under my coat, and lifted me up. His stubble scratched my cheek and his body shook with laughter that boomed in my ears. My whole body shook, too, with the effort of holding in tears, my skin white hot with fury and humiliation. God, I'd hated him then. I hated him so much it felt like only his grip kept me from exploding. I hated him as I wrapped my little arms tight as I could around his neck and wrapped my legs around his ribs. I buried my face in his shoulder. I hated him and I held on to him for dear life, suddenly terrified of falling, suddenly terrified that he might let me go.

I set the photo down on the table and turned off the lamp beside me. I curled up on the couch, the family photos tumbling onto the floor. I turned over, burrowing away from the edge, pressing my face into the cushions of the couch. I could barely breathe. I wrapped my arms tight around my chest, pulled my legs up against my belly. I tried to be still, but I shivered. No matter how small I made myself, the air at my back stayed cold and empty.

FIFTEEN

THE NEXT MORNING, WAKING WAS LIKE RESURFACING FROM A coma. For a full thirty seconds, I couldn't remember who or where I was. My body felt impossibly heavy, like it had been buried at the center of the Earth. When Julia yelled to me from the kitchen that coffee was ready, I was on my feet, swaying in the middle of the living room. I swear I fell asleep standing up in the bathroom and nearly pissed all over my feet.

When I staggered into the kitchen, Julia handed me a full mug. She was ready to go, all dressed and made up. I had the vague recollection that I smoked. Before I could confirm the fact myself, Julia handed me my cigarettes. I put the coffee down and lit up. I didn't think I could do anything without both hands. I had the feeling I should be in a hurry.

"We need to go," Julia said. "It's time."

I wandered into the den. The rest of my suit, what I wasn't still wearing, was where I had left it. I dressed quickly. I skipped the shower and shave; it was the easiest way to go from hopelessly late to almost on time.

Julia straightened my tie for me then glanced at her watch.

"You think Dad's there yet?" I asked.

"Probably." she said. "Get undressed. I can iron for you real quick."

The doorbell rang. The limo was outside. It was time to go.

"Forget it," I said. "Who's got a better reason to look bad than I do?"

I pulled my leather jacket on over my suit, grabbed my coffee, and followed my sister out the front door. The sunlight blinded me, and I searched my pockets for my sunglasses. I couldn't find them, had no idea where I'd left them. There was no time to go back inside and search. I ducked into the limo as quick as I could, sloshing precious drops of coffee onto the seat. I was grateful for the tinted windows.

ST. STEPHEN'S WAS EMPTY when we got there. Empty, unless you counted my father. His casket rested in front of the altar, surrounded by the flowers and shamrocks brought over from the funeral home. The flowers from my father's office sat off to the side, where they wouldn't block the congregation's view of the priest. I dipped my fingers into the well of holy water by the door and blessed myself, more in the hopes the roof of the church wouldn't collapse on my head than for what I was about to do.

Father McDonald, already dressed in his robes, appeared out of some alcove behind the altar. He placed a Bible on the lectern and gave us a modest wave. When I waved back, he gestured for us to approach. I glanced at my sister and we walked, hand in hand, up the aisle. Father shook hands with both of us. Two altar boys fluttered about, lighting candles and sneaking glances at my sister and me.

"Are we ready?" Father asked. He folded his hands across his belly. "Is there anything I can do for you before we begin?"

"We're ready," Julia said.

"Good," Father McDonald said. "As I understand it, John Jr., you'll be eulogizing your father. You're prepared? Would you like me to have a look at your notes?"

"Oh, well, I think I'm all set," I said. "Thanks."

Father nodded. He knew I didn't have word one written down. "Will there be anyone else speaking on your father's behalf this morning?"

"Just me," I said.

"That's fine," Father said. "Take your time. Don't be afraid. Speak from your heart."

"I will," I said, wondering if I would go oh-for-three.

"We'll wait a few more minutes for the others to arrive," he said, "and then we'll begin." He made the sign of the cross over us. "God bless you, children. Be strong." We thanked him and promised we would. He disappeared back into his hideaway.

Julia excused herself to the restroom, leaving me standing alone with the casket. I looked around. I couldn't hear the priest or the altar boys.

So there he was. In there. Silent and still. Like I'd never, ever known him to be in life. There he was. Closed up in the big brown box I'd helped pick out for him. I watched my hand reach out and touch the casket. I swept my hand along the lid, dancing my fingers over the cool, smooth wood. Here lies my father. Here. Lies. My father. Just inches below my hand he was, and utterly unreachable. I wanted to open the lid. Not because I wanted to be sure he was in there, but because I knew he was. Not to touch him. I wanted to look at him, but not to see how badly he was hurt. I was about to speak to him for the first time in years, and I really wanted to see his face when I did it. I wished there was a way he could see mine.

I turned around and saw Molly sitting in the first pew, watching me. I hadn't even heard her arrive. She patted the space beside her then held out her hand. I lifted my hand from the coffin, stepped down from the altar, and slipped my fingers through hers. She didn't say a word as I sat beside her. Julia joined us moments later, kissing Molly on the cheek, then sitting on my other side. Nobody spoke. In unison, each slid her arm across my shoulders. I felt folded in the wings of a great bird.

As we waited for Father to come out, I could hear the creaking of the church door, the shuffling of footsteps as others arrived and took their seats. I didn't turn to look. Neighbors, maybe. Possibly a few guys from the office. What did it matter? I didn't care who else was there. The last of who I wanted and needed, Jimmy and Rose, arrived just as the service began. They sat in the front pew with the rest of us.

When my time came, I made the short walk to the altar. I gave the casket a wide berth. I spent my first few seconds at the ambo watching the blood drain from my knuckles as my hands gripped its sides. I moved the Bible down onto a shelf and stared at the blank space where my notes would've gone, had I brought any. I could see the casket out of the corner of my eye, just behind me, almost over my shoulder. I recognized a few of the faces before me from the wake; most were strangers. Fontana and his wife were there. Waters sat alone in the back.

I looked up at the ceiling, trying to catch a breath and clear my head, breathing in the perfume of the flowers, and the sour scent of my own nervous perspiration. I knew the people sitting in front of me would think I was fighting back tears. That was all right with me. As long as they couldn't tell I was trying not to laugh. Years of Catholic school, years of Irish Catholic guilt, a lifetime of Irish temper. I looked over and down at my dead father, flat on his back in the casket. I found I had no trouble seeing his face. So here we were. The father, the only son. Two devils. What a sloppy, intolerable pair we'd been. What a fucking mess we'd made. How in God's name did we end up at the altar together?

A multitude of sins between us, so many of them unforgiven. If I ever went to confession, I'd have to book that dark closet for a two-week engagement. I swallowed hard. I couldn't look away from him. There was only one of us left now to do any forgiving. How many of the ugly things that had lived within us would die on their own, of old age? How many would I have to kill? It was all on me now, the two of us. I was us in the world now. This was what I had inherited in his death.

I looked out at the small gathering of people in the church. Some fidgeted in their seats. I needed to start speaking. I covered my mouth with my hand, squeezed my jaw, scratched at my stubble. It was tempting to finally have a public forum at which I could attack my father and have him unable to attack me back. I had what I'd fantasized about for years. I had my chance to get even.

I patted my suit jacket, looking for my cigarettes. Should I ask for a little sacrificial wine? Then I could really do it up. I could. A smoke for my nerves. Pour out a little wine on the altar. One for my homies. Take a wee nip myself. Drop a few F-bombs during the eulogy. I could do it. I glanced over at Father McDonald. He looked nervous. Did he know what I was thinking? Would the priest have the spine to cut me off? To make a scene, if I really forced his hand? It'd make a hell of a story back at the rectory. It was probably what everyone expected. It was what my father would've expected for sure. But what about the rest of us?

I looked at my sister. Her eyes were big, her mouth rigid and colorless. She and Molly held hands across my seat. In the empty space between them, I saw it would one day be me on an altar. Not at the ambo, but in the casket. Would they be there then, holding hands? Who would be at the podium for me? What would I have left behind for them to remember, to say about me? I took a deep breath. My pulse pounded in my temples. My eyes burning, I looked at Molly, and Julia, and Jimmy and Rose, looking back at me. What I said wouldn't ever matter to my father. He didn't expect anything from me; he was gone. It was my sister, and my friends, and me, it was those of us still here who would have to live with what I did with these moments, and the moments and days and years to follow. The living would have to contend with the fallout, if I chose to be ugly. The dead keep their own counsel.

Slowly, Julia swept a lock of hair from her right eye and pinned it behind her ear. She straightened in her seat. She knew what I was thinking, every last thing. I knew that she was waiting, a hard, painful knot in her stomach, for my choice. She was waiting for me to decide where my loyalties would lie—with the living or with the dead. Across the silent church, we held each other's eyes. I folded my hands on the podium, but they wouldn't settle. I stuffed them in my pockets. I decided to do what my father never did when given the chance to inflict pain. I passed.

We could go, the three of us, one day without making a mess. We could. A thin line of sweat broke out on my forehead. I took a deep, deep breath.

"Though I am his only son," I said, "there is not much I can tell you about my father that you don't already know. I can tell you these things. My father was a New Yorker. He was born here and raised here. He lived his whole life here, growing up in Brooklyn, working in Manhattan, raising his children on Staten Island. He rooted for the Mets in Queens, booed the Yankees in the

Bronx. He was a lot like the city of New York, and in that way, he was a lot like the rest of us.

"There are sides of him we know, and wish we didn't. There are sides of him we didn't know, and wish we did. There are things about him we wish weren't true. There are things about him we hope are true. There were things about him, things he did, that had he lived to be two hundred years old, we would never understand. And now, there is much about him we will never know, or understand, or be able to figure out. The person who knew him best, for better or worse, my mother, left us even before he did. I, for one, never took the time to ask her about him. For a long time I was dumb and scared enough to think I had him figured out. I wonder as I stand here if I haven't made a terrible mistake in that.

"My father put all he had into making his way through the world the way he felt was best, no matter who disagreed with him. Life was a . . . a . . . full-contact sport for him. That attitude was his strength on some days, his weakness on others. Sometimes it benefited him. Sometimes it pained and punished those of us close to him, and maybe him, too. But along his . . . turbulent . . . path through life, my father did bind us into a family."

I paused and swallowed, my mouth and throat dry. I looked at my sister.

"Julia, I know," I said, "is here for our mother as well as our father. I am here today first for my sister. My sister has always done her best to be close to me, even from far away," and I smiled at her, "no easy task, for sure. Our mother, Susan, was the warm one, the nurturing one, but it was my father, it is my father who binds us together.

"Like the city, when we just look at the many different, contradicting parts of my father on their own, it is impossible to see how they all fit together into one man. It defies logic. It doesn't make any sense. But if we do the best we can to stand back and see him as a life, one life, maybe we can see that, though we may not understand how, the parts *did* fit together. Not always, maybe not ever neat or pretty, but the parts made a whole. They made a life. And that life is what we are left with now that he's gone. What we do with it, how we carry him forward from here is up to us.

"So what I'm going to try to do, when I remember him, is to stand high enough and look long enough to see the whole man, the whole life. All I ask of you, in his memory, is that you try to do the same."

I brought my hands out of my pockets and let them rest on the podium. I searched for the next thing to say. Then I realized, surprised, that I was done. I wondered how much of what I had said I would remember, how much of it I would still believe if I did remember. I guessed I'd find out, when I thought of this day. But that was for the future. There was nothing left to do right then but go back to my seat.

AFTER THE SERVICE, Julia and I climbed into the limo and followed the hearse as it delivered my father to the same sprawling cemetery where my mother and her parents were laid to rest. I spent the ride with my eyes closed and my head back against the seat. Julia rested her head on my shoulder. She twisted a rosary through her fingers but she didn't pray. She just quietly cried. Molly and Jimmy and Rose followed in their cars. Nobody else came with us.

After Father talked of ashes to ashes and dust to dust, I watched, my arm across Julia's shoulders, our friends gathered behind us, as the casket was lowered into the ground. I felt my stomach sink with it. The scene reminded me of *Raiders of the Lost Ark*. The last scene. Where the ark is sealed in an anonymous brown box and wheeled into the back of an enormous warehouse. All that awesome power, hidden away in a plain brown box and forgotten.

Like my father. Carefully sealed in a box of his own, lowered into a hole in the ground and buried. Packaged clean and neat, and put away. All that had emanated from him, bled or poured out of him into the world and into me; the fury, the frustration, the flailing violence—it was all gone. It walked no more halls, charged no more air, boiled no more blood. Not even, at least for the day, mine.

Julia broke away from me to thank and to pay the priest. I walked a few steps off to the side and lit a cigarette. Molly, Jimmy, and Rose approached the grave. Each plucked a flower from the arrangements. At the grave, one at a time, they dropped the flower in, and blessed themselves. They gathered at a respectful distance to wait for Julia and me.

Julia took two flowers. She dropped one into our father's grave. She carried the other to our mother's headstone, a few feet away. She laid the flower down at the foot of the stone, then knelt and prayed, her eyes squeezed shut. A bird sang in the trees. It was the only sound. When Julia was finished, she stood and made the sign of the cross. Then she kissed her fingertips and wiggled them at the headstone, a little grin curling the corners of her mouth.

I didn't take a flower. I walked to the edge of the grave and looked down at the casket. Burial seemed to me a cruel ritual. Cheap. We bury garbage. Why do we bury each other? What made burial any more than throwing someone away? A plain box and a pile of dirt. Some greenery over the top, just to pretty up the ugly truth. Just enough dirt to keep you from stinking up the neighborhood. Was this what we got for our troubles? For our fury and pain? For our agony? For the love and home we made? Was this what awaited us? The same fate as the garbage we dragged to the curb. Was there a way to cheat that fate?

From the pocket of my suit jacket, I pulled the photo of my father and me on the ferry. One more time, I studied the two of us, burning the scene into my mind, making it into a memory, something, one thing I could carry away from the edge of his grave. Other scenes materialized behind my eyes. He and I at the top of the Towers. His football team, his wedding day, he and my sister on a carousel pony. The fights with my mother, the fights with me. My father and Fontana. The scenes and the memories, good and bad, ran and swirled together. Like the colors of a kaleidoscope, all the images and colors blurred at the edges where they touched. I could not think of one moment, it seemed, without seeing all the others.

In the pocket of my leather jacket I found the scrap of police tape I'd taken from the murder scene. I wrapped the photo in the tape, tying the tape in a knot. I held the bundle in my fist. With the same fist, I tore a bunch of shamrocks from their pot. I kissed my fist. Then I took a deep breath and tossed the whole lot into the grave. Stray shamrocks stuck to my fingers. I shook them off and watched them spiral slowly down and settle on top of the casket. I got down on one knee, my leather jacket creaking at the shoulders, my cigarette burning low between my fingers. I spent a few long, last moments looking down at my father and his son.

I wasn't throwing them away, I decided. I was just changing the way they continued to live.

SIXTEEN

JULIA AND I MET THE OTHERS BACK AT THE CHURCH. JIMMY SAT
on the hood of his car, the girls standing at either knee. Except
for them, the parking lot was empty. The church was locked up
and dark. As I got out of the car, I caught a whiff of exhaust from
the traffic cruising by us on Annadale Road, the rest of the island
going about their normal afternoon business. Otherwise, it was
a beautiful spring day.

"Now what?" Jimmy asked as Julia and I approached.

We looked to one another for ideas, none of us having given
the rest of the day much thought. It was a good feeling, having
the day wide open and free before me. I held up my car keys.

"Get in the car," I said. "There's something we need to do."

Nobody moved.

"Trust me," I said.

Jimmy bit first, hopping down from his hood, shrugging at
Rose and climbing into the backseat of the Galaxie. Rose got in
beside him, shaking her head. My sister patted my shoulder,
opened the passenger-side door for Molly, and squeezed in beside
Rose. I stopped Molly before she got in the car.

"Long overdue as this is," I said, "it's still gonna take some nerve."

"I'm up for anything," Molly said, taking her seat beside mine. "Besides, I always was tougher than you."

I walked around the front of the car, climbed into the driver's seat, and started the engine. I turned to the others in the back.

Jimmy poked Rose in the shoulder. "Are we there yet?" he asked, several times. "She's on my side," he whined. "Tell her to stay on her side."

Rose whacked him playfully in the temple. "Where are we going?" she asked.

"Let's put our backs to this place for a while," I said.

I WATCHED HER CAREFULLY, BUT Molly didn't seem the least bit nervous as I parked the car in the pay lot beneath the ferry terminal. We made our way up the dingy concrete stairs to the terminal, where the scent of the ocean disappeared beneath the mingled odors of fresh urine and stale wine.

"You always take me to the nicest places," Molly said as we crossed the landing and turned up the last set of stairs, a single lightbulb flickering over our heads.

Finally, we emerged into the pale fluorescent glow of the train depot. Warm orange light pouring from their open doors, half a dozen of the silver trains sat idle on the tracks. They looked like a kid's play set, fresh out of the box. The electricity waiting to power them crackled in the air, tingling in my nose.

"Up here," I said, leading our entourage away from the trains up the wide ramp to the ferry terminal. Single file, we passed through the turnstiles.

The vast, high-ceilinged room was quiet, dimmed sunlight tumbling in through the dirty skylights. The coffee stands and fast food joints ringing the room did no business. Cashiers leaned on their elbows, flipping through newspapers or just staring off into space. A few tourists crowded together at the pea-green double doors that led to the next boat, clutching shopping bags and purses to their chests, nervously glancing over their shoulders into the yards of empty space behind them. A Port Authority cop shook the shoulder of a homeless man passed out on a bench.

We crossed the room, our dress shoes clicking on the marble floor. The big digital clock above the double doors read "Next Boat: 03 minutes." The five of us lingered in a patch of sunlight, well away from the tourists. Molly and I held hands. Snatches of conversations in French and Spanish drifted back to us.

"You want a coffee or something?" Jimmy asked me. "A beer?"

"I'm good," I said. "But we've got time if you need something."

"Anyone?" Jimmy asked.

Everyone declined. Jimmy stayed put, rocking on his heels with his hands in his pockets.

The big clock hit zero and the doors rumbled open. We let the tourists get a head start, took our time moving down the hall, emerged into the sea air, and boarded the squat orange boat.

The other passengers had disappeared inside, heading up the stairs to the second deck. We stayed on the back deck, leaning on the railing. Seagulls perched on the pilings all around us, watching the proceedings, beady eyes glittering in their tilted heads. The whole boat shook as the engines rumbled to life beneath us, churning the brown water to froth, kicking trash to the surface then swallowing it again. The deafening groan of the horn sounded, chasing the gulls airborne. The smokestack at the center of the boat coughed up a cloud of smoke, and we heaved forward. The pilings shrieked and rocked as the ferry muscled them aside and headed for open water.

Jimmy shouted something at Julia, but she just raised her hands and shook her head, unable to hear him. Molly put her arm around my waist, leaning into me so I could hear her over the engines. "Let's go upstairs," she said. "It's too loud back here."

"You're sure?" I asked. She nodded and walked away from me.

I smacked Jimmy on the shoulder and pointed toward the doorway. He passed the message to Julia and took Rose by the hand. We followed Molly, who was already waiting for us at the top of the stairs.

Her shoulders set straight, her chin tilted up, Molly led us the length of the boat. Pigeons and sparrows scattered out of her way, puffing their feathers as they cooed and chirped their complaints at the rest of us. An abandoned *Daily News* blew in pieces over the tops of the benches, its pages caught in the wind off the sea. Molly turned out the door onto the observation deck. I held up my hand and we all stopped just inside the door.

"Give her just a minute," I said.

Through the windows, I watched Molly part the tourists and walk to the front of the deck. She made the sign of the cross and bowed her head, gripping the metal railing. The wind tossed her hair wildly around her. It pressed her black dress tight against her body. As the boat plowed its way toward Manhattan, I watched the empty space where the Towers once stood open up over her trembling shoulders. She raised her head and stared straight into it. The tourists around her, oblivious, posed for photos as we passed the Statue of Liberty.

My throat tightened and my heart ached for her. Jimmy stood with his head bowed, his hands folded above his belt buckle. Rose had her arms around him, her forehead pressed into his shoulder. Julia wiped away one tear with her thumb then gave up and let them fall. She looked away from me, clutching her arms tight against her chest. There was no one to tell me what to do. I had no advice, no smart-ass remarks, no vitriolic speeches to offer in dismissal or as distraction. Nor did I feel the need.

Even in our most self-indulgently tragic teenage daydreams, we'd never imagined standing in such an ordinary place and staring into one of the great tragedies, the great crimes, in our country's history. A crime that stole the blood of one of our own. Of all the things we talked of doing together, grieving for and with each other never made the list.

Standing together on that boat, we were someplace far beyond anywhere we'd ever conceived of being while running the streets of Staten Island years ago. We were too young and bored then, kicking around dreams of the future like soda cans in the schoolyard, tilting them into the shine of the streetlights and tossing them aside like the caps off our beer bottles. Why pay attention? Tomorrow, there would always be more. Things never changed on Staten Island.

Our mothers always made our lunches, always bought our clothes at the Mall, always got home from work before we got home from school. The trains took our fathers to the ferry in the morning. The ferry brought them to the City, where every day they took their places in the sky, somewhere high up in those impossibly tall buildings, nested and safe like birds. The trains and the boats, like our mothers and fathers, would never stop working. The sky would never fall.

Our fathers, our families, the ones we loved, would never change, never betray us, never not come home. They would never die. Until they did. Until one day you woke up and your life was different forever, whether you were eight or thirty-one, whether you wanted it that way or not. And there was nothing left to do but take your place in the bucket line alongside the other survivors, helping to bear the loss and clean up the mess, the future suddenly a diamond clutched so hard in your fist its sharp corners drew blood.

I fought back the urge to run to Molly, to turn her away from the emptiness and cover her eyes with my hands, to promise her it wasn't really there. But I knew it wouldn't do any good. There wasn't any escaping her loss any more than there was escaping mine. She didn't look interested in running, anyway. She stood straight and tall against that expanse of blue sky, like she was trying to fill it on her own, a tower unto herself. A fragile, defiant skyline of one. It was too much for anyone to do alone. Without a word, I took my place beside her, making us two against the yawning, open sky.

The boat closed in on Manhattan and the looming skyscrapers surrounding the docks seemed to bow forward over our heads. The boat's engines dropped a gear. As the wind eased, all around us seagulls drifted down out of the sky like a fleet of crooked-winged escorts, rising and falling on the drafts. Molly's hair came to rest against her shoulder blades. She leaned into me for balance as the boat bumped along the pilings and settled into the dock.

"I wish I knew what to do for you," I said.

"You're doing it already," she said, stretching her arm across my shoulders. "You're here, warm and alive, with me. That's enough."

WE LET EVERYONE ELSE disembark then headed down the curving ramp to the street. Jimmy bought us hot pretzels from a curbside vendor and we wandered back toward the water, over to Battery Park, breaking our pretzels into steaming pieces and eating as we walked, licking mustard from our fingertips. Julia ate the entire thing and a piece of mine. We found a couple of empty benches and sat gazing across the gray water at Staten Island. I handed out cigarettes to Molly and Jimmy.

"I hear they've started laying the foundation for the Freedom Tower," Jimmy said.

"It's about time," Rose said.

"Are the families still fighting over the memorial?" Julia asked, looking at Molly. "I heard people are suing to reopen the search for remains at Fresh Kills."

Molly stretched her legs in front of her and leaned over them, running her hands over her knees. "I assume so," she said. "I haven't paid much attention to everyone's big plans. I'm sure people will be suing each other over that memorial fifty years after it's finished.

"My folks and I, we're not involved in any of that. We found what we could of Eddie. We said our good-byes. It needs to be finished for us."

"I hope that damn tower at least goes up in our lifetime," Jimmy said. "I want to see it, a great big middle finger from New York to those savages across the ocean."

I rubbed my hand over Molly's back. "It'll get done. It won't go the way anyone has planned. There'll be delays and mistakes, but it'll happen. These things take time. They're complicated."

Molly smiled up at me. "You're exactly right."

"Well then, that's settled. Good work, everyone," Jimmy said. "I have renewed hope for the future." He rubbed his hand over his belly. "But as for the present, those pretzels only got my stomach rumbling. Let's catch a cab to Little Italy and eat ourselves stupid. My treat."

Jimmy didn't wait for an answer, striding off into the park. The rest of us, one by one, turned our backs to Staten Island and followed him toward the vast canyons of the City.

NOT LONG AFTER SUNDOWN, back at my apartment, jackets and ties abandoned to the back of the couch, Jimmy and I watched the Mets run up an early lead on the Houston Astros. A win lifted them into first place. Jimmy and I both knew it, but neither of us mentioned it. Both of us understood that if we did say anything out loud, a jinx powerful enough to undo all the Mets' hard work would stream straight from my apartment to Houston and infect the team. It was the girls who made all the noise.

At their request, we'd stopped at a liquor store on the way home. Molly, Rose, and Julia, shoeless and giggling, flitted about in the kitchen, arguing and experimenting their way to what I knew would be a supremely awful round of martinis. They'd tried to enlist my help, but I refused. I made drinks for a living, I told them. It was hardly what I wanted to do with my last night off before a long weekend of returning favors and covering shifts. I was more than willing to drink bad martinis, I told them, if it meant I could stay rooted to the sofa and watch the game. What I didn't tell them was how good their laughter sounded floating out of my kitchen, and that the longer they played, the longer I could enjoy the sounds of it.

During a commercial, Jimmy asked when Julia was headed back to Boston.

"She's going back tomorrow, on the train," I said. "I'm taking her to Penn Station in the morning. She doesn't have to be back in class till Monday so I asked her to stay for a while, here at the apartment, but she wants that couple of days to settle back in."

"Makes sense," Jimmy said. "I bet both of you feel like you've lived a lifetime in the past few days."

"For sure."

"When will you guys see each other again?" Jimmy asked.

"Soon. She's coming back in two weeks. We'll spend the weekend trying to get things going with clearing out and selling the house."

"Sounds grim," Jimmy said. "You'll need to relax. Call us up. We'll take you out to dinner." He bumped me with his shoulder. "Bring Molly. Think she'll be available?"

"Oh," I said, smiling, "I get the feeling she will be."

"So she's really getting rid of David?" Jimmy asked.

"She is indeed. She figures he'll be relieved more than anything else. They've been just going through the motions for a long time. They've been on life support too long. It's past time to pull the plug."

"Strange choice of metaphors," Jimmy said.

Somebody knocked hard on my door.

"Pizza's here," Molly yelled from the kitchen.

"Heard that," I said, standing. Jimmy dug for his wallet. "I got this," I said.

To my surprise, it was Waters at the door, and he wasn't holding a pizza.

"Howya doin', Junior?" he said. "Nice work at the funeral today."

"Afternoon, Sheriff. Thanks for coming."

"No problem."

I realized he was still standing in the hallway. "Come in. We're just relaxing a little, waiting on a couple pizzas." I stepped aside and let him in.

The kitchen had gone quiet. The three girls stood motionless in the doorway, Julia with a dish towel wrapped around her hand. Jimmy stood and walked over to Waters.

"Jimmy McGrath," he said, extending his hand. "I'm an old friend of the family."

"Detective Nat Waters," the detective said, shaking hands. "Me, too."

"You know my sister, Julia," I said. "That's Jimmy's girlfriend, Rose, and my friend Molly."

Waters nodded. He still hadn't come far enough inside the apartment for me to close the door. "Detective Purvis sends his regrets," he said. "He had every intention of coming to the funeral. It was me that advised against it."

"Tell the detective we appreciate the kind thoughts," I said.

"Do," Julia said.

"I will," said Waters.

"I'm guessing that's not what you came to tell us," I said.

"Well, that's true. If I could talk to you and Julia alone for a minute, I have some news."

"Come in and sit down," I said, settling my hand on his shoulder. I guided him into the room and closed the door. "We have martinis, I think."

"No martinis for me," Waters said. "All due respect, this is really a family-only conversation we need to have."

"You caught someone," Julia said.

"We know who did it," Waters said. He was sweating, fidgety.

He pulled out a handkerchief and dabbed at his forehead. In fact, he looked slightly sick. Not at all like a sheriff who'd got his man. It made me nervous. I wished for a moment that I'd been alone in the apartment when he arrived. But it wouldn't have changed the facts.

"There's nothing you can't tell us in front of our friends," I said.

I looked at Julia. She nodded, stepping away from Molly and Rose and into the living room. "We're gonna tell them exactly what you tell us," she said, "as soon as you leave, anyway."

Waters shook his head. "Have it your way."

"Out with it," Julia said. "Please."

"It was a mistake," Waters said. "It was a bad hit." He stopped.

My jaw dropped. I heard Julia gasp. "Whadda you mean a mistake?" I asked.

Waters squirmed. "Turns out I wasn't wrong about the gambling, but it wasn't your father that was supposed to be shot." He walked into the middle of the room, looking at his hands as if he were still putting the pieces together. "Apparently there's a less than upright South Shore bookie that looks a lot like your father and frequents the same deli." He looked around the room at all of us. "I don't know what to tell you. It was an accident."

"When did you find this out?" I asked.

"Last night," Waters said. "That's why I missed the wake."

"You were arresting the shooter?" Julia said.

Waters stared at his hands again. "All I've got is information. Like where to find the shooter's body out at the Dump."

"Another accident?" I asked.

"He won't be missed," Waters said.

"You said it was a hit," I said. "That means somebody gave an order." I stepped to Waters, Jimmy grabbed my arm. "What about him?"

Waters looked dead at me. "It's being looked into. It's being taken care of. It may have been already." He looked away from me, at Julia. "Look, there are people out there who feel real bad about this. You know how some people are about family. You two won't have any trouble selling the house, for a good price. Scalia's gonna get paid. You give me an okay to pass along, Julia, and I don't think you'll need to worry about your school loans. With your permission, there are a number of things that can be done, easily, to help make your loss a little easier to endure."

"I don't want anybody's blood money," Julia snapped. "You tell your friends I said that."

"They're not my friends," Waters snapped back. He paused, gathering himself. "For the record, I demanded the guy who gave the order be handed over to me."

"And?" Julia asked.

"And I got laughed at. Quietly, gently even, but I got laughed at. These people are way beyond my reach. I'm lucky I got what I did."

This was a humiliating conversation for him, I realized, playing message boy for charitable gangsters. That was why he had wanted to have the conversation alone. I felt bad for making it harder on him than it already was.

"I appreciate the effort," I said.

Waters didn't acknowledge me. He just stared at the floor, looking disgusted. "There's no debts incurred with any of this," he said. "You don't have to talk to or deal with anyone. All the choices are yours." He dabbed again at the sweat on his brow. "Including how this ends."

Molly brought him a cup of ice water. He thanked her. She sat on the edge of the couch, Jimmy on one side of her, Rose on the other. Julia walked to my side.

"Walk me to the car," Waters said to me.

I looked at Julia.

"Give me five more minutes of your time," he said.

I squeezed Julia's hand and followed Waters into the hall, closing the apartment door behind me. His eyes looked everywhere but at me.

"So, you're gonna sell the house," he said.

"As soon as possible," I said. "We want to sell it cheap, to a family with a pack of kids that needs a break."

"That's a kind gesture," Waters said. He coughed into his fist. He still couldn't look at me.

"C'mon, Detective," I said. "You didn't ask me out here to talk about real estate."

"There is one more thing," he said. He reached under his jacket. I heard him unsnap his shoulder holster. "What happens next will never leave this hallway. Understood?"

"Understood."

He held out my gun. "My returning this to you is in no way connected to what I'm about to tell you."

"Understood." I took the gun from him. The weight of it pulled at my shoulder when I dropped my hand to my side.

"Arrangements can be made," Waters said, "for you to spend a moment or two alone with the man who called in the hit." He handed me a slip of paper. I took it in my other hand. "Call this number by ten tonight if you'd like to have that meeting."

I squeezed the handle of the gun. I looked at the number. "By ten," I said.

"If that's what you really want to do."

I thought of the man who'd made the call, sitting in a room, in a single chair, maybe on the edge of a bed, chain-smoking, guards behind him at the door, counting down the last hours of his life. Would whoever held him let him hear the phone call? I thought of him, sitting there, waiting for me. Not knowing who I was, where I was coming from. Only that I was coming for him.

I'd wanted so bad, back at the beginning, to put my eyes and hands on the man who shot my father. But that man was dead. Now I was being offered the man who made it happen. Whether or not I made that call, no matter who finally put the bullet in him, that man would never see the sun rise. Both men were dead as my father. I looked at the gun in my hand, wondering if I could really kill a man. I'd sworn to myself a thousand times I wanted to kill my father. But I knew now I'd never meant it. Could I really kill a man? Jimmy had asked me at the beach. I thought, even now, that maybe I could. It made me sick. Was that a question I really needed to answer?

What I knew or didn't know, did or didn't do, wouldn't change anything. When that guy died, or even if he somehow lived, nothing would change. I looked over my shoulder, at the apartment door, and then at the gun in my hand. Staring at the gun, I could feel Julia, and Molly, and Jimmy and Rose, waiting for me on just the other side of that door.

We'd made our way to the end of this thing. It was over. The old man was dead and buried. Jimmy was with me. Molly was with me. Julia was with me. The war, the violence, was over for good. Unless. Unless I started it up again. Unless I embraced it again, now in a way maybe worse than ever. Unless I picked up the violence and all that came with it again and carried it all with me, where it would find its way into Julia's life, and into Molly's and Jimmy's life, and Rose's. Until they, one by one, were all gone. And what then would become of me?

As it had been all along, the choice was mine. I held, as I always had, the answer in my hands.

"Detective, if you speak with your associates again, tell them Julia and I appreciate their generosity, but we decline." I crumpled the paper in my fist and dropped it at my feet. I handed him back the gun. "I politely decline all their offers."

Waters took the gun, tucking it under his jacket. He nodded.

"Tell them that we've made our peace with our father's passing," I said. I backed toward the door. "I gotta go. My sister and my friends are waiting for me."

ACKNOWLEDGMENTS

THE LIST OF PEOPLE who helped this book and its author into their present state could go on for quite a long time. I can't mention everyone, but there are some who cannot go unnamed. Apologies to those whose names I have omitted.

Big love to the families McDonald, Murphy, Loehfelm, and Lambeth; especially to my dad for taking me to those Saturday-morning writing classes; thanks to Barbara Baracks, my first writing teacher, and to Stevie D'Arbanville, my first muse. Props to Doug Bailey for always being there, no matter what. You are a great man.

Thanks also to Jerry and the staff of Rue de la Course, where I wrote most of this book. Thanks to Bruce, Sue, and the mighty crew at Lucy's Retired Surfers Bar for coming home and sticking it out. Make it rain. To Darrin, Cali, Sarah, Jeff, Justin, and Kevis—live the dream.

Love to my New Orleans tribe: Joseph and Amanda Boyden, for support, advice, and vacations, and for keeping the faith when mine wavered; Jarret Lofstead, Joe Longo, and everyone at nolafugees.com and the International House of Jolson for a voice, a lot of laughs, and a healthy dose of perspective; the UNO

MFA crew, including but not exclusive to Arin, Dave, Chrys, Sarah and Simon, Jen and Jeremy, Neil, Matt and Rakia, Adam and Ashley, as well as Rick Barton, Joanna Leake, and the late Jim Knudsen for giving us a place to let the freak flag fly.

A raised lighter to Vince Booth, for helping me keep my head on straight and for the gift of music.

Deep, deep gratitude to Matt Peters, a fine writer and reader whose input was invaluable in my writing this book. Thanks also to Barb Johnson and Dr. John Cooke for great advice.

Thanks to Parkview Tavern, Balcony Bar, Pals, and Handsome Willy's for putting up with us. Fine establishments all.

A toast to my home, the invincible city of New Orleans, Louisiana, and her brave, fierce people. There's nowhere else I'd rather be. Geaux Saints.

Sláinte to the members of U2. Thanks for twenty-two years (and counting) of hope and Big Ideas.

To Chris Pepe, my editor, and the staff at Penguin, and to Barney Karpfinger, my agent. All a man can ask for is a shot—thanks for helping me take mine.

Last but not least, all my love to my great treasure and the best writer I know, AC Lambeth, my extraordinary wife. You are my strength and inspiration. You are my great love. My soul bows, humble, grateful, and joyous, before you.